# Crown of Dust

# MARY VOLMER

# *Crown of Dust*

Published by Soho Press, Inc.
853 Broadway
New York, NY 10003
www.sohopress.com

Library of Congress Cataloging-in-Publication Data

Volmer, Mary.
Crown of dust / Mary Volmer.
p. cm.
ISBN 978-1-56947-861-5 (hardcover)
1. Gold mines and mining—California—Fiction. 2. Frontier and pioneer life—
California—Fiction. 3. Women pioneers—Fiction. I. Title.
PS3622.O645C76 2010
813'.6—dc22
2010031283

Paperback ISBN 978-1-56947-986-5
eISBN 978-1-56947-862-2

Printed in the United States of America

10 9 8 7 6 5 4 3 2 1

For my mom,
Cathy Volmer

# Acknowledgments

This book would not have been possible without support from the Rotary Foundation's Rotary Scholar program and the Jim Townsend and the Agnes Butler scholarship programs at Saint Mary's College.

Heartfelt thanks to Patricia Duncker for all of your wisdom and generosity, especially in the earliest stages of this book. Thank you to Rosemary Graham for your early encouragement and your continuing support; to Lysley Tenorio for your mentorship and your superpowers; to Ann Cummins and Gloria Frym for your inspiration.

Special thanks to John and Linda Higgins, to Bill Fritz and Diana Travis and to the Rotary Clubs of Grass Valley, California and Aberystwyth, Wales, for your support, friendship and hospitality. Many thanks to Chris Kilgore and to my colleagues at Saint Mary's College, especially Crystal Carey, Ammon Torrence, Drew Ancel, and Joseph Kim.

Thank you to David Comstock and JoAnn Levy and a host of other Gold Rush aficionados and historians whose books inspired and informed this novel.

Thank you to Susan Watt for taking a chance on this first-time novelist; thank you to Anne O'Brien for your patient effort. Many heartfelt thanks to Victoria Hobbs at A.M.

Heath for all your boundless enthusiasm, hard work and expertise, and to Sara Fisher who so generously adopted me for a time.

Lastly, thank you to my parents, Phil and Cathy Volmer. Mom, you are my sounding board, my first and last reader, my nutrition guide, my lending library, my confessor, my confidante, my friend.

# 1

Emaline searches the sky for storm clouds from the doorway of the Victoria Inn. The man snoring at her feet grunts, rolls over, and curls himself around an upturned bottle of whiskey. She picks up her skirt, steps over him onto the porch. Can't predict the weather this time of year. Fools even the wild flowers. Mistake three days of sunshine for the start of May when one hard freeze will snap the petals right off and kill the early batch of mosquitoes already swarming.

Across the road, the chapel's canvas roof sags like wet clothes on a line. It won't take another snow like the last. Klein promised to fix the damn thing, but he's probably knee deep in the creek with the rest of them. It's no wonder nobody in these parts has struck pay dirt yet, what with their canvas tents and frame cabins so easy to desert. Why would the earth give up its gold just to be abandoned on rumor of another strike? The soil is a shrewd old whore and has learned better than to give her gold for free.

A person should have a solid foundation, Emaline always says, some sort of permanence in her life, a place for luck to grow. That's why she's insisting on having the chapel finished. Nothing establishes a place like inviting God to stay. She imagines a tidy steeple with a sensible wooden cross, a simple oak pulpit and rows of sober pews. No stained glass. No gaudy ornamentation. Save that for the Baptists who mistake the sound of their own voices for the word of God. Behind the chapel she pictures a cemetery with graves surrounded by white picket fences to keep souls from drifting. Emaline is tired of drifting. That's how she thinks of it; not pioneering, certainly not running, but drifting. True, Motherlode isn't much to look at. Not yet. But she has a feeling about the place; call it intuition.

The ravine walls stand at attention on either side of her valley and the cedars that brush the rim are a feathered fringe in the glare of the afternoon sun. A movement up the road catches her eye. She squints to see better.

"Preacher," she says. The man at her feet grunts but doesn't move. Emaline nudges him with her toe. "John." She kicks him harder. Another grunt. "Goddamnit, John! Wake your sorry ass up and look down the road."

She reaches under him with her toe, lifts with all her might, and John rolls sideways down the steps to land in a stupor at the bottom. A stocky black man steps out of the building behind her and stares in the direction of Emaline's gaze.

"T'ain't no one but Randall, missus. And his mule."

"I can see who it is, Jed." But her shoulders slump and she lets out a breath, slowly, hoping Jed won't notice. "And don't be calling me no missus."

Jed crosses his arms in front of him and places his hand to his chin, a common posture for him. It's hard to tell whether he's deep in thought or simply hiding a smile. Emaline sits down, knees apart on the steps above Preacher John and glares back at Jed.

"Whatever you say, Miss Emaline," he says, retreating into the building just as another, smaller figure appears around the mass of manzanita marking the edge of Motherlode.

\*       \*       \*

2

"Randall, I tell you," says Emaline, "if God ordered wine on Sunday you'd bring it a week later Monday."

"Now, Emaline," says the muleteer. His beard hangs to his waist and the tobacco stain blooming about his lips is the only way she can locate exactly where the whiskers end and his mouth begins. "You know I can't make the wagon come. Sacramento ain't no closer now than it were a year ago – 'less you want me to come without the molasses and the mail."

Preacher John moans at her feet. She nudges him with her toe for no other reason than to remind him she's here. Sober on Sundays, he'd said. At least he's that, sober on Sundays. She shakes her head and is happy to let Randall believe this gesture is meant for him. She heaves herself from the steps and Randall stumbles back, regains himself. The mule behind haws its pleasure, or displeasure – hard to tell with mules – and the sound ricochets off the ravine walls and falls below the squawk of the scrub jays.

"Dangerous work I'm doing," says Randall. He rubs his toe in the dirt. He spits. The mule brays again, louder this time. "Man's – A man's gotta be careful, take his time."

"Careful? How much time you lose playing five-card between Sac' town and Grass Valley?" She's yelling now above the mule and she can see its ears rotating, its neck straining to look behind.

"Ah hell, Emaline."

"Ah hell, nothin' . . ." Her voice trails off. She pinches her eyes to slits, thrusts her neck forward to see what the mule sees.

"Who are you?" Emaline says. The mule goes quiet.

The stranger shifts under his load, pulls his duster hat low as if he could hide there beneath it, as if my piss-poor eyes can see anything but his shape anyway, she thinks. She can see that he's small. Narrow shoulders, his pack just about as wide as his whole back, his trousers and flannel draping over him like they have only bone to cling to. She's known too many men to judge this one's threat by his size.

3

"Randall?" she asks.

"Hell if I know." He shrugs, but seems content that he is no longer her focus.

The mule's ears rotate as if it too is waiting for a response, and the stranger seems to shrink down inside of himself in a way that raises the hairs on the back of Emaline's neck. The mule shifts its weight foot to foot, shakes its halter.

"I'm talking to you! Who are you?" Emaline charges forward and the mule rears its ornery self, eyes wild as if she'd struck the damn thing. Packages jar from the animal's back and slap the ground. Some burst open and precious flour thickens the air and powders the red mud of the road. Randall's beard trails behind him as he hustles after the frenzied animal, tripping in a wake of pinto beans and hollering, "Goddamn you, Contrary Julie!" Red-speckled hens poke their heads round the side of the inn, pick up their skirts and run toward the mess of oats and beans. Scrub jays descend in blue streaks to scold and scratch. Emaline bustles about the muddy road, shooing chickens, flailing at jays, salvaging what she can: a sack of potatoes, a side of salt pork. By the time she charges back to the stranger she's sweated clean through her dress. At least, she thinks, catching her breath, at least he's seen fit to pick up a sack of flour. He holds it there like a shield between them.

"I suppose you can pay for these goods?" No response. Up the road, beyond the grove of manzanita, the echoes of a braying mule and a swearing man do battle. "I don't take credit nor scrip, and – Look at me." Small black eyes peek out beneath the duster hat. "And I ain't here to nursemaid no runaway mamma's boy. Your name, if you got one?"

But his mouth pops closed. Flour sifts from his shoulders as he rummages in a small pouch at his waist.

"Alex?" he says, but it sounds like a question, a question she forgets when he holds out what looks to be a gold coin, San Francisco mint – double eagle, no less. The potatoes thump to the ground. She snatches the coin. Such a pleasing weight, twenty dollars. She gives it a bite, finds herself softening.

"Well, Alex," she says, placing the coin in her dress pocket, patting it twice, "you got the voice of a choirboy."

"Haven't got a sign up yet," says the woman, closing the door firmly behind her. Her voice fills every inch of space her body leaves open and she moves with an agility surprising and a little frightening in such a large woman. "But that's what I call her – the Victoria Inn."

She thumps the pork and potatoes on a plank table, or rather a series of tables held as one by a grubby cloth. Alex follows suit with the sack of flour and a puff of white escapes.

"Victoria, like the Queen," the woman says. She dusts her hands on her apron and motions with her head to the water-stained portrait of a crowned woman on the opposite wall. Two windows of distorting mason glass offer the only light in the room and the painting's features are indistinct. The face of a youthful older woman, Alex thinks, or an aged young woman, with round cheeks to match her chin.

A ramshackle bar traverses one corner and three-legged stools are scattered about. It smells of alcohol, yeast and strong burned coffee, and Alex's stomach grumbles with hunger, clearly not the response the woman is waiting for.

Emaline puffs a curl from her eyes. It catches in the frizzy halo framing her angular face. She turns on her heel and charges up the stairwell into a shaft of hallway light without pausing to see if Alex follows. She stops by one of eight doors in the narrow corridor, her hand on the latch, and squints in the same probing manner she used on the mule-teer, the scowl on her face made deeper by crease lines like poorly healed scars.

Alex pulls the duster hat low, makes an effort to look aloof, would have spit as the muleteer had done if they hadn't been inside.

No one, yet, has taken her for a girl. No one, yet, has looked this closely.

"You're from where, you say?"

Alex hadn't said, and is so relieved by the question she fails to answer.

"That's a question," says the woman.

"Pennsylvania."

"Don't talk much, do you?"

Alone in the room, the darkness is complete and endless, even as Alex feels the closeness of the walls, the low ceiling. Little by little her eyes adjust and the corners of the room take shape. The bed smells sharply of cedar. The only other furniture is a three-legged stool resting at a slant on the uneven floorboards. There is no window, no need for curtains; a single candle burned nearly to the nub sits on the floor by the bed. The woman's heavy steps descend the stairs. Victoria, like the Queen, Alex thinks, and sees again the whitewash peeling down the inn's face, the unpainted balusters, the ornamental balcony propped precariously over the porch. She eases down to draw a line in the dust with her finger. A few days is all she needs, to rest, to think.

How far had she come since stepping off the steamer into the frenzied chaos of the Marysville docks? Was it only three days ago that she'd stood there on the river bank amid that sea of canvas sacks, barrels and boxes? Delicate chairs, end tables and bookshelves looked out of place perched alongside kegs of black powder, stacks of picks and shovels, piles of hydraulic tubing coiled like earthworms. Alex pulled her duster hat low, avoiding the eyes of the men scurrying back and forth, hauling skeins of fabric and barrels of whiskey. She wanted to be back on the boat, surrounded by the hissing blast of steam and the clank of pistons, away from cursing muleteers and braying donkeys and important-looking men dressed in black. But after Marysville the river split in two, the Feather shooting north, the Yuba branching east, both too rough for riverboats.

Alex followed the Yuba because it sounded foreign and far away from San Francisco, because those men she had seen on the boat – lawmen, perhaps, with their trimmed mustaches, their pressed black trousers – were heading north. She'd joined the line of wagons rolling east, kept her head low, spoken to no one, and stopped briefly at a shanty store on the edge of town. It was here she'd learned of her need for boots.

"Best there is," the merchant claimed, stroking the blackened leather with an arm that ended in a rounded stump of flesh. As he spoke, he gestured with the arm, as if forgetting his fingers were gone. "Made special for a colonel. Small man – they all are. Killed by Comanche, 'fending women and children. For you, forty dollars. Boy don't deserve boots like this. A man's boots. War hero's . . ."

Gaps in the wall behind him let in streamers of light and the roof shuddered with every gust of wind.

"The hell kinda shoes are those? You steal 'em off your mama's feet? Won't last the week. Not half a week," said the merchant. His cackle turned to a cough. Alex stepped back.

"Wait now, thirty dollars then," said the man. "Can't believe I'm saying it – three kids and a wife back home . . ." He bowed his head, rubbed his salt-and-pepper beard with his good hand. "Should just save 'em for my son, but with his one leg, won't do much good, see."

Alex said nothing, fearing the high pitch of her voice. She shook her head no, turned to leave.

"Goddamn! Goddamn, twenty dollars," said the merchant, dangling the boots from his stump by the laces.

She had rested in thickets, when she rested at all, and followed the twisted path of the Yuba to Rough and Ready, a town whose citizens had looked both rough and ready for all manner of mischief, staring openly at any passers-by as if assessing their worth. Here she bought a loaf of bread and a gold pan from what could have been the same grizzled merchant, apart from the missing arm. She put the bread in her pack and the pan under her arm as if it strengthened her disguise, as if gold had been the reason she'd come to California, as if, when she turned off on to a narrow road to the northeast, she was confident of a destination.

The land became steeper, the earth darkened to an iron red. Lonely scrub oaks in tall grass had long since given way to ferns and evergreens; the towering pines pinched off the sky and on the crest of every hill she found the gleaming teeth of the Sierra Nevadas growing larger, more menacing. By the time the trail split again – one tail coiling its way toward those mountains, the other dipping down into a valley – her legs were quivering protest with every step, her feet throbbed, her shoulders ached. All of her bread was eaten, her canteen empty, and the coil of smoke snaking its way from the valley floor called to her above the distant murmur of running water and the coughing protest of a donkey.

The gold pan in her pack clangs against the floor as she sits. She frees herself from the straps, rolls her shoulders front to back. Her leg muscles have already begun to tighten, but her body feels numb, distant – as foreign as the river she'd followed. She pulls her shirtsleeves to her elbows, straightens her arms in front of her to find the bruises there mere smudges in the dim light. As if a bit of soap and water could wash them clean, she thinks, but she doesn't touch them. She doesn't touch the knots on her lower back or just below her collarbone. She can feel her heartbeat pounding in the blisters on her feet. She loosens her bootlaces, peels away the woolen sock. The skin of her heel is pregnant with white fluid, but disappointingly intact. She wants blood, proof of pain.

Below, a door opens and closes, and male voices seep through the floorboards.

"Alex," she says to herself. The voice of a choirboy. She pulls her chin into her neck, scrunching her vocal cords. "Alex," she says again, and is still practicing when a black man sticks his head through the door.

"You don't come now, it'll be gone. They ain't fixin' to wait for you."

Downstairs, she finds herself trapped by the eyes of eight men hunched around the plank table, their expressions masked by facial hair and layers of dirt. The black man sits down opposite the head, but no one seems the least surprised by his boldness. The only sound is heavy breathing and the silence pricks the hairs on her arms. She tries to sit and finds a muddy boot planted on the only unoccupied stool. The owner's beard is yellow and a twisted smirk reveals teeth of the same color.

A giant oak of a man to Muddy Boots's right lets out a long curving whistle that rises upward to the low-beam ceiling and spills in a puddle on the floor. The kitchen door bangs open and the woman bustles through with a large iron pot.

"Look out," she says, brushing Alex aside, and slams the pot on the table. Muddy Boots moves his feet.

"You need an invitation?" she asks. Alex sits, feels her cheeks flush hot.

"All right, Preacher," says the woman.

"Dearly Beloved," says a dark-haired man with just a hint of whiskey in his voice. He stands, as if it just occurred to him to do so, and runs his hands up and down his flannel. His eyeballs search for words beneath his lids and his hands clasp so tightly his knuckles show white. "We are gathered here today, Lord, to thank you for your wondrous bounty."

"'Cept when it comes to gold," says a baritone to Alex's right; the whistler, she thinks. A low chuckle catches, then dies. She bows her head, but lets her eyes dart to the pot mid-table. A large round loaf of bread sweats under a cloth and she begs her stomach silent.

9

"And lead us not into temptation, Lord. No, lead us far from temptation, our Father who art in heaven. We hallow thy name, giving glory, Lord. Thanks for health, we ask for wealth. Hallelujah, let's eat."

Preacher's plate is half empty before Alex is allowed to scrape the bottom of the iron pot for the last chunks of rabbit stew. What bread there was has already been snatched.

"Don't get used to it, boys," says Emaline. Her tone is thick with disappointment, and men pause mid-chew to listen. "Be cinching our belts by the end of the week, thanks to our new friend here."

The serving spoon and nine faces point in Alex's direction. Alex looks down at her plate. Alex chews. She has to tell herself to do these things.

"But damned if he ain't offered to buy drinks all round to make up for it!"

"Attaboy, son," says the baritone and slaps her on the back, propelling the chunk of rabbit meat across the table and into the bowl of a beardless man with expressionless gray eyes. A drooping auburn mustache curtains his thin lips and frames his cleft chin.

"No forgiveness like whiskey. Ain't that right, Preacher?" The baritone stands, nearly brushing his head on the cross-beam. A grin fills his face. Alex flinches, afraid there's another slap coming, good natured though the first one seemed. The mustache man fishes with both fingers for Alex's meat in his stew. His eyes flit to Alex and away.

"Don't think we've been properly introduced," the baritone says. "Mighty hard to be polite on an empty stomach, you know. No excuse, mind you, but the truth. I 'spect you met Preacher John yonder, but don't ask him to remember it. The one-eyed fella next to you is Micah Daniels, also a resident here at the Victoria. Owns a sore excuse for a general store and assay office just down the walk. Claims he can figure fine, but you watch him careful when he's weighing your gold. Been known to lighten the load some, yah know what I mean, and grows his fingernails long enough to get two dollars in one pinch of gold dust.

"Harry Reynolds there lives in the first cabin as you come into town, along with good Mr. Fred Henderson, self-proclaimed expert on rocks, animals, plants and all things natural. Next to him is our German friend Klein, master builder and jack-of-all-trades – when he feels like doing 'em. Got no other name, so don't go asking him. Just Klein. You met Jed –" he nods to the black man – "and Emaline; Miss Emaline, if you know what's good for you.

"My name is Samson Limpkin, but most call me Limpy on account of, well, let's say a crooked limb. And the man you so graciously shared your stew with –" he nods to the mustache man – "is my cousin, David Trellona, fresh out of Cornwall and thinkin' he knows more about mining than those Empire folks over in Grass Valley. Why work like a dog for some other man? Aye, Dave. Why indeed?"

Limpy takes a swig from his cup, wipes his mouth with the back of his hand, and with the same hand points at Muddy Boots, still bent over his bowl as if intent on ignoring him.

"And that there is John Thomas. Not much on manners, but . . . well, not much on anything."

"Damn you, Limpy," says Muddy Boots, his mouth full of food.

Alex can feel the big man's breath down her neck. He pulls a gold pouch from his pocket, holds it like an egg in the palm of his hand.

"And you are . . . ?" Limpy asks.

The curve of Emaline's brow, the curl of her lips, tells Alex these men know very well the name she gave.

"A simple question, son," says Limpy. "Name?"

Men lean forward, listening, and names and faces swim as

11

mismatched pairs through Alex's mind. She pulls her head into her neck, says as deeply as she can manage:

"Alex."

"Hah!" says Limpy, his paw slamming down again, this time square on her back, forcing all the air from her chest. "Eighteen, my ass. Who said eighteen? John Thomas, trying to hide? Alex what?"

"Shee-it," says Micah, thumping a small pouch of gold on the table and giving Alex a close look at the concave indention of skin where his left eye should be.

"Why thank you, Micah. Alex what?" Limpy asks again. Outside, a scrub jay screams the sun down.

"Ford?" Alex says, hearing the doubt in her own voice. Emaline's arms cross before her and her eyes narrow to slits, but Limpy doesn't seem to notice.

"Alex Ford," he says. "Solid name. No more than sixteen, if that. Pay up." Leather pouches thump on the table. "Pay up, John Thomas," says Limpy.

"Now just hold on a goddamn minute," John Thomas says, his fair skin turning the red of Micah's empty eye socket. "I'll pay you later."

"My ass."

"Hell yes, your ass – you calling me a liar?"

"Both of you better sit yourselves right back down," says Emaline, barely raising her voice. "Y'all know I don't permit no gambling at the dinner table. And you, Alex –" the serving spoon again jabs her direction – "finish up so I can get to getting done with dinner."

With the plank tables separated, the room feels smaller, cluttered. The ramshackle bar at the far end of the room now dominates, the counter lined with tin cups and a few glass canning jars, and now the elbows of Limpy and the one-eyed Micah. Bloated whiskey jugs on shelves behind the bar are blurred in the orange lamplight and look, to

Alex, like a row of rotund women. Several card games are already in progress when Alex eases her way up the stairs.

"Hey," says Emaline, pushing through the kitchen door. She thumps a stool down next to her own. "Stick a while."

And something, the weight of her filling that doorway, or the calm authority in her voice, triggers an old habit of obedience. Alex sits, but remains above on the stairwell with her chin tucked into her knees. She hadn't liked the suspicious glances the woman had been casting through dinner. She prays the woman's eyes are as poor as they seem.

"Whatever suits you," says Emaline, dismissing her with a wave of the hand.

"'Scuse me, gents, Emaline . . ." Limpy's voice and body rise as one from the bar and the saloon goes silent. "A toast. To Alex and his gentle way with mules. May his way with women be less costly, but just as exciting!"

He tips his glass, leads a collective swallow, motions to Jed to fill his cup again. "Now don't you dare smile there, Alex, don't." Alex does not feel like smiling, makes no attempt to smile. Six coins left, she thinks. She'd felt so rich with twelve.

"And speaking of costly," says Limpy, downing the next glass, "how 'bout it Emaline? Nearly hit it today. Sho' 'nough pay dirt. Pay you double price. I say I'll pay you double, tomorrow –"

"Now hold on there, Limp. You know the woman doesn't take credit, and I'm a hell of a lot prettier than you anyway – and richer," says Micah, winking his one eye.

"The hell –"

"And I can hold my liquor."

Alex is only vaguely aware of what they're saying. The rest of their banter is lost beneath the groan of the accordion in the corner – a tune that just might be "The Old Oaken Bucket" or "Clementine," or a wobbly combination of the

13

two – and as if called by this racket, miners begin to trickle into the saloon. No less than thirty, if she had a head to count, and she doubts whether some of those mud-stained canvas pants and holey flannels had ever been, or would ever be washed. It would certainly ease the competing stench of rotting canvas, stale tobacco, whiskey. The men lean on the bar and against the walls and against each other. They swear and laugh with their mouths wide open, chew plugs of tobacco, smoke cob pipes, and soon the air is thick and yellow. Their hands stroke leather pouches of gold dust, arrange and rearrange dog-eared playing cards, fiddle with the worn visors of discolored hats and punctuate speech with herky-jerky movements in the air. To Alex they are a collection of parts, of hands, feet and hats, interchangeable with a few exceptions: John Thomas; the big man, Limpy; the black man, Jed; one-eyed Micah; the mustache man, David, whose broad-angled shoulders give him a stocky compact appearance next to Limpy, even as he tops Micah by inches.

And there, sitting apart from the rest by the kitchen door, is Emaline. In her lap, a pair of trousers, needle, thread. Her fingers are busy, but she glances down only so often at her work.

Her weight is not so much the round softness of other women Alex has known, or the wire sinew of her gran. Emaline is solid, with wide, square shoulders and thick vein-tracked forearms. A fringe of dark hair feathers her upper lip. Her only softness appears to be her generous bosom that strains the front of her dress like mounds of rising sourdough. Emaline's hands work the cloth. Deft, confident movements, and Alex finds her fingers moving of their own accord, with life and memory of their own.

She forces her hands to fists, stuffs them in her pockets. Gran, too, could sew by feel alone, her fingers unconscious of themselves and of the bent-wire body to which they were attached. Gran was never so patient with Alex as she was with cloth. "After three boys," she liked to say, "three foolish, foolish boys, God at least could have given me a proper granddaughter."

Proper, Alex thinks. What would Gran think of her now, after all she's seen? After what she's done? She rises unnoticed, climbs the stairs. Thigh muscles catch and pull with every step. She slips across the hallway and closes the door of the dark little room behind her.

Mountain lion, Emaline thinks, and close by. She curses and grabs the shotgun by the bed. It won't be the first time she's been roused in the middle of the night to protect those damn chickens. Bothersome old biddies, scratching through the leaves all day, dining on leftovers. Women should be valued so much and paid so well for their monthly cycles. A dozen eggs brought her five dollars on Tuesday, more than that bigmouthed Limpy and his cousin David made together digging in the mud all day.

She hears the scream again – high pitched, like a woman – and hurries out of her bedroom door. The hall is morning dark, but Emaline has memorized the irregularities in the floorboards like the lines of her mother's face. She knows the sound of Micah's high nasal snoring escaping from the second room on her right. She'd thrown him out at midnight and listened while he clumped down the hall in unlaced boots. They never spent the night, her boys. She refuses to do business after midnight. They all know it by now and don't even grumble when she lights the lantern and hands them their boots. Grumbling costs extra.

She offers a product in limited supply in these parts, which is one of the reasons she moved to this little mud-hole town in the first place. Too much competition in the cities. Younger women, girls really, with exotic slanting eyes, or skin of rich amber – girls with pliant rubber bodies, born

15

with their legs wide open. They monopolize the market. They work cheap, happy to sell themselves on street corners. Or they work for someone else, leasing their bodies for a fancy costume, a place to stay and a tiny fraction of the price paid. Emaline is not cheap. She is experienced. She has the touch and can tell what a man needs by the length of his stride, the angle of his grin, the shape of the erection through his trousers. Her callused, muscled hands transform from tough and insistent to feather-soft, almost tender, and she knows that in the dark she is more beautiful than any of those city ladies.

She's halfway down the stairs when she hears the scream again, above her this time. Her arm hairs stand straight. The snoring stops, sputters, then begins again, softer. She grips the gun with white knuckles. She eases up the stairs. The hall is empty. She creeps on. Her ears twitch. A soft, high murmur from the first room. She opens the door. It whines.

Young Alex is lying tangled in his quilts. His head is thrashing back and forth, and pellets of sweat roll down his forehead. Emaline eases the gun to the floor, folds her arms in front of her and watches.

In the hallway, a floorboard creaks. Arms encircle Emaline's waist. A fuzzy head rests on her shoulder.

"Should we wake him?" Jed whispers in her ear.

"No," she says. "Better to deal with demons in sleep."

She closes the door and follows Jed back to her room.

# 2

Alex wakes to an empty cocoon of darkness, oblivious to all but the steady thump of her heart, the coarse wool blanket twining around her legs, hot breath against the skin of her arm. Last night she'd smelled bourbon, woke herself screaming. But for a moment she lingers in the pleasant fog of half sleep. For a moment there is no morning, no dreaming, no smell but the musk of her own sweat. There is only her pulse pounding at her temple, only the sheet beneath her head, and now unmistakably, unforgivably, the need to pee. She stands too fast, steadies herself against the wall. Her hair sticks out at all angles, perpendicular to her head, and she smashes the duster hat over the mess, stumbles to where she remembers the door to be and flings it open to the shock of sunlight.

Emaline's voice meets her at the stairwell.

"You heard me, John. You want, I'll yell in your good ear and pull your left right off your head, I will, preacher or no."

Her wide frame is bent at the waist over Preacher, spread-eagled in the middle of the doorway. She holds a whiskey jug by its eyelet and Preacher's red eyes follow its bobbing movement. He mumbles a response and she raises the jug high above her head.

"I don't care what the Lord tells you to do," says Emaline. "You get drunk on my whiskey, you pay for it."

Every bone, every muscle of Alex's body is stiff. She tiptoes down the stairs, bent like an old woman, clutching her pack to her chest to quiet the metallic jangle of the gold pan against the canteen. She pulls her hat low over her eyes, but this does nothing to prevent the last step from moaning beneath her.

"Well," says Emaline, "if it ain't our newest prospector."

With her hands on her hips, Emaline is as wide as the doorway.

"You missed breakfast," she says, and moves aside. Alex squeezes past her, steps over Preacher and out the door.

The outhouse squats forty yards beyond the inn. Alex crouches over the wooden hole, careful not to wiggle and get splinters. She holds her breath against the smell. Flies knock themselves against the walls. A wasp makes circles near the ceiling as though anchored with a string and Alex watches, glorying in that blessed release when a branch snaps. Her bladder freezes. A shadow blocks the slices of sunlight piercing the open spaces in the plank walls. Something slides beneath the door. A newspaper? No, a magazine: *Godey's Lady's Book*, the same Gran read, sometimes aloud in her high northeastern rasp, pointing out details of different fashions and pooh-poohing the poems. "All trying to be clever. Just say what needs said," she'd say. Or, if she really liked a poem, "Bunch of foolish fancy, that one."

All but two of the newsprint pages have been torn out. On the cover a woman with hollow eyes smiles primly. She wears a dark gown embroidered with gray flowers. The sleeves are long, ballooning slightly at the wrists, and the corseted waist tapers to a triangle, cutting the woman into two halves. The skirt billows like a napkin doily, the layers of petticoats beneath forming a womb-like vase of fabric, accentuating the very region they profess to protect.

"Hogwash," Gran would say. "One for her hips, one for her husband and one for the Holy Ghost. If a woman can't keep her peace with three petticoats, she won't do with ten."

She looked at Alex when she said this, as though imparting some great knowledge. Alex could only nod, never quite sure what "keeping the peace" entailed; she suspected it had something to do with walking slowly and with "proper reservation." Gran wasn't one to be questioned or contradicted, especially on her topic of expertise: women. She spoke in a removed manner of confident authority, as though age had absolved her of the vices of womanhood, leaving her only with the burden of virtue to pass on to her granddaughter, who, even as a young girl, especially as a young girl, found sitting still and walking slowly the most difficult virtues to master.

From Gran, Alex had learned the true nature of women – deceitful, manipulative, full of the sin of Eve – and she'd wondered more than once what kind of woman her mother had been, wondered if she too had been stricken with a wandering soul. Gran spoke little of Alex's mother, obviously did not think her worthy of her youngest son, Charles. Alex knew her only as the gold-etched daguerreotype by her bed.

Her mother's lips, thin and straight. Her mother's eyes, looking out but seeing nothing. Her body, a thin, flat frame.

Instead, Gran related her own family history as a moral tale. She told of her husband Nicolas, who insisted on fighting and, by Gran's telling, insisted on dying, in the Battle of New Orleans. Nicolas left her with three sons and no income, apart from her father's dairy farm, and the boys grew fast and foreign to her, each one following their father's reckless lead into military life, and eventually military death. Charles left behind baby Alex and a consumptive wife fated to live but three months longer than her husband. Alex had always understood that her existence was in itself a "burden endured" – had heard it put just this way by Minister Bosworth who, on occasion, was called upon to confirm Gran's low estimate of female virtue.

"A girl, from the time she is born, is at battle with her natural inclinations," the minister confirmed one day at tea while Peter, his son, made faces at Alex through the living-room window.

Alex had fidgeted in her chair, scowling at Peter and staring past him into the fall day. The leaves were just turning rose-brown. The apples were ripe.

"She must, growing and through adulthood, quell the evil spirit within her and, by her submissiveness, gain eternal redemption."

Gran's head was bowed when the minister said this, and did not see Alex stick out her tongue at Peter.

Alex looks up from the picture, suddenly aware that the shadow is still there. Gran fades into the nitric fumes of the outhouse.

"It's not for reading," Emaline barks, "and you're welcome." Then the shadow is gone.

Alex wads the front cover of the magazine, scrunching the dress, smashing the woman into a mass of crinkled paper. She wipes with the soft inside pages and drops them down the hole. But even as she makes her way along the road to the creek, the model's hollow eyes take the form of the rough-cut windows of canvas shacks, giving her the disconcerting sensation that the town itself is somehow following her, closer and closer toward the sputtering edge of the creek until the town too is swallowed by the sound of rushing water. She turns to face the silence behind her.

The windows of the frame and canvas cabins are not eyes. The splintered gray walls are not inching closer. The clouds gathering on the lip of the ravine look as if they are brushing the feathered heads of cedars, but the ravine walls are not collapsing around her. The brown-butted chickens, worrying their way up the road, scratching for worms and other treasures, ignore her completely. It's only the Victoria Inn, with its ornamental balcony, splintered balusters and peeling whitewash, that reminds her of an old woman's crumbling face.

At the creek the tops of men's heads bob from holes in the ground. They gather beside long wooden sluices, washing soil down hollow slat-lined boxes. Most work silently, adjusting to each other's tempo, and the few that stop to watch as she passes make no effort to speak. Better to keep her feet ahead of her thoughts. Better to fill her senses with California, once a word light with hope. She keeps step with the thump of an axe, pulls her hat to the very bridge of her nose, tries to ignore the blisters pinching the skin of her heel. Biting air fills her lungs. Her aching legs begin to warm and loosen.

Further upstream, the path narrows. Her eyes begin to wander. The overcast sky allows the ravine above the thinnest of shadows, while brambles and thickets form dark impenetrable outgrowths of branches and leaves. Fallen limbs, black with mold, litter the trail. Mushrooms grow from the fermenting dead leaves, and the crevices of lichen-covered rocks. The clank of metal on rock becomes distant. Men's voices are all but swallowed by the rush of water, the squawk of scrub jays. She pauses for breath at a flat outcropping.

She likes the way the valley opens here, offering a shelf of gravel and sand that gives way to a carpet of grass and clover running to the ravine wall. The clearing is buttressed on either side by a twisted thicket of red brush bursting with pale, coin-sized leaves. Black-skinned scrub oaks reach arthritically outward, and above, on the ridge, fir trees stand rigid.

At the creek, a row of rounded boulders protects a calm

enclave of frigid water. She skims her hands across the slippery green skin growing on a rock. She rummages in her pack for the gold pan, past the tin cup, the canteen, the money pouch. How heavy these few belongings had felt, how light she feels now, alone here by the creek. She scoops up a brimming pan of sand and water, remembering the old prospector on the outskirts of Rough and Ready.

FROM $10 TO RICHES, his sign had read, and beneath it a stack of gold pans rose one on top of the other like tortoise shells. She'd choked down a bite of the old man's barley bread. "The first fortune is always the hardest, wettest, coldest, meanest son-a-bitch you ever chase," he said. His voice was a gravel rasp, high pitched, and in this way reassuring to Alex. Already her shaking hands had stilled some. "They don't tell you that in those shipping fliers, do they? They don't need to. Gold! That's all they need, save the ink and paper. A man's not bound to read between the lines with a word like that to tempt him."

He emptied his pipe on the stump next to him and pointed up at her with a finger more bone than skin.

"I see myself in you, is what I'm saying, and I'm telling you it's not as easy as they make it sound, finding gold, getting rich. Nothing is, is it? A man can lose himself in the search – forget anything else ever mattered to him but gold, forget who he was and what he valued 'fore he came. It's a danger, like scurvy – sneak up and take your teeth 'fore you know it."

He bared a set of blackened incisors, yellow at their roots, but Alex's eyes lingered on the gold pans, and the word *gold* rested there on her shoulder as if it meant to follow her wherever she was going. She found herself reaching for her money pouch, giving the man a coin from her precious stash, though she knew better by now than to put faith in words, even those as shiny as gold. A crooked grin tugged his whiskers as he tucked the coin into his boot.

"What you do is, you find a likely spot, one that smells rich, like a rusted wheel axle. Hunch down, like this –" He eased off his stool and bent down to demonstrate, his knees jutting on either side of his shoulders. He mimicked scooping up a pan of soil and water. "Then you just rotate it round in a little circle. All in the wrist, see –" His hands were small and slender with brown sunspots dotting the backs like islands. The crease lines in his hands were mirrored in his face, and a thin white beard was the only trace of hair on his head. He moved the pan in circles. "The lighter stuff, sand and such – worthless. That'll slough off first, so what's left at the bottom, see, is the black sand, the heavy stuff. And the gold." When he stood, the man's back remained curved like the keel of a boat, and he had to crane his neck to look directly at Alex. "'Course, most nowadays is using the rocker and long tom, if they don't want to go down a hole, but thems require at least three to work right. Not long ago, miner by hisself only needed his pan. I know, I was here in '47 taking gold 'fore anyone know'd the name Cal-i-for-ni-a."

She takes a deep breath. The smell is organic, cedar bark, fermenting mud and mushrooms. No rust. She rotates her wrists clockwise. Small flecks of white, black, gold and gray swirl in suspension, spilling over the edge of the pan, staining her crotch and the front of her flannel. She sucks in her breath at the chill, dusts off the sand and silt, and bends down again, allowing her knees to jut on either side of her as the old man had done. She scoops less sand this time, less water.

She sets the pan like a boat on the water and watches it float downstream, catches it before it's swept away. She gives the pan a spin, it twirls like a top, throwing flashes of sunlight into her eyes. She scoops another bit of water and sand, this time angling the pan away. She works slowly, biting the end of her tongue, losing herself in the water and silt. Her forearms burn and she uses the pain to keep her mind from wandering back into memory. The manzanita rustles behind her.

She turns to face the teardrop ears of a doe frozen mid-step. Its tail twitches; its ears rotate, listening. Its pregnant belly is stretched taut. Liquid eyes fix beyond Alex, beyond the end of the clearing. Alex turns to look and the deer, even with her big belly, springs forward in two arching leaps before again halting, motionless.

Alex's ears twitch. Her heart begins to thud. She follows the direction of the doe's gaze to find herself in line with the muzzle of a rifle.

All she can see now is the gun, the tip round and glinting silver, and she thinks, how quickly, how effortlessly they found me, before I even knew where I was going. She rises to her feet and the doe braces to run, every muscle and ligament tense. The gunshot shatters the stillness; the metal whizzes like a breath past her ear. She hears metal strike flesh and flesh thump to the ground, and only now does Alex begin to shake, the instinct to run so strong she is paralyzed.

John Thomas leaps from the manzanita grove. "I got 'em, Jed," he yells, eyeballing Alex.

"You get 'em?" says Jed, crashing through the brush behind John Thomas.

"I said I got 'em."

The two men crouch over the body as it slides into death. Its eyes stare, too pained for fright, and Alex can't help but look down where the bullet has pierced the belly. The taut skin has split around the wound and a small, hoofed leg twitches through the hole.

"Cut the throat," says Jed.

"Be dead in a minute."

"Cut her now, goddamn it," says Jed. He grabs his own knife and slashes the doe's throat. Blood surges crimson from its jugular. He stabs the belly and the fawn's leg stills. He pauses a moment, letting the blood drain, then guts the animal, leaving the rope-like entrails steaming on the grass, and thrusts the small body of the fawn behind him, out of his line of sight, directly in front of Alex.

There are memories here, gathering like flies on the vein-tracked birth sac.

"Alex?" says Jed.

The smell of blood, thick enough to choke her . . .

"You all right? Alex?" She opens her eyes. The doe's legs drape about Jed's shoulders like a shawl.

"Nearly cost us the kill," says John Thomas.

"Well now . . ." says Jed, and then, grunting under the weight, he heads down the trail to town.

"Don't know what the hell you're doing up here anyway. Hey – you deaf?" says John Thomas, waving his hand in front of her face.

He's only just taller than her, but far bigger through the shoulders. The pupils of his eyes are no bigger than pinheads. The curl of his lip disgusts her and for a moment it is this man dead on the grass before her, his belly ripped throat to gullet.

"I hear you," she says.

John Thomas steps closer, as if hearing the challenge in her tone, and she's not so sure he won't shoot if she runs. She's not sure if she cares, but finds herself backing away, splashing into the creek. Cold water tugs at the hem of her trousers, soaks through the toes of her boots. John Thomas grins.

"Claim jumping's a hanging crime. You ever see a man hanged? No? Dangles there, like a dead fish. Broken neck, if you're lucky. Quick that way. Don't cry, though, don't piss your pants," he says, and he aims the rifle at her water-stained crotch. "I'd shoot yah if you was to live through the drop. First in the balls. One POP, then the other – POP, POP. And then in the kneecaps –"

"Then the toes, then the elbows, then the stomach. Seems

to me I heard this before sometime, Johnny. Seems to me David, here, has too," Limpy hollers. He emerges from the upstream trail and David follows, his shoulders alive with compact energy.

"Limpy, this ain't no goddamned business of yours," says John Thomas, but the gun falls to his side and Alex steps away.

"Yours neither, if I remember right," Limpy replies.

"I made this claim four months ago."

"And ain't been back for two. Ten days, Johnny. It's the law. Right, David?"

David's large hands strain white around the pick. His nostrils flare. Beneath the upturned brim of his Panama hat, his eyes pierce John Thomas.

"And don't try and tell me you was here workin' this claim all the time, 'cause me and David been by every day and never seen you. You ain't even staked it."

Limpy winks at Alex, and John Thomas's face turns red to the roots of his eyebrows.

"Ain't no gold here, nohow," John Thomas says. As he stomps away, he kicks the fawn with the toe of his boot, and Alex's stomach seizes. She wants them all to go, but her thoughts, her desires, go no deeper than this. She's wading shallow on the surface of her mind, afraid to slip deeper into the current of her memories.

Limpy ambles up as though a friendly hello was his only reason for being there.

"You ain't planning on getting rich with that, are yah?" he says, and she finds she is clutching the gold pan to her chest.

"Ah hell," says Limpy, "never mind. Just stay out of the way of that fella. Them little ones is always the meanest, yourself excluded, 'course." He chuckles a bit, raising his hands as if in surrender. "Come on, Dave," he says, and lumbers up the path.

"You listen to Limpy, yeah? Stay out of the way of John Thomas," David says, his voice tipping in a funny foreign lilt. He lingers for a response. He shifts his weight in the silence, transfers his pick to the other shoulder, and turns to follow Limpy, leaving Alex alone with the steaming carcass of the fawn.

Stay out of his way? She drops the gold pan to the grass and steps toward the fawn. Her eyes sting, but stay dry. Impossible, she thinks. Flies scatter as she bends down. Everywhere is in the way.

The little body is much heavier than it looks, the flesh warm to the touch, the blood and placental fluid slick like the green ooze of the rocks. She holds the fawn away from her, sits back on her haunches, squatting above the branching stream of blood. She imagines that it's her blood, thinks it should be her blood. The damp mercuric smell fills her head and the insects swarm about her, taunting, whispering, mimicking Gran's hissing breath. "Natural inclinations," Gran says, shaking her head and rocking, rocking by the side of the bed.

Alex doesn't bleed as she should, not any more, not since the night her blood filled that bed, soaking through the mattress to the wood beneath. She lay there as her insides shredded themselves, and she bled and bled until there was no blood left, and Peter never came, and Gran just sat and rocked like Alex rocks, holding the fawn away from her as the flies surround them both. In California she's learned that there are many ways to bleed. The smell of bourbon . . . Don't think. She moves to the side of the creek, holds the fawn underwater, lets the current tug and take it away.

She washes her hands.

"Got a brother about that age," David says when he catches up to Limpy. "At least, he was when I left. Must be near a man now, working underground with the rest of them."

27

"We all got someone, somewhere," Limpy replies, and David says nothing more.

They settle down to work a half mile upstream from Alex at a claim that has yielded modest yet steady returns of an ounce a day for the nine months they'd been there. But David is not satisfied. There is gold in this creek, more than an ounce a day. He can feel it like some men feel storms coming. He can smell it in the iron-rich soil, taste it when he puts the soft igneous mud to his tongue. So different from Cornwall, this country. Soil the color of dried blood. Trees rising like the giants of Cornish legend. Clandestine peaks and valleys breaking the horizon into pieces. He misses the sound of the ocean, the pebble beaches and flat expanses of crab grass interrupted by white seven-lobed flowers, feathery, yellow dandelions and sun-sensitive bluebells in spring. He misses the salt smell of the air, and watching storms appear and then recede into the Atlantic. He misses the insistence of the wind, at times soft like a fluttering kiss, and at others brutal with an angry intensity, refusing to be ignored or even merely appreciated. Demanding respect and fear, like God.

"Without the wind," his father told him, "a man might forget just how small he is."

Over time, his father had shrunk, and not just in relation to his second son's growing body. Only forty years old and already the tin mines had blackened his consumptive lungs and bent his back like a man many years older. His hands were hard-cut stones and his arms wire sinew blanched pale in the pitch darkness of the mine. Soon he would be restricted to the crushing grounds, sorting the pulverized ore in the wind and rain with the women, girls and young boys, while one by one his sons descended underground.

David imagines them waking before dawn, choking down a thin gruel, trekking three miles down the Penzance coast in a ragged line with father in the lead and mother in tow. Six boys, five now with David gone, and a baby girl, a

28

three-year-old who runs screaming with the other children, kicking clods of ore like other kids kick cans. Two miles off, the ore stamps move the ground in a steady rumble the family hardly feels. Then they part. The four oldest boys and father climb an hour down into the belly of the earth, with its damp, black walls. Climb down with only a candle for light, a pick for work, and a pasty for lunch to:

*earn enough money*
*to buy enough bread*
*to get enough strength*
*to dig in a hole*

Unending. Such a future makes any man feel small, wind or no. David wanted more. But his father was a stubborn man.

"Follow in the paths of greed and find sorrow in the next life as well as this."

"It's not greed. It's a new life, a chance to work for yourself."

"It's a metal, like any other." He grabbed the flier from his son's hand and tore it down the middle, separating the *Cali* from the *fornia* and the *G* from the *old*.

"You planning on working today?" Limpy asks. David shakes himself into the present, bends and sets his pick on the ground by a wooden contraption. A rocker, they call it, or a cradle, like an infant's bed made from an old whiskey barrel cut in half and fitted with a row of wooden slats. It is not an elegant machine. The sides of the barrel are splintering and a pungent black fungus has begun to eat away the bottom. More a coffin than a cradle, David thinks. He picks up the hopper with its perforated metal bottom and places it back atop the cradle. Limpy dips two buckets in the creek as David shovels a load of earth into the hopper. While David rocks the cradle,

Limpy pours water over the agitated soil, making several trips to the creek until the dirt has washed through the hopper. The lighter, worthless minerals wash away, leaving the gold trapped in riffle slats at the bottom. Same idea as the gold pan really, only more efficient; if efficient is a word rightly used to describe alluvial mining. Returns have been too low. David didn't come all the way from Cornwall to dig in the mud, freezing his knackers off in the winter, frying them in the summer, all for one or two ounces of gold a day. He came for the lucky strike, the rich vein, the motherlode. Be damned if he'll ever again climb down a hole to make some other man rich.

After a while, they switch; David totes the water and Limpy shovels and rocks. Their faces are pink. Little beads of sweat gather at their temples, mix with the mud and streak rust-brown tracks down their cheeks. Downstream, the steady clank of picks and shovels mixes with the noisy murmur of the creek. The sun is directly overhead, and most of the birds have muted their songs till evening time. On flat, worn rocks, winter-stiff lizards rouse themselves to bask.

"Wouldn't hurt to have some help. Someone to shake the cradle," Limpy says, as David pours a bucket into the hopper. The water splashes, speckling his trousers. "Been thinking 'bout a long tom or a sluice box. Need more men to work one of those." He rocks the cradle until David returns with another bucket of water. "Said yourself he reminded you of your brother."

"My brothers are in Cornwall." David dumps the water. "That boy's too scrawny to hold a shovel. He probably wouldn't know gold from pyrite."

"I don't know. Got me a feeling about that boy." Limpy stares off down the creek.

"You got a feeling about anyone you made money off," says David.

Limpy only acknowledges this remark with a gesture.

"'Sides," he says, "bound to fill out working claims, ain't he? What with Emaline feeding 'im."

"I'd like to know how he's paying for that."

"City boy with a face for theatre," Limpy says.

David glances at him, looks away. "Not that pretty."

# 3

The saloon door squeals open and footsteps clump toward the stairs. Emaline sticks her head through the kitchen door.

"Alex," she says. The boy stops but doesn't turn. "Come on back a minute, have a seat at the table."

It's not a request, but when she returns from the kitchen with two cups of coffee, he's still standing in the stairwell, bracing himself with a hand on the railing, a hand on the wall.

"Sit," says Emaline, and he slinks to the stool across from her. "I don't allow hats inside the saloon." He sweeps it from his head and his hair falls forward into his face. He sits on his hands as though they were tied behind him.

She doesn't mind the quiet ones, to a point. David is quiet, but the silence is natural on him. This one sits on his words same as he's sitting on his hands, and she doesn't like the way he won't look at her. Up close, she can see his face is narrow, his nose and chin slender, his eyes, when he shows them, are the same black color as the hair hanging shaggy and jagged before his eyes. I've got more whiskers on my face, she thinks, and scratches at the patch above her lip. When she was living in the city, she'd pluck them out, the thick black ones bringing tears to her eyes. Shedding tears over a few silly hairs. But she was younger then. Not stupid, or even vain, so much as inexperienced. Maybe that's what bothers her about this boy: that spooked look of experience.

She pushes a cup in his direction. His hands remain beneath him. She leans forward, places her forearms on the table closer to Alex. He looks up, down.

"I'm gonna ask you what you're doing here," she says.

"I'm looking for go –"

"That's not an answer," says Emaline, shaking her head. "Everybody's looking for gold. What are you doing here, in Motherlode?"

But the boy clamps his mouth shut. Something close to defiance hangs there over his head, and his eyes look off beyond her.

"Listen," she says. "You listening? You paid me enough for the week, and I understand you got a bit more stashed away. I ain't even going ask how you got it. But let's be clear right here and now . . . You listening?"

She slams her mug down, leaving an opaque ring of coffee on the table. She's not used to being ignored. She never did like it much.

"Look at me. We don't want no trouble around here. If you're running from something, best just keep on running, hear?"

She can almost feel the tension in his shoulders, can see his jaw clenching. His feet cross at the ankles and he hunches down, as if trying to be even smaller than he already is. If she were the mothering type, she'd act on this impulse to hug him.

"I ain't meaning to throw nobody out, 'less they give me reason. You give me reason, you're gone. Understand? Out of the Victoria. Out of Motherlode. Understand?"

Alex nods once.

"Good. Now, if you got something to claim, I suggest you do it before John Thomas gets himself to the assay office.

He's already been here complaining like a son-of-a-bitch, but I know you wouldn't jump nobody's claim." She lets the statement arc into a question. Alex doesn't respond. "The back of Micah's general store. Sign reads 'Assay Office,' though it ain't much more than a counter."

She drinks down her coffee in four gulps, leaves him sitting there.

When she returns, Alex's full cup is blowing steam to the ceiling. Thankless little snot, she thinks, as she carries the cup back into the kitchen. She wishes she knew what he's doing here. Spoiled little rich kid, running away from daddy's expectations with daddy's money, most likely. Yet she doesn't detect the usual arrogance of the moneyed little pricks she's known in the past. Cocky young things, strutting around like a bunch of banty roosters 'cause no one ever told them they shit out the same hole as everyone else. And why would any rich kid come to a canvas town like Motherlode when Grass Valley and Nevada City were only miles away and fit to burst with pretty girls, theaters, saloons, restaurants, hotels, brothels and countless other ways to spend money? No, silent Alex had to be running from something.

She glances out the window at Jed bringing the day's water from the creek. He sets down the buckets just inside the kitchen door and gives her one of his big-toothed smiles. Emaline walks over, takes his head in both hands and kisses him on the lips. They linger, exchanging air, grinning so their teeth click together. He leaves without a word and Emaline props herself in the doorway to watch. We're all running from something, she thinks, but she stops her thoughts there.

The kitchen is a pine-sided addition to the back of the inn and can get mighty cold in the winter before the stove is stoked, and mighty warm in the summer when the heat puckers its dry lips to suck the energy right out of you. It's the heat that gets you, she thinks, rolling her sleeves to her elbows. There are only so many clothes a woman can take off, though she's sure the boys wouldn't mind a certain amount of flesh exposed on a hot day. They walk around with their trousers rolled to their knees and their shirts in hand and wonder, at the end of the day, why they're burned to a crisp. Alex is bound to make that mistake as well. The new boys always do. A ball of gray fuzz scurries across the floor. Emaline stomps after it, misses. In the potatoes again. Just when she patches a hole in that barrel, the mice go and chew another one. With the raccoons getting into the beans and the mice in the 'taters, it's a wonder there's any food left at all. Must be feeding half the county's critters.

She takes the lid from the flour barrel, pours a measure into a large ceramic bowl with a bit of sourdough starter, adds a generous dollop of lard, an egg, a pinch of precious salt, and begins to knead. Someday she'll have a proper kitchen, free of mice, with walls that keep the heat in over the winter and out in the summer. A cast-iron stove with a smokestack that doesn't leak blackness into the place, and doesn't blow itself out the minute she turns her back. There'll be a cellar to keep wine, apples, cabbages, root vegetables and the dairy, if she ever gets a cow, and her floor will be polished flagstone that a once-over with a broom will keep clean. She'll have polished oak counters to replace the splintered pine planking, a great big larder and a separate scullery and, oh, an indoor pump, so they can stop toting water from the creek. She wipes a line of sweat with the back of her hand. Lord knows what's in the water with all those filthy miners wallowing in it every day. She hefts the iron pot from the floor, fills it with a bucket and a half of water, and stokes the fire.

Outside she hears the steady thump of Jed's axe and looks up from her dough to watch. With his shirt rolled she can see his corded forearms ripple. A bead of sweat trickles down his cheek on to the chopping block. His muscled thighs press against the skin of his trousers and she imagines his back, hard and smooth under her touch, and his voice, a soft rumble in her ear. Who needs a nice kitchen when you have Jed? She smiles, adding water a trickle at a time to the bread bowl. Certain things in this life you can do without. She supposes running water is one of them.

The wind has come up on the ridge. The cedars brace themselves and Alex can hear the squeal of air through the crags and the branches. It sounds like an accusation; a noxious mix of guilt and indignation swirls within her. Who is that woman to throw her out of town? As if it were her right to do so, as if this muddy valley, that dark little room, is somewhere she wants to stay. There had been nothing to keep her from leaving, from following the direction of her gaze around the grove of manzanita and out of town. Nothing, that is, but the steepness of that trail, the blisters on her feet, the thought of shivering the night away in a thicket, and now she finds she wants to stay, for a while at least, until it's her choice to leave.

The rain begins to fall, bringing men from the creek. She retreats within the general store – dank with layers of dust, dark for lack of a window.

Every square inch of wall space is covered with rows of empty plank shelves propped with metal rods. Piles of picks and shovels, barrels of black powder litter the floor, and scatterings of mateless boots lie prostrate like rotting carcasses. With the dust and the leather the place smells of a tack room and Alex holds her nose against a sneeze. Along the back wall, behind the counter, are tins of tobacco, bottles of large blue pills marked QUININE and CALOMEL, jars of brandied fruits, and a mound of clothing, heaped like boneless bodies.

Alex sits, resting her head in her hands. The gloom of the place is quickly turning angry determination to self-pity, when a blast of cold air and light rush into the room.

"Well, hello there, Alex. Heard you been claim jumping a claim jumper. No, no need to get up," says Micah. He closes the door behind him and scratches at that empty eye socket. "Might as well make use of them clothes."

She stands anyway as raindrops thwap one by one, each making its own indention in the canvas roof. Lightning flashes blue and the rain begins in earnest.

"Lordy, here we go," says Micah, looking skeptically at his roof. He wears canvas pants like the other men, but he keeps a pencil in a pocket he's stitched to his flannel. He stands with his hips thrust out as if his back hurts him. His brown hair hangs shaggy over his ears, and his low round forehead and bulbous nose wrinkle in a smile, friendly even with the one eye.

"John Thomas can be an ass – don't I know it. Gave me hell my first week as well, so don't take it personal. Challenged me to a duel for sitting in his chair at supper, and probably would have done me in, too, if Emaline hadn't put a stop to it. Foolishness, she told us. Grown men going around killing each other when there are plenty other things in this country to do it for us. Makes sense, doesn't it? That put us straight, of course. That and the double-barreled shotgun she likes to tote around with her. There is wisdom in women, boy. And pure hellfire. A frightening combination, to be sure, but effective. Remember that. Between you and me, I think ol' John Thomas has got a thing for her. Not that most of us haven't, had a thing, now and again – you know what I mean? No?"

Alex feels her cheeks flush. Colored women, Gran called them. A colored woman was threatening to kick her out of town? She certainly didn't fit the description of bawdyhouse ladies Alex has heard about. Emaline's cheeks were unpainted, and Alex doubts that her shoulders, or any other part of her, would fit into the dresses they wore.

"Of course you know," says Micah, winking his one eye. "But John Thomas has got a *thing* for her." Micah rummages for a match, but the lamp on the counter produces only a yellow light, feeble and sickly.

"Now, what can I do you for? You got yourself a pan, though if Limpy isn't telling tales, you got some learning to go on how to use it. You're gonna need a pick and shovel, no doubt, a bit of quicksilver . . . You got a hat, good. Every miner needs a good solid hat. Keeps off the rain, keeps off the sun. Though both are good in moderation. In moderation, son, like women and whiskey. Remember that. Lordy! If you paid any more than fifteen dollars for those boots you got had. Now, don't go looking down, it happens to the best of us . . ."

Micah pauses as if he needs a moment to digest his own wisdom, then scuttles around the shop giving a verbal inventory.

"Limited variety, I know. But that's what you get in a town full of men. All a man really wants is his tobacco, a little salt pork and flour, and a new shirt when the old one falls off his back."

He hands Alex a pick. The wood is smooth and cool in her hands and heavier than she imagined from the way the men were swinging them this morning.

"Nice, huh? Try this one for size –" Micah takes the pick and hands her a shovel. "Man's got to be comfortable with his equipment. Feel good, yeah? Yeah?"

She can see the muscles of the empty socket twitching beneath his skin, trying to focus. He rests his weight against the pick.

"Women, see – real, civilized, lacy women – they bring variety to a place. Soon you're stocking fancy furniture and silk cloth and fancy plates and such. Women, son, the spice of life. Remember that. Should have seen my store in Grass Valley. Packed with trinkets and trifles from France, Chile, England, God knows where else. Barely had room for breeches."

Micah sighs and quiets for a moment.

"Mr. . . ." Alex begins.

"Micah, son, call me Micah."

"Micah. I suppose I'm meant to, well, a claim?"

"'Meant to well a claim.' Nearly got yourself a sentence there, boy. But the answer's yes. Limpy came in here not ten minutes ago, made that claim for you, in your name. Took care of it, is what I'm saying, and not a minute before John Thomas came in here whining about it. Be thankful to him, if I were you, but not too thankful. Limpy's got his ways of getting more than he gives out of folks, remember that.

"'Course, you got to go to Nevada City and file in the county court to make it official, but we like to keep our own selves straight. More of a formality till someone finds something worth claiming. I doubt the county even knows we're up here."

A shout sounds from the road outside, and another answers.

"Anyhow," says Micah, "it's typically done the other way round, see. Find the gold, then make the claim. I'd do my own staking, too, if I was you. Later. Right now it's looking –" Lightning flashes again, the electric energy stands tiny hairs on Alex's neck and arms on end. "I say it looks like the weather's gonna keep us all in for a while. 'Bout time, too. Been a dry winter. Mark it clear, when you mark it. Each corner. Sell you some of these, if you want –" He brandishes four wooden stakes. "And a sign nearby stating your right. The law says one hundred feet by fifty, but no one really follows that round here. Just as long as it's clearly marked and not overlapping anyone else, which shouldn't be a problem up there. Nobody's found enough gold to waste the water on, in truth. But, hell, luck's no predictable animal. Remember that."

He pauses and Alex fills the space with a nod. "This all you need? 'Cause I'm not usually open but two days a week, the other being day before last."

Alex nods.

"Fine. Now, gotta ask for cash I'm afraid. Credit comes with a strike you understand. Only reasonable."

It rains for three days, and for three days Alex sits on the staircase staring down into the saloon as if watching a Christmas pantomime. She has no part in it. She is above, looking down, finding it difficult to remain aloof and indignant with solitude's cold hands curling around her, making the walls feel very close and the people below very far away. No one seems to see her there. No one says her name.

Rain, as it falls outside, traps old air in the saloon. She thinks, every breath I take is someone else's breath discarded. I am eating other people's air. She thinks, this should make me full and larger than I am. She thinks, if I stay in this place, I will eat enough man breath to become a man, and I will play cards and drink whiskey and they will never find me. She thinks, it would take two of Gran and two of me to equal one of Emaline, standing there with Jed behind the bar, now mending a sock, now bringing bread from the oven, everywhere at once, and occasionally she heads upstairs with a slack-jawed miner with money in hand. Alex moves over to let them pass.

She thinks, the smell of whiskey is sweeter than wine; but she's only tasted wine, and then only sips. Nearly a week on her feet, nearly a week of constant movement and now no place to go but her thoughts. She tried to escape to the creek that first rainy day, stood cold and wet on the edge with her claim stakes and shovel as a liquid train of water crashed downstream, covering claims, filling coyote holes and toppling the windlasses into the gutted sink of soil.

Jed said, "You don't play games with a river in heat – if you was thinking 'bout working today." He shouted this over the water and over the rain, and she watched and shivered while he dipped a water bucket, holding on as the current gripped and yanked.

Now the road is a river, or many tiny rivers all running toward the creek, a thousand strands of motion, and Alex trapped inside on the stairwell thinking about the four gold coins left in her money pouch, how rich she'd felt with six coins.

Limpy is telling the same story he'd told two days ago, but with a few details added for variety. Three whores instead of the two, and he changed the place from Grass Valley to Nevada City. No one seems to notice or care, and Emaline just nods her appreciation. The jealousy takes Alex by surprise.

She thinks, if I were a man I would be loud like Limpy, and tell stories and everyone would laugh; or I would be very quiet like David, with everyone listening real hard those times I did speak.

She notices the way David moves from his stool to the bar and back again, filling space, not taking it like Limpy. His legs bow outward a bit and he walks on the outside of his feet. He looks it next to Limpy, but David is not a small man. He's at least six feet tall with broad shoulders that angle from his neck. His drooping mustache calls attention to a small lipless mouth and cleft chin. His hands are always folded or at his side, different hands altogether than the ones straining white against the handle of his pick a few days ago. "Stay out of his way next time," he'd said, and now she sits alone on the stairwell, out of everyone's way. She thinks, I would become a man who fills space and I would not be afraid to leave this step. And sometimes, when she loses focus, loses herself in the yellow smoke of the room, her thoughts turn into memories.

The hemlock grove and apple trees of the Hollinger orchards back home. She's climbing as high as the apple branches will bear with Peter on the ground looking up. "Not so high," he says. And Gran poking a knobby knuckle through a tear in Alex's petticoat. "Natural," Gran says, shaking her

41

head. "Natural inclinations." Klein heaves the accordion into another song, and a lanky miner with the ears of a much larger man stands near the bar to sing a sad song about lovers and loss. As his voice trails off from a soft, flat tenor to a forced vibrato, the room is silent.

"Uplifting as always, Mordicai," says Limpy. A clap of thunder takes his voice and the day outside flashes bright, and dulls as quickly. "Who's next then? Bible verses allowed, but not recommended till twilight, ballads are capital and stories divine."

The one called Harry folds a hand of cards, pushes his stool back, and sweeps down in a dramatic bow all but lost on his audience. He's a stocky man, with thick coarse hair and fleshy cheeks. She's never seen him without Fred, the gaunt-faced fellow to his right. Captain Fred. Captain Fred Henderson, if the cavalry cap he wears is his own. She's heard stories of cavalrymen, and Fred looks anything but broad chested and daring.

"A poem . . ." Harry says in the voice of someone used to being heard above a crowd. Around him card games and conversations continue, some in strange languages Alex couldn't understand even if no other sound competed. ". . . by Harold Daniel Reynolds."

"The third!" says Limpy.

"Why not? The third!"

> *Old Bob Blue got his heart broke in two*
> *When a lady, the love of his life,*
> *Ran off with a stranger in snake-skin boots*
> *And a gift for throwing the dice . . .*

And the rhythm of the poem, the way one line ends in expectation of the next, bring the walls of the inn even closer around her. The second ceiling of smoke and ash rises and falls with his voice, until the laughter and words are magnified, mixed and unintelligible.

Harry finishes his poem with a flourish and bows again, his balding head pointing to the floor. Alex claps with the rest. Emaline's eyes scrunch at the sides, her mouth open, her big teeth crooked yellow. Women shouldn't laugh with their mouths wide open, Alex thinks, but wants more than anything to feel that good, to be included. Outside, the rain continues. On the ridge the wind moans through the cedars and into the valley, and Alex feels the cold through her flannel. She thinks, I will grow a skin thick enough to fight the cold, tough enough to join the men below. But for three days she stays alone on the stairwell.

"What do you think?" David asks, surveying his claim.

Limpy jabs his shovel into the mud, folds his arms over his great chest. A wash of silt covers the rocker and the fungus-eaten bottom is now a gaping hole. The hopper and apron lie twenty feet away, wedged between a granite boulder and a wall of shale.

It would feel so good to rage, David thinks, to punish some tangible and contained foe. But the weather is neither tangible nor contained. Its neck cannot be snapped on a gallows rope, or safely imprisoned behind stone and mortar. A Cornishman knows that the weather will always be at large. And here in California there are no giants of legend to blame for it, no magic.

"What do you think?" David asks again.

Limpy shoves his hat back and scratches his receding hair. A half dozen miners packed and left this morning, looking for richer claims upriver, east to Nevada, or north to Vancouver Island. Long-legged Mordicai had been among them.

"Been hearing things about the Fraser River," he told David. "I aim to get there *before* the rush this time." He glanced back once at Bobcat Creek, tipped his hat to Emaline, and strode stork-like out of town.

David bends down and picks up a broken riffle bar. He

will not write home about this. He hasn't written in months and won't until he has the gold to prove himself a success, to prove his father wrong. *It's a metal like any other.* He's been away two years now. Two years with nothing to show, and he won't return until he can buy himself a farm in a quiet, out of the way valley and raise the wheat that refused to grow in that salty Land's End air, that rocky Penzance soil. A heretical ambition for a fourth-generation miner whose family had always dug for their dinner.

"I think . . . I think I'd like to try a sluice this time," Limpy says.

David nods and hurls the splintered wood into the creek.

Alex has fleas. They invaded two nights ago when the rains began, emerging from the cloth tick of her bedclothes and taking happy bites ever since.

She slaps and misses a black speck, gone before she's even sure it was there. The sun's white light is tearing a hole through the cloud cover. She slogs through the red mud, sucking in the fresh air as if she's been underwater. The creek crashes by.

That morning, several miners had left town. They blamed Motherlode for their bad luck.

"Luck don't have a location," Emaline told Mordicai, the lanky man who sang the sad songs.

"Gold does," he said, and tipped his hat goodbye.

Alex had followed him out the door of the inn to the porch. She stood out of the way, but close enough to be noticed if Emaline wanted, close enough, she thought, to warrant some acknowledgement. "Got to build luck around you," is what Emaline said, more to the chickens clamoring about than to Alex, even as the heat of the woman's body reached out to brush away some of Alex's coldness. Alex waited. Her eyes wandered from Emaline's wide posterior to the reed-thin man disappearing around the row of manzanita. She even scuffed her feet as a chicken might scratch for a worm, but Emaline had nothing to say to her. Alex could stay. Alex could go.

She thinks about the way Emaline laughed with her mouth wide open, how Limpy's stories grew larger and longer with every whiskey, how David held his cards to his chest as if they were sacred things, and how Preacher sat with his Bible and mumbled to himself, slipping drinks when he thought no one was looking. Alex was always looking, so that at night, warm in her little room, hugged by darkness, she could recreate those images and suffocate other pictures that crept into her dreams. Her mind had a skin too, and she could already feel it thickening. Stay a few more days, she thinks. Just a few more days and then I'll go.

She picks her way up the narrow trail, past the wreckage of abandoned claims, over fallen trees and branches. Mud and gravel have slid from the ravine, forming a tongue of earth that sticks like a wedge from the wall of her clearing. Scrub jays and robins streak down to snap up earthworms wriggling in the red clay. Slivers of pastel grass poke through like fingers to the sun. One of the granite boulders protecting the cove has washed yards downstream and her quiet pool is now a mass of charging water. All remnants of the carcass have been washed away. She takes a wooden stake from her pack. She pounds it in at the water's edge. She hefts her pick to her shoulder, looking for a spot to place the next stake, and allows her mind to travel back to another spring day, or one of many that featured her and Peter climbing trees in the Hollinger orchard. Back then the whole of her life took place tomorrow.

"I want to be a soldier," Peter told her as he pulled himself up into the apple tree.

"So?" said Alex, straddling a branch, enjoying the friction between her legs. "Be a soldier."

"Pa says I'm meant to be a pastor."

45

It must have been spring. The wind was colder than the air and the smell of mountain laurel and apple blossom made her eyes water. She wiped her nose and rubbed the snot across Peter's leg.

"Stop." He punched her in the arm and fought to stay balanced. She'd begun to enjoy teasing him like this. She didn't know why.

Alex dropped to the ground, scanned the rows of apple trees for Farmer Hollinger, who hated children in his orchard even more than birds. "My Pa was a soldier," she said, and Peter swung upside down by his legs. His hair fell on end and she could see up his nostrils. "My Pa's dead."

Peter knew both of these facts, but she often dangled the death of her parents above him like a prize gem, though she never understood his fascination.

"You can be anything," Peter said once in explanation. "Anything you want to be." They both knew it wasn't true.

She swings the pick, ducks as metal rebounds off rock. Chunks of granite and shale cascade around her. She swings again.

She used to lie in bed wondering what it would be like to be Peter. What would it be like to call someone mother and someone father, to wake each morning to organ music and hymns, for as a small child this was how Alex imagined Peter starting every day. Alex held no such illusions now.

Down comes a satisfying clump of red clay and a chunk of granite, speckled black like dirty rock salt. Again and again she swings, finding a haunting satisfaction in the crumbling mountainside, as if she were tearing away pieces of herself with the chunks of rock and sand, as if digging far enough would bring her face to face with . . . Who? What? She doesn't know any more. Perhaps digging is enough; to make a small indention in an unknown mountain. She digs until her breath comes hard, and her shoulders and back burn. She sucks in cold damp air, rubbing rough stones back and forth in her hands. Drops them. Olive-colored plants with velvet lobes nearly a foot long grow out from the hillside. Root stems, some thick as a man's arm, course the wall as if holding it together or clawing to get out. And there, wedged in the crook of a wooden elbow where bits of rock and dirt have gathered, is an egg-sized stone. Lusterless yellow and much heavier than it looks, she thinks, rolling it back and forth in the palm of her hand.

"Alex?"

A shadow drapes itself across her. She whips around, but it's only David, squinting up at the crater, down at her hand. He'd come up so silent.

"What is it you have there?"

David steps closer. Alex backs away a bit, opens her mouth to answer, then looks down at the rock in her hand. She holds the solid mass out to David.

"Gold?"

# 4

Of course, as soon as she says the word *gold* she begins to doubt, and while David does not deny her statement, he does not confirm it either. He drops to his knees and bows his head as if in prayer, rubbing ore between his fingers. He touches his fingers to his tongue, and his eyes grow round. His eyes track the angle of the ravine from base to skyline.

"David?" says Alex, but he's up now and striding out of the clearing. He looks back once, a gesture she receives as an invitation to follow.

Men attach, like links in a chain, as they weave down the trail. The only sound is the sucking of boots in the mud; even the birds are silent, watching this strange migration. The afternoon sun, magnified and reflected through drops of water beading from tree leaves and rooftops, creates a million shimmering lights dripping to the ground. Alex jogs to keep up with David and ahead of those boots behind her. She's surprised to find a small knot of men already waiting outside the general store.

"What in the Sam Hill is going on? Back in ten minutes, you said. What is everyone . . . ?"

Limpy pushes his way through the men. He wipes snot off

his nose and mustache with the back of his hand and spits a mass of yellow to the ground at Alex's feet.

"David?" he says.

The crowd contracts, tightening around her like the constricting segments of an earthworm, becoming one animal with eighty eyes. She's afraid to look and find a fist full of mud. The gold she's seen came in flakes of color, or minted coins with heads and letters stamped like epitaphs, or gleaming nuggets filling the pages of the steamship fliers and travel bills. This had been a lump of jagged edges, just the size of her palm, a heavy lusterless stone like any of the hundreds she'd thrown as a child. She looks to David for reassurance, but David's teeth clamp over his lower lip. His arms are crossed before him.

"Best just to relax," says Micah, even as the vein of his empty socket strains through the skin. He swipes his hands down his apron. "Can't tell by looking."

"Hell, I know gold when I see it," says Limpy. "When I see it, Alex . . ." A murmur of agreement ripples through the crowd. She steps back and up the first step of the general store, and every head follows.

"Now, shit, son, shit. Think this is funny? Think gold is funny business?" says Micah.

"Could be all you got is pyrite, make fools of us all," says Harry.

"Wouldn't want that, would you, Alex?" says Limpy, his heavy hand on her shoulder. "To make fools of us?"

"Best just to relax," Micah says again.

She opens her fingers, slow for the stiffness, expecting something larger, more substantial to match the way she suddenly feels.

Emaline has a drawer full of men's clothing, shirts mainly, for it's easier to walk out of a room without your shirt than your trousers. She has moth-eaten flannels with frayed collars

49

and missing and mismatched buttons; silky-white dress shirts with embroidered initials, looking very official and somewhat smug next to blue muslin and tough, weathered buckskin. There are ruffled sleeves and holes in seams and stains in unusual places. Orphans all, which might explain why she can't bear to throw them out, or even give them away. Lord knows, only a fool keeps more than she needs, but she smiles now as she digs through the musty pile of cloth, looking for one article in particular. Her ears prick and tingle at the sound of gunshots fired skyward. The echo rebounds back and forth between the ravine walls with the sharp unnerving staccato of firecrackers. Somebody gonna be bitten by one angry mosquito if they're not careful, and she's in no mood to be plucking bullets from a miner's ass. She closes the drawer with her hip and holds up a blue calico shirt, remembering the bucktoothed young man she'd taken it from.

He was just off the boat from Italy or Chile or some such place and had tried to slip away without paying. "Everyone pays," she told him, catching him by the scruff of the neck, "even if it is with the shirt off your back."

She'd laughed as the scrawny little bloke hightailed it down the hall, his backbone sawing holes through his skin. But as the evening wore on and the night howled cold and angry off the bay, she found herself clutching the shirt. Three days later, when the city of San Francisco was coated in a thin sheen of white, Emaline huddled warm by the fire as her stomach churned ice cubes, and resolved that, from now on, she would demand payment first. Of course, there was no way to tell if one of the fifty frozen bodies found the next morning was her Italian, but she'd kept the shirt just the same, carrying it to Sacramento, and now to Motherlode.

She spreads it on her bed, running her hands over the wrinkles. She'd washed it twice, but never managed to get rid of the smell of him. Cloves, was it? He had been chewing on cloves, and his black hair had streaks of brown that matched his eyes. He should be, he would be, too big for the shirt now, with broad shoulders and muscles filling in the wiry sinew of his arms. She shook her head and blew a curl from her face. It will be a relief to get rid of the thing, a redemption of sorts – the only motive she considers as she knocks on Alex's door. She flings it open to the sickly glow of the candle, half expecting, hoping in fact, to find him in all his newborn glory, skinny as the Italian.

Alex sits fully clothed on the bed. He wrenches himself upright. The boy is skittish, Emaline thinks, but as she becomes accustomed to the dark, her gaze falls upon a solid lump nestled like an egg on the blanket. The Victoria hatches before her, shedding its rough skin and primitive décor for a dreamed-of elegance. She'll have the downstairs floors redone in smooth milled redwood, stained dark brown to hide whiskey spills; replace the make-do bar with a hard oak one, with shelves beneath to keep the good stuff and new shelves on the wall to hold the cheap. She'll build a proper kitchen, add a cellar and a dining room with a long maple table. A wonder of woodwork. Oak for the doors, sweet cedar for the chairs, ash for the two upholstered settees that will sit by the new stone fireplace. Plush carpeting. Green with red roses and dyed canvas tapestries to cover the plain wooden walls. Glass for all the windows, a mahogany nightstand with a finished ceramic washbasin in every room. A new bed for herself, four-poster, with sheets of pure silk and – Alex snatches the golden lump from the bed and holds it to his chest.

Emaline's mouth closes with a pop and curls to a frown. Might as well just accuse her of thievery. She crumples the calico shirt in a ball and crosses her arms before her chest.

"Now, if it were me," she says, her voice cooler than she intended, "I'd wrap it up as good as I could and leave the damn thing here, hidden under the bed, wherever. Unless it's worth your life protecting."

His eyes grow to wide, moon-like disks, but she doesn't

care if she scares him. It's dangerous holding things of value too close to you. And grown men have been killed for smaller hunks of metal. She shivers at this, and squints down at the clear complexion, the hairless lips, the slender shoulders of Alex, feeling suddenly protective of the thankless little snot.

"I brought this. For you," she adds, taking the calico from beneath her arm. She holds it before her as though judging fit. "The one you got's a bit rank, you don't mind me saying."

Alex says nothing, but ventures cautiously forward, his feet very light on the floor. It strikes her just how small he seems now with his shoulders hunched, his arms tucked in as though his guts would otherwise spill out. He'd waltzed into town today like the crown prince himself, a trail of men following after him, practically falling at his feet. But she can't recall anything about his expression. Her attention, as now, was fixated on the gold. The devil himself might as well have been carrying it. She lays the shirt flat upon the bed and smoothes the sleeves over the chest.

"Try it. Bound to fit you," she says, and waits. His eyes flit from her to the shirt, as if either will bite him. Emaline shakes her head, waves away her disbelief, and turns to leave in one motion. She's got better things to do than wait for a thank –

"Emaline?" Emaline turns round. "Thank you?"

She closes the door behind her, ignoring the heavy lump in her gut. He was forgettable before, without the gold. Safer for it.

Downstairs she finds David leaning against the wall on a stool and staring out at the foolery in the road. He's lit the lamps and the fishy smell of the oil permeates the room. On the far wall, across from the kitchen, the portrait of Queen Victoria gazes out across the saloon, her complexion all the more pale in the yellow light. "Damn fools," says Emaline, and the third leg of David's stool thumps to the ground. "Don't want to join them?"

52

"No, thank you," he says. Emaline pauses, holding the kitchen door half open, looking back up the stairs.

"David?" she says. "Do me a favor?"

As she expects, he nods a quick agreement. She points to Alex's room above them. "Watch out for him for me." She doesn't expect the ashen look that falls across his face. He sits up straight. "Yes?" Emaline asks. Before he can answer, the door of the saloon slams open and Limpy ducks beneath the doorframe holding two bottles by their glass necks.

"Rum!" says Limpy, an exclamation and a statement. Behind him, the street is a flurry of movement. The shadows of evening spread like fingers through town.

"Thank you, David," Emaline says, and pushes through to the kitchen, leaving him with his mouth open.

Limpy met Alex at the stairwell, called her the Golden Boy, bought her a drink and whiskey isn't nearly as sweet as she'd imagined.

"Drink it down, son," says Limpy, leaning with his back to the bar. The taste lingers in her mouth like the fuzz of a peach. She squirms on her stool and readjusts the nugget where it hangs hidden in the pouch between her thighs.

Klein muscles the accordion to life and a man in the corner stands on his stool singing, "Mine eyes have seen the glory of the coming . . ." in a wavering Scottish brogue. It takes a rag to his face to sit him down, but the song has caught here and there, and while none of the singers agree on a verse, all come together in time for the truth to go marching on.

"Whiskey," Limpy says, "is not meant for sipping, am I right? Micah? Show the boy how it's done."

Micah tips his head back, barely swallowing. He orders two more drinks, offers one to Alex. She shakes her head. "No, Micah. Thank you."

"Do well to accept gifts given you." He sets the cup down anyway. "Remember that."

53

"Women and whiskey, son, rarely come free," says Limpy.

"Not that I blame you," says Micah, "what with this rotgut-mule-piss whiskey Jed's been serving. Jed? Jed, a cup of your best for the boy. New England rum."

"And don't tell us you ain't got any," says Limpy. "Carried two bottles in myself this very afternoon. Got the good stuff in your own glass – that's what I thought."

Jed is wiping a clean spot on the bar, but his eyes follow Emaline as she circles the room, talking, laughing, gathering cups as she goes. If Emaline feels eyes, she ignores them.

Alex adjusts herself. She takes another sip of the whiskey in her hand and finds it empty. The rum smells of sugar beets, but she doesn't trust the sweetness until she tastes it, soft on her tongue, slipping down her throat so easy.

"Good, huh? What I tell you? New England rum," says Micah, separating *Eng* and *land*. "You're welcome." He winks his eye and she watches him totter back to his poker game.

She'd practiced walking about her room, adjusting the knot around her waist to still the anchor-like swing. But as she watches the Scotsman approach the bar, she wonders if her nugget hangs a bit too low. She couldn't leave it in the room, didn't quite trust the heavy look in Emaline's eye at the suggestion. Nor was Alex ready to part with the flannel, her adopted skin.

She ducks low over her drink, now, every time the woman passes.

The tobacco smoke rises layer upon layer to the ceiling and the room feels smaller, more cluttered even than it looked from the stairwell, as if each clump of bodies sections off its own living, breathing room. Man breath, she thinks. Men springing from rocks. What would Gran think of that? Men from rocks. She takes a sip. Water from wine. Her head feels very large. She pulls away from the hand tugging at her flannel. New. She feels new. The Golden Boy Alex. She turns

54

to find Preacher John pointing at his Bible as if trying to spear the words with his fingernail.

"You read?"

Alex nods her head yes and Preacher says, "'Course not, no," and begins pointing out every word as he reads, tugging on Alex's arm now and then to regain her attention.

"Whoever sows sp-spar-sparingly," Preacher reads, "will also reap sparingly, and whoever sows gener-ous generous-ly will also reap generously. God loves a cheerful giver."

Preacher nods furiously and Alex finds her head bobbing right along. "A cheerful giver," Preacher says again as Limpy leans over.

"Now, Preacher, you're not bothering the boy, are you?" He takes the empty cup from Alex's hand and gives her another rum. "Me and Alex have business, you understand. Business."

"Business," says Alex, and *s*'s tickle her tongue.

"Generosity and righteousness," Preacher says, still tugging on Alex's sleeve. Limpy pulls her away. He drapes his great arm like a yoke across her shoulder.

"Generosity. All well and good," he says. "But men like us have to look out for our own interests, Alex. Drink up now, attaboy. Been thinking real hard 'bout you, son, all night, real hard. Always had a good feeling 'bout-chah. It's a gift. Always could tell an honest man by lookin', and I liked the look of you. From day one, boy, ask anyone, ask David. 'Got luck riding with him,' I tells him. David's got skill, but you need both."

"I say I was feeling lucky tonight?" yells Micah, and a groan sounds from the men at his table, David, John Thomas, Harry and Fred among them.

"See there?" says Limpy, pointing to Micah's table. "David thinks he's got some sort of talent for cards, but he only ever wins enough to keep him playing. Now what's that tell you?"

She's not sure that tells her anything, but she hears the

word *boy* wafting from the table and smiles because boy means her, Alex, Golden Boy.

"You listening to me, son? Alex? Could be very important to your future. Partners, you understand, but not equal. No. I understand you was the one found the gold, and that's most important, no doubt. But can't do much on your own, can you? Wouldn't know where to begin, would yah? Thirds is what I'm thinking, with you keeping any nugget bigger than a chispa, as should be. Know what a chispa is? No? Anything bigger than your big toenail, in my book. Now, some will tell you big as the whole toe, but I'm a fair man. An honest man. Like you.

"Look at me when I'm talking to you, boy, 'cause some would have you sell the claim, see. Them over there –" He waves his hand in the general direction of Micah's table. "Give you pennies for it. Already planning to scoop up all the land on either side, which is yours by right, once you strike gold. And with me and David claiming side by side, sure to keep that gold in the family, you understand. That's how I think of you: family. David, too. Said himself you reminded him of his brother back in Cornwall."

"Jed," Micah hollers. "Jed, you send that boy over with a dram o' rum. And fill it good, too. Hell! Can you smell the luck, boys?"

"Here now, Alex – look here, Alex," says Limpy. "Wouldn't have saved your ass in the clearing if we didn't think fondly of yah. It's what's important. Family. Trust."

"Come on, boy! Don't have all night, and no telling when the luck runs out!" yells Micah. Alex finds the word *family* lingering between her ears and a fresh cup in her hand.

"You ain't saying no to it, then?" Limpy asks as she slips from the stool. She navigates toward Harry, edges between shoulders and around stools with the nugget pulling her down, making her bowlegged. The racket of the room pokes her with individual sticks of conversation, so unlike the solid mass of sound that met her on the stairwell during the rain.

56

"Likely to be nothing but pyrite from now on," says Harry. She stops short of the table to listen, minding the cup.

"Way it goes, sometimes," Harry continues. "Fate. Now don't look at me like that, Fred. You know it too. Get all excited for a hundred dollars of poverty and heartache. But, hell, that's life, right?"

"You done?" says Micah, and Alex takes a sip of his rum.

"Just an old wives' tale, Harry," says Fred. "You can't kill luck with hopeful talk. Micah and I went back and it looked rich."

"What you know about it?" John Thomas asks Fred.

Fred discards four. David folds.

"Fred here fancies himself an expert in all things *natural*," says Harry. "Tell them the name of your book, Fred, tell them."

"Hydraulicking," says Fred, ignoring Harry, "would clear more earth in a week than a hundred shovels could in a year. You watch, if we don't do it, someone else will. I heard they just got a load of hydraulic tubing down there in Marys—"

"That is bull-sheeit," says John Thomas. "Woulda been up there for yourself if you'd know'd there was gold." He discards one, slams all five to the table when he sees his draw. Alex feels her lip curl. "Bullshit," he says again.

"*A Geological and Floral Survey of the Greater Alta California*," says Harry, holding his cards in front of his laughter, revealing to Alex a pair of sixes. "That's what he calls it, and that's all he's got, other than a bunch of weeds smashed between the pages."

"I never said I could find it," admits Fred. "Just recognize a find. Was me that told them Empire boys to stick it out, and look at them now."

John Thomas slumps back in his chair. "Boy don't deserve it," he says to no one in particular.

"Exactly why we need to buy the claim right up. Follow it to the quick," says Fred.

"Jed!" Micah yells. "What about my . . . W'hell – Alex!" and suddenly the whole lot of them are looking her way.

"Sure!" booms Limpy behind her, and she nearly spills the drink. His great paw clamps down on her shoulder and she does spill some. "Just take the claim, fellas. Boy won't care, will he? Don't know jack about mining and can't work alone. He'll take his luck to some juanita in Grass Valley and be all the better for it. Am I right? Am I right? Alex?"

Limpy's words chatter back through her head. Alex finds the drink in her hand and a mush of words in her mouth and for some reason needs to deliver the drink first. She holds the cup in front of her, too intent on keeping the liquid level to notice that John Thomas has thrust his leg out.

Alex is falling, flailing her arms to stop herself. Fails. Collides with the card table. She feels her nose crack and blood pour into her mouth, warm and bitter after the rum. She opens her eyes to red splintered wood and whiskey-drenched playing cards spinning in a kaleidoscope of color. She gulps down blood, tries to rise. Fails.

"Clumsy son-of-a –" John Thomas begins, and Alex feels the strength of rage surge through her. She wants to stop it, the voice, the tone of the voice, the man speaking. She lunges, misjudges the location of the stool, lands hard on the ground. Laughter bounces off the inside of her head. She opens her eyes to silence, a frayed hemline, thick ankles. Emaline's cool hand on her forehead.

"Out," says Emaline. Out of the Victoria, out of Motherlode, Alex thinks. Tries to rise. "No, no, now easy," says Emaline, tipping Alex's head back.

"And Jesus came to the temple," Preacher yells from some-where above her. "He came and saw the sin of the Farsees and overturned the tables of wickedness . . ."

"Emaline, I –" says John Thomas.

"Out," Emaline says, "before I decide you can't come back."

58

"Out, out. Can't come back," someone parrots in the corner.

"Forty years to build what was demolished in a day, the word of –"

"Preacher! Shut your mouth and get this boy outside 'fore he bleeds a river on my floor."

"Your mouth, Preacher. Shut your mouth," says the parrot, and the voice recedes into laughter.

Alex feels herself hefted. Her knees can only bend. Through the haze she sees Emaline float across the wreckage to John Thomas. Men step out of her way. Jed jumps over the bar and stands ready. The room is silent, listening, but Emaline has said all she will. She nods to Jed, and then to David. They hustle over to flank John Thomas. John Thomas opens his mouth to protest, shuts it as if he can think of nothing to say, yanks himself free from Jed.

"Get your nigger hands off me, boy," he says, and Jed gives him a shove out the door, past Alex who stands bleeding on the porch planking.

"Stupid fool," David mumbles from the doorway. "And you," he says to Alex. "Told you to stay the hell away from him."

Her eyes blur and she feels as if part of her is hovering there above the porch, watching John Thomas stumble down the road, watching herself bleed to a puddle on the floor.

# 5

"Your hands," Alex says, as David helps the boy up the stairs. Below them, Limpy's tuneless baritone leads a round of "Turkey in the Straw," a silly song that David has never liked.

"Turkey in the straw, turkey in the hay," the men roar, with Emaline's voice raftering up an octave higher, just a bit more in tune. "Roll 'em up and twist 'em up a high tuckahaw . . ."

The boy joins in, obviously doesn't know the words, reverts back to the "Battle Hymn of the Republic."

"Shhhh," David says as they near the top of the stairs. "Your voice is shrill."

"Such big hands," says Alex, making a fist, holding it up for David to see. "Gran says, she said, men have big hands."

Alex erupts back into giggles, wrenches from David's grasp to totter and stare squint eyed down the hall. The boy's right hand inches down to adjust himself through his trousers. David looks away. If the boy would pass out, he'd make it easier on them both.

Instead he thrusts his chest out, pokes at the bloody liquor stain with one rigid finger, as though his own chest is foreign to him. And before David can react, the boy swivels and grabs the collar of David's flannel, pulls himself close. He lays his head over David's heart, breathes in and out to the beat.

David tenses. The boy smells of liquor and earth. His hair is fine and oily and his skin is flushed, emanating heat. David's arms hover just over the narrow shoulders, as if repelled.

"Terrible things," Alex hisses, his body shaking now in dry sobs and David's arms lower themselves of their own accord until his fingertips touch the coarse flannel of Alex's shirt. Alex's shoulders go limp. He slips to the ground, wraps his arms around David's leg. He squeezes, as if David's leg were a ship's mast. He sways as if the floor were rocking.

Voices bounce up the stairs. Moonlight shines through the open hall window, painting Alex blue.

"Get up now," David manages. "Get you to bed. Found gold today."

He shakes his leg, but Alex holds tighter, presses his head into David's thigh. David's breath catches. He grits his teeth, focuses on those voices downstairs. Preacher sings a hymn about repentance and God's saving grace. "Three kings and a joker makes four," yells Micah. Groans all round. Another layer of tobacco smoke and liquor fumes rise and settle and to David's tired senses, the moon-streaked hall takes on an orange-red glow. He closes his eyes and holds his breath. It's the time of night, the liquor in his veins. Only this.

Alex lets go and sits back on his hands, raising his eyebrows as if to keep his eyes open.

"Gold," Alex says. His lips curl in a reluctant grin, then harden. "Golden Boy."

David gathers himself, reaches down and pulls Alex to his feet, drags him a few yards, then scoops the boy up into his arms. Two doors down, he plops him on the bed, and flees the room with shaking hands.

Long after Limpy has stumbled back to their cabin, David sits at the bar, whiskey in one hand, rubbing the soft, worn rim of John Thomas's forgotten hat with the other. Besides

Emaline, only Jed, Micah and Preacher John remain in the saloon. Stools are overturned with their legs wide in the air. Queen Victoria hangs crooked on the wall above Emaline, who sits staring off into nothing with an absent smile on her face, as if posed for a portrait.

She shakes from her stupor and makes eye contact, her smile now for him. David looks away. He hadn't realized he'd been staring.

"'Bout time, isn't it, boys?" she says and Jed jolts upright behind the bar.

Micah groans his agreement and stands up to stretch his back. Preacher continues scribbling notes in the margin of his Bible as though he hadn't heard.

"Lord, Emaline," says Micah. "Think you could get some proper chairs in here? My bones feel near twenty years older than I am."

Emaline ignores him. She maneuvers between tables, through shattered whiskey jugs, around the rust brown puddle of blood, to stand over David. She places her hand soft against his cheek as if checking for fever. He boosts himself to his feet, away from her.

"Yah all right, my dear? You look a little down," says Emaline, squinting up at him. "Been playing with that hat an hour now. It's past midnight, I know . . ." Micah turns round with a questioning glance. "But if you need me . . ."

"No, thank you . . . no, Emaline," David says, and Micah dismisses him with a disgusted wave of the hand, mumbles something under his breath.

"Well, won't bite yah, you know," says Emaline, just a hint of hurt in her voice.

"Does, too," says Micah from the first step. "But worth it, believe you me."

Emaline gives a "humph" and Micah escapes up the stairs.

"Nevermind," she tells David. "Appreciate you opening the chapel tomorrow, like usual. Sunday, and no work need be done before some thanksgiving, bonanza or no. And, David . . ." He waits, but she doesn't finish her sentence. "Goodnight," she says.

He pushes out the door, into the night.

It isn't as though he wouldn't *like* to go upstairs with Emaline, though the reasons why still evade him. She is not a beautiful woman. Her hair is rarely, if ever, pulled from her face, and at night the fringe on her top lip glows in the candlelight. Her wide hips take the space of two women and make her pumpkin-sized breasts appear almost proportional. Her shoulders are too thick, her posture too straight. She struts around the saloon like the Queen herself, issuing orders as if she were born to it.

David has never fancied plump women. He isn't fond of facial hair, and has never reacted well to orders. Yet, even to David, Emaline exudes a salacious energy that moves before her like a second self, announcing her presence in any room. No man in Motherlode is immune to this energy. Only he has been strong enough to resist.

He was raised to know better, has abstained for too long to give in now. Sex is sacred to marriage alone, and prostitution – for that's what it is – is a sin, just as murder is a sin, and those who encourage Emaline by slipping into her bed every chance they get are paving paths to hell. David does respect her. Respects her in a way he'd only respected men before, in a business sense. He simply refuses to take part in her hypocrisy. Sunday service, giving thanks, saving the souls of men she soils week after week. The sign of a guilty conscience, if you ask him. Already he has sinned with her in his dreams. He blames her for this. He'd like very much to blame her for this new conceit lingering and polluting his mind. *Watch out for him,* sure. David can see the boy even now. Alex hugging his thigh. Alex clinging to his flannel.

He looks back at the Victoria. Emaline's lamp is lit and

her body throws shadows on the curtain. He gulps a lungful of biting air, clears his mind on the exhale, and follows his steaming breath forward over hills and valleys of frozen mud, pauses in front of John Thomas's canvas tent.

At the card table tonight, John Thomas had been as agitated as David's ever seen him. He didn't think it *fair* that a boy found gold in the very spot he'd worked and found nothing. Didn't think it was fair that a boy had found gold after they'd *all* been working for years for broken backs and empty pouches.

He was right. It wasn't *fair* for a skinny, soft-handed boy to find gold where others failed. John Thomas was saying just what everyone else was thinking, or at least what David had been thinking. But that's the reality of the diggings. Stories like this brought David to California in the first place. Gold for the taking. Nuggets plucked from riverbeds and hillsides. Poor man to rich man in a day, if you were willing to work hard, willing to believe sulphur sweat would translate to solid gold. David had worked, suffering through snow-choked winters, mucking through spring mud, frying in summer heat, far away from his home and his family, his mum's rich clotted cream, her flaking pasties, her thick potato pancakes. Away from the happy chatter of his little sister and his cheeky younger brothers and their impromptu wrestling matches on Sunday afternoons. Away from his father's low rumbling voice reading the Bible each night by the fire. All of this seems so distant, part of another life that David yearns for, but to which he no longer belongs. He should write to his father, but he's afraid of the words that might come, afraid that in writing he will confirm his own failure and prove his father right. *A metal like any other.*

He places his cold hands under the waistband of his trousers, warming skin on skin. The night is still. The cedars make moonlit silhouettes at the tip of the ravine.

This new claim could play out in a few weeks. John Thomas

is probably working himself up over a bit of color, nothing more. Speculation did no good. They wouldn't know anything definite about the ore content until the digging started. And the boy alone is sure to have slow goings, especially if this lode is as narrow and unpredictable as other California lodes have been and covered with the same thick layer of topsoil. Take him all summer just to dig through to the granite, if he doesn't bury himself first.

Limpy has forgotten to cut the lamp in the cabin again and the canvas roof glows like a luminary, attracting a colony of moths. Guttural snoring bounces off walls as though four men sleep instead of the one. He'll never wake Limpy, doesn't fancy turning him on his side. He puffs out the lamp, closes the door and ventures back into Victor Lane, pulled toward the Victoria like a moth. His thoughts veer stubbornly back to Alex; the boy's small body slung around his leg, the heat of the boy's breath on David's thigh.

All lights are out in the Victoria. The windows, like eyeless sockets, stare blindly into the night. Still David feels exposed in the moonlight, as though the eye of God were viewing his obdurate thoughts, judging his body's weakness. He steps into the shadows of the cedars just beyond the inn. He leans his head against the sweet-smelling bark, focuses on the sound of fieldmice foraging in the undergrowth, on the owl calling into silence, but cannot will his mind blank. He settles for a lesser evil, takes himself in hand. His breath quickens. His toes curl in his boots. He shudders and his shoulders reach for his ears, then sink. He is wiping his hand on a frosty patch of grass when a shadow slinks toward the Victoria.

David follows, guarding his step against snapping branches. The figure eases the door open, squeezes inside. David counts twenty breaths, and edges in after. He stands in the doorway as his eyes adjust to the darkness. The stools again stand right side up, the broken pieces of a whiskey jug have been swept to the corner and the blood has been mopped, leaving only a dark misshapen stain like spilled paint. Queen Victoria is still crooked on the wall, but it's the kitchen door, swinging softly on its hinges, that steals his attention.

David peeks his head in the kitchen, sees nothing. Floorboards creak above him. He tiptoes to the stairs. He grasps at his belt for the bowie knife he left in the cabin. He climbs the stairs, his hand against the wall for support.

The figure stands in front of Alex's room. A dagger glints in the weak window light. A hand reaches for the latch and David takes two giant steps forward. The body and blade swivel his direction. David steps forward again, wishing for a revolver, or a knife, something to give him authority.

"Forget your hat?" David says, his voice as flat and frigid as he can manage.

"Shit. Now, David . . . Shit. Somebody gotta do something about it. I'm gonna do something about it."

Another step forward. John Thomas takes a sharp breath. His knuckles strain white around the knife handle. David hunches down, both hands in front of him.

"Not right. A boy. Ain't worked."

Footsteps on the stairs behind them. A rifle is cocked. Jed's voice comes in a snarling whisper.

"Get out."

"We share the gold. All of us, Jed. Equal. Boy don't deserve gold like we do." John Thomas's words come fast but make no impact, and his hopeful face becomes scarred with hate. "No good fucking nigger, taking airs. I shoulda –"

Jed rushes forward, leveling the rifle at John Thomas's head. Jed's face is obsidian, his brow beaded with gleaming sweat. His hands tremble.

"Get out. Get out and never come back. I shoot yah. I see yah, I shoot yah."

John Thomas pants shallow airless breaths. A puddle steams on the floor beneath him.

"I shoot yah, hear?"

John Thomas jerks a nod and eases forward as if to pass. "Ah!" says Jed. "The knife."

John Thomas nods again, places the knife on the floor beside the puddle of piss. He squeezes past David, down the stairs and into the night.

# 6

Emaline opens the shutters to a sharp March chill and fills her lungs. The road below is a bustle of chicken banter and she squints toward the mass of feathered streaks clamoring after a hen-pecked Rhode Island Red. The poor thing's rump is already a balding mass of blood sores where feathers used to be. Half plucked already, Emaline thinks. If the ground were thawed enough for earthworms, they'd leave the old girl well enough alone. Funny, how boredom in chickens breeds cruelty, just as in men. Might as well put the old bird out of her misery. They won't stop pecking until she's dead, and Emaline hasn't made chicken and dumplings in a while. That makes ten chickens down from twenty last May, and spring is just beginning. A hungry coyote or mountain lion could take the rest in a matter of weeks, might have already if she'd kept the hens fenced like a damn city fool. No fence gonna keep out a coyote or mountain lion. Gathering all the victims in one enclosed space just makes the job of killing easier. Weren't too smart, chickens. But given room to run and roost high they had a better chance than penned. What's a little chickenshit splattered around town when fresh eggs and the occasional chicken dinner were at stake? She'll tell Randall to bring a rooster next time he makes the trip up. Chicks do well in the summer months.

She turns from the window, leaving the shutters open to vent the stale air. On the bed, Jed's head is nestled to the nose beneath the patchwork quilt and she's tempted to snuggle back into his warmth. She doesn't know when he came in last night. Either he couldn't wake her, or didn't care to, which was just as well for Emaline who finds no greater comfort than his closeness. Closeness, even without the urgency of desire. Closeness in the delicious exhaustion of Saturday nights.

Jed groans. His eyes open in tiny downward slits and are met by the upward curve of his smile.

"Morning," he croaks and clears his throat. "Morning."

Emaline says nothing. He shouldn't still be in the room, but then no one is likely to be up early on a Sunday, even after yesterday's find, especially after yesterday's drinking.

"Emaline?" She shakes herself, focuses on Jed.

"Just thinking. That's all. People start coming in here, we gonna have to pen them chickens. People start coming, things are gonna change."

"Not everything."

"No? I hope. I was waiting for a strike, same as all the rest of 'em. Got plans, you know, but . . ."

In the room down the hall she hears Micah retching into his chamber pot. A long wet belch resounds on the street below.

"Best get on outta here," she says, "'fore the whole town wakes."

"Ain't no secret no more."

"Ain't common knowledge, neither."

Jed looks dubious. He scratches his scalp through his tight curly hair and runs both hands down his face, wiping sleep away.

"Get on up and rouse that boy down the hall," she says,

hoping the task will give him motivation. In the daylight, in Jed's company, this room has never felt safe. Regardless of what people knew and what they pretended not to. Free state, sure, but no one ever looked kindly on mixing. There were plenty who'd string Jed up just for that, even in this town, her town, and Jed is no longer someone she can live without. She clutches her nightgown tighter to her chest and tries to warm herself against the chill that is creeping into her mind.

She and Jed had stumbled on this valley on the road from Sacramento. They were traveling light, heading north to the gold fields, aiming for Rough and Ready, or a camp outside one of the more populated towns like Grass Valley or Nevada City. She meant to set up her own establishment where city laws and the men who made them had yet to take hold of everyone's business.

The June heat pressed down on them from all angles and the sound of running water called them down from the lip of the ravine. There was no way of knowing what manner of men had made the camp they found. Two canvas tents squatted in the sun-scorched grass. The bedding was rolled, and a pair of tattered underclothes hung on a line to dry. A neat circle of stone marked their campfire; but the tidiest of men could still own the most wretched of souls.

Jed didn't think it safe to stay, but Emaline had no desire to climb back out of the valley in the June heat. Besides, she knew she could handle a few wretched souls. Setting her bundles down, she dug into her satchel for the breathing terry cloth of sourdough starter, flour, lard, and water; mixed them all in the pan she found by the fire. While the dough rose, she scrounged with Jed for long flat rocks and built them into a precarious little oven. By the time the miners tramped up from the creek at dusk, a steaming loaf of bread, a pot of coffee, and fried salt pork awaited them.

There were just three of them: Mordicai, the lanky singer; a scurvy-stricken fellow named Jake who's long since gone his own way; and a solitary German who took his plate and ate outside the reach of the fire's glow. "That there's Klein, he calls hisself," Mordicai told her by way of apology. "He doesn't say much of anything to anybody, but I 'spect he's 'bout as grateful as me and Jake."

Already the place felt like home.

When the men offered to pay her, she didn't think twice about taking their little bit of gold. For this Emaline knew to be true: gold don't ease a belly's hunger, calm a man's urges, or know how much he's afraid to miss his mamma. These boys were getting far more than they were giving. She didn't think a thing about changing the name of the place to something more hopeful, accommodating. "Destitution Valley" implied a pessimism she couldn't live with, and it certainly didn't do justice to the beauty of the place. Motherlode filled her whole mouth with hope, and she wasn't at all surprised by the steady stream of miners who found their way into and out of her valley. The walls of the Victoria rose even as the level of the creek and the number of men fluctuated and has stood much as it does now for a good year and a half. She likes to think she'd foreseen this partic-ular future from the ridge above, likes to think she had looked down and seen a town sprouting like a sapling from the valley floor and gold oozing like pine pitch from the ravine wall.

And here she is, crushing a good thing by letting a few bad *what if*'s get in the way. Silly. A gold strike is just what her town needs, what the Victoria needs. More people, more customers, fancy fixings.

Jed throws the quilt from his body and his legs over the side of the bed, wiggles his bare toes on the chilled wood floor. He slips on his trousers, tucks in his shirt. He kisses Emaline gently on the forehead and tiptoes down the hall to Alex's room.

Emaline forces her thoughts to follow him out the door and strips to wash.

71

Stale water in the washbasin. She'd meant to freshen it yesterday. She dips a rag, watching the fabric expand, places the rag on her face, tips her head back and lets the moisture seep into her skin. Her skin. So much drier than it used to be. In the mirror, she can see lines invading, making her look older than her thirty-five years, older than she feels. Lines. Signs of wisdom, experience, character. Lines gave personality to a face. Wrinkles, she knows, are something else entirely. Emaline has no wrinkles. She breathes slowly in and out through fabric and moisture, runs the rag along her neck, behind her ears, enjoys the chilling tingle of evaporating water on bare skin. Then down her front, encircles one breast, then the other, and her nipples perk in the damp cold; scrubs the dark mats of hair growing full and free under her arms. She dips the rag again, wrings it, scrubs her legs, beginning with her right calf, working her way up to her groin, pauses at the pleasure of cloth friction between her legs.

A knock on the door.

"Emaline, Emaline, he dead to the world, that's the truth. He breathing, but I can't wake him for nothing. Won't hurt to let him sleep, yah think?"

"If he's gonna sleep under this roof, he's going to Sunday service. Try again, and if he don't get up, you tell him I'll come in and wake him good."

Jed's steps recede down the hallway. Emaline plaits her hair into a manageable rope and pulls on her Sunday best, a faded yellow dress with one small torn patch in the sleeve and a strip of off-color lace at the neck. Nothing compared to the silk fantasies worn by rich men's wives. Nothing to be proud of, but she is. The dress defined the day, setting Sunday apart from the drudgery of every other day, with a splash of color, a bit of lace. She fastens the buttons, holding in her gut. She'd already let out the waist seam when she threw her corset away. Be damned if she'd extend it again. Another knock on the door.

72

"I'm on my way," she says. She's halfway down the hall when inspiration strikes. She leaves Jed waiting, bustles back into her room, hefts the washbasin, careful not to slosh water on her front. She nods at Alex's door, waits while Jed opens it.

Alex is curled into a fetal ball, his arms around his head to shield the light. He doesn't stir as Emaline approaches.

"Gold or no gold, I make the rules in this place and everyone goes to Sunday service. Give you one more chance to get up on your own."

He doesn't stir and she feels a smile warm her ears. Jed waits, biting his lower lip, his eyebrows raised. She dips her hand in the water and flicks her fingers at his face, turns back to Alex and dumps the whole basin, washrag and all.

Alex leaps from the bed, his eyes wild and his filthy flannel drenched. Emaline's whole self shakes with laughter, and she's trying very hard not to pop her buttons. She doesn't notice how green his face becomes, how his cheeks puff. She isn't prepared for his eyes to roll back in his head, or his body to lurch forward. He seizes the empty washbasin and sloshes the liquid contents of his stomach up over the rim, and down Emaline's yellow dress.

Emaline is not laughing. She stands, arms out, mouth open, looking down at the vomit on her dress. Before Jed can curb his grin, she turns, glares death at his half-contained amusement and slams the door behind her.

When she charges back into the room wearing her usual brown dress, Alex is still holding the basin before him and Jed's expression is nearly neutral. She focuses on Alex, just a shade less green.

"Change your clothes. Breakfast downstairs in half an hour, if you can stomach it. No one misses Sunday service."

The door closes, but the hallway light fades slowly from her eyes, leaving an ambient glow that breaks apart into colliding shards of light. Alex has to swallow every time they burst. She wraps her arms about her stomach to find the front of her flannel slimy with globs of rewetted blood. In another instant the flannel lies crumpled on the floor, and sweat freezes dry on her chest, so suddenly, so completely exposed.

Her breasts, never very large, now mere impressions of flesh, erupt in goose bumps and it's the chill that makes her cover up so quickly. It's the chill that forces her hands into fists, preventing her fingers from touching the clammy cold of her own skin. It's the chill that clenches like a hand to the back of her throat. This is what she tells herself – even as she kicks the bloody flannel away under the bed, out of sight – just a chill.

She clutches the calico about her, careful not to miss any buttons. It smells familiar: spiced pie, a little too sweet for her stomach right now. She adjusts the nugget between her legs, ties and reties the knot until it presents a modest bulge beneath her loose trousers.

Morning light washes the hallway a sickly yellow-orange and walls of green wood sweat sap. Her arms and legs are distant, heavy, attached to the wrong head, and her thoughts take their time in forming. The muted rumble of voices in the saloon below is only Preacher arguing with himself. His cheeks are a flaccid shade of gray, and he looks up as she passes, holds his finger up as if preparing to speak, lets it fall with a puff of air.

"Shit!" Emaline's voice from the kitchen, the resounding clang of an iron pot hitting floorboards. Alex has no wish to see the woman. She pushes through the front door, but ventures no further than the porch before cold air, a mix of woodsmoke and damp earth, slaps her in the face. She blows the old air out, and out again, until there's nothing left to do but suck the new back in, pressing her fingers gently to the lumpy bridge of her swollen nose as she does so. She sinks down to the porch bench. Chickens puff and preen in the road, and Harry and Fred urinate in two arching streams off their front porch, straining for height and distance.

"Hell, that ain't nothing." Limpy's voice from the other direction. Alex glances away, embarrassed he'd caught her staring. His long legs make short work of Victor Lane and he steps straight from the ground to the porch.

"Now, David there," he says of the Cornishman apparently deep in thought behind him, ignoring them both as he climbs the stairs and pushes past Limpy into the saloon, "he's the reigning king of us all. Could piss from here to the creek," Limpy says. "You're young yet. You'll get there."

"You and Limp make some kinda deal with that boy?" Emaline asks, setting a cup of thick coffee in front of David. Her scowl is angled such that he decides to accept this morning. He even takes a sip. It runs like boiling acid down his throat, and he wakes enough to find the place empty but for Preacher, bent over that tattered rag of a Bible. His hat is off, revealing a strip of gray just above his deaf ear, and his eyebrows contort in time to his moving lips. David takes another sip of coffee, delaying an answer. Limpy's deep gut laugh sounds from the porch.

"We talked," he lies, and drinks down the coffee, grounds and all, before Emaline can question him further.

"Don't be forgetting to open my chapel," she calls after him. He's out the door in time to see Limpy with his thick arm draped over Alex's narrow shoulders, disappear up the creek.

He and Limpy had talked this morning, to an extent. David wanted to stake a claim just upstream from the boy, but Limpy wouldn't have it. Luck's with him, he said, and crossed his arms in a way that said he was going to be stubborn.

"I shoulda talked it over with you, I know. But I gave the boy my word. I shook on it."

"You shook on it?" asked David, making no effort to hide

the incredulous tone of his voice. Limpy gave as many hand-shakes as a politician, kept about as many promises. Dishonesty was the one thing you could count on from Limp. Even accounts of his past – especially accounts of his past – grew layers with each telling, until it was impossible to determine which details might be true and which were merely convenient. Limpy could be married, single, Republican, Democrat, or American Party, Presbyterian, Lutheran – even Catholic, if it suited his purposes. Most times David didn't say anything. Most times Limpy's purposes also suited David.

"Gave my word," Limpy said again.

"It's a Sunday."

"Sunday? Ain't no such thing as a Sunday after a strike. You surprise the hell out of me, standing around here like you got something better to do. Do you? Now look, I understand piety, saving Sunday for God, and all that, but . . . you're either with us, or you're not."

It was the "us" that gave David pause.

Across the road, Klein pushes through the door of his cabin. He arches his back to give full volume to a mighty yawn, shoots snot from one nostril, then the other. A raw-butted chicken hops up to the porch, scrutinizes David's bootlaces with one eye then the other. David gives the bird a gentle kick just as Jed rounds the side of the inn.

"Aw now, David! You know how long it took to corner that damn bird?" He bunches up the potato sack in his hand and steps onto the porch. The hen runs up the road and back before stopping in front of them as if daring Jed to lunge. Jed sighs, cusses.

"Easier to just shoot the damn thing," he says. He kicks a rock from the front step and the hen fluffs up and runs a few harried steps. "Been by his place this morning and I ain't seen him. I ain't told Emaline. Don't plan to tell her."

David's eyes wander down the road to John Thomas's

76

cabin. A squirrel's bushy tail twitches just inside the open door. "He'll be back," he says.

The two men stare as though the hen is still their focus. The clashing ruckus of birdsong surrounds them. Woodpeckers pound percussion in the digger pines, robins belt melody from the underbrush, vireos sing harmonies from the manzanita. Loud-mouthed scrub jays throw the whole ensemble into tunelessness. Jed takes a breath, blows it out.

"How you feel about rabbit tonight?"

David smiles, slaps Jed on the shoulder. He jumps from the porch. Right to the chapel, left to the creek. Each call with different voices. His hands itch for a pick. The sound of metal on rock clatters through his head.

Surely God will understand his absence this particular Sunday. It could even be God's will.

"I had a brother once. Still have a brother," says Preacher, leaning his elbows on the pulpit, his voice a drink-worn rasp.

Emaline crosses and recrosses her legs. Through the open windows she can hear the Sabbath breakers, their voices rising over the creek, their picks and shovels moving at a faster tempo than usual. Jed fidgets by her side. His eyes find the window, even as his head bows in prayer. His body is in the chapel, but his mind is swinging a pick, and in her experience God don't care so much where your body is if your head's not right there with it.

God has found her body in the most remote of places, where the only sight in any direction was yellow-brown grass bowing in the wind, or in the crook of Devil's Gate or lost in canyons so steep on either side that only a sliver of sky was visible. God was with her in Salt Lake City and San Francisco, and in other places she'd never want her mother to see.

Here in Motherlode, she's built a place for her body and mind to worship together. She'd thought these walls would

77

make her closer to God. She thought of the pine planks as an offering of sorts, a gift for the gift of herself. But nowhere has she ever felt as full of that presence as when she was walking step after labored step behind the wagon train, a mere tick on the hide of the great plains.

Maybe a steeple will help; hard oak pews with back rests, a real carved pulpit, maybe.

"When we were little, lads, you know, young, Pa gave Sal – that was his name, my brother, Sal. Pa gave him a pony to raise and train all on his own." Preacher straightens, bracing himself against the pulpit. "And was I jealous? Did I ENVY him?" Preacher licks his lips. Emaline leans forward on her knees. Jed's hand finds the base of her lower back and she shakes him away, even though only Preacher is there to see.

"Damn right I hated him!" booms Preacher. He looks up as though shocked by the power of his words, and continues with a flourish. "Getting a pony when I got nothing, not even a puppy or a piglet to raise. Not even a chicken. Nothing! Wanted to kill him, or the pony, just 'cause I ENVIED him so much. See what I'm saying? It's natural. Like passing wind. Human. Just gotta get over it somehow, like me. Get over it, 'cause it don't do you no good, none. And people that have ponies and such, be advised to be generous, let others ride 'em. See? Let us read . . ."

Emaline's foot is tapping. She stills it. Jed shifts in his seat, sighs heavily, puts his hands over his lips as if embarrassed by the sound. The chapel door is open, inviting any latecomers. She's made a point of not turning around to look, but she knows there's no one there. No one is coughing or breathing too loud, or whispering to their neighbor. When she does turn, she finds that raw-butted hen peeking its head through the doorway. Its toenails click down the aisle. It stops to peck at something of interest as Preacher continues:

". . . if I have made gold my hope, or have said to the fine gold, 'Thou get my confidence . . .'" She looks up, but Preacher is turning pages as if looking for the rest of this passage somewhere else. The chicken stands at Preacher's feet, its head a-tilt, this way then that, utterly unconcerned that the man who was trying to kill it is sitting just yards away, a wide grin on his dark face.

"Son-of-a-bitch," says Jed under his breath, and Emaline elbows him in the side. He's biting his lip over a smile, but his ribs shake under the strain of laughter. He elbows her back, much more gently than she did him. She stares straight ahead, trying to focus on Preacher but seeing only that chicken shift its weight foot to foot as if getting comfortable.

"'He that hath a bountiful eye shall be blessed-ed . . .'"

Pages turn. The chicken is unmoved. Emaline is laughing silently, holding her hand over her mouth so her teeth won't show. Showing teeth is defeat, and this is Sunday. A shout rises from the creek and her ears strain, but no more comes of it. Preacher sounds out another word and is on to another verse on another page, and she's struck by how focused his sermon has been by comparison.

This Sunday his usual choice of verses, one from Genesis and one from Revelations, and other creative, or perhaps haphazard, combinations, seem governed by a recognizable theme. Too bad no one is present to hear it, she thinks, and this thought brings with it a sobering sense of righteous indignation that even the chicken, pecking now at the worm-like laces of Preacher's boots, cannot break. Not even David came. She could usually depend upon David. The set of his shoulders this morning had been telling. He'd been tense as a rattler last night, tense and distracted this morning. He'd even drunk her coffee.

"'If you harbor bitter envy and selfish ambition in your hearts . . .' No, wait," says Preacher, staring down at the Bible, tapping the chicken away with his foot. He deters it only a minute from the tough leather worm bobbing there.

79

Emaline finds tears streaking down Jed's cheeks. A falsetto *he-he-he* escapes his lips. Pages turn.

"Oh, here –" says Preacher, beginning again, "'For where you have envy and selfish ambition –'"

"Ah hell! Save it, Preacher!" Emaline stands as she says this, ruffling both the chicken and Preacher John, who looks about the room as if noticing for the first time the size of his congregation. She picks up her skirt, climbs over the pew into the aisle. There is bread to be made, wood to chop, a dress to wash and, if she were the betting sort, she'd bet even God himself was down there at the creek, swinging a pick with the rest of them.

White light meets her at the doorway. Her eyes adjust and follow the sound of hooves up Victor Lane.

"Preacher?" she says, then turns to stick her head back through the door. "No, Jed, you stay put."

She ignores the way his cheeks darken. His smile vanishes. Preacher sets his Bible on the whiskey-barrel pulpit and follows her outside, laying a hand on Jed's shoulder as he goes.

In the gullet of the ravine, the sound of hooves has multiplied, but she sees only one man on a horse. Sitting so straight in the saddle, full to bursting with his own self-importance, Emaline would have guessed he was a military man. But as he gets closer, the cocky tilt of his head and the set of his shoulders remind her of someone.

"Emaline?" says the rider, crossing one arm casually over the other.

She barely recognizes him, his boots so shiny black, his frilly shirt so white next to that purple waistcoat. But, most striking, his bushy beard has been trimmed to a perfect square of whiskers on his knobby chin.

"Jackson Hudson." She spits the name out at him.

"Good to see you, too, Emaline," he says, and licks his lips as though preparing for a meal. Preacher John nods hello, but Hudson ignores him.

"What are you doing here?" says Emaline.

"Heard you were living up here in a mudpit, and I thought, sure, she'd need a kingdom of her own ..."

The horse throws its head for a shake and Hudson cusses, gives the reins a violent yank.

"I'm a changed man, Emaline."

"You changed your clothes," she says. The animal adjusts its mouth painfully over the bit.

The last time she'd seen Hudson was in Sacramento, nearly two years ago. He'd been one week off the overland trail and looked more like a beggar than a doctor's son from Ohio. She'd made him wash and comb his matted beard and hair before she would serve him. Of course, back then her bodice had been silk, and she'd been working from a rented room.

Emaline wraps her arms across the tattered cotton of her dress.

"Light attendance for a Sunday service, ain't it?" says Hudson.

"A find!" Preacher says, then lowers his head as if it was a secret he should have kept. Hudson's shoulders lift, his eyes follow the sound of digging to the creek.

"Is that right?"

"Might be poor," Emaline says, but knows as she says these words that he hears their opposites. "What is it you want, Hudson?"

"I have come to ..." he pauses to doff his hat. "I have come to offer my services. My protection –"

"Your *protection*?" she says.

"I am a servant of the citizens of Grass Valley. Elected." He brandishes a flimsy badge, glinting cheap copper rust.

"The only thing you ever protect is your own interest."

"Bandits!" he says, and his eyebrows flatten across his forehead. "Thieves, Emaline. Foreigners and celestials – all sorts of undesirables running round since the water strikes."

She shakes her head, "Don't need your kind of protection."

"And fugitive slaves, Emaline. Niggers taking what's *ours*," he says, thumping his chest. His voice takes a lower pitch. "Where's the nigger, Emaline?" A shadow darkens the doorway of the chapel.

Stay put, Jed, she's praying. Stay put.

"Knew you'd get rid of him sooner or later," says Hudson and chuckles, sits straighter in his saddle. Emaline hears floorboards give. Goddamn, goddamn, Jed, stay put. Preacher John's flaccid cheeks color beneath his beard.

"Got rid of you, didn't I?" she says. She steps close enough to run her hand down the leg of Hudson's black trousers, but Hudson is already turning in his saddle. His hand edges toward his holster. A scratch of footsteps on the porch behind her; her breath skips. Her eyes are focused the level of a man's shoulders, so when the chicken pokes its head sideways through the chapel door, it takes Emaline a moment to see it. The bird takes two tentative steps forward, stops, clucks a salutation, and Emaline remembers to breathe.

"Haw!" says Hudson, waving his gun at the bird. The horse frights, jerks its bridle, wide eyed, nostrils flaring. But the bird just stands there cocking its head, unimpressed.

"The lady wants you to leave," says Preacher, puffing himself up like the chicken.

"Woman don't know what she needs," says Hudson, and stays there a moment, staring at the chapel door. He gives the reins a jerk, digs his spurs into the horse's flank.

Emaline stands listening as the sounds of hooves multiply then fade; listens to the metal-on-rock sound of digging, to the gutter caw of crows, and the swirling song of blackbirds. This time the groan of the floorboards brings Jed from beyond the shadows of the doorway. He runs his hand down the back of his neck, presses his head against the doorframe. His face, half in, half out of the light, is two-tone – tan and black. His eyes flicker white. He opens his mouth to speak, but Emaline cuts him off.

"I've got dinner," she says, and hurries away to the Victoria.

The shock of it, grown men, their trousers to their ankles, one bent over the other, clinging to a barrel of beer, pale skin only just visible as his eyes adjusted to the light. David should not have been there so late at night. There were reasons for rules, and the captain had told them the very first day: "Passengers will be confined to their accommodations by ten o'clock." But the night was humid, the smell of puke and shit suffocating, so he'd crawled from steerage down to the luggage hold, bracing himself against the steady rise and fall of the water.

A movement caught his eye. A rat, or the ship's cat on the prowl, he thought, except there was rhythm to it, a frantic pulsing rhythm, and as his eyes adjusted, his breath caught in short panting breaths.

Living so close to the ocean, seeing the ships appear and disappear on the horizon as he trudged to the mine each day, well, of course he'd heard stories. Violent bloody initiations into sea life or dramas of capture and punishment, designed to shock the sons of miners, to keep them away from the ocean and under the ground where they belonged. But the stories had never had this effect on him. These sailors were friends. He'd seen them talking on deck, slapping each other on the back as lads do. Even now, there was no anger in their dance. It was a satisfied grunting duet. David shuffled back the way he'd come. He told no one. He pretended to sleep on the hard wood of his bunk until morning, afraid to dream. He's dreaming now, his body rising and falling with the waves.

"David?"

Limpy, naked to the waist, sits on the side of the bed. His eyes are coal indentions in the dim light. It cannot be past midnight. Limpy's breath and voice are thick with whiskey.

83

"Hope I didn't tear you away from a good one," he says, shoving David in the shoulder. David doesn't answer.

"Golden Boy, what I tell you? Ha! Sho' 'nough pay dirt. How many ounces a' color you think we washed today? Twenty, thirty dollars' worth, I'm thinking. And washing with pans? With a sluice we'd make five, six times that, easy. Easy," he says, spreading his foul breath over the bed.

"Go get some sleep, Limp."

"There it were . . ." Limpy sits back on his haunches and the bed groans relief. His head tilts back to the canvas roof and a toothy grin shows white. "There it were, sitting there in the ravine all along, winking at us. Was I not the one what told you? I told you I got me a feeling about that boy." He clears his throat, spits on the floor, sings, "I got me a feeling . . ."

David rolls away to face the wall. "Go on, Limpy!"

"All right. Hell, sleep, sleep," says Limpy, crawling on hands and knees across the room to his bed, humming the same tuneless jig. The humming turns to silence, the silence to snoring. David takes himself in hand.

# 7

Through the kitchen door, Emaline watches the sun set on cotton clouds, purple-white against a pink sky. Can almost hear the grass growing, she thinks, and she does hear the blended orchestra of insects swarming the puddle of water outside the door. With the number of new faces in town it seems as if twenty-eight days have passed instead of four since gold was found. It seems to her that the poppies should be blooming, but time always did have a funny way in California. Hatches miners like insects. Bends a young man's back and gnaws at his knees, doing ten years of damage in a sliver of the time. She can hear them now, trooping up from the creek. Her boys, hungry, smelly. Still she languishes a moment more.

The saloon door opens. Familiar footsteps pause in the kitchen doorway.

"Been meaning to talk to you," says Jed, his voice soft but firm.

"No one stopping you," she says, but doesn't turn to face him. She has been avoiding him with busyness, baking twice as much bread, boiling four times as much coffee and using her cycle as an excuse at night, which she never does. Her cycles were short and violent, and Jed knew the moon wasn't right for them. He is a patient man, but also a persistent one, and that hangdog look of his is dragging her down.

"Since Hudson come, I been thinking."

"You been thinking what?" she says, fumbling in the potato sack.

She refuses to worry, resents the energy it consumes while contributing nothing, not a damn thing, to the things that need getting done. She chooses six good-sized potatoes, thumps them one by one on the tabletop.

"Hudson just here to piss on what was never his territory," she says, pointing with her rag. "Wonder who he paid to make him a lawman? Just a feckless shit, more guts in a chicken – and when that chicken came strutting out, tilting its head like it saw Hudson for the worm he was? Ha! I coulda kissed the damn thing." She scrubs a potato. Dried mud flakes on the tabletop. "Fugitive slave, my ass," she says and sweeps the dirt into a pile. "Those politicians making laws in little rooms way off in Washington, expecting people a continent away to follow? We all seen what a mess those laws are making of Kansas, sending neighbors to killing one another over slaves only the richest white folk own anyway. Drawing lines on a map and expecting folks to mind them. Laws like that are only enforced when they suit the purposes of men like Jackson Hudson. What quarrels there have been here, I have dispensed with, quick and fair, and a man can leave if he don't like it."

Jed shifts his weight. He's letting her thoughts play their course, always so damn polite. She closes the back door, steps across to the table. She picks up the paring knife and a potato – just holds them.

"Do you think I should go?" he asks.

"I'm not going anywhere," she says.

"That's not what I asked."

"It's not?"

"Emaline . . ."

86

She shakes her head.

"I was just thinking," he says.

She puts the knife down, places the potato next to it. She pushes past him into the main building, pauses a moment as the heat of him touches her, closes her eyes to the scent of him. That she has no purpose being in the saloon doesn't strike her until eight or so faces look her direction. From behind, she can feel the weight of Jed's eyes upon her. She looks down the line of men. Alex looks up, then away.

The first evening all week he's graced them with his presence instead of crawling up to bed without even eating. Never yet thanked her for washing his flannel or for cleaning the vomit from the floor of his room.

"Alex," says Emaline, and his head jerks up in that shocked way of his. She searches for something else to say, angry at Jed for making her this way, at herself for letting him.

"Know what to do with a broom?" she says and holds open the kitchen door. She needs him to do this for her, to put a body between her and Jed's words.

"Boy been working a mine all the long day and you telling him to sweep?" Limpy says. He stretches his arms behind him and winks at Alex.

"Right, then you can do it. You, David?"

The wrong thing to say. Their eyes move as one to Jed, still standing beyond the door and she can hear their thoughts. Woman's work, man's work, slave's work. It's all work. Think they're the only ones working all day? Think she lazes, sitting on her fist and leaning back on her thumb? She's about to tell them this, tell it good, when Alex stands up.

"It's all right," he says, "I don't mind sweeping."

"You don't mind sweeping? Blisters the size of sixpence on his hands and he don't mind sweeping!" Limpy says.

"Remind him of that when his pick stops swinging

87

tomorrow," says David, his tone much sharper than Limpy's playful banter.

"What else you going to do there, Emaline? Sweeping, huh! Go on then." He catches Alex with a boot in the ass as he passes.

In the kitchen, Jed is scrutinizing the floor for evidence of filth. He won't find any. She'd swept up just minutes before he arrived. Alex stands with the broom in his hands, looking from Emaline to Jed to the floor. Jed's nostrils flare. He picks up a handful of potato dirt, as though he plans to give Alex a mess worth sweeping. But his shoulders fall, his face changes. His fingers loosen and brown sifts to the tabletop. He leaves a trail of dust as he walks out the back door.

He'll be back. He'll be back tonight at her door and she'll let him in. She nods, trying to reassure herself. Alex peeks out beneath his duster hat.

"Right – blisters," says Emaline. "Let me see."

She grabs his hands before he can pull away, feels the shiver that flutters through his body. Such cold hands. Small. She's never been close enough to see how small. His palms are raw and red, except in those places where blisters fill dead skin with clear fluid. A dark shadow peeks just below the cuff of his sleeve. She pushes the cuff up, finds an oblong bruise, brown and fading, but roughly the size of a fist. A frightening blankness clouds his eyes. For a moment she thinks he's stopped breathing.

She pulls his cuff back down and rubs her fingers softly over the blisters. "Some beauties," she says, not sure what else to say. "Nothing much you can do for them really. Just wait till they harden up and become part of you for good."

He nods, and she's relieved he responded. When he pulls away, she lets him go.

"Probably need more of a sweep tomorrow," she says, taking the broom. "Thank you, though."

He opens his mouth, shuts it. His hands fidget. She waits, not sure she wants to know what he's going to say.

"Go on then," she says. She leans her weight against the broom and watches him go.

Her first morning at the mine had passed in complete and utter exhaustion. Each bone and muscle, only thinly connected to the fog of Alex's head, chanted its own special tune of protest. Her nose felt the size of her head, her head the size of her entire body. A throbbing ache began at her tailbone and stretched over both shoulders like the straps of a heavy pack. For the next three days, as her head shrank in size and the cartilage of her nose began its crooked realignment, this heavy pack of fatigue remained with her and sent her straight from the mine through the yellow light of the saloon to the darkness of her room each night. Any thoughts she had of quitting, taking what gold she'd found and moving on, were extinguished by the safety of that room and by an unexpected pride that greeted her with the sun each morning. She would not give the regulars at the saloon, who watched delighted as she crawled up to bed, the satisfaction of watching her quit.

Now, a week and some days have passed since she became the Golden Boy, and her legs are lighter than they have been. Her shoulders are sore along their ridges, but her back is loose. Her eyes wander over the blood red face of the ravine as she follows close behind David and Limpy down the trail leading back to town.

New claims pock the mountainside and miners hunch over their sluice boxes, picking out the larger flakes of color by hand from the wooden slats before collecting the finer grains of pay dirt in a bucket to be washed with a gold pan. Today she spilled only one pan down her trousers and David barely raised an eyebrow in response. It's rare for him to miss a chance to criticize.

"Widen your stance," he lectures. "Bend at your knees – more. Keep your hands a shoulder-width apart on the shaft – a shoulder-width, wider. Use your legs and back next time, not just your arms. Are you aiming, or just swinging?"

All of this to swing a pick at a mountain she hadn't struggled so much to hit when she'd found the gold. David seems intent on forgetting this and she hasn't yet found the nerve to remind him. Even when his back is turned, it feels as though his eyes are on her, looking for the chance to quibble. She had loaded too much raw ore into the sluice box so that pay dirt washed away with the slag, and then after the river water had rinsed the slag away down the creek, she'd failed to wash each black grain of pay dirt from the sluice slats into the washing bucket. "Each grain is money down the creek when you're careless," he told her as Limpy stood in the shade of the ravine, picking his teeth with an oak twig. A scrub jay squawked from the manzanita bushes. She stood impassive to both voices, staring just past him as she used to do with Gran.

The trail curves sharply to the right, around a towering pine. She steps high over the root stems radiating from the trunk. How easily David's legs carry him next to Limpy's graceless clomping. She moves her arms swiftly front to back like David and mimics his stride. His voice comes in chunks of words between the sounds of night birds. He's speaking of the mine, already making plans for the next day when this one is only just ended. His hands are animated in a way they never are when he speaks to her, in a way she's never seen in the saloon. She adjusts the nugget between her legs. The trail widens to Victor Lane.

At least two more canvas shacks have sprung up since this morning, quick as new mushrooms, and the road is littered with discarded canvas sacks, broken pick handles, a pair of mud-crusted socks. Long underwear hangs from a clothesline stretched between tent stakes.

The speed with which men have come to Motherlode surprises her a bit less than the state in which they are willing to live. Four, sometimes five, at a time sleep in bunks, one on top of the other like sailors, and every room in the Victoria Inn is full. At night now the walls of the inn reverberate with the sound of men snoring, retching, coughing. They do nothing quietly, it seems to Alex, as if they were afraid of the invisibility she sought through silence.

Yesterday at this time a crowd was gathered in a circle before the Victoria. Their cheers and shouts reached her ears long before the sound of fists on flesh, and before she got close enough to see the two men tangled at its center, Emaline stepped from the Victoria, shotgun in hand. Alex couldn't hear what she yelled over the ruckus, but everyone heard the shotgun boom, and all heads turned in the shocked silence that followed.

"You going to kill each other, you do it somewhere else," Emaline said, and as if this were an invitation the stockiest of the two fighters stepped forward. A bruise bloomed on his cheek, and blood colored his teeth red. He pointed at his long-legged adversary.

"From the digger pine to the bend in the creek, I said. Wrote it and filed it myself, and this, this – *sonbitch* jumped my claim."

"Weren't no digger pine on the land I'm mining," said Long Legs, holding his left shoulder.

"Well, no shit! But there's a stump, right? Cut my tree, jumped my claim, is what he did. I filed the papers official in Nevada City this last Sunday. The big fella was there. He saw."

Limpy stepped forward, nodded but made no effort to hide the grin on his face. "Saw him when I filed our claim," he said. "But I didn't read it for no tree."

Emaline cradled the gun before her. She squinted from one

bloody face to the other and a murmur was the loudest sound from the miners watching.

"You cut his tree?" she asked Long Legs.

"I cut *a* tree –"

"You cut *his* tree?" The man didn't answer but rubbed his toe into the dirt, chewing on his lower lip as though he'd have liked to cry. Alex was struck by how young he looked, how fine and soft his beard. No older than Peter before he rushed away to the seminary.

Emaline thumped the barrel of her gun down on the porch. "Right, then. *You* find your own claim or find a way to work this one together. Otherwise, I got whiskey to sell and nobody drinking it."

Today, there is no crowd and Emaline stands on the porch of the Victoria, the chickens a flurry of feathers beneath. She scatters oats, clucks and coos at the birds, speaking as if their clucks and chuckles were replies. "Hello, ladies," she says. "How was our day today?" And then, stomping and shooing away a crow, "Git now, git, you old nasty thing!"

David and Limpy disappear together into their cabin. From here, thirty yards away, Emaline could be any number of women, and for a moment she is the woman in the daguerreotype by Alex's bed in Pennsylvania. From this distance, her lips are thin and straight and the dust-brown hair swirling about her head is a deep charcoal-brown, just a shade lighter than Alex's own. Emaline steps off the porch and around the side of the inn, the chickens still pecking at the ground behind her. Alex follows, intending to watch from afar, as she's done the last several days. Watch and listen without knowing why.

Rivers of rainwater on Victor Lane have dried to muddy ruts and crags. She stays to the opposite side of the street where the shadows are longer, and then to the cedars beyond the Victoria. She watches through the open door of the kitchen, listens to the clang of pots and pans. The faint melody of a song wafts out with the smell of rising sour-dough. Alex creeps closer than she has before, crouches low beside the woodpile, and the song reveals itself as a made-up tune, a personal melody that makes Alex want to hum along.

Gran would sometimes hum in the kitchen, usually while peeling potatoes or apples, or some other task that required more patience than focus. It was a pleasant sound of absent contentment, weak but clear, and without the strain that Sunday service seemed to demand. Gran's voice, so gravel thin in speaking, strained for volume in church, wobbling up and crashing into the careful harmonies of Peter's mother, who sat to Alex's right, as if only by being heard by all would Gran be heard by God. Her kitchen-humming lacked urgency, and listening to the soft waft of that voice, Alex could almost envision the young woman invited to sing at weddings and funerals all over the county.

The humming stops. Emaline's dark shape fills the doorway and Alex tumbles back over a stick of firewood and lands with little grace on her rump.

"Well," says Emaline, a smile in her voice. "If it ain't the Golden Boy."

Alex is suddenly very sorry for being sick on Emaline's dress, regrets nothing more at this moment than that dress. Emaline turns back to her stove and, though this is not exactly an invitation, Alex picks up the kindling, follows her through the open door. Heat touches her face. She's struck with an overwhelming sense of familiarity. There the stove, throwing raw heat into the room, there the washtub and the plank table dominating the floor space. Pots and pans hang from hooks like an iron fringe along one wall. Dry twists of herbs, wild rosemary, thyme and mint, are strung from threads in the window. Alex knows this place, or a version of it, knows the feel of bread dough, the smell of pie baking in the oven.

93

She knows the singular satisfaction of sweeping a floor, the simple consolation of ordering the daily disorder of breakfast, lunch and dinner.

Emaline's rump bounces as she pulls the bread from the oven.

"You still here?" she says, and sets the steaming loaf on its side to cool. She tucks a curl behind her ear, wipes her hands on her apron. "Of course you are. Turn your head – the other way. Yeah, well," she says and touches the bridge of her own nose, "no sense being too pretty. And the . . . the blisters?"

Jed clears his throat from the doorway and Emaline's head snaps in his direction. He sets two buckets of water down softly, as if afraid they'll break.

"I'll come back," he says to Emaline. The door swings shut behind him. The fire flares with the blast of oxygen, an open mouth waiting to be fed, but Emaline is staring after Jed. Alex has seen the smug private grins that pass between them. Sitting on the stairwell during the rain, she saw everything.

"They're better than they were," says Alex. "The blisters."

She feeds her kindling into the stove and finds the broom leaning nearby on the wall. Some things aren't allowed, not even in California, but Alex doesn't care to think further on this. She picks up the broom, unsure why this is such a comfort to her. She sweeps, allowing the heat of the stove to engulf her. She won't think about Jed, or anything else outside the heat of this room. She's content to watch the potatoes boiling in the pot, content with the broom in her hands even as she feels Emaline watching her. The outer doors of the inn slam shut. Male voices leak beneath the kitchen door, but come no closer. Just outside, a chicken squawks at some indignity, then quiets, and Alex sweeps.

*      *      *

Yesterday, when David arrived at the mine, he heard a knocking, very like the sound of rats scuttling through the cabin walls at night, and then louder, more distinctly, like a tiny pickaxe on solid ground.

It had become his habit to arrive before Limpy and Alex, if only to enjoy the rare quiet. He'd stand or sit in the middle of the clearing, watch the flycatchers dive from scrub oaks to feed on mosquitoes hovering invisibly over the creek. They made no sound as they dove, not like the cliff swallows back in Cornwall who shrieked their pleasure as they plummeted down toward the rocks and waves, swooping up at the last possible moment.

The knocking continued, louder than before. His shovel leant against the ravine wall, just as he'd left it, the shallow mouth of the mine gaped wide and silent. He blew the air from his chest, ran his hands through his hair. David was not a superstitious man; he and his father agreed on this if nothing else. There was no such thing as Knockers, leading men to rich lodes and then demanding tribute; no such thing as Spriggans, defending those same lodes, upsetting the soil, collapsing mineshafts. "The little people live as sloth inside us all," his father told him. "Men just need a reason for their fortunes. Poor man wants to blame his luck, rich man wants to claim his merit."

Yet a day never passed without his father leaving a bit of his pasty on the ground where he ate his supper, just like the men who swore they had heard the sound of digging coming from the bowels of deserted mine shafts.

He needed a full night's rest, a wash, a shave. He settled for the shock of creek water on his face and sat back on his haunches. He let his head drop back and found a redheaded bird pounding away at the bark of the digger pine above. He must be tired. Of course he knew the sound, knew it belonged here in California. Even so, he stayed away from digging, busying himself with other tasks, until he heard Limpy's voice down the trail.

\*          \*          \*

95

Today, David resigns himself to a late start and follows Limpy to the Victoria for breakfast and coffee.

Less than a month after the find and Motherlode writhes with activity. The trail leading into town has been widened and wagons bring lumber and supplies and merchants eager to take advantage of poor men with new wealth. He's amazed at the speed with which buildings rise from the ground; a foundation laid on Monday is an open shop on Friday. But the buildings lack – what is the word? – permanence, he thinks. They lack the permanence of stone and mortar. They are shoddy, quick constructions with false fronts offering only the impression of elegance.

When he walked the streets of Penzance, David had been surrounded by whispers. He heard whispers in the bustle of Market Jew Street, whispers from standing stones older than the oldest grandparents, whispers from the ocean as the tide rose and fell with the moon. These were voices of the past and while he could never quite comprehend words, they offered him a sense of history and stability. There are no such whispers here in California, or if there were, they weren't talking to him. No such history. Only now and tomorrow – and tomorrow was never certain.

A man retches in the cabin to his right, and hopping along before him a scrub jay scolds, hops and scolds. Behind him the thump of metal on rock calls him to work. He steps up on the porch of the Victoria, pauses a moment, holds his breath. No whispers.

History here walks in living men's shoes, men known for the wealth they accumulate, men more admired for their resourcefulness and luck than their honesty: swindlers, bankers, businessmen, and criminals crowd the same pedestal. Lucky Baldwin, Lord George Gordon, Joaquin Murrieta. The Golden Boy. David sniggers at this last addition and steps through the saloon door to find Alex at a table.

Their eyes meet. Alex stops chewing and David looks

away. Emaline bustles through the kitchen door with a pot of coffee.

"Alex, could use you in the kitchen?" she says, and Jed flashes a quick, sideways scowl.

"I'll go," says Jed, pushing past both Alex and Emaline.

"Emaline sure having a lot of help these days, huh, Alex?" says Micah from behind his newspaper. "Must enjoy taking orders from a woman."

"Feet off my furniture, Micah," says Emaline, and his feet thump to the ground.

"Ha!" says Limpy.

Alex smiles, showing a row of white pearls that quickly disappear. David focuses both eyes upon his food, sips his coffee, letting the bitter taste turn his thoughts to the mine. From the mine and back to Alex, from Alex to the sound of wagon traffic rumbling down Victor Lane. The day must be further along than he realized. Micah rouses himself to meet his supply wagon. David stands and Alex follows him out the door with Limpy. All three linger on the porch.

Behind the wagon is a sight yet to be seen in Motherlode: a sleek iron buggy bouncing along on rusty springs. It's driven by a man in a gray cotton suit and a bowler hat. Behind the man sit two women. No, David sees, a woman and a girl. The gray of their dresses catches a silver seam of light. A wide straw hat obscures the woman's face. David swipes his own hat from his head.

It had been six months ago, on a trip to Grass Valley, that David had last seen a woman – not counting Emaline. Even then he'd kept his distance. There are so few women in this land that chances are, if they aren't married, they'd be of a sort a good Methodist didn't consort with.

Emaline joins them on the porch.

She nods to the man, who offers back a split-toothed smile and earns a sour look from his wife. The girl is handsome, David thinks, but not pretty. Her face is too long, favoring her mother, but her smile is full and her eyes are large and set wide apart. She's staring at Alex. The girl waves. Alex waves back, sheepish, blushing. The woman sits so straight her head doesn't even bob with the ruts in the road.

"That one'll stir things up," says Emaline. David agrees, though he's not entirely sure which of them she's talking about.

# 8

The tail end of April had proven dry; a few lightning bolts slashed jagged signatures across the sky, a few thundershowers, a few days of misted rain, but nothing like the torrent that welcomed her to town. Nothing could have prepared her for the corrosive heat to come. It's now the first week of May and already the long grasses of the valley have yellowed, and even in the shade of the ravine ferns curl to fiddleheads. Miners have been talking drought, eyeing Bobcat Creek suspiciously, as if at any moment they expect the flow to cease, the creek bed to dry and crack.

But inside the mine, walls sweat, and within an hour of digging Alex's flannel has soaked through. *A gallon of sweat for an ounce of gold.* She'd thought the limerick an exaggeration.

"Water . . ." says Limpy. He leans his big body against the mine face and watches Alex dig. "A miner's lifeblood." David returns from the sluice with two empty buckets. Sweat darkens the brim of his Panama hat and clay streaks like war paint down his face.

"Water bringing folks to town as much as the gold," says Limpy. Alex swings her pick. "Talk was nothing but water when I went to Nevada City to file. Ditch companies, charging men fifty cents a day to bring a measly inch of water to dry diggings, just 'cause they can. A hell of a way to make a buck." Alex swings. Limpy brushes bits of shale from his hair. "Fifty cents for a spigot of water from a hole this big –" He makes an "O" with his thumb and forefinger, looks through. "How'd you like to be washing your gold for fifty cents an inch of water? Take all day to get as much as comes down Bobcat Creek in half a second. Fifty cents an inch . . ." His voice trails off as if caught in the thought. Alex places the pick between her knees to wipe sweat from her eyes.

"Break time again, is it?" says David, very close behind her. "The mountain might move itself if we all took breaks as often."

Limpy chuckles. "Luck don't take breaks, David, you know that." His pick plummets with the force of all three of Alex's blows. "Me, on the other hand, I need a breath or two every once in a while." And with that he steps out of the shadow of the ravine into the midday haze.

Alex can feel David's eyes boring into the back of her head, while Limpy, casting a diminutive shadow, stretches his arms to the sky. She lifts her pick, grunts a little, so David can hear the effort. He acts as though this were *his* claim, gives orders as though he was the one who'd found the gold and Limpy just allowed Alex to tag along.

She brings the pick to her shoulder. Her hands are grimy with sweat and mud, and she seeks a better grip. David's voice is just the caw of crows, deep, ornery, everywhere. She raises the metal head, but as she swings, the shaft slips. The pick sails backward. She turns to find David doubled over, clutching himself. Limpy's face contorts in sympathy.

"David!" says Alex, rushing to his side, only to be shoved away.

Limpy pulls her to her feet "Now, if he woulda meant that, be a whole lot better with a pick than we imagined. Dave? You all right?"

David doesn't, or can't answer. He hasn't said a word to her since, and now, in that moment of quiet after dinner, before the plank tables are separated for poker and the bar officially opens for business, David has separated himself from the rest of the regulars. He leans instead against the bar with Jed.

"Extortion," says Micah, sitting on Alex's right at the table. "That's what it is." He leans back on his stool and the vein of his empty socket pulses blue.

"It's not extortion to sell at a *lower* price, Micah," says Harry.

Fred, who's in the habit of disagreeing with everything his partner says, rubs the faded blue felt of his cavalry cap. "Things are changing," he says, then nothing more. His eyes flick to Harry, then down, and Micah continues to scowl into his cup.

The first month after the strikes, Micah nearly sold himself out of business. Every day he raised his prices on mining staples: quicksilver, black powder, picks, shovels, mealy flour, and sprouted beans. Miners kept paying. But two weeks ago Simon Waller rolled into town with his wife, her sister, and a wagonload of goods, intent on starting a livery stable where Victor Lane meets the creek. And a week after that, Gerald Sander set up a dry goods in a shack across the road from Micah's store. Both men sell shovels, picks, and quicksilver, in addition to their usual stock. Both charge the same price; both charge less than Micah.

Limpy's booming guffaw sounds from the porch and Alex leaves the men to their sour moods, and David to his whiskey, and joins Emaline in the kitchen.

At the back door, Emaline fans herself with a tin plate and stares out at dusk. Sweat stains make dark ovals under her arms, and something in her stance suggests a frown.

Alex picks up the broom. Emaline turns to the sound of sweeping.

101

"Alex." She nods. Men's voices filter in from the saloon. The fermenting sweetness of manzanita blossoms seeps with cool air through the open door.

"Alex? What do you hear about Dourity?"

Alex holds the broom silent. She's not yet entirely comfortable with the sound of her own voice. When she speaks, she speaks of the mine, regurgitating what David taught her about soil types, vertical riverbeds, and mineral deposits deep, deep within the earth. These harmless words released a pressure in Alex, made other words unnecessary, made Alex feel more useful with a few swipes of a broom than she ever did at the mine, though with each passing day, she's getting stronger. Not even David can deny that. Emaline never presses. She speaks of the Victoria, or rather of settees and cast-iron stoves and flagstones, and Alex is happy to pretend that life begins and ends in Motherlode.

"Dourity?" says Alex. "He's a lawyer . . ." Emaline shakes her head and Alex offers more: ". . . and some sort of politician? Harry knows him, or knew him, I think."

"*She*," says Emaline. "The wife."

Alex closes her eyes on the word, sweeps away the smell of bourbon.

"Alex?"

"She – Mrs. Dourity – she's got a daughter."

"Well, I know *that*." But she doesn't say what she wants to know, lets the subject drop with the plate to the countertop. She turns to stoke the coals and batten the oven door for morning.

Until Emaline asked, Alex hadn't realized just how carefully she'd been watching Mrs. Dourity. She saw with eyes seduced not only by a gesture, a word, a tone of voice, but by the skill behind each of these. Mrs. Dourity's every step carried a sense of deliberate purpose, as if unseen obstacles lay waiting to trip her. She says *could not, will not, have not*, and flinches when these words are contracted in her presence.

102

She wears constricting dresses, bordered with a deep flounce, and gauntlet cuffs fastened tight about the wrists, and never ventures outdoors without that ponderous straw hat. The only color on her person, apart from the dun-colored mantilla that drapes her head, are the rosebuds stitched into the lace border of her bodice.

In the three weeks since Mrs. Dourity rolled into town, three other women have followed. First Mrs. Waller and her sister Rose, carted up on the back of Simon Waller's supply wagon, then the twittering Mrs. Erkstine, who introduces herself as "the Reverend Mrs. Erkstine." Like Mrs. Dourity, they are living among the miners in canvas shacks along Victor Lane. But already foundations for larger, more permanent homes form a separate growth of town beyond the livery where the cedar stumps rot.

Alex has seen men stop mid-sentence when one of the women passes, preferring not to speak than to swear in her presence. Pissing contests have been restricted to the mines. Hats are doffed and muddy feet step to the churning dust of the road, leaving the fresh pine of the new sidewalk clear for the women to pass.

And more than once Alex has forgotten herself and allowed her legs to cross at the ankle instead of flaring wide. This morning she woke to the sensation of hair falling heavy down her back, and her dreams have become thick with layers of petticoats. Dangerous dreams, for they pick their way indiscriminately into memory, bring the smell of bourbon with the word *wife*.

She watches Emaline out of the corner of her eye until she realizes Emaline is doing the same. She turns her back and attacks the corner in earnest, though she knows the stain is water damage and a broom will do no more good than a word.

There are times when Emaline wishes to sit among women, to talk about something other than gold, to exchange recipes

103

and secrets, and she must admit that part of her, perhaps a large part, is lonely for this company. The company of ladies who might appreciate her efforts with the chapel, the fine silk of the curtains she's ordered, the labor of a good meal, the unending demands of men.

A fly bobs in the air before her. She would swipe at it, but her hands are a muck of butter and flour. She is making a pie. Two of them, actually, for she wouldn't hear the end of it if the boys discovered she'd neglected them. The butter, golden yellow, brought in just yesterday from the Storm Ranch, slips through her fingers, mixing with the powder-soft granules of flour and a pinch or two of salt. She rolls out the dough, spreads it thin, adds only enough flour to stretch it.

For some reason her crusts are never as flaky as she remembers her mother's being. Too much flour, too much kneading, always too much of something. She wants this pie to be perfect, and wishes that there were fresh berries in season. Preserves will have to do. Boysenberry, she thinks, and unscrews the lid of the mason jar to the tart sugary smell. She dips her finger for a taste.

Four ladies living in Motherlode, she thinks, and none of them, not one, has come round the Victoria. Mrs. Dourity, at least, should have introduced herself by now. Emaline closes the oven door, wipes her hands on her apron. Got nothing else to do, squatting there in Mordicai's old place, the pine planking just as leaky as it ever was. She smiles at this image, a gray patterned dress, ruffled shoulders, high neck, forced to squat over a stone fire pit and rest on a wooden bunk. It's easier to think of Mrs. Dourity this way, as a dress. Lord knows, her husband has been by, though only to drink and stand at the bar jawing about community and county elections like he's running for governor of California. Emaline isn't angry with his wife, exactly. But she is not above applying a little congenial guilt, portioned out in the form of a pie. She'll make her rounds to the other ladies later.

She drapes the crusts in pans, shapes them to fit, slices off the excess. In go the preserves, a design on the top crust with her knife, and egg yolk and butter for a golden brown. Later, she stands over the finished pies, scrutinizes one, then the other, decides the one on the left is just a bit overdone on top.

She ties her hair up, wishing she had a mirror, but refuses to go upstairs to have a look. She pulls at a curl here, tucks a curl there, runs a kitchen cloth along her teeth. She takes the apron off, smoothes the folds of her dress, clean but the same ugly brown. No time to sew a new one. It's this or the stained calico. She picks up the perfect pie on the right, heads for the door, but stops with her hand on the knob. Goddamn, she says under her breath. She walks back. She switches pies. She takes a breath, blows out all her air, forces her shoulders down. She'll be damned if she'll try to impress. She opens the door and ventures out of the Victoria to introduce herself.

She waits for a wagon to pass and steps down on the new sidewalk. Micah is busy inside his store, arranging and re-arranging new merchandise. None of the ready-made dresses he'd ordered would fit her big toe. A damn waste of money, you ask her, carrying clothing that fits only a few shapes. Used to be, you bought the cloth and made the dress to suit the woman. The way it's going, they'll need to start making women to fit the dresses.

In the May heat the ridgeline above town takes on a purple hue. The wild strawberries behind the Victoria will soon be ripe, the heart-shaped fruit still white, bloodless, but plentiful. She can almost taste them, fresh with the chill of morning, or baked up hot in a pie. She looks down at the pie in her hands. Preserves will have to do, for now.

Hard to believe eight weeks ago everybody and their uncle

was heading north. She hasn't heard a thing about the Fraser River since Alex found that nugget, though she's heard news from just about every other corner of the world. News rolls up on wagons. News walks behind pack mules, or by its lonesome self, taking the varied form of miner, or miner-turned-merchant, or lawyer-turned-miner, or merchant-turned-pharmacist. Seems like every one of these men, new hat or tattered, claims to be this, and also this, and on occasion that. Believe everything or nothing of what they say, it would make no difference. Gold just opened the place up, spanned the world like a guitar string plucked a little different by each man walking through. Wars, rebellions, famines, floods – the usual fare, with added local complaints: miners striking against water companies, and President this or Governor that promising to do more than General this or Judge that, if you just elect him. She heard they finally got that railroad running through the Sacramento Valley. "The Sacramento Valley Line, twenty-two miles, through to Folsom," a curly-headed fellow told her one night, acting proud like he was personally responsible. And some fools in San Francisco were talking about bridging the bay. No such thing as an unreasonable goal here, she thought, as she looked about the town growing solid around her.

A muleteer slows his team to pass and shows his scurvy-blackened teeth. "Whoa now," he says. His eyes flit from Emaline to the pie, back to Emaline. He tips his hat. "Gee up," he says, and the wagon leaves behind the sap smell of timber.

Banging and sawing join the busy noise of birdsong as the open spaces along Victor Lane are filled. She rather liked the cigar shop, the musky scent of tobacco drifting out into the street, though the haberdasher could do with more than bowler hats and farmer's straw hats. They were cutting a side street just up from the new livery stable, which is fine with her since it didn't intersect at the Victoria Inn. The new street curves around behind the inn, paralleling Victor Lane, forming a funny little horseshoe, with the chicken coop like an island in the middle. A sawmill is what we really need, she thinks. More than side roads or this other inn she's heard talk about.

With the improvements she's planning, won't be any place better than the Victoria. Takes time, is all. She's already ordered the furniture. Rich maple settees with velvet upholstery and rounded oak tables stained dark amber-brown. Klein is building tall stools to match a new oaken whiskey bar, but she's told him that his first priority should be the chapel, guaranteed him a written contract, no matter how many carpenters come to town. Looking back, it would have been wiser to let him compete for the job. Loyalty is not always the best thing for business.

The heel of her shoe slips off the planking. She wobbles, rights herself. She debates whether to drop in on Micah, but the pie is still warm in her hands and she knows by the way her mind is skittering from one matter to the next that the best thing is just to do what she came to do and then get back to the Victoria. She takes a breath, letting it out in one long blast, and a lone chicken, the raw-butted Rhode Island Red, scuttles out of her path. She smiles at the gray weather-stained wood of Mordicai's old cabin. The uneven steps squeak and groan as she climbs up to knock, one, two, on the door.

The door opens.

"Lou Anne Dourity, where have you – oh," says Mrs. Dourity, looking both directions up then down the road.

On the occasions Emaline has seen Mrs. Dourity, her face has always been in profile and hidden by that over-large hat. Hatless, from the front, the woman's long, hooked nose is offset by a pair of large brown eyes, which manage to appear neither pleased nor displeased by Emaline's presence. Her mouth, straight and thin from the side, gives way to soft pink lips from the front. The sharp line of her cheekbones in profile is softened with the curve of her eyebrows. Emaline has never seen two such separate faces on the same woman before and it takes her a moment to figure out just who is greeting her. Perhaps she judged the woman too quickly. She feels tension giving way to a smile.

"I was looking for my daughter, Lou Anne," says Mrs. Dourity. She doesn't return the smile.

"I haven't seen her." Emaline holds up the pie. The sweetness teases her nostrils. She wouldn't mind a bit of this now.

"How nice," says Mrs. Dourity. She takes the pie, but holds it straight in front of her like a soiled child. A crashing sound draws both women's attention down the street to the livery stable where men unload lumber.

"Might be for your new place?" Emaline suggests, meaning the wood, but Mrs. Dourity shakes her head.

"We'll be building in oak and brick. Hard wood is far more resilient, don't you agree?"

"More expensive."

"Yes."

Emaline shifts her weight in the silence that follows, looks back up the road toward the Victoria. It would be nice to sit for a while, take a bit of coffee with someone else serving.

"I'm right up there at the Victoria Inn, should you need anything," says Emaline, and hears the words repeat themselves inside her head. *Should you need anything.* Her mother's words. "Emaline's the name," she says.

"I've heard," says Mrs. Dourity, and Emaline's smile goes flat.

"Ah well . . ." Emaline takes a breath, raising herself up to look down on Mrs. Dourity. "Since you've *heard*."

But as she turns to go, the sound of voices stops her. Mrs. Dourity glances back through the half-closed door.

"We were just having some coffee," she says, then, "Won't you join us?" with an expression that begs, *Please don't.*

If she had been forthright with her hospitality, Emaline might have graciously declined. *How nice of you, no. Thank you, but I really should get back, bread to bake, drapes to mend, men to fuck*, she'd say, just for the shock of it. But the sound of female laughter, a high twittering blending with an alto chuckle, issues from the cabin. That, combined with the shade of guilt coloring Mrs. Dourity's cheeks, convinces Emaline to stay.

"Why, thank you. I think I will," says Emaline, pushing past Mrs. Dourity into the cabin, immediately regretting this decision.

It has been years since Emaline has been alone in a room full of women. She pushes through the doorway, harking back to her mother's tea parties and quilting sessions for courage. The hushed voices, the condemning tones and well-intentioned advice, the short blasts of laughter, quickly swallowed. Mrs. Dourity comes in behind her. The door shuts, muffling the slams and bangs of the livery stable, nearly blocking the sound of wagon traffic and the constant pinging of picks and shovels at the creek.

The only light in the room filters in through the crescent-and-petal-shaped lace of the curtains and shines, as if trained there, on the white tablecloth around which three women sit. They look her up and down. And let them look, thinks Emaline, drawing herself up, tucking a curly strand behind her ear. She notices the whalebone rigidity of the women's backs and her chin, as if on a string, strains higher.

"Ladies," says Emaline, nodding, noticing the two empty stools.

"We're expecting my daughter, Lou Anne," says Mrs. Dourity, her eyes also on the stools.

"So you said. Well, not to worry, the boys'll take good care of her." Mrs. Dourity cringes. "Won't do her no harm, at least," says Emaline, easing herself down upon one of the stools, pulling her skirt out from under her.

Mrs. Dourity says nothing to this, turns instead to her other guests. "A pie," she says, and places the plate in the middle of the table. She leaves the cloth over the top.

"Oh, my," says the woman closest to the stove, but Emaline's not sure she's commenting on the pie. Her hair is a straight, sandy-colored blonde, gathered into a loose braid, and her big eyes blink out beneath thick lashes. Emaline would have thought she was the owner of the twittering laughter, but her voice is rich and warm. Her face, like the faces of all of these women, is young – younger than Emaline, at least. Not even out of their twenties. But the confidence of seniority is not forthcoming. It's their dresses that hamstring her, the high necks, the frilly lace, and more buttons than weeks in a year. She shifts on the stool, nods her thanks when Mrs. Dourity offers a cup of coffee. The blonde woman takes a deep breath in through her nose.

"Blackberry?" she asks.

"Preserves," Emaline says, hoping this doesn't sound like an apology. "And it's boysenberry." She wasn't expecting to meet the whole of Motherlode's female population in one day. Gathered here, excluding her, no doubt discussing her. On the other hand, at least all introductions will be over and done with. One pie for four women, not a bad exchange. She sips the coffee, weak, watery stuff. "You are . . . ?" she asks.

"May I introduce Mrs. Ely Erkstine," Mrs. Dourity says of the sandy blonde, as though just now realizing introductions are necessary. "Mrs. Simon Waller," she says, motioning to the woman in the middle, a tight-lipped lady with stripes of premature gray coursing through her hair. Her left hand rests on the round bulge of her stomach, the only weight to her. "And her sister, Rose. And this is Mrs. . . ."

Morgan was her father's name; Sweeny had been her husband's. "Call me Emaline."

Her eyes fix on Rose. The woman's black hair is secured in an eye-peeling bun. Her body is bone and sinew. Her dress reveals little in the way of breasts.

"I own the Victoria Inn."

"Own?" says Mrs. Erkstine. "We thought, I thought, didn't you say the big fellow . . . ?" she asks Mrs. Dourity.

"Limpy?" says Emaline.

"I thought he was . . . or at least owned . . ." stammers Mrs. Erkstine. She blushes. "We heard you, well . . ."

"I own the Victoria," Emaline repeats, then, "I'm a widow."

"You are," says Mrs. Erkstine, stretching the "are" to twice its usual length.

Emaline regrets this last admission, is angry at this sudden need to justify herself, but appreciative at least of Erkstine's sympathy. It seems genuine. Mrs. Dourity and the other two – sisters, did she say? – have yet to thaw.

"It was years ago . . ."

"Where is that girl?" says Mrs. Dourity, staring out the window, content to ignore the conversation.

Mrs. Waller speaks: "The West is really no place for a young lady. If she were mine, I'd be on the first ship back to Boston, away from *influences*."

"The moral character is never so vulnerable than at this age. Don't you agree?" Mrs. Erkstine asks Emaline, but doesn't wait for a response. Emaline's neck hairs prickle. Maybe not so genuine. "But if the civilized keep running back East, what kind of Christians would we be? My husband's a pastor." The woman spits out her *p*'s as if they were distasteful, and Emaline can imagine her sitting in the front row of a fancy church, playing the moral paragon. "He's been friends with good Mr. Sargent, the DA up in Nevada City, since childhood. Chose different paths to justice, but it's the ends that matter. They've already shut down that Applegate place. One less bawdyhouse, and fourteen women liberated." Her face is flushed, exultant, but Emaline glows with secret knowledge. She has already been introduced to Mr. Erkstine, though he was a bit too preoccupied to mention that he was a pastor, or that he was married.

"He'll be holding a service this Sunday at ten."

111

"Where?" asks Emaline, setting down her cup.

"Must be terrible, the only woman in a place like this," says Mrs. Waller.

"Ely wanted to come up here alone," says Mrs. Erkstine, "but I said, 'No, I will not leave you alone to face the trials of your calling.' Walking with God, I call it, though Lord knows I didn't want to leave Sacramento, the pleasures and comforts of a city . . ."

"Bless," says Mrs. Waller.

"The law's a calling like any other," says Mrs. Dourity, just the slightest bit defensive, then goes back to searching for Lou Anne out the window.

"Where is he planning to hold his Sunday service?" asks Emaline again, beginning to wish she had more than coffee in her cup, weak coffee, at that.

"Why, the chapel, of course," Mrs. Erkstine says. Then, to Mrs. Dourity: "Do you plan to save that pie?"

Mrs. Waller sits up straighter in her chair and Mrs. Dourity gives up on the window. "No, no sense in saving –"

"My chapel?" says Emaline, and Mrs. Erkstine catches her breath. Mrs. Dourity halts with a knife poised above the pie. Mrs. Waller licks her lips.

"Surely it is the Lord's chapel?" says Mrs. Erkstine. "And without a proper preacher, if I'm not mistaken."

Mrs. Dourity's knife plunges into the thick, flaky crust and deep purple jam oozes through the open wound.

"John does just fine."

"When he's sober." Rose says this, but her lips barely move, and her expression does not change, so that for a moment Emaline wonders if she really heard her speak.

"Smells lovely," says Mrs. Waller.

"He's sober when he wants to be," says Emaline. "He's sober on Sundays."

Rose remains sitting upright in her chair. Black eyes, her only animate feature, fix upon the pie.

"Well now, it's not unusual to hold more than one service," says Mrs. Erkstine. "If the Methodists and Presbyterians can share, then surely we can share with – what are you? Oh, just a bit bigger piece, a little more. Perfect." She presses the flat of her hand to her stomach, and digs into the pie on her plate.

"I . . . Motherlode is not affiliated. And Preacher John is –"

"Heavenly," says Mrs. Erkstine, taking a small bite. Emaline looks down at her slice of pie, the sugar of the jam suddenly too sweet for her stomach.

"Motherlode," says Mrs. Erkstine between bites, scrunching her nose. "Who on earth names these places? Rough and Ready, You Bet . . . The first thing we should do is give this place a proper name."

"I named this place!" says Emaline. "And who's 'we'?" Who the hell is "we" she means but holds herself back, letting the rest filter through her head. With men you could say anything you chose. They'd only hear half, anyway. Women heard what was said and then a whole lot more that wasn't. She shoos a fly away from her slice. Rose has declined a piece. Emaline takes this as a personal insult.

"Nevada City was Coyoteville, of all things," says Mrs. Dourity, ignoring Emaline completely. "And Placerville? Hangtown! Can you imagine sending a letter home from Hangtown?"

The fly takes advantage of Mrs. Dourity's preoccupation and dips into the slippery red jam.

"Lewiston?" Mrs. Erkstine suggests.

"No, there's a Lewiston just south of Sacramento, I'm sure of it," says Mrs. Waller.

"It has always been Motherlode," says Emaline, standing up from her stool. All four women look in her direction as if they'd forgotten she was there. "It was Motherlode from the day I arrived, and it will be Motherlode until the day I die." A drastic statement, but her voice is calm, matter of fact. "Now, if you'll excuse me."

113

The door closes behind her before she again hears voices from the cabin. Men stride this way and that, busy or faking it, and Emaline chews on the inside of her cheeks, ruminating, remembering. She steps back into the road, heading for the chapel, a fury not unlike religious zeal building with every step.

Freedom is what these women lack, and ambition – though in Emaline's mind, they are the same. In California freedom is defined by a price, and its price is ambition. It is not enough simply to celebrate freedom, to dig a hole and hide it from harm, or build up walls of rules, protecting your idea of what freedom should be, while damning other versions. You have to invest in freedom, she thinks, to put it in the bank of blind faith and draw interest on strength and effort. Goals are dangled, like bread to the starving, and you could find your-self crawling, walking, running forward, grasping for cotton on the wind, not so much to catch it, but to call it your own, to say you tried and will keep trying. Ambition gave shape to freedom, a purpose, a calling. Take this seed and grow a forest. Take these nails and build a town. Emaline walks on, watching for cracks in the sidewalk.

These women are bound by more than corsets. They are bound by the rules they brought with them, rules Emaline had left behind, first out of necessity by her husband's grave near the Continental Divide, and later by choice. She raises her head now, trusting her feet to find the boards. She swings her arms. Moral character, they say. By whose standard? Tight-laced, corset-bound matrons of the East. Too harsh, she knows, for her mother had been the same cut as these ladies. So constrained by the rules she'd lived by that she never had the time or energy to dream of anything more. So paralyzed by what was proper that she'd never considered what was possible. Refused to see why Emaline craved the West, though at the time not even Emaline understood what the call meant, and what the cost would be. The West was a land of dreamers

114

whose pasts were mere shells, foundations for greater aims. And the dreamers were not just men. And only the dreams were easy.

She finds Klein pounding away on a pew, the pulpit already reworked with simple vine-shaped decorations. Sawdust floats, catching streams of light through the windows. He looks up, his black hair littered with wood chips.

"I need a sign," she tells him, holding her arms wide. "This big, or bigger."

"All right," he says, scratching his back with the blunt side of his chisel.

"MOTHERLODE, in big letters."

# 9

"Up a little, your end, Alex," says Limpy.

Alex strains on her tiptoes, edging the bracing timber upward another inch. The backs of her arms and shoulders ache. David supports the other half of the timber, laboring only slightly under the weight. In the shadow of the infant mine, his skin is translucent.

"Hurry, Limpy," says Alex, feeling her arms deaden, the weight shift.

"Almost got it. Just one more . . . Okay."

Alex's arms fall to her sides. Her hands are leaden pincushions that prick and tickle as the blood rushes back. She leans against the damp wall of the shaft. She listens to the tap and crash of picks and shovels a mile upstream, a half mile down. Windlasses groan under the weight of ore buckets hauled to the grass and ever present is the hum of the creek. Purring, Limpy calls it, but Alex still remembers how loud it roared, how violently it pushed its way downstream during the rains; how, when filled with rage, the creek upended boulders and tore trees from their roots. She thinks about this when her shoulders ache and her hands throb; how much stronger this little creek could be than any man. For some reason this thought allows her to continue, as if she sensed that it was some strange grace that allowed her to hear the river and liken it to a purr, allowed her to linger here in the fading afternoon and think these thoughts.

"Don't know about that last timber, Limp," David says. "All right for now. But that crack isn't getting any smaller."

"Be fine. One of many, you know," Limpy says. "Not gonna hold up the whole mountain on its own, is it?"

"I'm saying I've seen whole shafts caving in around one faulty timber. We're not working with solid rock here."

"Superstition's what that is."

Limpy leans on the timber to prove his point, and Alex grins. Superstition is a sword Limpy often draws against David. "Be fine till tomorrow, at least. Besides, don't think Alex is up for another one today."

She lets out an acceding breath and sinks down against the wall. Downstream, someone detonates a lodeful of black powder. Bits of earth shower down and the tendons of her lower back tighten. Digging holes with picks and shovels is frightening enough. The thought of blasting terrifies her. The smell of the char-silicon powder that the miners pack into drill holes bears a terrible resemblance to cauterized skin and, at any moment, Alex expects the entire ravine to tumble downward in pain or protest. Perhaps David is right about that last bracing timber. But she doesn't feel like admitting this.

"It'll wait till tomorrow, won't it?" Alex asks, addressing Limpy more than David.

"We still got some daylight left," says David. "We have time."

Limpy wipes his hands down his trousers and lowers himself to a crouch.

"Daylight's one thing, energy's something else. I got no more poop."

He winks at Alex, and she gives a conspiratorial sigh of agreement. David's frustrated scowl follows her out into the fading light. The grass chokes under a layer of clay and the

117

manzanita bushes on either side have been cut to make way for digging. The dead, graying limbs, still too green to burn, are piled across the creek, and heart-shaped leaves carpet the ground. Every cedar and pine within a half mile has been cut for support beams and sluice boxes, for the cabins and shops thriving where trees once stood along Victor Lane.

Limpy joins her outside and together they wait for David to concede, which he does only after washing one more bucket of ore through the sluice and gathering every tool scattered around the claim into an organized stack, with all pick handles facing the same direction and shovel heads spooning.

"Quite done, then?" Limpy asks as David rinses his hands in the creek. In reply, David strides off ahead of them downstream toward Motherlode.


That last timber moved a good inch when Harry blew his charge. No way it will hold in a local explosion, and David wants to be blasting by next week; would be blasting now if Limpy didn't insist on wasting daylight's last hour gabbing in front of the Victoria. A town full of new faces and Limpy thinks he had to be on first-name terms with everyone. They'd be another twenty feet deeper by now if the man moved his shovel as much as his mouth. But he never could sway Limpy, and the boy . . . Well, David doubts if Alex even bothered to listen to what the big man said before agreeing. He cannot shake the suspicion the boy did this to spite him.

He passes claim after claim, the freshly turned soil like festering blemishes on the ravine face. He stops to watch two greenhorns hacking away at the mountain. He can see by the way these fellows have laid their shaft that they'll have trouble with drainage. He should say something – let them know the load of work they'll save by cutting up into the mountain, let the water run out on its own – but feels no need to help another man get rich. Likely, they'll spend their profit as fast as they dig it for a fancy new hat, a night in Emaline's bed.

David could use a new hat. His panama smells as rank as he does. But he hates the thought of spending money, and doing business in raw gold dust still baffles him. One pinch from a man's pouch was never equal to a dollar, whatever Micah said. Depending on the size of a man's thumb and forefinger and the length of his nails, one pinch could take closer to two dollars, or more. And you had to watch careful that a fellow didn't press buckshot into his fingers, increasing his yield with the indent, or lick his thumb or rub his nose before dipping in your pouch. Micah was a master at this. Pretend he was itching that ugly socket, make a detour past his tongue, and rid you of a few more flakes than dry fingers would have.

Across the creek, the valley grass rises tall and brown. A few of the newest arrivals have settled for the flats downstream. He can see the conical hats of Chinamen bobbing over their pans, adding ounces of slag at a time to the mud-choked creek. Ten or so have made camp there. They packed in silently at night, and he can't see one without remembering the hundreds landing on docks in San Francisco when he arrived two years ago.

"You stay away from them," a woman's voice had called from the window above, but for a moment all he'd seen were the screaming gulls. Human bodies of every size, shape, and color bumped past him as if he were but a box in the sea of boxes stacked along the wharf. After months at sea his legs shook on the solid ground. "Up here, honey, haloo," said the woman at the window. "Hey, Jenny," she called behind her. "Come look at the face of this one."

"I seen all the faces there are," came the answer, and the woman on the railing leaned out further. Her breasts swelled round and bare as moons before him.

"You stay away from them—" she gestured at the

119

Chinamen. "'Less you want to smoke your pecker off." She held up her finger, wiggled it around. She made a perfect circle with her mouth and bit the finger at its base. "HA!" she said, and disappeared through the window.

His letter home mentioned only the hundreds of Chinamen – Celestials, they called them in San Francisco.

He should write home. No reason to be hesitant now that he's making a profit. A hundred dollars in gold dust a day, split three ways. More money than his father saw in six months of wages. But when he sits down to write, there is always more to say than he can put into words on paper. He sends only gold, and even the act of scrawling his name feels dishonest.

He trips over a fallen log, keeps his eyes to the trail. When I have enough gold, I will return to Cornwall. I will sit with my family surrounding me and I will show them a place in stories – evergreens standing taller than the giants of Cornish legend, the violent stillness of the Sierras in winter, San Francisco Harbor choked with the bulk of hundreds and hundreds of ships – I'll show them a place.

He stops. A Chinese man stands knee deep in water ten yards downstream. He grins and points. Another man, his long black queue hanging to his waist, tugs at the grinning man's shirt. His eyes flit from David to the grinning man. His frown is that of a frustrated parent or an older brother.

"Gold," Grinning Man says, or something like it.

"He simply man, sir," says his partner and bows. "Simple man," he says, correcting himself, and leads Grinning Man away by the arm.

Enough gold, David thinks, as he watches them go. How much is enough gold?

Grinning Man looks back. He shakes his head and his queue swings back and forth across his chest.

Alex passes the livery and Heinrich's shoe store, a solid wood building that has sprouted and grown to overshadow David and Limpy's cabin on its left and the cigar shop on its right. Shopkeepers are just shutting their doors. They linger outside to talk and sweep dust from their storefronts into a choking fog that settles back in much the same place. Alex loiters a moment in front of the haberdasher, staring at the assorted headwear, at the panama hats in particular. Their straw-colored brims turn down at a pleasingly jaunty angle and, if David didn't wear one, she'd already have bought one for herself. She might still, she thinks, and ducks between Sander's dry goods and the Victoria Inn, to be alone among the dwindling cedars.

Even here, with the jumble of wagons and construction and human voices buffered by the body of the inn, Alex can hear Emaline's voice from somewhere near the chapel.

"Won't have a leaning steeple, Klein," says Emaline, and Alex smiles, imagining the woman's arms crossed, her foot tapping, and Klein squirming. "You look there and tell me it ain't leaning."

"Jesus H. Christ, Emaline!"

"Three other carpenters in this town now, Klein, most charging less than you, so –"

"All right now . . ."

Klein's voice falls below the level of the hammering and the exploratory squawks of the chickens who tiptoe around the edges of their pen, testing the extent of their new confinement. Alex eases down onto a log and closes her eyes on the outhouse and the chicken coop.

After two months, her body is just now acclimatizing to the daily toil of the mine. She no longer minds the fatigue, the rough calluses forming on her hands, the solid indentions developing where she never dreamed muscles lurked. With each new ache, she discovers a new, living part of herself. Filling out, the men call it, but to Alex it feels more like filling in, for she's not becoming much bigger. Her arms are still spindly, and her stomach has lost its former softness and shrunk to a firm, flat surface. She now simply feels more complete. The dirt beneath her nails, the tough layers of skin hardening on her feet and hands, and the veins showing thick and blue through the darkening tan of her skin, is rooting her, establishing her in this place, and in this body. With every muscle formed and every ounce of sweat lost comes an unaccustomed sense of self, independent of her past. Even her nose, healing just off center with a bump in the bridge, fits her.

She runs her hands down her nose, her aching arms, as much out of curiosity as comfort and is sinking deep into the pleasant exhaustion of evening when she becomes conscious of someone approaching around the side of the inn. Graceful steps, too quiet for Limpy, too casual for Emaline.

The girl, Lou Anne, appears, her red hair barely contained by a lacy blue bonnet, a wilting batch of wildflowers in her hand. Not more than thirteen, Alex thinks. The girl advances, not coyly, but cautiously, as though Alex might bite. Alex closes her eyes to slits, hopes the girl will go away. Instead, she lays the flowers in the dirt, produces a small ball of twine and throws it, thump, thump, thump against the wall, edging ever closer to Alex. Alex opens her eyes.

"I'm not supposed to be here," Lou Anne says, throwing the ball just above Alex's head. It rebounds into Alex's lap. The girl grins.

"Mother, she doesn't want me here. Says she'll tan me good. She thinks I'm picking flowers. I am . . ." She looks down at the pile at her feet. "Was."

She selects a long-stemmed lily, blue petals with yellow tongues, and holds it out for Alex. The wildflowers in the valley are almost all dry. She must have ventured downstream. Past the Chinamen's huts? Alex takes the flower.

The girl giggles and her face reddens to match her freckles. "She says only coarse men and fallen women come here. That's what she says."

Emaline's voice again, barking orders at Preacher John.

The girl turns toward the sound, then back to Alex. "Like her."

"Emaline," Alex blurts, unthinking.

"Living in sin. No right to build a church if you plan to go right on living in sin. They all say that: Mrs. Erkstine, Mrs. Waller, her sister Rose. All of them. Should let other than a drunk do the preaching, too. That's what *they* say."

Alex's neck warms at the collar. Who are they to say anything? Emaline's presence is like a quilt around Alex's shoulders. Emaline's hands heal blisters.

The girl stands with her hip jutting to the side, her toe tapping. Her very presence is loud and reminds Alex of Gertrude Mellon who came to Shackelford just after Alex's fifteenth birthday.

Gertrude wasn't a pretty girl, at least not to Alex's eye. Her hair was a strange sort of blonde that looked as if she'd washed it in red wine and was pulled back into a maze of clips and braids. Her body was soft and pasty white, like bread dough. The white gloves made her hands look like small, boneless decorations. But she was a year older than Alex, and seemed to carry with her a strange confidence that drew invitations to tea and supper all about town. She was from New York City and had gone to boarding schools, her manners fashioned under the eyes and expectations of other young girls expected to marry well and live comfortably. Her laugh curled upward like a climbing vine, remaining in a room like a scent, hours after she'd left. When she sat down in a chair, it seemed as if she were floating in midair, and she could drink from a tea cup in a way that demanded an audience: her finger pointed just so, her lips poised, but never slurping, never a drop of liquid escaping to dribble down her chin. And when she walked, she swayed, the layers of petticoats whispering secret messages Alex heard but couldn't interpret, not like Peter seemed to.

She watched him when Gertrude came into the room, the

way he pushed his shoulders back, held his head at an angle, like his father. He laughed loudly at Gertrude's jokes – much louder, Alex thought, than the jokes themselves warranted – and made a point of sitting beside her at services, his leg carefully aligned with hers but careful not to touch.

Gran insisted that Gertrude come to tea at least once a week, as if hoping these manners, this grace, this impeccable dress, would somehow lend themselves to her granddaughter, would somehow linger in the room like the sound of that laugh.

"A beautiful girl," Gran would say. "Quite charming." And Alex would remain silent, unable to disagree, but not willing to agree. Silence had become her only true protection, especially since Peter was spending less and less time with her in the fields behind Hollinger's place and more and more time studying for his seminary exams. He still spoke of soldiering, but his words had lost that dreamy ring of possibility, coming out like a nursery rhyme repeated so many times that it was only the rhythm that mattered. Alex would climb to the attic to escape Gran. She'd look upon the dusty remnants of her family: wooden soldiers and toy hammers, readers with little-boy scrawl, and clothing of various sizes documenting the growth of three boys. And in the corner of this room, whose slanted ceiling offered only enough headroom for Alex to stand bent at the waist, hung her mother's wedding dress, wrapped in a protective dustcover of terry cloth and muslin.

Alex would sit here among the trunks and hatboxes and talk to her mother. She would run the satin sleeve of the dress down her cheek, feeling in this the tips of her mother's fingers. She told her mother. All the things she would have told her if she was alive, and many things she wouldn't. She'd told her mother about stealing apples and climbing trees, how bright the teacher said she was, how misshapen the s's always turned out on her stitch sampler, looking more like a coiled serpent than a letter. She told her mother of the fliers and editorials about the West that she and Peter had read behind the rabbit hutch.

But one day, nearly three months after Gertrude imposed upon her life, Alex took the dress down from its hook. It was heavier than she'd anticipated, as if she were folding a real body over itself, the whalebone stays of the bodice like a woman's ribs. She hugged it tight in her arms, careful not to expose the silk to the dusty floor, and eased her way down the ladder, back to her room.

The neckline was round, edged with pearls and bits of lace. The heavy train pulled her back and down, making every step forward an act of strength and balance. There were satin panels on either side of the skirt, accentuated with layers of pleating and lace, and pearls were stitched along every seam. She closed her eyes and let her fingers explore the flared sleeves, slipping over the satin, sticking on the lace, bumping over the pearls. She filled out everything except the bodice, but this was no matter to Alex. She could not tighten the stays, so she left them hanging as she practiced walking about the room. She twirled, she swayed, loving the whispering sound the fabric made as she moved. She claimed sickness at dinner, waited for the April sun to set and Gran's door to click shut, then tiptoed from the house, picking up her skirts so their whispering wouldn't wake Gran.

"Peter," she hissed through his window. His light was still on. She knew he was awake. He liked to make her wait. "I'm going to the rabbit hutch. I want to show you something . . . Peter?"

She heard his chair scrape back against the floor. She ran before he could see her, picking up her skirts, her feet very light even as the dress dragged her down, her lungs drinking in the cool spring air. She waited at the rabbit hutch a very long time. She wondered if he hadn't heard her after all, or if he'd heard and was simply ignoring her. The ground was

125

getting damp and she was tired of standing there, holding the skirt and train off the ground, careful not to brush up against wood and snag the fabric, which wasn't nearly as warm as the layers would suggest. Hollinger's dog was howling, and the moon was full enough to see all the way across the field where the orchards began. And beyond that the creek, and beyond that the Alleghenies, and beyond that . . . ? Alex didn't know. She wanted to, but also wanted Peter to look at her like he looked at Gertrude, wanted to be able to move her hips like that, and hold her cup and laugh in more than her usual choppy giggle.

"Alex?" He startled her. She hadn't heard him coming. His nightshirt hung just below his knees, and he'd pulled his socks high over his boots. She noticed a sliver of dark hair feathering his lip. "You look . . ." His eyebrows were sideways question marks. He wiped away a string of shiny snot.

"Yes?" she said, moving closer, sashaying her hips right, then left, as Gertrude had done.

"You look silly."

He was taller than Alex now, but skinny. His arms were ropes attached to knotted joints, and when she rammed him, shoulder to chest, he fell back upon the ground, pulling her with him. She could feel the dress tear on the edge of the hutch, could see mud branding the train. But his lips were touching hers now, his hands exploring the many layers of that dress. She kissed him back. She helped his hands by casting aside the veil still clinging to her skull, and she shed the petticoats from the inside out, no longer cold. Later, she hung the dress back inside its protective covering, the rips in the fabric like cuts, the mud stains like bleeding wounds on her mother's body.

She was careful not to sashay after that night. To Gran's dismay, she was even more unmannered, more defiantly disheveled, and now enjoyed Peter's eyes in the crowded room, his touch behind the rabbit hutch. In bed at night, she'd touch where he touched, but softer, and the next day showed him how. Until that day she bled and bled, this was just another kind of play; to Gran, just another torn petticoat; to Peter . . . ? She still doesn't know.

Her insides pinch and curl around themselves. A man's breath, bourbon. A man's weight. The Golden Boy, Alex. I remember nothing. I feel nothing. She thinks of David, how his eyes, too, seem to find her in the saloon.

No. His eyes find Alex. The Golden Boy, Alex. I feel nothing. She stares past the girl into the fading light.

"*You're* not coarse, are you, Alex?" says the girl. "You're not a sinner." The last word slides off her tongue.

Alex shifts on her log and the girl speaks faster.

"It's because you're quiet, is all. Boys aren't supposed to be quiet, like you, and I talk entirely too much for a girl. Everyone says so. 'Lou Anne,' Pa says, 'if you were a boy, you would have made a cracking lawyer.' I don't want to go back East with them, when they go. I'm not going. I'm gonna stay here in California, marry a miner and go to saloons and never wear a corset. She doesn't, does she? Mrs. Erkstine says there's not one that could contain her."

The girl takes a breath and Alex leans back against the wall. She is standing too close.

"Do you like my dress?" Lou Anne asks, swaying so the fabric brushes Alex's legs.

Alex stares down at the hem under which peeks an ankle. The material is a peach-colored cotton with silk embroidered flowers, no less than six starched petticoats. The girl edges closer. Her breath is warm on Alex's neck, her hand trembles on Alex's shoulder. Too close.

"Lou Anne?" A woman's voice from around one side of the inn, a chipper whistling comes from the other. Jed appears with a bucket of chicken slop.

"Kiss me," the girl commands, mere inches away. Jed stops whistling.

"Miss Lou Anne Dourity!"

Alex turns toward the voice and the girl leans down and plants a kiss on her lips. Alex's eyes go wide. Mrs. Dourity's long face contorts like one stung by a bee. Alex shoves the girl away, springs from her log, runs past Jed, heading back toward the creek.

# 10

"Good Lord! I'm fit to burst!" Limpy roars.

His great shoulders spasm with an infectious laughter that spreads through the saloon and tickles Emaline's backbone. She loves a full house, new faces and old, a collection of teeth shining like coffee-stained stars. Alex sits before her at the bar, red faced, hunched over a glass of whiskey. He's taking it well, Emaline thinks, a bit surprised by the pride that accompanies this thought.

"Micah, feet," she says.

"Ah, Emaline. Charge me an ounce of gold per meal *and* you gonna tell me what to do with my feet? Bother me when the ritzy chairs come."

"Break the habit now, no need to break it later. And you can feed yourself, you want."

". . . Nearly begged him," Jed manages, gasping for breath, for once the center of attention, obviously enjoying it. She loves his smile; it fills his whole face but is usually reserved for her alone. *"Kiss me, kiss me, Alex!"* Around the room a chorus of falsetto voices joins the chant. Alex grins into his cup.

"And the look on her mamma's face! Could have skinned a grizzly." Jed mimics the face, opening his eyes wide so his pupils are dots in the whites. Emaline wishes he would sit down, or meld as usual into the background of the bar, unremarkable, unmemorable.

"Lucky her daddy didn't catch you!" yells Fred from across the room. "Might be in some Grass Valley jailhouse right about now."

"Or rip you a new asshole," comes a voice from the corner.

"Limpy, feet off my furniture," says Emaline, and Limpy's feet thump to the floor.

She hasn't seen David yet tonight, not since dinner, and he was sulking then, or at least thinking. She worries about him. He works too hard. The lines beneath his eyes tell her he's not sleeping and he won't let her help. She wipes the bar, fills a man's glass, drapes the towel over her shoulder. She almost feels like drinking herself.

"Dourity? Hell no! Why do you think the poor bastard left Grass Valley?" Harry sneers at Fred, his voice that of a man half drunk or half sober – a dangerous state for Harry. "That man changes political parties more often than a woman changes clothes – a Whig, a No-Nothing, now a Republican? Kisses the ass of any docket that will nominate. The fact is he's a piss-poor lawyer. Don't hush me, Fred. He couldn't win a case if the judge was there to witness the crime and take names. Wants to be a politician? Congress? Shit! The man's got the personality of a tree frog. Looks like one too. What's that, Fred? I heard that, Fred. What'd you say to me?"

"Easy, Harry," says Emaline, as she pours another drink. Never seen two men argue so. She ducks behind the bar for another bottle of whiskey.

"I said," says Fred, "got himself elected county counsel, didn't he?"

Nothing like politics to sour a night. Emaline puts a whiskey beneath Harry's nose, but already feels the energy in the room changing with Harry's face. Especially personal politics, she thinks, and sets the whiskey down with a thump. Around here, it's always personal.

"Just goes to show you, doesn't it?" Fred continues, addressing the whole room but looking at Harry. "Don't go kissing the judge's wife." Then, turning to Alex: "Or a lawyer's daughter."

"I didn't . . ." Alex begins.

"Sure you did, boy," Limpy chimes, and Emaline is grateful. Limpy has that ability to diffuse conflict – even when he's the cause. "Don't have to want the attention, or even deserve it. Some men have that irresistible flair. Women flock." He puffs his chest, licks his hand, and slicks back his hair, preening like that new rooster in the coop. Still the scowl on Harry's face lingers. Emaline knows a few secrets he hasn't told her, but they have nothing to do with another man's wife.

"She a good kisser, Alex?" Micah asks.

"I don't –"

"Long and wet, or a bit of a peck, lip smack?" asks Limpy.

"She laid it on him, all right," says Jed. "Thought her mamma'd have to pull 'er off."

"Nothing to be ashamed of, boy. Get Emaline to educate you. My treat," says Micah, winking his one eye at Emaline. The thought strikes Emaline strange, almost incestuous, but the impression has no time to linger as Harry is standing now, jabbing his pointer finger into Fred's skinny chest.

"You know full well that I didn't kiss Judge Debb's wife."

"Hell, why not?" comes a voice from across the room. "I know four others who did."

"All right, all right." Emaline steps round the bar. "Less jawing, more drinking."

"You never kissed ol' Debb's wife?" says Fred.

"No, I did not."

"That so? W'hell, why don't you tell . . ." Fred pauses and

looks about. A ratty smile cuts a line across his sallow face. "Why don't you tell us all what did happen? Who *did* you kiss, Harry?"

"His son?" roars Limpy, pounding the bar for emphasis. But the round of hoots and hollers that follows ends in an abrupt and expectant silence.

From outside, the cry of a screech owl as David comes through the door. He stomps his feet and looks about, sensing something amiss.

Fights are so much easier to predict than the weather, Emaline thinks. She should break in now, offer a round on the house, or call for a song, but she doesn't. She watches with the rest of them as Harry wipes his mouth with an exaggerated gesture. He turns to Alex, but his eyes remain on Fred.

"Want to know how to kiss a woman, boy?" The boy's eyes open wide, but he doesn't say no and a smile sweeps Harry's brow upward. His eyes track sideways to David on his right, who takes his hat in hand and prepares to sit.

Harry moves quickly, engulfs David in a sweeping embrace, and kisses him full on the lips.

David's arms dangle behind him in shocked helplessness. His back is rigid. Then his arms find motion and he flails. Harry lets go and David falls gracelessly to the floor, holding his mouth as though stopping blood. Harry stands above him, arms held high in victory, with a sneering grin directed at Fred.

"You son of a bitch," says Fred, his red face revealing, Emaline thinks, something more than surprise. "You're a son of a bitch."

His cheekbones seem to grow more prominent on his gaunt face. His eyes glaze with moisture as he rushes out the door, knocking the portrait of Queen Victoria to the floor with the slam. But Harry holds his pose a moment, soaking in the silence as if it were applause, then sweeps into a bow, lingering at the bottom until the first hoots begin. The miners roar, pound him on the back, offer him drinks in payment for his comic bravery. No sense making more of it than it is, right? A well-executed practical joke. Emaline allows a puzzled smile to twitch her lips, but her eyes are on David, and David is not smiling.

He sits stiff on the floor, the vein on his temple pulsing. She can almost hear his breath over the hilarity, can see the subtle coil of his body, can only watch from across the room as he springs from the ground, knocking Harry flat on his back, heaving him up again by his waistcoat, slamming him down again before Limpy can pull him off.

The new faces in the room, a red-headed Virginia boy, not much older than Alex, a saucer-faced Frenchman with a bent back, and nearly a dozen others, are caught between adulation and shock. Emaline can almost hear their thoughts. All in good fun. Fellow can't take a joke. As soon pound you as laugh with you. While others, the dark-headed Georgian, perhaps, and the thick-lipped Maryland man, would have liked to see Harry beaten bloody. You can joke about most everything, says the arch of Maryland's eyebrow, but a man's dignity. And she knows this is true. Out here, where a name means nothing and no one cares who your daddy is, dignity is the one thing that separates men. That and gold.

She moves through the crowd, parting men like water, barely conscious of Alex following in her wake. All David needs to do is smile, she thinks. Call Harry a son of a bitch and help him up. Tell him he kisses like an old woman, make a joke about his mother . . .

But David struggles mightily, a man possessed, and to step before him would not be the smartest thing to do. She's not in the mood for a black eye, and Harry might just benefit from one. Both of them take themselves too damn serious. It's not healthy. And as she thinks this, Alex

133

slips around her, placing his body between David and Harry.

"David, don't," Alex says, barely a whisper.

Emaline only watches; seeing, but not sure she's seeing everything.

"Out of the way," David breathes, but the will has gone out of him and Alex seems to grow larger, more solid.

"No," says Alex. "I'm not moving."

Emaline looks, and looks again, squinting her eyes to see better. David drops his fists and stomps out, leaving the door gaping behind him.

The chapel tonight has a witch's profile, the crooked steeple silhouetted like a bent black hat against the full moon, the unfinished front stoop edging outward like a broken nose. The door swings open quietly on new metal hinges and David closes it softly behind him, keeping the silence undisturbed. He takes a seat in the very back, as far from the crucifix as possible, and lets his head fall into his hands. Rough calluses scrape across his skin. A pounding ache rises just below his temple. He lifts his head to a room lit with moonlight.

Dear Father, he thinks, hoping other words will volunteer themselves and purge him. "Dear God," he says aloud. When he was a child, those two words, Dear God, brought warmth to his entire body. He had a connection that was immediate and unconditional, and he cannot remember when or how that connection left him. Tonight the words slap benignly off the walls and land on the floor, as useless as river sludge.

He'd just turned fourteen when he first went down into the mines at St. Just, tallow candles slung round his neck and the hard felt hat slumping a size too large over his ears. He had been so proud as he climbed, hand over hand, down into the mine, expecting to emerge at the end of the day a man and a miner. But over the pounding of picks upon rock, the metal upon metal of the hand-held drills, and the hissing blast of steam engines, David heard his father's labored breathing and the consumptive hacks of other miners echoing through the damp, narrow tunnels. They were dying down there in the humid heat of the mines, choking on dust and asbestos, the walls ever poised to cave in and end their labored chorus. He felt death reach softly around him, inviting him to stay as he dug deeper and deeper into the furnace of that pit. And the hole he dug, like the pick he swung, was not his, would never be his. Even in death, his bones would belong to the pit boss. In the glow of his tallow candle, his father's unquestioned authority cracked. David knew he could not spend his life as his father had, singing about heaven every Sunday, just to climb into hell every Monday. He did not reject his father. He did not reject God. Each still maintained the power of condemnation, but now they were useless to comfort, useless to forgive his irrational ambitions. His unnatural desires.

Is desire the word?

He wipes his mouth with the back of his hand. The tips of his fingers are warm. He sees Alex before him, head down, shoulders slumped, black hair flecked with mine dust. David feels his cheeks flush, his ears pulse. He shifts in his seat. I might have killed Harry – would have killed him, he thinks. He needs to strike something, to exert his own will, his own force.

He slaps his face, softly at first, then harder, until both cheeks sting. His hands form fists and he pummels his thighs, then his chin, his forehead, the thin membrane of his upper ear. His temple throbs. His knuckles ache. Tears ooze from his eyes.

"David?"

Emaline's voice behind him. He wipes tears from his face. "Go away," he says.

Her squinting eyes pierce the back of his head.

"Go away!" He slams his fist against the pew before him. His knuckles bleed. The door closes, and he's left with moonlight.

He leaves the chapel and crunches through the brittle, thirsty thicket, up into the ravine. Brambles and bushes grab like thousands of pinching fingers. The sound of crickets is everywhere and nowhere. A screech owl flutters from a tree branch. He climbs faster until his legs ache.

He nears the top of the ravine and sits exhausted on a jutting granite boulder overlooking the valley. The wind whistles softly through the cedars above him and the moon casts shapeless milky shadows. The remaining canvas roofs in the town glow like paper lanterns. Gone is the noise of the saloon. The wail of the accordion is replaced by the high-pitched whine of crickets. Sweat dries cold on his brow and his breath slowly evens.

He will leave. He will take his share of the gold, go back to Cornwall and marry a nice Methodist girl. He has more than enough money now for the passage and would return, in all eyes but his own, a success. He will buy his mother a milk cow, a small plot of land to grow potatoes and corn, inland where the soil is less salty, less congested with granite. Limpy will be fine without him. And Alex? To hell with Alex. If the boy were a woman . . . if the boy were a woman, David would suspect sorcery, like the witches of St. Buryan, condemning men to hell with strange enchantments, evoking sinful waking dreams and ungodly urges. David will return to Cornwall, join his brothers below ground, where at least his soul will be safe. He'll leave his unholy desires to scorch in the California sun.

David takes a deep breath, eager for the anxiety to dissipate. He slaps at an insect scaling his forearm and watches the lights go out one by one in the town below. Perhaps peace will come with morning.

\*　　　\*　　　\*

Mrs. Dourity believed in God and her husband, though both, at certain times of her life, had proved equally ineffectual. Neither, for instance, had seen fit to give her another son. Not that she would ever presume to replace Marcus, whose fever never left him even after they had cleared the humid climbs of Panama. As the steamship chug–chugged up the coast of North America, her baby son's heart slowed with each breath, then stopped, and she thought grief would take her too. It was her daughter, Lou Anne, who gave her reason to live, and it was the society ladies of San Francisco who lent her purpose.

"Mrs. Dourity," said Mrs. Fareweather one day at tea. The women had never stooped to the vulgarity of addressing one another by their first names. "Our upbringing offers us a singular opportunity." Mrs. Fareweather's head looked puny without her broad hat. Her hair was dull brown and her eyes lacked the luster of her voice. When Mrs. Dourity closed her eyes, she always imagined a much grander face. "There are boys and girls here – your girl, Lou Anne," she added pointedly, "who are without the benefit of a Christian education." Together they joined the local Ladies Temperance League, raised funds for an orphanage, and worked to establish an academy for young ladies, which, for most of its six-month existence, boasted only two students: Lou Anne and a flatulent young girl whose face was ever contorted in an effort to contain unladylike essences.

Mason was tolerant of his wife's charitable activities, even after she suggested he take lawful action against houses of ill repute, especially those established next to the finer hotels and galleries in town. But he wasn't entirely comfortable with his young wife's constant activity.

"Next," her husband teased, slipping into bed one night, "you'll want to take to the polls yourself." She slapped him for his silliness, then pushed him away. The noises from the couple one door down slipped embarrassingly through the thin walls and she would not return the indignity. "I have no interest," she said, "in the public sphere of men."

Mrs. Dourity was thankful Mason never suggested that her constant involvement might have something to do with their son's death. If he had, she might have given in to the pessimism she tried to keep from sullying the tone of her correspondence home.

Her mother had not been happy when her son-in-law stole her daughter a whole world away from her, and so Mrs. Dourity made an effort to focus on the positive aspects of her adventure. "Really, Mother," she wrote, "the variety overwhelms the senses. In the dead of winter I eat apples and squash, tomatoes fresh from the vine, all floating up from Chile and the Hawaiian islands. Lou Anne is growing into, shall I say, a wild flower. I fear the effect of this country on an unshaped constitution. But the civilized among us here have, under the wisdom of God, banded together against a plethora of vice, and I have no doubt that she will emerge of stronger moral character than a sheltered and untested Eastern schoolgirl.

"Still, I wonder if you might inquire at the seminary about boarding situations. Your loving daughter, A.D."

She'd meant these last lines to convey a more confident tone, but her mother knew her better than that. When Mason informed her that they would be moving to the gold fields, her optimism had faded further.

From Nevada City to Sacramento. From Sacramento back to Nevada City. From Nevada City to Motherlode. Motherlode – she doesn't know why the name bothers her so. She does not fully understand her husband's business here. His law practice had failed in Nevada City. Surely, this town is not the place to further a political career?

She sits up in bed, chilled from the loss of Mason's heat. His snoring is muted tonight, and she knows from the smoky smell of him that he's been in that woman's place. She wishes the morning would bring a bracing fog, that the bay would open up before her eyes and Mrs. Fareweather would be waiting at four for tea. The women here are well intentioned, but Mrs. Erkstine speaks loudly on all manner of subjects she does not understand, while Mrs. Waller and her sister are intolerably reticent – Rose to the point of impudence. Still, she finds hope in the very presence of these women, hope that had nearly been dashed upon finding her daughter in the clutches of that boy.

How could you? she'd asked her daughter. How could you let that boy kiss you? "I didn't *let* him," Lou Anne replied. And yet Mrs. Dourity had seen it with her own eyes.

Rats scuttling through the walls send pinpricks down her spine. An owl's call strikes the exact tone of her melancholy. Lou Anne traipses about any new place, flush faced, pulling her skirts up to run. She talks as fast as words come to her, exhibits none of the restraint Mrs. Dourity has tried so desperately to instill. Perhaps she has been a fool to think this restraint would come with womanhood, like a mantle or a crown. She is no longer sure what to think. Lou Anne's sudden admiration for *that woman* frightens her nearly as much as catching her daughter kissing – catching *that boy* kissing her daughter.

Mason snuffs, rolls over. He raises his head. "Up again?" he asks, but is soon back to sleep. She watches the small of his back rise with his breath. His scalp shows bright through his thinning hair. She wonders if love is a duty for everyone.

Too many nights she has lain awake. Too many nights of prayers. Dear God for guidance, perseverance, deliverance for every soul spare one, she prays. She will not share heaven with a woman who sells the very gift God gave her. Corruption – this, too, was woman's power, if she used it such.

She cannot shake the image of her daughter, bent over that boy. That boy? Her breath catches and she holds it.

She eases herself from the bed, steps over her snoring daughter to stare out into the night.

In the morning, she informs her husband of her plan for Alex Ford.

# 11

Even after a sleepless night, Alex prefers mornings. It is one of the few solitary times in her day and lends itself to a strange beauty that dissipates with the heat. The scrub oaks manage to look sleek in the morning, the flaking bark a shade darker, nearly black beneath the vivid green of their spring leaves. The mineshafts gaping from the side of the mountain, and the slag heaps piling up like giant gopher mounds, seem almost natural before the miners arrive in force to grunt and swear the illusion away.

But this morning she feels as if she's being watched.

Her trousers make a swishing sound as she picks her way upstream. She stops to listen.

She'd lain awake last night rehearsing an apology she's not sure is warranted. She did nothing but stand in his way. She should be apologizing to herself. Dear Alex, sorry for putting you in front of a man angry enough to relieve you of your life. But even as she thinks this, she knows David would not touch her. She flinched out of reflex alone.

For all his ready criticism, David seems intent on never touching Alex. Limpy will lay his hand on her shoulder, nudge her with his elbow, slap her on the back, but David maintains a distance, avoiding contact. If Alex is working to

Limpy's right, David will work to Limpy's left. When Alex sits down at the dinner table, David sits down two chairs over where she can't even see him. If she didn't sense that his avoidance was intentional, it might not bother her so much. She's not sure why it bothers her at all.

She continues, slower now, making an effort to look at ease – which is difficult in the India rubber boots she'd bought the day before from Heinrich's store. "A pinch more," Heinrich demanded, which meant he wanted another dollar of gold for the boots. He was a Prussian man with a short, stubby mustache and long, flat fingernails that were sure to gather more than a dollar of gold from her pouch in one pinch. He grumbled only a little when she demanded he weigh the pinch with the dust already resting on the scale, which likely meant he'd doctored his scale as well. She should have gone to Micah's store. He grew his nails long like the rest of them, but at least he didn't lie about cheating you. She feels disloyal for having gone across the street in the first place, drawn by the smell of the leather, the variety.

She runs her fingers over a tough, heart-shaped manzanita leaf, considers humming, but doesn't. The few miners already at work pay no attention to her, and she tells herself that it's her imagination making her skittish. Even so, she's relieved to hear Limpy's tuneless whistle growing louder behind her. She stops to wait, nods good morning. David is not with him.

Harry and Fred are already hard at work, showing no sign of continuing last night's argument. Harry is smiling even, and Fred hums his own nasal rendition of "Amazing Grace." Harry raises his hand in welcome as Fred sets off the first charge of the day, sending a red-brown cloud of dust into the air. On the ravine above Alex's claim, two small rocks dislodge and tumble harmlessly to the ground near the sluice. Alex picks them up, hoping for hints of gold. Nothing. She flings the pieces one at a time into the creek where Limpy splashes icy water on his face and neck. There is still no sign of David.

"I tell you," Limpy says, unbuttoning his trousers. Alex studies his shadow until he hikes them back up again. "Ain't nothing in the world like springtime in California. We had our seasons in New York, you know – couldn't beat the fall for color, but spring? Hell. Sun's warm enough to heat yah, but not so hot as to burn yah. Ground is still nice and soft, and the air, can almost taste it." He spits, rubs his toe in it. "Where the hell is David?"

Alex is wondering the same thing. She shouldn't have confronted him. She wasn't drunk or even close, but there she was doing a foolish thing she didn't understand.

"Didn't come home last night," Limpy says. "Does that once in a while. Not your fault. Moody son-of-a-bitch, I tell you. Always was."

She dips her hands into the creek, splashes her face. She should have let well enough alone. She's done nothing but draw the wrong kind of attention to herself. She remembers Emaline squinting down at her, the crooked angle of her mouth.

"The water is going through here too fast, isn't it, washing some of the gold out?" she says for something to say.

"Bound to lose some to the creek. We move enough ore, won't have to worry," says Limpy. He's a believer in quantity over quality. If David were here, Alex would bet he'd agree with her assessment, even if he wouldn't acknowledge it at first.

The flume was David's idea. They'd spent two days away from the mineshaft, digging this artificial watercourse, diverting some of the creek into a narrow trough that runs right past the mine. They no longer needed to lug buckets of ore down to the creek to wash.

Limpy and Alex both glance down the path, stalling. It doesn't seem right to start without him. Alex hears the open-mouthed cry of baby starlings and in the forked pine on the ridge a woodpecker knocks. She shades her eyes and looks up but sees only the glare of the sun shunting around the branches.

"Well," says Limpy, slapping dust off his legs.

Alex grabs her pick and pulls her hat tight on her head. Another explosion shakes the ground. Limpy bends and walks into the mine.

Fifteen feet deep and already Alex can smell the change in the earth, from fermenting vegetation to a metallic odor, like axle grease and rust. The air, too, is dense, tasting of mud and mold. The walls are slick and black. They work in silence, picking away at the soft red clay and chipping at the larger pieces of granite embedded within. The wooden supports above them stand at attention like soldiers at the mouth of a mausoleum. They have yet to hit solid granite and, until they do, the black powder David bought from Micah sits unused on the floor of his cabin. An hour passes and Alex's arms cramp, her back strains. She glances sideways at Limpy, still uncharacteristically quiet, his face streaked with red clay and the black carbon of fermented root stems.

"I'm going to load the sluice," Alex says.

Limpy sets his pick on the ground, squats on his haunches, the ceiling too low for him to stand upright. "Not like him," he says, and the concern in his voice unsettles Alex. "Ten minutes, I'm going to town. Emaline will know, if anyone will."

It never occurred to her to be worried about David. Annoyed, yes, for it's David who is constantly preaching a full day's work, the more ore to grass, the more gold in their pockets. It's as if he's two different men: one who works the mine, rubbing ore between his fingers, tasting for richness, so confident of his movements as to be connected to the soil itself; and the other, the brooding, nervous man in the saloon, flashing irritated glances. She prefers the man at the mine, driven by the habit of hard work, and by hope. Alex needs that hope, feeds upon it. And there were times when David's silence proved a hundredfold more comfortable than Limpy's chatter.

Alex steps outside with a bucket of ore in each hand. The sun is at eleven o'clock and the moisture in the air has all but evaporated. Alex squints in the brightness, staring off across the creek. The grass of the valley leans away from an imperceptible breeze. She pours the first load of ore into the sluice. Downstream, Harry is waving and mouthing something Alex can't hear. Alex waves back, used to responding without comprehension, but the hairs on her neck rise. Someone is behind her. She turns to find David staring toward the mine.

"David?" says Alex.

"Is Limpy in the shaft?"

Alex looks toward the mine and David grabs her shoulders, then yanks his hands away again, fixing Alex's attention on the stubble beneath his mustache and the bitter stench of his breath.

"The mine – is Limpy inside?"

An explosion shakes the ground. Alex and David turn as one to see a cloud of red earth billow from the tunnel entrance. For a moment, neither moves, their eyes fixed upon the spitting dragonhead of the mine. Then David is sprinting to the shaft, shouting Limpy's name. Alex follows. No sound from the tunnel. No movement beyond the swirling suspension of dust in the air. The entrance is blocked with a wall of earth. Together, they claw at the dirt, afraid to swing a pick.

"Limpy!" David screams, his voice filling Alex's head. Alex digs faster, scraping at the earth with numb intensity, the tips of her fingers bleeding, her fingernails clogged with mud. Her pulse slows and every heartbeat feels like a fist to her chest. A figure, dark against the rust-red background, stands above her. Its arms reach out and with them comes the thick warm smell of bourbon. She flails, striking, clawing, stabbing the figure with her empty fists until blood warms her hands and moistens her upper arms. She gasps like one who's been trapped underwater. And then the figure is gone. The only moisture on Alex's hands is sweat. Her heartbeat quickens and her ears perk to a frantic intonation.

"Help me!" David yells. "Alex!" An arm is exposed like a tree root. Alex digs, flinging dirt behind her. Another arm. A head, pale and alien next to chunks of red rock.

"Pull!" David screams, pushing with his legs against the wall of fallen earth for leverage.

Alex pulls. A torso is revealed, then legs, and Limpy squirts from the cave, red clay enveloping his body like a birth sac. They drag him to the grass just as Harry and Fred come sprinting up. They lean over the body.

"Limpy!" says David, slapping at Limpy's face, harder and harder until the pale skin reddens to match the clay.

"Stop," Harry says, grabbing David's hand. "David stop, he's breathing. Look. He's breathing. Stop."

Between them they are able to pick Limpy up. David and Harry heft his shoulders, Alex and Fred each take a leg, and they struggle down the trail to Motherlode.

"Ladies," Emaline says curtly. She passes Mrs. Dourity, Mrs. Waller and her sister Rose, with long purposeful strides. Their skirts billow around them like protective cocoons that will never hatch to butterflies. If they, too, were heading to Micah's store, they decide against it now, stopping in the middle of the road, putting their heads together and chattering like squirrels. Only Rose is silent, her expressionless eyes making contact with Emaline's, betraying little in the way of emotion or opinion. Her hair is pulled back into a bun so severe that it seems to reflect the light. Her small mouth looks inadequate for anything other than taking dainty bites of food. She seems a creature devoid of passions, perfectly suited to be her sister's lapdog. A pitiful waste of a woman, thinks Emaline. She climbs the steps of the store and tugs the door. It swings halfway open, catches, and springs back, nearly slamming Emaline in the face. She steps back, startled.

"Micah, what the hell?"

"Hold on, sorry, hold on," says Micah from inside. "Just let me get this out of . . ." His grunts are accompanied by the sound of wood against wood. "There," he says breathlessly. "Come in."

Emaline steps through the door but can go no further. The floor is a shambles of boxes, barrels, and sacks, in no recognizable order. Cider, dry goods, tobacco, potatoes, molasses, pork beans, hatchets, a stack of ten or so axes . . . The shelves are cluttered with bottles, copper doorhandles, layer upon layer of starched trousers and flannel shirts, earthen bowls, tin pans, two giant porcelain wash bowls. Emaline's eyes sweep over the bountiful disarray, and come to rest on the skeins of calico, cotton and muslin cloth leaning like robed royalty against the wall.

"I ordered it, just like you said," says Micah, following her gaze. "Even wrote it down. Look here –" He retreats to the counter, rummages through a scattering of loose papers. "Iron lanterns, quicksilver, window glass, wool ticking, ah, wall velvet – tapestries, if you like. Red with green foliage and yellow chrysanthemums. Right here, see? Ordered it three weeks ago. Bound to be on the next wagon. I ordered it three weeks ago. Look."

He flashes the paper in front of her face, and she snatches it away, scowling and squinting at his illegible scrawl. She runs her fingers over a skein of calico, relishing the interwoven softness against her work-roughened hands. Micah fidgets. He steps behind the counter, putting a physical barrier between Emaline and himself. She hands the paper back.

"Micah, how on earth you afford all this stock? And don't tell me you're buying on credit."

"Now, Emaline, my word's as good as any man's, and I don't appreciate . . ."

"You selling on credit too, then? Are you?"

A squirrel scampers noisily across the roof and leaps into a nearby pine. Needles fall, tapping the ceiling like a shower of cut fingernails.

"I ain't one to scold, Micah," Emaline says, ignoring his *humph*, "but isn't this exactly how you got yourself thrown out of Grass Valley? Damn lucky they didn't jail your ass. Can't be buying on credit, and if you are buying on credit, sure as hell can't be selling on credit. Pay outright, or don't pay at all. And no sense ordering so goddamn much at one time, neither. Only a few claims producing like they should, and no telling how long it'll last."

"I know –"

"Gotta plan for the future. Not just tomorrow. Not just next year. Settle down and build little upon little, till you have something worth calling your own. No one finds their weight in gold in one go. Not any more. Maybe not ever."

"Emaline –"

"Lord, I tell you . . ." Emaline bites her lip. Her gaze falls on a stack of wishbone-shaped tree branches, their edges rounded and smoothed with a hasty lathe. She takes one in hand, glares skeptically at Micah.

"Divining rods. Only for gold," he says. He takes one in both hands and simulates the movement of the stem as it plunges down, pointing to gold. "Guaranteed to work nine times out of ten – providing the one doing the divining is sensitive to the movement. That's what the fellow said. Sensitive. Gonna sell like water to the thirsty, remember that."

"On credit?"

Micah reddens. "Now, Emaline, a man's gotta go with his gut instinct on these things. You just wouldn't understand."

Emaline's eyebrows raise. Micah blanches and changes the subject.

"The boys are wondering what you're gonna do about the Chinamen."

147

"What?"

"The Chinamen. Already started building downstream of us . . ." Micah pauses. "I don't know if you'd noticed."

"Of course I've noticed."

Hadn't she noticed? She throws the divining rod back on the stack like a stick of firewood. With the new furnishings coming and the saloon filling up every night, and the liquor to be stocked and the floors to be cleaned . . .

"Panning Mordicai's old diggings downstream. Making good returns. Patient as hell, they are."

She isn't one to be biased when it comes to color. No, sir. But Celestials can't be trusted; those strange clothes and long hair, and the slanted eyes God gave 'em to warn others of their dishonesty. A well-known fact. She's heard that the Chinese never smile. They are a small, hardy people, perfectly suited to a life of hard physical labor and are prone to murderous skirmishes between themselves. Just months before hundreds of Chinese had fought and killed each other over in Weaverville for no reason anyone could see. Not that most men need a reason, she thinks. But the Chinese bind and deform their women's feet, then sell them into slavery. And before long they'll open their opium dens, and she fears this more than the women they might bring. She's seen what that stuff does to a man. Makes him forget he's a man, dominates his mind *and* his body even more than a woman could, and holds on tighter. Drives a man insane with need, though it didn't seem to affect the Celestials. They pray to a round devil-god that makes them immune to the effects of their own drug. And they steal gold. And chickens.

Chickens. Emaline scratches the patch of fuzzy hair on her upper lip. Can't abide that, stealing chickens. No. Worked too hard setting up the Victoria to let a streak of good luck be ruined by a bunch of slope-eyed foreigners.

"You gotta sell to 'em, or someone else will," she says with a sigh. "We'll figure something out. They can't stay."

148

Micah hides a smile, but Emaline, still thinking, pays no attention. "John Thomas," she says under her breath. "John Thomas," she says again, this time addressing Micah. "Haven't seen him for a while now. You?"

Micah shrugs, shakes his head in ignorance. John Thomas always did have a way of disappearing and reappearing over the course of a year. You'd hardly know he was gone before he turned up again. Could use a man like him in getting rid of Chinamen.

"Might just need your help, then," she tells Micah.

"Emaline!" It's David's voice echoing off the walls of the ravine. Emaline jerks her head in the direction of the call. "Emaline!" yells David again, even more frantic than the first time and Emaline rushes out the door.

The men hover, breathing heavy and hot on Emaline's neck as she kneels by Limpy's side. His head lies flush against the wall, but his feet hang off the end of the bed, jutting into the air in the same pigeon-toed manner in which he stands. Since carrying him through the saloon, up the narrow staircase to Alex's bed, no one has spoken. Their worry closes in around Emaline like the walls of this boxy, windowless room, and the air is stagnant in her lungs. She wipes sweat from her forehead and tries to ignore the silent petition of the men behind her. Make it better, they beg her. Make it better, they demand, and her shoulders tense. She stares down at Limpy's face, places her hand on his forehead, looking for signs of color to fill his ash blue cheeks. His breath is regular but shallow, and she's afraid to take her eyes off of him. She knows how gently death can come, how quickly, even to big men like Limpy. She stands up, bumping against the man behind her.

"Move," she says, rolling up her sleeves. "Back, David," she commands again, taking her eyes only briefly from her patient. She does not want this responsibility, would rather confront almost anything than do battle with death, a battle she's already lost once on the trail to California. But this is no time to be thinking about the past, and that's what Harold is now, bless his soul: part of her past. She waits for the tightening of her throat that his name always brings. She hasn't thought of him in weeks, months even. She clears her throat, purses her lips, but she can feel only the stress of the six men behind her, all sweating, breathing hard, wiping their eyes as if it's sweat they're dabbing away.

She grabs the lantern, lights it with a match from her pocket and leans in for a closer look. A cut oozes a steady trickle of blood down Limpy's cheek and a fist-sized lump is forming at his temple. His fingers are cool to the touch, but twitch slightly when she blows on them. What else can she do? What do they expect her to do? Bring him back with a touch, with some magic words? She hates not knowing what to do. But she's not a doctor, and there's no one else. Four lawyers, four merchants, even a clockmaker, for heaven's sake, have clattered up Victor Lane in the last month and a half, but not a single goddamned doctor. She bites her lip, knowing that Preacher John won't return with one from Grass Valley before the morning. If Limpy makes it until morning, then she imagines he'll pull through with or without a doctor. He'll pull through with or without her.

"Is he . . . ?" David's question trails off and she suddenly needs them all out of the room. Fred and Harry stand to David's right, their contrasting features pinched in the same worried expression. Micah places a reassuring hand on Alex's shoulder as the boy edges ever closer to the bed, closer to David, who moved back all of an inch at Emaline's command. Jed stands as though holding up the doorframe, his arms outstretched, his features backlit and shadowed by the light from the hall.

Emaline's throat constricts. She doesn't like feeling helpless, likes it even less in public. Control is becoming as rare as gold once was, even within the walls of the Victoria, where she is accustomed to some measure of ascendancy.

"Out," she says, drawing the word into two syllables. But the men remain. She turns on them, rising to her full height, nearly hitting Alex in the head with her elbow. Her eyes narrow as she squints at his smooth, muddy face in the lamplight. "Out! Out!" She points to the door this time, her eyes still focused on Alex, and he steps quickly back, knocking Micah toward the door. "All of you, out."

They stumble backward over each other, out of the door. All but David, who lingers, his arms crossed in the hopeful, defiant manner of a small boy. His eyes meet hers briefly, then return to Limpy's prostrate figure.

"I told him yesterday. I told him it wouldn't hold," says David, and Emaline closes her eyes. She breathes in fresh air from the hall.

"David," she says, softly now, "I need water and a rag, and then I need you to leave."

He brings water, a rag, a stool for Emaline to sit on, and a cup of steaming coffee. Then he stands again by the bed, arms crossed, chin lowered resolutely to his chest. Emaline can almost feel the unfinished question digging holes through his lips.

"He'll be fine, David," says Emaline, hoping he doesn't hear the uncertainty in her voice. "Close the door behind you." She looks back at him again, forcing eye contact, and he finally leaves her to the lamplight.

Her shadow flickers and sways on the bare walls, the rough-cut pine dotted with so many knotty eyes, each staring out at her. She works her way down Limpy's buttons, peels the soiled shirt off his shoulders, revealing the red wiry hairs on his chest and belly. She runs her hands up his arms, beginning at the fingertips, feels each digit, each knobby joint for breaks, shudders at the clammy chill of his skin. She wipes the blood from his cheek, presses a soft cloth to the cut and holds it there with one hand while scrubbing off the layer of

151

dirt and mud with the other. The face that emerges is drawn and gray, but she can almost see the knot rising, a blue volcano of bruised flesh on his forehead, and this reassures her somehow – as if a dying man's body would not bother to bruise. She watches, hoping for a healthy pink to grace his cheeks. "Four bloody lawyers," she mumbles under her breath, as though afraid to wake him. And their wives, she thinks. She might prefer lawyers, who at least reserve their self-righteous bullshit for the political arena.

She pulls a blanket up around his shoulders. She waits. She watches his breath make bubbles of spittle around his lips, and drops the rag back into the basin of water. Blood and grime loosen and bloom outward until the water is covered in a thin red-brown film. Downstairs she can hear none of the usual noises. No accordion, no swearing, no boots stomping.

They expect so much. Bring her their problems, big and small when, sometimes, the best she can do is clean up. She brushes the hair from Limpy's forehead, picks a lump of dried mud from his crown. Clean him up and wait for him to die. Clean him up and wait for him to live. There is no one else. She waits. Her eyes grow heavy in spite of the coffee. Her arms cross over her bosom. Her head nods forward then jolts up. The fresh air is all but exhausted and the lamp flickers. She adjusts the wick. She wipes the spittle from Limpy's mouth with the corner of her apron. She eases her head down and rests her ear upon his chest, testing the cadence of his heart against her own, and falls asleep.

"Emaline?" A hand upon her shoulder and her head jerks up. A small pool of drool darkens Limpy's chest hair. The door is open, but the hallway is now pitch dark and the air carries a midnight chill. She bends down again. Limpy's heart is beating. His lips are pink with blood and oxygen. His cheeks are flushed and his breath comes deep and even. The raised bump on his forehead is a healthy purple-black.

152

"I'll watch for a while." Jed's voice is a whisper.

Emaline's eyes sting, but she does not cry. Her ears are filled with the silence of the room. She lets him ease her up by the shoulders and, as she stands, she regains herself, wipes her mouth with the back of her sleeve, breathes in the blast of fresh air from the hall.

"They're still down there – Alex and David. I told them was no use in staying, but they're still down there."

Emaline nods, looking down with a sad half smile at Limpy.

Alex wonders if it is a dream or memory that plays across David's face. His shoulders are straight as a scarecrow's. His foot taps out a quick, even rhythm as he runs his finger around the rim of his cup.

"Well," says Jed from the bar. His back and neck crack like knuckles as he straightens. "I'm off to bed, y'all. Sure you don't want something? A drink – David?"

But David is answering only to his coffee cup.

"No. Thank you, Jed," says Alex. She sips cold, stale coffee.

"Wouldn't hurt to sleep some. Limpy ain't going nowhere."

"Goodnight, Jed," says Alex.

Jed takes a lamp, leaving the other one on the bar and climbs the stairs, skipping the creaking third. Without two lamps to cancel the shadows, Alex and David's dark shapes overlap on the saloon wall. Outside a coyote howls. The chickens squawk nervously, then all is quiet and objects in the room blur. Alex's eyes close. She's standing on the edge of Bobcat Creek, shin-deep in icy water, the gold pan in her hand filled nearly to the brim with glittering gold dust the consistency of ash. She holds her breath, afraid to upset the dust, afraid it will catch in the breeze and be gone forever. And then it is gone, swirling about her in the air, and scattering to nothing. A voice penetrates the clear sky, replacing it with the Victoria's wooden ceiling.

"He's not my cousin."

Alex jerks awake. David is still looking in his coffee cup, his shoulders still rigid, and she wonders if he's really spoken. She stretches her back, rubs sleep from her eyes. David speaks again.

"I met him in Nevada City. Years ago – almost two years. He talked me out of a mess."

He runs his finger along the rim of his cup.

"We came to Motherlode for the gold. Always knew it was here. I could feel it. I still do."

"And now?" Alex says, and he looks her full in the face, his jaw clenched, his eyes hard. It's not so much his words but his tone and expression that feel like an accusation.

"Now? I'm staying. I'm staying for the gold, for Limpy, understand?"

Footsteps down the stairs. Emaline hovers on the fourth step, the upper half of her body still in shadows.

"Y'all may as well get some sleep." From Jed it was a suggestion, from Emaline an order. "Got Limpy in your bed, Alex. Go on home with David."

"No!" David blurts. He clears his throat, says softly. "Alex, you go. I'm staying."

"Be fine, bump on the head and some bruises, David," says Emaline. "There's no sense –"

"I'm staying here. Alex, go."

# 12

Gathered around Alex is David's square-patterned quilt. Its softness enfolds her in a warm and unconditional embrace, and she imagines David's mother in a rocking chair or porch swing piecing the fabric together, discovering new patterns in the colors of old cloth. She is portly with soft inviting arms, David's wide gray eyes and straight red-brown hair, and a voice as soothing as owl song. Or perhaps she is an aunt, rigid and tough, but only in love, with David's long nose, his sloping shoulders and awkward, silent manner. A sister, an older sister, teasing him about the mustache that struggles to emerge from his pallid mine-boy complexion. They'd kiss him goodnight, each in turn, these women of Alex's imagination, and hold his baby-boy self against their chests so he can hear the beat of their hearts. Alex sinks within the rhythm of their tenderness, tracing the trochee cadence out of her imagination and back into memory, until the rhythm weakens and slows. The arms that hold her shorten and dehydrate. She recognizes this solitary embrace. The smell so familiar: candle wax and dead skin, chrysanthemums. Alex knows this is a memory from childhood, a memory from before. "You're not to see that boy again."

She shakes free from Gran and Gran falls into a quilt on

155

the bed, leaving Alex shivering. She pulls her knees to her chest, wraps her arms round her shoulders, closes her mind to thought, her ears to the self-important calls of the rooster.

She slides off the bed and the floorboards send a chilled shock from her toes to her fingertips. Goosebumps erupt on her arms. She pulls on her boots, and David's buckskin jacket, which swings just above her knees and completely covers her fingertips. She stands a moment, imagining that the leather is a body, that the sleeves are arms. A portable hug, and it didn't matter who you were or what you had done when you were someone else. Perhaps as close as she'll ever get to unconditional love exists here in the limp arms of someone else's jacket, or someone else's quilt. She tucks that thought away behind her ear with her hair and looks about.

Across the room lies Limpy's bed, a gnarled mass of flannel atop a cloth mattress. A deck of playing cards sits on a planed log table, the jack of spades face up. Alex pours some water from the bucket by the stove into a coffee-stained tin cup and sits lightly on the stool. Is there anything more intriguing than someone else's home? Her eyes touch on the long-barreled rifle resting on rungs above the door and the tanned deer hide taking pride of place on one wall like a fine piece of art. Next to the stove, a iron pot rusts, and on a shelf above the stove a small set of scales is balanced by two stones. She picks up one of the stones, upsetting the equilibrium. One of the two round copper plates clatters to the floor, and whatever small animal was sleeping on the roof scurries off. She rushes to right the scale, thankful nothing is bent or broken, but lingers with one stone in her hand.

It's like nothing she's ever seen. The same blue-green color of the seawater off the coast of Brazil, but spotted with black specks like the unsprouted eyes of a potato. She knows it to be David's from the careful way the two pieces were balanced

156

just so on the scales. She wants nothing more than to drop the stone next to the nugget in the pouch between her legs. The exaggerated shadow of a bird darkens the canvas roof and in the chill of that shadow she feels David's anger. Still she holds his stone, warming it in the palm of her hand, running her fingers and thumb over the rounded edges until it gives heat back to her. She replaces the stone and shoves her hands into the pockets of her trousers.

They should put on a new roof, or build a new place, behind the Victoria, on Providence Street. She nearly thought "we," we should replace the roof, but banishes the thought by easing out of David's jacket. She smiles, imagining Limpy with his high waders and muddy pant legs nodding good morning to sour-faced Mrs. Erkstine. Would probably invite himself over to Sunday lunch at the Douritys', talk too loud with his mouth open and eat all the meat from the stew. Someday. Someday, Alex thinks, I will build myself a great big house with a second-story balcony and carved lattice-work, and watch as Motherlode becomes a proper town. A town and then a city as famous as San Francisco, as rich as New York. I'll buy Emaline rows and rows of fancy chairs, and Limpy a top hat to make him even bigger, and David . . . ? I'll buy David a long golden chain big enough to hold one of those green stones around his neck. The Golden Boy will disappear within the sprawling activity, changing her name like her clothes in perfect anonymity. One day this, another day that.

Alex hangs David's jacket by the door, shaking the sleeve in introduction. "Hello," she says several times, trying out different tones of voice. "Hi. Hello. My name is Alex. Alexander. Alexandra. Rebecca. My name is Rebecca. David, Jamie, Sam, Henry. My name . . ." She catches her breath, surprised by a sudden wave of desolation. "My name is Alexandra," she whispers, and again, louder: "Alexandra."

*     *     *

The doctor has already come and gone by the time Alex steps through the door of her room. Apart from the purple knot on his temple, Limpy looks none the worse for wear. A smile lifts his face. His feet extend off the thin mattress of Alex's bed, and a straw-colored corn advertises his left big toe. David, however, with dark, half-moon circles beneath his eyes, his hair a matted tangle, his cleft chin invaded by two-day stubble, slumps upon the stool as if he lacks a backbone.

"Alex my boy, my hero!" Limpy booms. "Good thing Emaline been feeding you right. Might still be sucking soil."

"You all right?" Alex asks David.

"Shit, nice to see you too. Just trying to give my thanks, boy." Limpy sits up and the bedframe groans. His feet disappear beneath Alex's short blanket. "Takes more than a mountain to send Samson Limpkin to the great down under. I ever tell you about the time –"

"You feel good enough to be telling tales, you should be getting your own breakfast," Emaline says from the hall. "Morning, Alex. Trust you got more sleep than the rest of us." She hands David a cup of coffee and eggs to Limpy. "Damn, but it's dark in here." She looks across the room to where the window should be, adjusts the lamp and opens the door wide. The brighter light of the hallway squeezes around her wide body. Outside a wagon rumbles by, a horse shakes its halter and a man's voice yells a greeting. The rooster still has not tired of his own voice.

"Lost another two chickens last night," Emaline says. "Taking 'em off somewhere to kill 'em. No blood, few feathers."

"Raccoon?" suggests Limpy.

"Or human. That buncha Orientals in the clearing across the creek. I've seen them sorts eat chicken feet raw." She dismisses the worry with a wave of her hand. "You want breakfast, it's still hot," she says to Alex and disappears down the hall, leaving a column of light in her place.

158

David arches and yawns.

"Is he okay?" Alex asks Limpy this time.

"David and I were just discussing business. The future. Wondered what you thought."

The future. Motherlode the city. Streets and side streets radiating off Victor Lane. Refreshing thoughts. For months the present has been all her mind could handle. She wonders about this, listens to the empty ring of her own speculations, has trouble locating herself in this future place.

"What I'm, what we're thinking is, expand. Too much work for three people. With more help we could move more ore a day, wash more gold and be safer doing it. Keep it small, just Harry, Fred – maybe Jed, if he's interested. A regular core-pore-a-tion, what I'm thinking. Small, though, like David says. All equal shares but you, 'course, finding the vein, you keep the big chunks. Bound to be more of them the deeper we go."

David sits up in his chair, attentive for the first time. "You don't really believe that, Alex? Do you? That there's likely to be nuggets of that size just lying around, waiting for you to find them?" He looks at Limpy with a strange tired grin on his face. "He really believes that?"

She looks to Limpy for reassurance.

"Now, Dave," he says, but David leans back in his chair as if evading Limpy's words. He speaks up at the ceiling.

"This isn't acting like any lode I've ever seen. What gold we've found has been random. Scattered. I'm just not sure. No, no," he says, shaking his head. He sits upright. "No, it's not stable. We haven't even hit bedrock yet."

"Details, details, you understand." Limpy waves dismissively. "Was his idea in the first place, about the extra help. Just likes to be disagreeable. So, what you think, Alex? 'Cause you got the final word, being the finder. Wouldn't want to step on your toes none by telling you how foolish it'd be to continue as we were. Could use the extra muscle.

"Now, don't be all offended. No offense meant. You're young yet," Limpy says. "Who's to say there aren't a bushel of nuggets even bigger than the one you found, just a pick-swing away. Who's to say – well, he said himself, it wasn't acting like any lode he's seen. We just gotta use what we got. I'm thinking of you. Your best interest."

Alex wants to believe that it is possible for Limpy – or anybody, for that matter – to act in her best interest. But she knows Limpy well enough now to understand that he'll say whatever he has to say to get his way. Progress is only measured in profit. And David? He folds his arms before him, looks at the wall as if there were a window there. He hasn't actually discounted Limpy's plan. Last night he'd said there was gold in the mountain. Last night, in the glow of that lamp, there'd been no doubt in his voice.

"You don't think we should do it then, get help?" she asks, and his head jerks up as if surprised she's asked him. His hand tugs at the twin tails of his mustache.

"I didn't say that," he says after a time.

"What are you saying?" she asks. He sucks in his lower lip, spits it out again. "David?"

"I . . . we," he says, and looks away from her. "We can't go on as we were."

"HA! You stubborn son-of-a-bitch, couldn't just agree with me!" says Limpy, ignored by both Alex and David.

"Take us two weeks, by ourselves, just to dig back through the fall to where we were," says David. "And then we don't know if we'd find enough to make the labor worth it."

"And with more help?" she asks.

"Maybe."

"Maybe what?"

"Maybe we find a rich vein in the granite, maybe the gold is scattered throughout the topsoil, maybe we find nothing, maybe it caves in again . . ."

Maybe was better than quitting entirely, disbanding, moving on, the unsaid alternative dragging David's face to a frown. Beneath the growing pessimism of each of these statements, Alex is listening for and hears hope – the chance to continue the life that gold made possible, a life that depends upon the men in this little room, on Emaline, and the Victoria, on digging away in the gutted clearing. Cleaving any part would feel like an amputation. It had never been those nuggets Limpy promised that kept her digging in the first place.

"Maybe's good," she says. "Maybe is worth a try."

"Attaboy, Alex," says Limpy. "Spoken like a true Californian. New England Mine Corporation, we'll call her."

"No," says Alex, growing weary of Limpy's presumptions. David's eyebrows rise and Limpy gathers himself to speak.

"No," she says again, before he has the chance. "Victoria – I'll call it the Victoria Mine Corporation. Klein will make me a sign."

Alex finds Klein in the blacksmith shop with Mexican Jack. The door is open. Hot air billows through with every puff of the bellows and her eyes water in the dry heat.

"What she want now?" says Klein, his German accent relaxed and difficult to decipher.

Alex steps over the threshold into the room, shakes her head to show she hadn't heard. Frightening ornaments litter the walls: iron clasps and hay hooks, bridle bits, chain links, tools of various sizes. A wheel axle lies broken in three parts against the wall and the dirt floor is gouged in places where steel has fallen. Apart from the open door, the red glow of the forge offers the only light in the room.

"Want, want – what does she want?" Klein says, his hands making circular movements with his words. When she doesn't answer quickly enough, he resumes his conversation with Mexican Jack, who studies his coals as if he could tell temperature by color alone.

161

Jack's bare arms are already streaked black and sweat beads along his forehead and collarbone. She's never said his name aloud; his eyes, beneath those thick black brows, seem, if not threatening, then at least intimidating. She's heard that his real name is Antonio and that he's from Valparaiso, but no one calls him anything but Mexican Jack and when she sees him on the street, this is the name that comes to her. The two men speak in a garbled mix of English, German and Spanish. She can't follow, but Mexican Jack finds something funny, roars with easy laughter. Klein stares straight ahead at the flame.

"I want – I need a sign," says Alex, and Mexican Jack's laughter flutters.

"You want a sign, you ask your ancestors. Ask their bones, you want a sign," he says, crossing himself once, twice and winking at Klein.

Alex recoils at the presence of Gran in the hot breath of coals, pushes the sensation aside. "A wooden sign. I'll pay you now," she says, and this gains Klein's attention.

Mexican Jack's laughter follows her out the door with a blast of heat, and the pride she thought she'd feel in the trans-action is lost.

Shopkeepers are sweeping the wooden sidewalks free of dust. Some smile, most ignore her. Even though the sound of building overwhelms all others, in her head Mexican Jack's laughter continues, and David's words come back: *I'm staying for the gold, for Limpy, understand?* She understands this now, and has no trouble understanding his tone this morning. *You don't really believe that, Alex? That there's likely to be nuggets of that size just lying around, waiting for you to find them?* It was the way he said "Alex," the way he said "you," the obvious pleasure he took in her gullibility that clutters her thoughts with indignation. The Victoria Mine Co., she'd told Klein, spelling each word in careful block lettering so there would be no mistake. It is my claim, after all, David.

162

My name on some paper stating my rights. She walks past Sander's dry goods, and Heinrich's shoe store, past the musk of the cigar shop. It occurs to her that she's never actually seen any such paper. "Limpy took care of it for you," – that's what Micah had said. And it was Limpy who'd gone to file in Nevada City . . .

Mrs. Dourity emerges from her husband's office, before the last thought gains purchase.

Alex pulls up short, squeezes into the crack between two shops. It's possible she hasn't been seen.

Mrs. Dourity peeks around the corner. "There you are," she says. If her hat would fit into the space between the buildings, Alex is sure she'd have the Golden Boy by the scruff.

"Come on out here."

Alex shakes her head no.

"I just want to talk, to give you something for that woman."

Alex doesn't budge.

Mrs. Dourity shuffles her bundles, holds out a leaflet. "We have met, and we have decided that we would like to cordially invite that woman to refrain from the selling of liquor and other . . . well, other improprieties."

Alex grins at the suggestion. "We?" she says.

"The local Ladies Temperance League."

Alex accepts a flier, hand-copied in a looping formal script, as refined as the most artful stitch sampler. Four names grace the bottom border.

"It says –"

"I can read," says Alex.

"Well, good. Then you can read this to –"

"She can read too."

This information seems to take Mrs. Dourity by surprise. Her shoulders fall with her breath as if she's made a decision.

"There is something else." She stares down her nose at Alex. "You do know my daughter, Lou Anne?" Her tone is not at all ironic. "Well, you can understand why I worry. I simply couldn't approve of a . . . of a man whose morals were governed by little more than his basic . . . urges."

"Approve of a what?" Alex asks, intrigued now.

"Why, a suitor, of course."

Alex's disbelief chokes her to coughing but Mrs. Dourity continues.

"My daughter can be quite . . . forward. She is young and full of lively mischief, but she is nearing fourteen now, and I was married well before my sixteenth birthday."

"Mrs. Dourity –"

"And my husband, Mason, he agrees that a boy your age – an orphan? Bless. An orphan with enough gumption and good grace to make his way in a mining town is the kind of man who will one day lead. And – let me finish – we, my husband, I mean, is prepared to offer you a place, an apprenticeship, reading law. You can read – that will make it easier. Naturally, you will come and live with us when the house is done."

Alex is amazed by the ease with which the woman has constructed this future. There it is, laid out in words as if written on the flier in her hand.

"My husband will be a man of some importance."

Alex hears resolve in this statement, a resolve she hasn't observed in the person of Mason Dourity. The man seemed to wear his title before him like a shield to hide behind. Before dusting sawdust off the porch, before checking the reliability of the roof, or the constitution of his desk chair, he held his placard to the wall in various locations about his new office, admiring the importance the bronze lent his name and title. MASON DOURITY, ATTORNEY-AT-LAW. He placed it finally just outside the front door, so that people passing by on their way to the shoe shop, or from Sander's dry goods, could admire it as well. This was a running joke among the miners, who made a point of rubbing their grubby hands on the thing when they passed on their way home from the mines. But seeing her own name there in her imagination: Alex Ford,

Attorney-at-Law? No. Golden Boy, Alex. No. Alexandra. No. Not any more.

Mrs. Dourity's pensive face, the hope in her voice, gives Alex a chill.

"And you'll come to chapel with us tomorrow, the second service?"

"Good day, Mrs. Dourity," Alex says, tipping her hat as gentlemen do, and pushes past into the road.

"There is redemption, Alex, in the loving hands of God. You won't forget the flier, now?"

*First meeting of the Temperance League of Motherlode, California. Sunday, May 25th following the service of the 1st Congregational Church. Reverend Erkstine presiding.*

"That woman," says Emaline, "has some elevated opinion of herself."

She hands the flier back to Alex, and it's hard to say whether Emaline or the pot boiling on the stove is more agitated.

"Now, Emaline," says Jed, his hands palms down as if to placate.

"'Now, Emaline?'" she says. "That woman is after more than liquor, and you and me, and Alex. We all know it. Alex, what else did she say?"

Alex feels her cheeks flush. Alex Ford, she thinks, Attorney-at-Law.

"Emaline," says Jed, his brow furrowed, his tone meant to temper, "I just don't think this is something you should work yourself up over."

"Work myself up? As if I just like to get worked up when there's enough goddamn work to do without getting worked up!"

Jed holds his ground, crossing his arms before him, but Alex backs away. There is a frantic tone to Emaline's voice she's not used to.

165

"They take the word *sin*," says Emaline, "and they stamp it on anything they don't understand."

"'They,' Emaline?"

"They, Jed. Those women. They come here after we cut and carve a little place for ourselves and they want to call us barbaric just so they don't feel so bad about taking our place and making it their own. Taking, Jed."

"I hardly think they –"

"You know what they want to call my town? Hartford. Hartford! Just want to recreate what they left back East, so they don't have to change themselves. There's a reason I came West, Jed. There's a reason you ain't slaving back in Mississippi. You want to go back to that place? You want them to bring that place to you? Women can't own their own land, or the clothes on their backs, but they can make others feel bad about it. Try. At least I own what I sell. And to hell with voting. This isn't about voting, or being heard. This is about being allowed to live without a lace collar around your neck, or a chain."

Jed's jaw is clenched. He eases his shoulders down, takes a breath. "You make it sound like all women. You a woman, Emaline."

"Yeah," she nods. "But not the same one I was."

He lays a hand on her shoulder and her head turns to meet his fingers. Their breathing links in the same rhythm. Alex turns her back, not willing to see what she's seeing. She thumps the broom against the wall and hears Jed's boots scuff the floor. When she turns around, both Jed and Emaline are looking at her with something close to worry.

"I'll get the water then?" says Jed.

"Hold on. Alex?" Alex looks up then away. Emaline pauses, chews on her sentence, spits out another. "Did she say anything else?" asks Emaline.

"She wants me to go to church with them tomorrow, the second service."

"She does, does she? And what did you say?"

"I didn't say anything."

Emaline shakes her head, wipes flour on her apron. She returns to the wild mint on the table, chops viciously. Alex puts the broom aside, looks up when the blade stops thumping the tabletop. A smile stretches across Emaline's face and Alex mirrors Jed's worried frown. "You're going," says Emaline, pointing with the knife.

"I'm what?" says Alex.

"You're going." Emaline walks over, smiles up at Jed. "We're all going. I could use some extra preaching this Sunday."

The second service always begins a half hour after the first, giving the members of each congregation ample time to avoid each other. Alex waits in the shade of the leaning steeple. She makes no effort to reconstruct Preacher John's sermon into a defined message. She appreciates the random leaps his preaching takes, as if the Holy Spirit were bouncing freely off the walls of his mind. But her purpose now distracts her. She resents this feeling of vulnerability, this exposure, but you don't say no to Emaline.

Across the road the doors of the Victoria are closed and the mood about town is subdued, reverent, in a way Sundays never used to be in Motherlode. The second-service parishioners don't seem to notice this. They trickle up the road in their Sunday best. Mrs. Dourity, Mrs. Waller and her sister Rose wear dresses buttoned to the neck. Mrs. Erkstine has seen fit to add a lace collar, like the one worn by Lou Anne, who skips along ahead. Extra petticoats billow beneath her skirts even in this heat. She spots Alex, and rushes back to her father's side.

"Why, Alex," says Mrs. Dourity, smoothing an unruly strand escaping her daughter's braid. "I – we are delighted that you have chosen to join us." She looks delighted, flashing a self-satisfied glance at Mrs. Erkstine to her left, and Mrs. Waller to her right. Rose is nearly hidden behind her sister. Alex barely notices her. She feels full of secrets, one of which, acted out before her yesterday, like a play, is not her own. Emaline said nothing about what passed between herself and Jed. She didn't try and explain it away or demand Alex's silence. Jed's hand on Emaline's shoulder, that weighted look lingering in their eyes, seemed almost natural.

"Aren't we delighted, Mason?"

Mason Dourity peers out from behind a pair of round spectacles. He is a head taller than Alex, but most of that height comes from the trunk up. His wide forehead funnels to a retreating chin, poorly disguised under a patchy beard, and he sticks that chin out when he speaks.

"Alex," he says with a nod, and rests a possessive arm around his daughter's shoulders.

"Sir," Alex says. She glances toward the chapel door. When they enter, the warmth of Mrs. Dourity's goodwill turns frigid. A short gasp escapes from Mrs. Erkstine. Lou Anne's mouth falls open, then curves into a grin, and both of Mrs. Dourity's hands latch on to her daughter's shoulders.

Miners occupy every seat. No room for the second congregation squeezing itself in the back. For the first time, Alex can see clear as a line in the sand, the division that had been growing as fast and solid as the town. The miners sit tight on the hard oak pews, their bodies grizzled and dirty and worn, their hair as sun bleached as their frayed flannel collars, their fingernails impacted with mud and clay. They outnumber the black slacks, stiff collars, and crinoline skirts two to one.

"Hell," says Limpy, from the front row. The knot on his forehead has shrunk to a nugget, but the bruise has spread into a black-and-blue mask down the left side of his face. "Glad you could join us. The Lord's a calling sinners in today. Isn't that right, Emaline?"

Emaline sits next to Limpy facing the crucifix, her head bowed. She looks back, as if surprised by the company.

168

"Welcome, welcome. Come on in and make yourselves comfy."

She beckons Erkstine forward with a magnanimous gesture, and Mrs. Dourity bristles. "Come on up now, Preacher," Emaline says. John stands up. "No, no, the other one. John, you had your go this week." She beckons Erkstine again. "Don't be shy now, we're all here for the same reason."

The reverend clears his throat, and it's obvious he's not at all happy about being invited to his own church service. He straightens his tie. He runs his hand down his lapel. His wife's eyes go wide and worried, and Mrs. Waller and her sister Rose part to let him by. He steps high over booted feet resting in the aisle.

"Well, go on." Emaline waves him on. "Let's hear some preaching!"

Mrs. Dourity's breath is coming harder than it did a moment ago. Her lips pinch tight, but she doesn't turn to leave as Alex thought she might. Nobody leaves, and the chapels fills with the stench of boot leather and body odor. Singing voices compete to be heard, and never before has Alex sung the "Battle Hymn of the Republic" with such passionate fervor. It's a patriotic zeal she feels – pride of a place and a people. The thought is shocking. Her people. She peels herself from the side wall. She nudges Fred and Harry over in the closest pew and sits down.

Erkstine soldiers mightily through his sermon. Words boom from him as if ripped directly from a stone tablet. "John," he says, "Chapter 4: 'There came a woman of Samaria to draw water. Jesus said to her, "Give me a drink . . .""'"

A smirk on Mrs. Dourity's face. A glance passes from her to Mrs. Erkstine, but, even as the ire rises in Alex's gut, Emaline sits expressionless. Reverend Erkstine reads on, stops to pontificate about everlasting thirst and eternal life, and reads again. Alex's eyes become heavy. The people left

169

standing shift from one leg to the other, and the miners fidget and whisper back and forth.

"'. . . "Go, call your husband and come here." And the woman answered. She said, "I have no husband." "The fact is,"'" his voice rises almost imperceptibly, ""'you have had many husbands . . ."'"

Sweat shines on Emaline's temple, but her face is not nearly as red as the reverend's. It seems he's suffering the very penance he seeks to exact. Emaline bows her head for the prayers, and during hymns her warbling soprano is heard above all other voices. But she doesn't say a word until the last "Amen" has rippled through the overheated congregation.

"Amen!" she says and stands up, holding her belly as if she'd just eaten a large meal. "Thank you so much, Preacher – excuse me, Reverend Ely."

"Erkstine. Reverend Erkstine."

"Don't be silly, Ely," she says and winks at him.

"Reverend," says Mrs. Dourity, stepping forward from the crowd, "I have an announcement."

"Well now, *I* was just going to say . . ." says Emaline, stretching the word long enough to face Mrs. Dourity in the aisle. Mrs. Dourity does not step back, and Alex isn't so sure Emaline won't walk right through her to the door. The faces around the room, those sitting, those standing, gawk. Limpy grins; with the bruise darkening half his face, it looks malicious. Jed hunches two pews over from Alex. He bites his lip, folds his arms before him, as if trying to hold himself down on the pew. Lou Anne's mouth is hanging open and she gazes upon her mother as if she were a brave and worthy stranger. But even Mrs. Dourity is caught like a fish on Emaline's last word.

"I was just going to say that I'm just about as thirsty as Jesus at that well. Anybody wanting a drink is welcome to one free on the Victoria." She takes two steps toward the door.

Stops and looks about. "Best come quick, before the spirit leaves me."

Alex joins the current of bodies following Emaline to the Victoria. She pushes through to the front.

"Alex," says Emaline. "Golden Boy." And she lays her hand on Alex's shoulder, her face so close there's no need to squint.

Alex laughs with her mouth wide open.

# 13

A week and a day later, Monday, Fred holds up a dark green plant with silver-dollar leaves surrounding the stem. "This one you can eat," he tells Alex. "Miner's lettuce, *Montia perfoliata*."

"Just showing off now," says Harry, who never had anything positive to say about Fred's mining ideas, either. Yesterday Fred had gone on and on about pressurized tubing and the power of the four humors in carefully controlled imbalance. "Earth, air, fire and water," he had said, pointing a bony finger of warning at Alex. "Mighty powerful, mighty destructive, and mighty useful – if controlled. River runs a levy and everyone swims. Wipes out a whole town, whoosh, in hours. How smart you gotta be to build the levy higher, wider? How smart you gotta be to let that water do the work of a hundred shovels? Thousands, maybe. Move more earth in a week than we could do in ten years of digging; wash that mountain away in great chunks."

Alex had imagined a gaping hole where the ravine stood, imagined the mountains leveled, the red earth baked and barren in sun. A frightening image, but somehow inspiring as well.

"Hydraulicking. Besides," Fred had said, speaking to Harry's incredulous expression, "someone is bound to make a whole hell of a lot of money."

Today he speaks of plants.

"Go ahead," says Fred, handing Alex the sprig of Miner's lettuce. "Tastes like nothing really."

Alex takes a careful bite, her lip curling up like a horse taking a carrot. If green has a taste, this is it.

"Not bad, eh? And this one here's a lily; in the same family, anyway. Star tulips, they're called, on account of their five ray-like petals." To Harry: "*Calochortus monophyllus*. But I wouldn't be eating this one."

She has begun to look forward to these lunchtime conversations; far more enjoyable than being caught between Limpy's constant stream of language and David's careful silence. It intrigues her that a man with a cavalry cap could be so fascinated by minute details of nature that most people stepped over, or on, without ever paying heed. Flowers and rocks and insects, the shelf-like growths that skirted the oak trees – Fred knew the names for all these things, and if he didn't know the name, he made it up.

"It is a named world, my friend," says Fred. "Most plants, see, they've got themselves names that describe 'em. White globe lily, red clover, wild pea. And the Latin names, they mean something specific, descriptive, more so than common names. Butter weed –" he holds up a tall plant with a yellow head of feathery flowers. "Butter weed all right to say unless you want to describe more than color. But you say the family name, *Compositae*, you know already the flower head's going to be made up of many hundreds of flowers all clustered together. See? And you say *Senicio*, you're going to know those flowers are probably whitish yellow, like an old man's beard, and covering the really important parts, the pistils and ovaries. The female parts you know. Hiding them like armor. Like a disguise. A better description, see, the scientific name. A more *complete* description."

"Providing you know Latin," says Harry.

"You don't?"

Alex wiggles her feet, letting the mud slip between her toes. The end of May had been dry, and as June nears its end, drought is on the horizon. This day is overcast but stiflingly warm, and there's little chance of rain to douse the parched and shedding pines. Fred and Harry have both abandoned their shirts, revealing the pasty white skin that represents their only physical similarity. Fred's chest is concave, his tiny nipples inverted, while his rib-racked stomach boasts a protruding belly button sticking boldly outward like a stunted finger. His shoulders are lean and bony, leading to a pair of thin but defined arms covered in a meager coat of dark brown fur. Harry is round and soft where Fred is thin and bony. He has recently shaved his beard and his jowls are a shade lighter than his cheeks. His shoulders are fleshy, but not without the density of hidden muscle, and his hands are like two starfish, each digit beginning thick and funneling downward to a nail nub. Diffuse islands of coarse hair populate his torso like oases of well-watered grass in a desert. Two utterly different species, in Alex's mind: a climbing vine and a shrub.

She's glad Emaline warned her about too much sun. It gives her a viable excuse to leave her shirt on, and the men no longer razz her about it. If Emaline is behind Alex's stubborn refusal to bare her chest, there is no reasoning. Besides, it's getting too hot to tease. Alex wonders whether the men envy the time she spends alone with Emaline, even if this time includes sweeping the floor, stoking the fire, or a host of other small jobs Emaline could just as well do herself. She wonders if the men listen in on any of their surface-level conversations, wonders if they, too, can hear how much is never said.

Limpy is the only one who seems to care. "Look at you, then," he said one day as Alex carried the bread to the dinner table. "A regular woman's helper. What would your mamma say if she saw this?"

"My momma's dead," Alex replied, and Limpy's mouth popped shut, his eyes angled down.

"I'm sorry 'bout that, son. Skin me up, will you?"

Alex wasn't looking for pity, but it felt good. "My pa's dead, too."

Limpy never broached the subject again.

Harry heaves himself to his feet. His stomach, resting in three distinct rolls upon his torso, melds into one drooping mound of flesh. "Excuse me while I get back to mining gold," he says, letting the current clean his feet before plunging them into his boots. Under his breath, he mumbles something about blisters.

"Now, take Harry, for instance," Fred continues. "What's his name tell about him? That he's got green eyes, a crooked left pinkie finger and a bald spot? No. It tells you nothing. Not even that Harry is a he. I've known a man called himself Jan – big barrel-chested fellow – and I've heard of a woman called Joe. Short for something: Jo Anne . . . Josephine. But that's what she called herself: Joe. It's all wrong, you ask me, backward somehow. Fred, now, that's a family name. Couldn't escape it. Fred Henderson III, if you want to know the truth. Don't mind the third part, but Fred don't suit me."

"Poor don't suit you, neither," says Limpy from behind. "Y'all planning on working today? David's getting a little agitated, you understand. Throwing things, giving me hell."

Alex turns. Beyond Limpy, David stands with his arms crossed and foot tapping with nervous impatience. His glance jumps from Alex to Fred and back to Alex. Let him wait, Alex thinks, and takes her time with her boots. She wonders what *scientific* name would suit David? What name would suit her?

That same day, near sunset, a reporter rode into town and demanded a room for the night. Alex couldn't help but grin as Emaline stared down her nose at the man, making him wait for an answer, reminding him it was her answer to give.

175

Now the man lounges in one of Emaline's new velvet-upholstered settees, one leg crossed easily over the other, looking just a bit too comfortable for Alex's liking. Over a bleached muslin shirt with pearl buttons, he wears a gray wool waistcoat with a short stand-up collar and lapel that matches his trousers. His oiled hair looks darker than its natural dusty blond, and is parted down the center, dividing his head into two halves, drawing attention to his long, pointed nose and the manicured square of mustache above his lips. Beneath his blond eyebrows and lashes are sunken eyes the color of old urine. Only a wide and ready smile saves his face from a sinister severity.

"I understand what you're saying, Mr. James," says Harry. "I simply cannot agree with your assessment. The law is put in place precisely so the line between good and evil, justice and injustice is maintained. Allow vigilantes to run wild, all you got is a mob that cares more about hanging than the truth."

"But California is a land of extremes. Take the weather," says Mr. James, clicking his front teeth together in the pause. His voice has a neutral, soothing pitch, good for putting babies to sleep. Alex slumps back in her chair, and stares at that patch of thinning hair on Harry's head. "Three years ago, floods," Mr. James continues. "Sacramento nearly washed down the river. And now we're looking at the worst drought in state history."

"All six years of it," Emaline says from above on the stairwell.

Mr. James clicks his teeth and continues in spite of the self-satisfied grin on Emaline's face. "She'd just as soon freeze you as fry you, drown you as starve you. And she's not too particular. Some get rich. Some get dead. She needs a quick, extreme justice. Justice," he says again, as if the word alone could prove his point.

Alex nods hello to Limpy, who makes a space for himself

between Fred and David. Her mind wanders happily back to names and flowers. She had walked in a tunneled fog all day, glaring down at daisies, scrutinizing dogwood blooms, looking for evidence of nature's disguises when she should have been sifting the sluice for gold. The camouflage, the deception, it was ubiquitous. A praying mantis posing as a branch, a moth holding motionless and leaf-like, a red water snake basking in the sun, impersonating river mud. She marveled at the relief she felt at this revelation, as though nature had somehow exonerated her for posing as someone, something she was not. Nature, a coconspirator, a fellow master of disguise, if survival demanded, and it so often did. Deception was natural, expected, even, making the disguises themselves defining features.

As the last of the afternoon light fades, she runs her fingers down the ridge of muscles along her forearms, comparing them to David's.

The days are getting longer. In Marysville and Sacramento, where flat land stretches out into the horizon, she imagines the sunlight lingering in the sky, fighting the urge to move time along. But in Motherlode the sun slips over the edge of the ravine and is swallowed every day by six. Sometimes she wishes the days would linger, that time would slow or stop, and hold her here in this moment, or the one before, working the claim every day, sweeping floors and sipping whiskey every night.

She watches David's face grow darker with the room, but pays scant attention to the presumptuous Mr. James, whose audience grows as men come in from the mines.

Emaline lights the oil lamps. Kerosene fumes, sweeter smelling than the fish oil, mix visibly with tobacco smoke. Fred is shaking his head and waving his finger in the air. "No, no, no. The opposite. Like I was saying earlier, about hydraulicking –" he appeals to Harry – "gotta have more control, not less, even if it takes longer. Build the levy up so it lasts. Get more lawmen, *real* lawmen, more courts. Never be safe if people are running round half cocked in the name of justice. Has to be more than a name, has to be ordered, or it'll all just go to hell."

For once Harry nods his agreement. "The courts are too slow, is that it?" he asks Mr. James.

"And too few and far between just now. Just now, I'm saying, not in five years or ten. We got Mexicans and Chinamen and Negroes running around like they own the place; got women and children robbing and murdering."

"The hell," says Limpy, nudging Alex in the side. Alex sits up to listen.

"It was in all the papers. I set both articles myself for the *Telegraph*," says Mr. James. He smoothes his oiled mustache with the pointer and pinky finger of his left hand, then produces a folded newspaper from his attaché case. Harry grabs it up, frowns at the small print. "I don't have to tell you that these are the kind of stories that establish a newspaper," says Mr. James. "Murder and politics – not necessarily in that order. Hate to say it, but gold is pretty old news nowadays. Two or three new strikes in every issue, and we wouldn't even print those except that it beats reminding everyone how much debt the city of Grass Valley is in after that fire."

"I tell you what news is," says Emaline. Mr. James turns. She's been standing by the kitchen door, her arms crossed just beneath her bosom, as though she's hefting a pair of flour sacks. "News is what's killing my chickens."

Mr. James laughs. His teeth are small, straight, and the bluish yellow of a blueberry eater. Eventually he realizes that he's the only one laughing. Emaline's foot taps. Mr. James clicks his teeth. "Now, now, I don't know much about –"

"I won't read any paper supporting Millard Fillmore," Harry blurts, thrusting the newsprint away as if it had suddenly begun to smell. "I don't care what else you print."

178

Mr. James clicks his teeth, fingers his mustache, then veers back to his original topic, as though that one moment of hesitation absolved him from responding to either of the last two statements.

"Yes, well," he says. "Story goes, Mr. Hanson Minford of San Francisco – a very wealthy man, imported furniture from England and France, owned a share of the Union Bank, sat on the city council . . ." Mr. James leans forward, speaking in the soft, confidential manner of one revealing secrets. "He comes home after a hard day's work expecting a little comfort – dinner hot, his feet rubbed, a kiss from his wife – when she stabs him in the heart with his own knife."

"Ah now, I already heard this one, months ago," Limpy says, folding his arms before him, obviously disappointed. "Slit him gut to chin and all that."

"Well, then she cuts off all his digits – *all* his digits, fingers and toes and his . . . Well, she stuffs them *all* in his mouth."

Alex's mouth drops open, her reaction mirrored by men on both sides of her, and this seems to please Mr. James enough for him to continue:

"The maid finds him next morning, lying face up on the floor, the bloody stumps buzzing with flies. No sign of his wife or a good sum of money Minford had just withdrawn from the bank. Now, this was no lady of disrepute, no whore, by any standard, but his lawful wife, pledged to serve and protect under God. One of Miz Eliza Farnham's imported brides, supposedly bringing Eastern values to us Western barbarians." Mr. James's voice betrays his disgust for this idea. He clicks his teeth, the sound grating now on Alex. She forgets flowers and disguises, focuses her whole attention on those discolored teeth. "By the time the law got around to looking for her, she'd disappeared, maybe for good. Maybe in these foothills."

The door slams and Jed enters, laboring under the weight of a whiskey barrel. He eyes the circle of listeners. He winks

179

at Alex, and she wishes he'd ignored her, walked by as if she were invisible or just one of the men, which can be the same as invisible in a town full of men.

Mr. James's audience has grown even larger as miners continue to trickle in from the creek. Alex forces herself to relax her grip on her armrests.

"Vigilance committee never would have let Mrs. Minford put so much distance between herself and San Francisco. We, ah, we . . ." Mr. James pauses as though losing his thought, clicks his teeth and cranes his head to get a look at Jed, who lets the whiskey barrel bump to the ground by the bar. Jed looks up, as though feeling eyes on him.

"And the other story?" Emaline asks, stepping quickly into Mr. James's line of sight, for the first time bestowing upon the reporter the full weight of her nameless appeal. "You had another story."

His forehead colors. He clicks his teeth. He reaches into his case, pulling out a sheet of newsprint. "Well, read it for yourself." He hands her the newsprint as his eyes follow Jed behind the counter.

"My eyes ain't so good," says Emaline, again placing herself directly in Mr. James's line of sight and thrusting the paper back into his hands. "All right?"

At this admission, David leans forward in his chair as if listening harder. Emaline's eyes were one of those things she didn't talk about, as if an unacknowledged weakness was no weakness at all.

A silent exchange passes from Emaline to Jed: a blink, a nod, nothing more. Jed slides quietly through the kitchen door.

"All right," concedes Mr. James, as Emaline hulks above him. "All right.

"'On Thursday, March 4th, at dusk, a Wells Fargo stage-coach en route to Sacramento from San Francisco stopped to offer a ride to a young boy alone on the road. In payment *for his generosity, the driver received a Colt revolver at his temple. Within minutes, the stage was surrounded by a hooting gang of bandana-masked bandits who proceeded to relieve the coach of all valuables, including twenty-five thousand dollars' worth of gold coins minted in San Francisco, and a crate of fine French wine. In future, citizens and stage drivers alike are advised, whatever their benevolent inclinations, to aid and assist only persons of intimate acquaintance.'*

"Now, I don't know about you folks, but how safe is a place when young boys are turning to crime?" says Mr. James as Micah takes the paper from him, frowning over the headlines. Frowning, Alex realizes, at her, or the Golden Boy. David's gaze follows Micah's and their suspicion heats the base of her neck.

"There's got to be consequences," Mr. James is saying, but all attention is on Alex, who can't keep her hands from trembling. She makes a fist as Mr. James slams his upon the table, jolting the whiskey glasses. "Consequences," he persists, looking about for support, his fist now suspended midair in the silence. Alex can't help but look to Emaline, whose eyes are searching the upper right corner of her mind. Emaline's eyes widen, and when she bites her lip Alex has to stand. She catches the corner of the table, hears the glasses fall, doesn't slow down, doesn't look back as she pushes past Klein and out the front door.

David's head swivels from Alex to Mr. James, whose lips have pursed themselves into a question all but swallowed by the sudden frenzy of the saloon.

Emaline storms from Mr. James to the bar and back again with a tumbler in hand.

"Care for a drink, Mr. James?" She lets the tumbler slip and brown liquid douses his crotch. She moves in front of him, places her hand just above the damp patch on his trousers.

181

"Oh, I am so sorry. No – stay put. I've got a towel." She produces a small embroidered napkin from her bodice.

David can barely watch.

"Ooee! Comedy you printing in this paper, Mr. James!" proclaims Micah, loud for all to hear. "Listen to this, David, listen: 'Minerva O'Fountain, a young "gentleman," or some other kind of animal dressed in a boy's suit, was arrested and brought before Justice Rolfe on Wednesday last for violation of the ordinance prohibiting females from appearing in the streets in male attire.' Says here she was fined twenty-five dollars and costs. You make that up, Mr. James?"

"Who was –" James attempts.

"I'll take a drink, sure, Emaline," declares Limpy, slapping a paw on the reporter's shoulder. "You hear of that fellow over in You Bet, claiming to be the second cousin to the King of England? Turned out he couldn't even spell 'Edward.'"

"Another drink, Mr. James?" asks Emaline, for the moment done dabbing his crotch.

"Thank you, no," he says, but Emaline hands him another anyway and stands waiting, hands on hips, toe tapping. Mr. James drinks.

"Not that that proves he was lying," Limpy concedes. "Might never have learned to spell. What you think?"

"Speaking of hydraulicking," says Fred, edging his way past David, back into the circle, "wondered what you thought about the use of sheet-metal nozzles over wrought iron."

"Yes, what about that hydro-licking," says Limpy, now cradling a whole whiskey jug beneath his arm. He offers David a drink. David shakes his head, no.

Mr. James is speechless.

"Music!?" says Emaline, turning full circle to find Klein already taking his accordion from its case. The first note brings more men from the street. Soon a fiddler joins the jig and a guitarist finds the rhythm. Limpy do-si-dos around the room with the jug, pouring whiskey and cracking jokes.

David sits back in his chair, watching, thinking, tapping his fingers on the table. He stands up and walks to the door, leans a shoulder against the splintered frame, half expecting, perhaps even hoping to find the boy on the porch, just sitting there. The night is moonless and dark. Wind buffets the ridge above. Trees squeal and moan in concert with coyotes, but Victor Lane is deserted. If Alex is gone, then he's gone. Nothing David can do. Better that way. No questions to ask, to answer. He plays with the ends of his mustache, drooping like a pair of inverted question marks. Boy Bandit – the thought is almost humorous. Alex, the Boy Bandit. But David is not smiling.

Behind him in the saloon, elbows brush elbows. Sleeves stain dark with perspiration, foreheads shine and body heat escapes through the door in musty waves. A banjo has made the trio a quartet. Emaline takes a seat by Mr. James, close enough to smell the liquor on his breath. "About them chickens . . ." she whispers, breathing hot air into his ear. She runs her finger along the seam of his stiff collar. Her hands admire the fabric of his waistcoat, then explore downward. He breathes in sharply as her hand moves to the bulge between his legs.

"Drink."

David struggles down Victor Lane with Limpy leaning heavily on his shoulder. The big man's sour breath surrounds David in a noisome mist. He can smell nothing else. He opens the door of the cabin, tugs Limpy inside, lets him tumble on to his bed, where he lands too drunk even to snore. Sleeping at that angle, his back will hurt him in the morning. He'll use it as an excuse to get out of work, but David doesn't feel like moving him. Instead, he sits down on the stool, tugs off his boots and lets the air tickle his fetid toes.

He massages the red, tender skin of his arch, then the

crusted white calluses of his forefoot. His toenails, yellow from lack of sun, need trimming. His ankles have been rubbed free of the coarse blond hair covering the rest of his body. His shoulders slump, his eyes stare at nothing, his mind slips between topics, resting finally on Alex. No, it's too late. He's too tired. His eyes adjust enough to cross the room where he sits dejected on the bed. A groan of protest rises from his quilt. A small hairless hand slips from beneath its layers.

Alex? David mouths the word. Embarrassment warms his earlobes. He can feel the vague impression of body heat, see the quilt rise and fall with each breath. He sinks to his knees by the bed. Slowly, gently, he pulls the quilt aside and reveals Alex's sleeping face, pale blue in the dim light, like a stone saint. Alex's hair is growing long around his ears. David reaches out to trace the crooked angle of Alex's nose, the soft chin, the narrow jaw, the high, rounded cheekbones. Alex stirs. David yanks his hand away. It hovers like a blessing.

"Alex," David says, this time giving voice to the word. Alex remains motionless. "Alex, what are you doing here?" Alex's breathing grows shallow. His lids open, revealing dilated black eyes like obsidian in granite. David repeats his question.

"What are you doing here?"

"I was tired," Alex whispers, and closes his eyes.

John Thomas arrived early at the Hughes Ranch arena to examine the beasts before putting money down. He'd lost weight since leaving Motherlode, and on the walk to the ranch decided to save half of the fifty he'd earned that week for food. That changed the moment the bull, a shadowed Brahma–Angus mix with a set of wide, pointed horns, a thick barreled neck and pair of densely defined shank muscles stalked into the ring. It pawed the ground, snorting clouds of dust like the horned devil himself. Sweat foamed at the animal's shoulder hump, and John Thomas stared, intoxicated with the sheer size and strength, two qualities he as a

184

small man had always envied. Even before he saw the challenger, the bull had earned John Thomas's full fifty-dollar wager. The sorry beast they called a grizzly was no match: one ear bitten clean off, a blind white shadow across its left eye, its fur matted and bald in places, revealing dark brown skin, scabbing and flaking. It favored its right front leg and it limped around the arena with a look of tired resignation. Damn thing was better off dead. A sure bet, John Thomas thought. Easy money, the best kind. A hell of a lot easier than working them lumber mills in Grass Valley.

The hillside from Grass Valley to Hughes Ranch was stripped of good lumber and as he'd made his way to the arena, John Thomas couldn't help but feel pride at his part in this drastic change. The rows of stumps, the sweet-and-sour smell of wood rot, even the sight of the white wood larvae boring happily into their feast, had given John Thomas a sense of accomplishment he'd never before experienced. Not back home in Georgia, tilling his daddy's field; not in Auburn, working his cousin's claim; certainly not in Motherlode. The very thought of that town made John Thomas scowl.

Goddamn whelp of a boy, stealing gold from John Thomas's own claim, putting on self-important airs when all he did was get lucky. And Jed? He's whipped niggers in his time. Not his own, of course, but Mr. Johnson's slaves from the plantation that bordered his daddy's farm. Every spring during the planting, and every fall during the harvest, John Thomas went over to Johnson's to help. He felt bad about the whipping at first. The blood oozed through their clothes, welled up from their dark, unnatural skin and leached outward. But pain was the only thing they minded. A word wouldn't do nothing but make 'em look at you, and John Thomas couldn't stand to have them looking. They stared as though they knew you and hated you. Or, worse, knew you and pitied you. Jed had done that a lot, looked down at John Thomas, shaking his head. He'd even smiled. That nigger had no respect. John Thomas didn't blame Emaline. She was obviously under a spell of some sort, making her pliable, as women will be, protective even. Now, with that boy stirring things up, making people gold-crazy, it had probably been a good thing to get out of town. He'd rather live with the Chinamen and the Mexicans, though their chattering gibberish and strange habits seemed to soak the luck right out of a place, or out of John Thomas, at least.

Not today, though. Today he'd woken up feeling different, lucky. Today, when he stepped from his tent on the outskirts of Grass Valley, the sky was a viscous black, and the coyotes sang just to him. He looked before biting into a weevil in his biscuit, he found an extra gold piece stuck with pine pitch to the bottom of his boot, and on the way to town he tripped but didn't fall over a tree root jutting in his way. Luck was with him, for sure.

His gaze traveled the arena, scaling the seven-foot walls from sawdust to seating. The bull was still making his rounds, charging at legs dangled over the arena walls, snorting dust into the air while the grizzly cowered in the corner, licking his tattered rump like a disgruntled kitten. Better be more of a show than this, thought John Thomas, jingling his pouch of gold and imagining added weight. He'd start at the top of Main Street, work his way down saloon by saloon. He held his breath, closed his eyes, anticipating the blessed delirium. He could still feel the rumble of the stamp mills in Grass Valley, three miles away. The mills hadn't stopped, day or night, since John Thomas had arrived six and a half weeks ago; hadn't even stopped during the fire, nine months before that. Three hundred buildings, flattened. Four hundred thousand dollars' worth of damage, and still the stamp mills rumbled on. Some said they would never stop, would continue crushing ore until the mountains themselves caved in upon the hard-rock mines below. John Thomas wouldn't mind seeing that.

Nearly every seat in the arena was taken. An expectant buzz traveled upward to the overcast sky. Directly across from him, overdressed and smug, sat councillors Tompkins, White and Wheeler. Officially, they were against such fights, denouncing them as "brutal amusements." John Thomas wondered how much Tompkins had wagered. With his straggly beard of gray hair, downcast eyes and shuffling manner, he looked like a close cousin to that bear. John Thomas jittered in his seat, absently kicking the bench in front of him and frowning at the bare toes that peeked through his cracked leather boots. A tall redheaded man turned, annoyed. John Thomas stopped kicking and looked deliberately in the other direction.

"John Thomas? Well, I'll be," said a familiar voice, and John Thomas returned his gaze.

"McLantry?" John Thomas said, more surprised by the man's tailored waistcoat, gold-tipped walking stick and polished black boots than his presence at the fight. The freckles on McLantry's well-fed face had multiplied, giving him a ruddy, healthy complexion. Time had treated him well.

"That's *Lantry*," McLantry corrected. He looked around him for eavesdroppers, then continued amiably: "Didn't think I'd ever see you again, but, hell – knew you wouldn't go far. Doubt they even remember, or care, up there in Nevada City. One less Indian – did us all a favor. Woulda just growed up killing white women, like his daddy. You shoulda stuck around. I work for Hughes now. And business . . . ? It's good."

McLantry held out his arms, showcasing the arena like an entertainer. John Thomas scowled. It was McLantry who'd said he ought to leave town and quick. It was McLantry who'd told him killing that Indian brat would give Sheriff Jones – who was never real fond of John Thomas to begin with – an excuse to lock him up. Or hang him. On account of an Indian, no less.

"Word of advice, between old friends . . . ," said McLantry, leaning over in a friendly manner. John Thomas looked suspiciously into McLantry's wide, confident eyes. ". . . Money on the bear." McLantry nodded, gave John Thomas a conciliatory wink, and turned back to the arena.

Never had trusted the son-of-a-bitch. John Thomas's lip curled at the thought. No way in hell that bear would last ten minutes. He was no fool, even if McLantry insisted on acting like the king of the arena. Thomas Hughes had built the place. Thomas Hughes would be taking all the profit from it. McLantry had probably stolen those new clothes on his back.

John Thomas settled back into his seat and crossed his arms in front of him. The bull, its ears twitching, its breath nearly visible, had turned to face the bear. The mounting tension of the arena pulled taut as a cinch. The bull charged and conversations ceased. The bear strained casually against his tether, allowing the bull to come, head down, horns level with its chest. The crowd cheered and eyes flashed with excitement. John Thomas gripped his money pouch, leaned forward and gritted his teeth for the horns' impact when the bear suddenly reared to its hind feet, sidestepped the bull like a matador, and clubbed it hard, leaving a track of four parallel gashes down the bull's neck. The crowd erupted, then went silent. For a moment, John Thomas forgot to breathe. The stamp mills rumbled in the distance. The bull charged again, twenty feet, ten, slammed into the arena wall, splintering the wood and breaking its right horn off at the tip. The bear sank its claws into the bull's exposed flank, its teeth into the soft part of the bull's neck. Blood stained the yellow sawdust. The bull's tongue lolled from its mouth, gathering bits of dust, and the bear returned to serenity, licking its coat, not even bothering to sample his kill.

John Thomas left the arena and began trudging back toward Main Street, the sounds of protest following him. The fight had been too quick, the outcome fixed. He heard the blows of fists against flesh. Gunshots shattered the air. But

John Thomas had no energy to complain. He glimpsed McLantry, who stood with an arm around a euphoric gentleman weighed down by gold. Tricked again. McLantry had known John Thomas wouldn't trust him. No one trusted McLantry.

The smell of fresh rolls competed with a bouquet of new lumber, damp ash, and sweating horseflesh as John Thomas neared Main Street. Luck? For him there was no such thing, only bad luck. That grizzly had just waited till the bull knocked its damned self silly, then finished it off. Lucky?

He kicked a stone up the street, resenting the good-natured bustle, hating the newly painted shopfronts. He edged by ladies in stiff, starched dresses, men in pressed trousers, and knew what they saw when they looked at him. They saw his threadbare canvas pants, his stained flannel shirt with two missing buttons, his big toe protruding from his left boot. A cursed man. A failure. He continued past Mill Street and Marshall's Grocery Store, came to an abrupt stop in front of a poster on the wall of O'Dunkel's Saloon.

John Thomas straightened and, for a moment, forgot to breathe. He counted the zeros printed below the familiar face and smiled. His lucky day.

# 14

Emaline is used to feeling clever in the morning, after that first cup of coffee has seeped into her veins, before the day's plans transform themselves into the day's duties. But lately her morning moods have been spoiled by strategically placed biblical verses on scraps of yellow newsprint. Jeremiah 5:3 on the lid of the flower barrel: *They have made their faces harder than rock; they have refused to repent.* Matthew 11:20 next to the water bucket: *He denounced the cities, because they did not repent.* And just yesterday, Jude 7 beneath her bedroom door: *As Sodom and Gomorrah and the cities around them indulged in gross immorality they are exhibited as an example in undergoing the punishment of eternal fire.*

If they were so goddamned worried about her eternal soul, you'd think they'd just say so in person. Treat her like the great unwashed, unworthy of a word, unless it be one of condemnation, and then only written on paper, as easy to burn as to read. She doesn't know why, but she's kept every scrap, noticing the differences in the slant of the lettering. One, a billowing, effusive hand with a fondness for large pregnant O's; another thick and slanted with letters nearly too pinched for Emaline's eyes; and the third, a careful, blocky style, utterly without personality.

Emaline stuffs the scraps in her apron pocket. She wraps her shawl around her, though she isn't cold. Flipping an untidy ringlet behind her ear, she walks out to inspect the damage in the chicken coop. A lone bird strides cautiously around the pen, scratching through the feathers which are all that remain of its fellow inmates. It cocks its head sideways in the jerky, graceless manner of chickens. Emaline sprinkles some oats.

"You're it, huh?" She scans the coop. No bones, no blood, just feathers, and not a sound the night before. Neat. Very neat. She leans over the rail, lays her chin on her hands. Crows hop among the feathers. A squirrel darts along the coop roof, vanishes over the edge. She can hear the town waking behind her, the buzz of human voices, the first clatter of carpentry. The chapel is nearly complete, though the steeple still leans a little to the left, and likely always will; brass-plated mirrors and porcelain washbasins grace every bedroom of the Victoria, and new four-legged chairs and upholstered settees with fancy armrests curling down like snail shells now adorn the saloon. But beyond these refinements, beyond the boundaries of the walls she built, the town is growing like a teenage boy. Growing too quickly – sprouting roads and buildings – out of her control. Jed is off at the mine most days now, and comes home tired. When they do talk, he can speak of little but gold, net yield, per-ton percentages. She's not sure how much longer she can manage alone, fixing the meals, cleaning the bedrooms, stocking the saloon ... And those women, swanning around Motherlode like a fleet of holy human barges, dispensing disapproval like manure on a bramble garden – who else but they would be placing Bible verses under Emaline's nose?

She puffs a curl from her face. Above, wispy clouds manage a few formless shadows. The chicken gives a cautious squawk, looks none too grieved about the disappearance of its comrades. It turns its back and reveals a plucked red backside, as if to say, "I didn't kill 'em, but I ain't sad they're gone."

"Didn't feel like squawking last night, did you?" says Emaline, eyeing the bird suspiciously. Not that it would have mattered. Emaline knows exactly what happened to her chickens, but isn't about to tell that to the bird. Fresh eggs. Such a sacrifice, but a worthy one. "Wouldn't have done much good anyway, huh? Might have woken up Mr. Reporter – Mr. Jamesesess and all his questions with him," Emaline says, though the chicken's attention is on its meal. "Hey!" she says, and whistles as though calling a dog. "Guess I won't miss that rooster none. You won't be doing any crowing, will yah? No. A whistling girl and crowing hen, Mama would say. 'A whistling girl and a crowing hen always come to some bad end.' Smart woman." She purses her lips and whistles a nonsense tune to herself. "Mr. James . . ." she says, pointing her finger at the bird, but doesn't finish her sentence.

Jed is none of Mr. James's damned business. And as for Alex . . . Well, she doesn't know what to think about Alex. Boy Bandit? She wanted to believe it. It would give Alex a solid identity, a past defined by actions. As it is, he's just the Golden Boy, the town luck, a mascot of sorts. Be more comfortable knowing exactly who he is and where he got the bruises he walked into town with, even if he is a criminal. The word sounded so much bigger than Alex. Criminal. If it hadn't been for those bruises and the way he shrank inside himself when she saw them, she might have asked . . . No. A man's past is his own damn business. He'd tell her when he was ready, just like everyone else. She takes a breath, chews her lower lip. She pulls another crumpled paper, a letter, from her apron pocket. She brings the page inches from her nose and squints her eyes to slits.

*My Dearest Emaline,*
*Because your last correspondence was no doubt lost, I will assume that you are healthy and receive this letter in good spirits. A rush of events marks the time since my last letter.*

*Your cousin Elma is now the mother of three, having brought a healthy little girl into the world not two weeks ago. She has her father's dark hair and her mother's dimples, and our prayers have seen her through a worrisome spell of fever. Elma's husband Daniel was elected to the county seat again, but professes no desire to stand for the Senate. So refreshing to find a man in this day and age with humble, reasonable ambitions. Rafe Gentry spent four nights in jail, fighting again, and Renton's fishpond had to be drained and dredged, but the cholera is better than it was. Only three deaths in the last three months. I do hope the orphanage is running smoothly. After trying for so long for a baby of your own, the Lord has blessed you with a house full of needy children. I have always said to trust the Lord. The Lord has a plan for each of us. You know we were far from pleased to learn that you would not be returning to us after Harold's death. But your mother died a happy woman, knowing that you had answered God's call to other ends. I regret that there is no money to send in support. Bless those dear children, and know our hearts and prayers are with them, and you.*
*With Love,*
*Aunt Florence*

Flo has no idea to whom she is writing any more. The Emaline she knew is buried with her husband somewhere between Utah and the Missouri River; a single unmarked wooden cross the only evidence of death.

So rarely, now, does she think of Harold as more than a mound of earth, but this letter has resurrected his belly laugh, the smell of his pipe, his boxy, chinless face. He was a forty-six-year-old widower when he asked her, an old maid of thirty, to marry him. She'd loved Harold for his kindness and familiarity, for his work-hardened hands and weepy eyes, for the silly stories he told to neighborhood children every Sunday after church. She loved him for the poetry he read her aloud each night; sometimes his own, often the words of William Wordsworth. Now, only one line remains: "a slumber did my spirit seal" – his voice sweeping through her memory like a breeze, for it's not the words so much as the resonate warmth of his voice and the rhythm that lingers. Lord knew he wanted children of his own to inherit the wheelwright shop and listen to his stories. Watching wagon after wagon of young families rumble West, Emaline had wondered if it was something in the Missouri soil that kept her barren. Watching that endless train of migrants, she'd felt a presence clawing her belly for release. She liked to think that it was another life, a separate life, a child doing the clawing. She didn't try to contain her enthusiasm when Harold suggested they, too, should venture West.

After leaving behind Missouri's wooded rolling hills and crossing horizon after horizon of prairie, endless as the early summer days, after braving rivers that snaked and meandered to parched earth and others that burst with the violent thrust of flash floods, she felt this presence growing stronger, slowly defining itself like the Rockies in the distance, punching granite fists into the sky. Even as Harold weakened, this other presence grew. If it was not a baby, it was . . . it was something, somebody she already loved. She loved Harold still for giving it to her.

Flo would not accept the woman Emaline has become. She, too, would be leaving scraps of paper to save Emaline's soul, would accuse her of having lost her faith. Emaline shakes her head, drops more grain for the chicken. Faith is one foot in front of the other, even if you suspect you might be going the wrong direction. Faith is letting a small lie alleviate the stress of a thousand unaccepted explanations. She wrinkles her nose, scrunches the letter into a tiny ball and lets it drop, inviting the Rhode Island Red to investigate. The chicken pecks tentatively, punching holes through the paper. A smile breaks the frown lines of Emaline's face. She bends for the letter, puts her finger through the hole in the middle and begins to tear, littering the coop with slivers of false expectations. She bites her lip, refuses the tears in her eyes, and tips her head back, breathing in deeply as if to suck the moisture back into memory. The chicken circles the strange paper worms, looking for something more substantial. Emaline pulls all three scraps of newsprint from her pocket. Jeremiah 5:3 is shredded and strewn, then Matthew, then Jude. The Rhode Island Red scratches and pecks the holy men like so many worms in the mud, bobbing its head for more. Forgiveness was never so simple.

"Nearly ate you," Emaline tells the bird. "Dumplings." A sound catches her ear. She turns to find a girl, almost a woman, peering around the side of the Victoria.

"Lou Anne, is it?" Emaline asks. The girl nods her head and pops her mouth shut. "Come on, then. I won't bite yah."

The girl bites her lip and ventures forward, tentatively, on her toes. She looks Emaline up and down with unveiled curiosity. They stand side by side, the girl's head barely reaching Emaline's shoulder. The sun has risen to nine o'clock and the clouds have evaporated to blue. Jays scream from a tree branch.

"You always talk to chickens?" the girl asks.

"Yep. You?"

The girl blushes, bites her lip again and opens her hand to reveal a wrinkled scrap of newsprint. She takes the paper between thumb and forefinger. Her nails are chewed to bloody nubs. She rips the paper in half, in half again, and throws the pieces to the wind. Emaline stares straight ahead, making an effort not to smile.

"Might just go to hell for that," she says, and feels the girl tense at her side, taking small careful breaths. A corset, Emaline thinks. Probably her first whalebone.

The girl holds her head high. Her dress is storm gray with a long skirt, impenetrable for its layers of petticoats. Her back is painfully rigid, her body yet to resign itself to the restraints of style. Her shoes are scuffed along the tops and covered in a thin film of river mud, and her braids are tight, woven around her head like a beaver trap. Pretty, but not happy about the sacrifice. A smile creeps across Emaline's face in spite of herself. She nudges Lou Anne with her elbow, allowing the smile to evolve to a chuckle, a chuckle to a laugh. On the second nudge Lou Anne sputters, slaps her hand over her laughter. Tears streak her eyes.

"I think you look very nice," says Emaline, serious now, and Lou Anne looks up, her scrubbed face glowing. "A real lady."

They watch scraps of paper do pirouettes on the wind. "You want to come in?" She motions toward the Victoria.

*Oh yes, please*, reads the girl's face. But she doesn't speak.

"Thought you was one to talk." The girl lowers her eyes, kicks at the dirt. "Won't tell your mamma." At the mention of her mother, Lou Anne balks.

"I have to go," she says, turning and rushing away as fast as the corset will allow, leaving Emaline standing alone with the Rhode Island Red.


Alex finds Emaline in the kitchen punching down the sourdough. Sweat rolls from her forehead into the bowl as she kneads and her face, below her right eye, is streaked with flour. Alex takes a breath of yeasty air, ignoring her lingering stomachache. She hasn't felt quite right in days. A large fly bobs heavily in the air before her. She brushes both away: the fly and the notion that she ever knew what it was to feel "quite right" in the first place.

"Throw some wood in the stove, if you're just standing," says Emaline, and Alex obeys. Emaline claps a cloud of flour from her hands and sneezes into her dress sleeve. Alex loiters by the stove, awkward without something to lean on, puts her hands in her pockets, pulls them out again, wishing she'd thought to pick up the broom. Emaline goes back to her bread, molding the dough into two oval loaves. Alex turns to leave, turns back, not sure if silence is worse than the words she has ready. Emaline scoops up the loaves, shoves them into the oven, closes the door with a clang. Her fists rest on her hips.

"For heaven's sake, Alex – what?"

But the words Alex was planning evaporate. Emaline shakes her head, takes a dozen potatoes from the barrel and begins to peel. She ignores Alex effortlessly.

No one in town has said a word, other than good morning, to Alex's face. But sometimes you just know what people are saying without having to hear it. She should have forced herself to stay still last night, to blend into the background of the Victoria or flee outright, leaving her pack upstairs, the gold in the mine, abandoning everyone to their own conclusions. She would have been miles away by morning – miles away with no food, no gold, no plan, nowhere to go. The thought alone had exhausted her. Instead, she had found herself snuggling down into the folds of David's bed and closing her eyes. She was tired. She is tired of running.

"Do you think I'm the Boy Bandit?"

Emaline doesn't respond. Alex wonders whether Emaline heard her, wonders if she actually spoke the words aloud. "A stagecoach robber . . ." she continues, just as Emaline turns, the knife in her right hand, a potato the other.

She points with the knife. "Fill the pot," she says.

Alex's mouth opens and closes. She skims a pair of moths from the water bucket, one long dead and sinking, the other still fluttering. The dead moth sticks to her fingers, leaving a gray film of dust behind, while the living moth quivers on the ground, flutters and rests, flutters and rests. Alex places her foot over the struggling creature, changes her mind, leaves it to survive or die, and fills the cast-iron pot.

"On the stove," Emaline commands, again pointing with the knife. Alex bends her knees, lifts the pot and sloshes water onto the floor. She looks around for a towel, but finds none. She'd been so eloquent in her head this morning, had Emaline convinced that the Golden Boy was no danger, that he should stay. Alex wants to stay, is happy to pretend this town, these people are all she's ever known, happy to live hidden within this body of new muscle, behind this crooked nose, guarding her secret forever in the pouch between her legs. But Emaline makes it so hard, consuming every ounce of confidence in a room until there is simply none left to go around. Alex wipes water and moth dust on her pants and knows she'll do whatever Emaline says.

"I'll leave," says Alex and wraps her arms around her stomach. "If you want, I'll go."

Emaline continues to work. Alex fidgets, tickled by the silence.

"You're not this Boy Bandit?" says Emaline finally.

Alex doesn't answer quickly enough. "No," she says.

"If you're not guilty, no reason to go. And if you was . . . If you are this Boy Bandit," she says, putting great emphasis on the word *boy*, "might not have a reason to go, either. Might be, here is as good as any place to be."

Her tone is morose, without the force and conviction Alex is used to. Emaline rests her hands on the counter. Her head falls forward. A potato peel drops to the floor. She ignores it. She has deflated before Alex, her wide shoulders caving in upon themselves. Tears suddenly dampen Alex's eyes. She hears the front door of the inn open. Male voices are muffled by the yards of decorative fabric tacked over the saloon walls. The velvet settees, the cedar chairs, the dark wood tables, suddenly seem out of place next to the makeup-caked complexion of Queen Victoria hanging on the saloon wall; artificial next to this coarse, imposing woman who, until now, Alex had only ever dared to respect and to fear.

"Emaline . . . ?" says Alex.

"Emaline?" Micah hollers through the kitchen door then bangs it open. Mr. James stands behind him. "Oh. Hi, Alex,"

Micah says. Alex nods to Micah and glances back at Emaline, who has regained herself, shoulders wide, chest out.

"What, Micah?" says Emaline.

"Morning, Alex. Feeling better? You left so quickly yesterday . . ." says Mr. James, and gives Emaline a lustful grin. His perfect mustache twitches up, and his teeth click.

"I'm feeling fine."

"Mr. James says he's going to stick around a few more days," says Micah. "For the paper."

Mr. James takes a notebook from his waistcoat pocket, looks Alex up and down, and turns an inquisitive eye to Emaline. Again his hair divides his face in half, the skin of his parting at least three shades whiter than his cheeks. His black shoes have managed to stay spotless.

"That right? Well, if you're sticking around, you can run and fetch me some water," says Emaline, and turns her back. Mr. James's neck reddens at his collar. He clicks his teeth. Micah begins to laugh, conceals it with a cough.

"Excuse my leaving so quickly, Emaline. David said something about needing something, from the store. Alex, you recall what that was?" Micah says. Alex doesn't mask her confusion. "For the mine, from the store. Why don't you come with me, to the store, and we'll find what it was he wanted. For the mine."

"At the store," says Alex tentatively.

"Yes, for the mine."

"The buckets are right over there," Emaline says to Mr. James, pointing with her knife.

Mr. James puts his notebook away and slides his pencil behind his ear. Alex bites back a smile as Micah ushers her out the door, leaving Mr. James at the mercy of Emaline.

A small crowd is gathered in front of Sander's dry goods. Micah cranes his neck to see better and tips his hat to Lou Anne, who loiters on the outskirts of the crowd. Alex makes a point of ignoring both the girl and Micah's prim sideways glance, pretending to take greater interest than she feels in the voice issuing from the thick of the gathering.

"I didn't know, ladies and gentlemen . . ."

Through the forest of shoulders Alex catches sight of a diminutive fellow with a pencil-thin mustache. His voice carries like a circus host. She can just make out the words stenciled on the handcart before him, DR. VINCENT HASGLOW'S MIRACLE ELIXIR. The man repeats himself for effect: "No, I did not know how sick I was! Days, moments away from death's door. I stood upon the very welcome mat of death, until Dr. Vincent Hasglow cured me."

Another man, presumably Dr. Hasglow, steps forward and distinguishes himself with a ponderous bow. He sweeps his top hat from his head and his coattails nearly touch the ground. The meager sputtering of applause brings him upright again, revealing a somber expression Alex could have mistaken for dignity, were it not for the barrel organ beneath his arm, the handle of which he suddenly feels the need to turn. Music, a sort of jig, resonates from the box.

"Step up, ladies and gentlemen, young and old, for a free diagnosis. Hasglow's Elixir will give women a shapely size and put hair on a man's chest! That's right, son . . ." He makes eye contact with Alex, winks, and plunges on. His partner continues his wordless accompaniment. Lou Anne giggles behind her hands and Alex glares.

It's not that she feels outright animosity toward the girl; Lou Anne has given no cause. Alex is actually a little flattered by the girl's attention.

". . . will cure all ailments, from scurvy to dysentery," the vendor continues. "It will ease the feet when mixed with warm water, lend a natural healthy shine to the teeth and gums, and prevent the ague. My friends, most people walk this world in a diseased haze, when health and happiness are but ten dollars away. Ten dollars, my friends, will –"

"Look at those two –" Micah says, nodding at the hand-cart duo. "Don't know if they're pharmacists, merchants, or jackasses pulling their own cart. Only a fool pulls his own cart, Alex, remember that. Come on."

Micah moves on a step, slips his finger beneath the cloth eyepatch he's taken to wearing "in consideration of the delicate constitutions of the ladies of the town," or so he said. But judging from his sudden conversion from miner's pants to black slacks, from flannel to white cuffs and waistcoat, Alex suspects that Micah is more concerned with keeping up appearances with the other storekeepers – the effortlessly elegant Gerald Sander, in particular – than he is about the six women in town. Five, if you don't count Lou Anne, and Alex doesn't.

"I was just wondering," he says when Alex catches up, "what do you know about hydraulicking? I mean, what have you heard?"

She picks a chicken feather from the tip of her boot, finds a trail of them leading toward Bobcat Creek, some white with specks of red and brown, some amber with dark tips.

"Only what Fred says," she replies, running her thumb against the grain of the feather. She'll take it to Emaline, though she has no idea what use she could possibly find for it. "Even if you was this Boy Bandit . . ." Emaline had said. Golden Boy, Boy Bandit . . . Just another name, Alex thinks, rolling the feather's quill between thumb and forefinger.

"That's what I thought. Well, never mind," says Micah.

A lumber wagon rumbles by. The horses snort the morning air, toss their heads toward the smell of the livery stable, and the handcart merchant begins another variation of his speech. Perhaps this *is* as good a place as any. A better place. The thought surges through her, warm like hope. There has been talk of a courthouse, a theater and a lumber mill. And while no one disputes that a mill is needed, as much or more than a courthouse, the debate continues about where to build it so as not to upset someone's claim. An unofficial town meeting was held at the Victoria, but quickly deteriorated into an argument. Randall was the only one staunchly opposed to the building of a new mill, but then he *would* oppose it, given the amount of money he's making transporting the lumber with his new wagon. Living in Motherlode but two days a week, Alex doesn't consider him a proper citizen anyway.

She pauses a moment by the general store, suddenly struck by Micah's last question. Any conversations Fred began about hydraulicking quickly became fodder for ridicule. "Just piss on the mountain, there, Fred," Harry told him once. "Might just move more earth than your shovel." Alex knew Fred was in earnest, but it was hard not to view him through the eyes of his critics, it was easier than really looking.

"Hi, Alex."

She looks up to find Lou Anne bustling down the sidewalk to meet them. The practiced smile spread across Lou Anne's face, her meager chest thrust outward, the hopeful upturn of her voice, makes Alex's insides clench. There is something Alex recognizes in the tone of the girl's voice and in the tilt of the girl's head, something that Alex wants to slap out of her, so that no one else would.

"Hi," Alex replies, trying not to stare at that pink patterned dress, the billowing skirts, trying not to remember what it felt like to have to stand so straight, to take such small breaths.

The girl's shoulders droop and her smile sinks, with her skirt coming to rest like a quilt on a sleeping body. Alex thinks of David, sprawled out this morning on the floor of the cabin.

"Good morning, Miss Lou Anne," says Micah. "You look very nice today. Doesn't she look nice, Alex?"

She'd watched David's breath tease the hairs of his arm. With her eyes, Alex had traced the lines of muscle and bone like a puzzle on David's back. It had been a chilly night, but David's blanket was gathered into a ball, which he hugged with his arms and legs. His boots were still on. It was painful for Alex to see him like this, in the way that beauty is painful when words come short of description. She wanted to touch him, to run her hands along the curve of his back, tracing each vertebra, to feel the coarse texture of his hair, the sandy stubble on his chin. Alex wanted to fold herself into a ball like that blanket, and feel David's body wrapped around her like another skin. Instead, she'd eased the quilt off the bed, draped it over him, and left the cabin. Golden Boys didn't think about men in this way, or ponder dresses. Her mind is growing heavier with the things she shouldn't think about.

"Alex?" says Micah.

"Nice," Alex says, and pushes into the store past the tears springing to Lou Anne's eyes.

"Might have given her a word. A little compliment wouldn't hurt you." Micah closes the door behind him, cutting the sound of the organ grinder and human traffic. "You feeling all right?" He places a hand on Alex's shoulder. Alex shrugs it off.

"I'm feeling fine," she says, harsher than she intended, but Micah just grins. Over his shoulder, on the far shelf next to the calomel, a few bottles of Hasglow's Miracle Elixir stand ready to work their many wonders. Perhaps she should try some. Maybe it would order her thoughts, calm her stomach, help divorce the reassurance Emaline had given her this morning from the doubt that lingers. Perhaps she just needs some hair on her chest.

"Don't take it for granted, is all I'm saying. There's a shortage of beautiful girls around here – remember that. Now, I know you're shy . . . Untried. Am I right? Huh? Boy Bandit, my ass! Look at me, son."

Alex finds herself holding one of the ready-made dresses. She sets it down. Micah chuckles, takes off his eyepatch and

203

puts it on the counter, rubbing his empty socket with his knuckles. He scurries around the shop, organizing the merchandise. Mining equipment no longer litters the floor in dusty piles but is segregated into the new annex, while dry goods, foodstuffs, gilded silver brushes, skeins of fine cloth, and ready-made dresses dominate the main room. Alex edges toward the door, suddenly anxious to get to the mine, to get dirty, to sweat out her thoughts. Micah speaks up as she reaches for the door handle.

"Could ask Emaline," he says. He picks up the dress Alex discarded, runs his fingers down the soft cotton seams. "You'd have to pay for it, no doubt. But . . . she's a good woman, Emaline. Remember that. Deserves a little gratitude. I'm sure she wouldn't mind, you know, teaching you a thing or two. You might even enjoy it."

Alex opens the door and steps outside. "Think about it," Micah yells after her.

# 15

The organ grinder is silent and at first Alex thinks the Hasglow Elixir crowd is staring at her. But when she looks toward Bobcat Creek, she finds herself in the path of Harry and five other miners dragging a grinning Chinese man. The man's hair is braided in a long raveled queue that falls limp and muddy over his slender shoulders. A bruise glows purple on his right cheek and blood drips from either side of his mouth. The seat of his loose blue pants is red with river mud, yet his eyes are full of mirth, apparently unconcerned with his captivity or treatment. His grin grows wider when he sees Alex, and his eyes narrow to slits. He bends as if to sit and Harry jerks him up again.

"Where's Emaline?" Harry asks Alex.

Where she always is, Alex thinks, but says, "At the Victoria," and the men forge ahead, prodding the smiling Chinese man from behind with a shovel. Alex stumbles along after, overwhelmed and a bit embarrassed by her curiosity. She can feel the heavy presence of the crowd creeping close behind her.

"What did he–?" says Alex, before another voice, strained, heavily accented, interrupts.

"Wait! Wait, please, sir!" and another Chinese man, whose lucid eyes hold the desperation she expected from the captive, teases his way through the crowd. "Wait, sir," he pleads. His voice cracks as if English forces his voice a half step higher than is comfortable. With his narrow shoulders and quick, light steps he looks diminutive next to the lumps of flesh and muscle that sit like cats on the white men's shoulders.

"Chicken thief," Harry tells Alex, turning his back on the pleading man to pound on the door of the Victoria. "Emaline!"

"Innocent," the Chinese man insists. And then, tugging on Alex's sleeve: "He simple man. Please, sir." She pulls away, but in his eyes she can almost see the dammed-up lake of words that English will not allow him. She opens her hand and her feather flutters to the ground.

"Six chickens' necks broke. Sound innocent to you?" Harry directs his reply to Alex but glares at the Chinese man as he speaks. "Emaline!" he yells again just as Emaline opens the door. Her face is flushed from the heat of the kitchen. Damp hair swirls about her head and when she sees the smiling captive, her face hardens in a way Alex hasn't seen.

"What the hell is he smiling about?" Emaline says. She's no longer squinting, but gazing generally over the crowd, as if she has already determined the look of everyone present.

"Wait, please, sir –"

"Harry?" says Emaline.

Harry produces the body of a chicken, holding it high above his head by its broken neck like a trophy for all to see. In the doorway of the inn, Mr. James scribbles away in his notebook. The crowd bunches closer. Alex's stomach clenches like a fist. She can see Limpy's red head bobbing near the back of the pack and she knows David must be nearby. Across the road, Micah steps out of his store onto the porch where Mrs. Dourity, Erkstine, Waller and her sister Rose flank Lou Anne, two on each side. Lou Anne stretches to her tiptoes to see better and her mother tugs her down again.

"I Kwong Ting-lang. Kwong, sir." The man bows, but

Emaline's expression is unchanged. He motions to the captive. "Chang," he says, bowing again for his companion. "His head. He simple man, he –"

"He thinks he can just go and kill my chickens?"

Kwong scowls at his feet. His lips move, but he says nothing and Alex bites her lip, willing the man to stay silent, sensing that, guilty or not, nothing he says will make a difference, except to make things worse. The other one won't quit smiling at her.

"I'm talking to you, Wong," says Emaline.

On level ground Emaline would still stand a head taller than Kwong, and for a moment Alex is conflicted. For a moment she is the young woman who walked into town dressed as a boy. For a moment she too is standing helpless before a powerful stranger. At the same time she is the Golden Boy, Alex, who loves nothing more than to sweep in the stuffy heat of the kitchen, to watch Emaline move with the robust efficiency of a woman Alex has always known, or wanted to know. "Here is as good a place as any," Emaline had said, and Alex loved her for that.

And Alex knew how much Emaline loved those chickens and if they *did* kill them – Chang picks up the feather Alex dropped, rubs it past his nose, holds it out to her as if to give it back. If they killed those chickens, then they deserve whatever they get. She's trying hard to believe this.

"He sleep all night," Kwong says, and bats the feather from Chang's hand, says a sharp word to the man in his own language. "Chickens there in morning."

"And I'm a Chinaman's squaw!" says a voice from the crowd.

"Hang 'em!" yells another and Alex's head jerks up with Kwong's.

"We pay!" Kwong says, and turns to Harry. "Gold we pay."

"No. You'll leave," says Emaline.

"I pay," Kwong says again, this time to Emaline.

"Got that right," says Harry, and shoves Kwong to the ground.

The crowd buzzes, squirms, and resettles like flies on a carcass. Kwong stays down on his knees, his head bowed.

"You will leave!" says Emaline to Kwong. "All of you –" She motions downstream to the colony of clustered huts. "*All* of you."

Chang's smile vanishes. His mouth falls open. He edges between Harry and Kwong, holding his arms out like a barrier. He screams high and clear, shocking even the birds to silence. He runs out of breath, gulps air like a drowning man and screams again as six men on horseback appear on the edge of town.

Alex's mouth drops open. Breath comes in panting gasps. She should run, should have run weeks ago, or last night, or this morning. Now her legs fail her, each seems to have its own separate agenda. Her knees shake. Her hands lose feeling, but her head swings from Chang to the approaching posse, back to Chang again. The crowd, too, has frozen. Men swallow their sentences whole, and Chang's pure tenor howl echoes back and forth between the ravine walls.

Alex's mind closes and opens within itself to memory. A bouquet on the side table, white layered flowers interspersed with yellow buttercups and blue drooping lilies. The smell of fabric and rosemary and something bitter, metallic. Blood.

Alex lying flat. Pain clamping her stomach in a vice. Gran's finger pointing downward like an arrow to Alex's forehead. Warm, salty tears down Alex's cheeks.

"Just looking for death, just like your father and his father. Want to leave an old woman all alone to herself. All alone," says Gran, so soft. "You're not to see that boy again."

Emaline slaps Chang hard across the face. Chang takes a breath, the silence more deafening than the scream, and Alex finds movement. She backs up against the porch of the inn, ducks quickly around the corner. Tries to think. The road? Blocked. Hide.

Behind the Victoria, past the chopping block, the feather-strewn coop, its lone occupant ruffled and agitated, to the outhouse. The door slams shut and shards of light through the plank walls slice her into pieces. Her insides chew themselves. Flies bash their heads into the wall. Thick, warm moisture between her thighs. She unbuckles her trousers, edges her hand down. Her fingers return red.

Emaline's hand hovers in the air above Chang, but her attention is focused on the six riders approaching along Victor Lane. She steps back up on the porch, straining to see clearly. Behind her, Mr. James's furious scribbling is amplified and grating. Someone sneezes. A murmur passes through the crowd, rippling outward as the riders force their way through.

"Well," says Hudson, leaning against his saddle horn, his wide-brim hat masking half his face in shadow. "Where is he?"

Emaline doesn't answer. He isn't speaking to her. He turns around, repeats his question and John Thomas spurs his jittery piebald mare forward, looking comically self-important in his filthy tattered trousers and sweat-stained shirt.

"We come for him, Emaline," says John Thomas. Emaline tilts her head to the side, folds her arms in front of her. A smirk spreads across Hudson's face. "You might as well stand aside, 'cause . . . we've come for him."

"You come for who?" Emaline says.

"You know who," says Hudson. "Dangerous criminal in your midst. A fugitive. Show her, John."

John Thomas pulls a paper from his shirt and a sly grin reveals dimples beneath the thick blond beard. When she first met him, he'd barely had enough facial hair to cover a flea's ass, and Hudson . . . Hudson was a bear-faced mountain man, and no better behaved for his pampered upbringing. Seeing the two of them now reminds her of men who put on masks for follies – except she finds neither one funny.

"Told you to get rid of him, told you nothing good would come," says Hudson, and he lowers his voice, making the crowd lean in to hear. "I told you I'd give you everything –"

"Dangerous?" she says, shaking her head, acknowledging only what she chooses. She hadn't wanted the everything Hudson had offered. She'd never loved him. He was lonely, and he was rich, and she was only doing her job. Yet he had been so sure of her answer. So sure that he went down on his knees in that crowded Sacramento saloon. He'd humiliated himself. She simply said no. And when he didn't accept that, Jed had told him no with his fists.

"Chicken thieves is what I got," she says.

Harry laughs, slaps Chang's face, leaving red marks on his cheeks and, strangely, another smile on Chang's face. The horses, always attuned to the changing moods of men, throw their heads and jingle their bridles. Harry slaps Chang again, harder, before Kwong rises up to grab Harry's hand with a strength that seems to surprise them both.

"Stop," Kwong says.

A pick handle to his stomach. A fist to his face. Kwong slumps to knees, gasping for air and Emaline's attention strays for a moment to the anguished man at her feet, his queue circling his neck like a noose.

Ridiculous to pity, she thinks, but she does pity. "Enough, Harry," she says, and Kwong slumps to the ground. The smiling one snarls at no one in particular then and bends to drape himself over Kwong and pat him stiffly on the head.

"Not talking chicken thieves," says Hudson, and sits back in his saddle, one arm crossed lazily over the other, an amused twitch teasing his lips. Never did learn a thing, did he? thinks Emaline. Still reckons he's God's gift to California. And John Thomas, holding that paper in front of him as if he expects me to fetch. Shit. Standing on the porch, she remains taller than the men on horseback. On the porch she will stay.

"Show the lady," says Hudson, his voice greasy with condescension, and John Thomas dismounts, becoming suddenly very small. His horse tosses its head, readjusts the bit in its mouth and bares its teeth as though laughing. The tall fellow riding next to Hudson does laugh, looks quite amused as he plays with the clasp of his gun holster.

Emaline ignores this, focuses all her attention down at John Thomas, scrutinizing him with squinted eyes until she makes him the size of a beetle she can step on. Presumptuous little shit, that silly look of righteous indignation on his face, squaring his shoulders, preening and strutting like a goddamned banty rooster. She suspected that leaving town hadn't been his idea this time, but she hadn't expected him to return with company, with Jackson Hudson. Before he climbs the second step, Emaline reaches down, rips the paper from his hands and holds it to her nose to read.

Emaline lets the paper fall, does an about-face and disappears into the Victoria. John Thomas's lips curl into something between a grin and a snarl. He steps on to the porch. He clears his throat. He holds the flier up like a prize, but Hudson speaks first.

"Looking for a fugitive slave, Jedediah Haversmith. Property of Mr. James Haversmith, deceased, and now the lawful inheritance of his brother, Amos Haversmith," he says officiously. The crowd quiets its murmuring and swivels its many heads, searching for a Jedediah.

"He's there, back there!" John Thomas shouts and points to the back of the crowd where Limpy looks to David and David looks to Jed. One by one, the heads of the crowd turn to see Jed as though for the first time. A black man. A slave. Property. Jed holds his shoulders back, his head high, and folds one arm over the other. Even now, dignity comes naturally. Limpy places his big body in front of him.

"Now wait a minute . . ." he says, just as Emaline reemerges from the Victoria, her shotgun cocked, ready and trained at John Thomas's skull. The crowd becomes one eye, focused on Emaline.

"Emaline," says Jed, edging forward, placing a hand on Limpy's shoulder as he goes.

"Stay put!" she commands without looking at him, and steps closer to John Thomas. The gun barrel kisses his ear. She's seen men die, slowly, battling their bodies for each moment of life, and fast, with a bullet to the brain. But she's never killed a man. John Thomas whimpers, like a dog, she thinks, hoping he'll continue. She could shoot a dog.

Hudson clears his throat and holds up his hand to silence the pistols behind him. He adopts a parental look of stern patience. "May I remind you –"

"No, you may not," says Emaline, raising her voice above him as he finishes his sentence.

"– that harboring a fugitive slave is a federal offense."

"Emaline," says Jed again, parting the crowd. "'S all right."

"I will decide when it's all right!" says Emaline, then bends to whisper in John Thomas's ear: "Now you just get back on that horse, turn and ride on out of here, and I may just forget all about this."

She shoves him down the porch and he stumbles over Chang, landing hard on his backside. Chang giggles, then howls, his teeth gleaming in the sunlight. John Thomas thrusts himself to his feet, and kicks Chang in the mouth. The grinning man falls unconscious to the ground, so John Thomas gives Kwong a few solid kicks in the stomach.

"Enough," says Emaline, and John Thomas straightens, out of breath and red in the face. Emaline levels her gun at Hudson; she's glad her eyes are too poor to see down the gun barrels pointing back at her. He sits up straight in his saddle, his hand on his holster. If it had been her, she'd already have drawn.

"No fugitives round here," says Emaline. But Jed has made his way through the crowd and steps up on the porch next to her, followed by Limpy and David. Harry joins them, wiping Chang's blood on his trousers. Micah and Fred come forward, leaving one of the regulars missing, but she's of no mind to count. She bites the tip of her tongue, glances at the men behind her, feeling, at this moment, neither gratitude nor discord. Her focus returns to Hudson. The crowd takes a collective step back.

"And you ain't no lawman. Am I right? Ah! Hands up," she says.

The men behind Hudson are young, boys almost, surely with no desire to shoot a woman if their mothers taught them anything, if California hadn't already unlearned it for them. "Y'all may get me, but I'll get him first," she says. "Tell 'em, Hudson."

Hudson purses his lips, his confidence failing. He gives a backward glance and a nod. The guns lower and Hudson chuckles with unconvincing mirth. "Now . . ."

"Now you're leaving," says Emaline. "Take them –" she motions with her head to Chang and Kwong, "or take nobody. Go on."

Hudson clears his throat, looks scornfully at the two Chinese men, then back down the barrel of Emaline's shotgun. He yanks the reins of his horse, motions the posse to back-track the way they had come.

"Wait!" says John Thomas, limping behind. His mare is already halfway out of town with the others. "The money! You promised me. You can't just . . ." He turns back to Emaline. "Emaline, I –"

Emaline fires one shot into the air. John Thomas leaps and hobbles after the retreating horsemen.

*    *    *

"They'll be back. They'll be back and they won't just be looking for me next time," says Jed. Emaline is hefting the stew pot, straining under the weight.

"Stop a minute. Stop a minute, let me talk," says Jed.

She turns to face him, but he remains in the doorway as though determined to maintain a distance. His features are a dark blur, but she has learned to read his expression from the tone of his voice. She wants to go to him, to put her hand on his lips, as though stopping the words would erase the problem. As though by refusing to think, by pushing that pulsing fear down, down, and down again, she could eliminate it entirely. As though it is words that make fear real.

She thunks the pot on the stove, pulls a forgotten loaf of blackened bread from the oven, slams it upon the counter. Her fingers are streaked charcoal black. She wipes them on her apron.

"You heard him," says Jed. "Harboring a fugitive slave is a federal offense."

"I'm not harboring anyone, am I? Not when you just come and offer yourself up. Didn't bring you up here just for them to take you."

"I'm not theirs to take."

"Damn right!"

"Yours neither."

Emaline places both of her hands on the counter. Her head falls forward.

"Emaline," says Jed, lowering his voice, "you gonna get yourself in trouble."

"Weren't real concerned with that when I got you out of Sacramento, were you?"

"That was before ..." Jed says.

"Before what?"

"Before ..." he says again, and looks away. Emaline thumps her fingers on the charred loaf of bread, hard as fired clay, and waits for him to speak. Instead, he moves behind her.

Pushes her hair aside and kisses the softness of her neck. He breathes in deeply, wraps his arms around her waist and presses himself into her.

"I . . ." he begins, massaging her belly, "I have to be a man." Emaline stiffens.

"A man? A dead man?" She picks up the burned loaf and places it in his hands. Jed looks bewildered at the charcoal separating the two of them, tosses it back and forth between burning fingers. Emaline rushes out the back door.

With a fistful of oak leaves, Alex sits scrubbing bloody underwear. The outhouse is alive with flies, bouncing themselves off the walls, basking in the warm nitric fumes. Spiderwebs span corners like suspension bridges spotted with decomposing insects. The sour stench of sewage overpowers the odor of menstrual blood and Alex pushes the gold pouch aside to rest like a growth on her hip as she works. The thin walls trap heat like an oven, and on these walls shadows take shapes.

Gran's face, dry, cracked and flaking like butter pastry. Gran's nose, as straight and severe as her words. A half-formed demon the size of a newborn kitten, with large unseeing eyes and shriveled appendages, dead on a towel before Alex. Proof of sin, of lechery, Gran said. "You're not to see that boy again." That boy whose lips never whispered the word *sin* when they lay together behind the rabbit hutch. That boy who said he'd love her if she swore never to tell, who left her in Gran's unforgiving home, waiting for the old woman to die. His face fades into that of a San Francisco businessman, his heavy cheeks flushed with liquor, leaving his mark in bruises on Alex's skin. This man gave a name to Gran's unvoiced accusations. "Whore," Minford called her, "barren whore," and hit her. Her womb remained dry while she bled from her nose. Her womb remained dry while she bled from her mouth. Alex grew tired of bleeding.

She clamps her arms round her stomach, squeezes as if she could somehow will both the memories and the blood back inside. A gunshot sounds, crackling off the ravine and down her spine.

Alex scrubs harder and faster, even after ripping a hole through the fabric. She's become too comfortable in this place, too accustomed to thinking of herself in terms of *he*. *He* didn't need to run. *He* hadn't lost his baby. *He* hadn't killed anyone, was far too timid, too innocent. *He* was lucky, a Golden Boy, *the* Golden Boy, Alex.

Elbows on knees, head in hands, Alexandra sits.

A moment, or a minute, or twenty minutes later, the outhouse door opens and cool air rushes to dry the sweat on her face. She finds Emaline standing in the doorway with tears welling like foreign bodies in her eyes. Emaline's gaze falls from the nugget dangling in the pouch on Alex's hip to the dark hair between her legs, to the bloody underwear Alex struggles to pull back up. Emaline opens her mouth to speak, surprises them both when no words come. Alex tries to escape and Emaline grabs her. Alex can feel the sinew and bone of Emaline's fingers making bloodless indentions on her upper arm. She can feel Emaline's unsteady breath on the back of her neck. The only sounds, beyond the usual commotion of Victor Lane, are avian. Alex wants to hear Emaline say something, to say, "Could use you in the kitchen." But Emaline lets go and Alex jolts forward, corners the Victoria Inn and disappears without looking back.

# 16

Preacher John is waiting inside the Victoria when Emaline bursts through the door.

"Alex," she says, out of breath. "Have you seen Alex?" She runs her hand over her hair, smoothing lumpy curls.

Preacher John removes his hat, scrunches the brim, swallows.

"Alex, Preacher – have you seen Alex?"

Preacher clears his throat and lowers his head. "Emaline, I came here 'cause I . . . well, I wanted to ask . . ." Emaline stares at him open mouthed. His beard has been trimmed, his face washed, the holes in his trousers mended. He wears a new starched flannel, pressed at the seams and smelling like the dry goods section of Micah's store. Most striking to Emaline, however, is the sight of his brown eyes showing clear and sober beneath his brows.

"What I wanted to say was, I know them Chinamen didn't steal no chickens."

Emaline's mouth pops closed. She forgets, for a moment, what or who she is looking for.

"You know that, do you?"

"And I don't think it's right or Christian of you to blame someone you know to be innocent. Do unto others, you know," he says, producing his decaying Bible from the pocket of his pants.

"You don't, huh?"

He holds the Bible under her nose. The pages are yellowed, smelling of tobacco, stale whiskey, and faintly of wildflowers. Not at all unpleasant, if the words and the scent weren't being shoved in her face like he was force-feeding a toddler. She pushes the Bible away from her and Preacher John clutches it to his chest.

"No, and I think that . . . well, Rose says . . ."

"Rose?" Emaline asks. "Mrs. Waller's Rose? What in high heaven are you doing talking with Mrs. Waller's Rose?" – who, as far as Emaline is concerned, is but a fixture on her sister's skirts, but she doesn't say this.

"Yes, Rose says she heard Micah talking, and Rose says those Chinamen never stole any of your chickens. Rose says you told Micah to –"

"Preacher!" He sucks in his breath, doesn't meet her eyes. "None of *Rose's* business, is it? No? Not yours, neither." An image of Rose passes before Emaline. A severe, small-busted woman with a meager mouth and a face devoid of expression. *Rose says?* She couldn't care less what Rose says. Emaline waves her hand in the direction of the bar. "Go. Go get yourself a drink." A thump against the ceiling brings her back to the task at hand. She hurries toward the stairs.

"Rose don't let me drink no more. Rose says the devil's in it, and Rose won't have any man the devil already owns, and them two Chinamen already left town, but Rose wanted me to tell you that them Chinamen didn't kill those chickens."

The words come out in a flourish and, when Emaline turns, Preacher looks relieved to be rid of them. "Wanted me to give you this –" he says, holding out a small scrap of newsprint like the ones she and Lou Anne had shredded that morning. He looks toward the bar, the shiny oak tabletop, the crystal-glass bottles bending the light, casting rainbow and amber

218

refractions on the far wall. Emaline marches back to him, arms swinging, eyes set. He retreats a step, but does nothing when she swipes the paper from his hands, rips it into four pieces, and stomps them into the floor with such force that the tumblers rattle on their shelves.

"Alex is up there," Preacher John says softly, and points to the ceiling. Emaline gives a "humph," turns and springs up the steps two at a time.

In the upstairs hall, hand over her heart, catching her breath, she starts to knock on Alex's door; stops. She strides to her own room, rummages in her closet and strides back. She knocks on the door. No answer. She knocks again and swings the door open, nearly hitting Alex, who stands with her pack on her back, ready to leave.

"Wait," says Emaline, and invites herself in. "Lordy!" She crosses the room to sit her hefty self upon the stool, leaving the doorway unbarred. "This day 'bout killed me already, and it's an hour 'fore supper." She squints in the light of the newly cut window, and Alex backs into the shadow.

"I brought you these," says Emaline, producing a bundle of torn rags from her pocket.

Alex's eyes sting, but don't tear. Before her, Emaline sits, knees apart, a line of sweat making a track down her forehead. Her hair is a frazzled disarray with wild wisps curling in a halo about her head, and the fringe on her upper lip is damp from her tongue. The rags hang limp from her outstretched hand.

She looks about her as if she were simply taking inventory of the washstand and basin, the window, the gilded mirror yet to be hung on the wall. For a moment neither woman moves, and neither speaks and to Alex both the stillness and the silence are pregnant. She edges forward into the light, feeling like a stray accepting a piece of meat. She reaches out, takes the rags from Emaline, who holds on only for a moment, then lets go. Emaline sits back on the stool, chewing on her upper lip as if holding back words or searching for them. If Emaline had tried to prevent her from leaving, Alex might have burst through that door biting and snarling like a stray. But the doorway remains open. She can feel the woman's myopic eyes strain over her body like a thousand fingers, peeling away her clothing layer by layer to reveal thin muscular arms, narrow hips, and small, fist-sized breasts. If this body were the only thing Alex was hiding, she might not shift under this gaze, might not hug her arms over her chest even as Emaline's eyes range lower to her trousers and the bulge of the nugget still hidden beneath. Alex turns away to face the window. The light is warm upon her face, the noise of traffic outside somehow subdued, almost lazy. She'd prefer the loud chaos of her imagined city, a place to get lost in, to go unnoticed, but this thought, too, brings a pang of sadness. She stuffs the rags in her pack and hefts the pack to her back. Emaline still says nothing. Alex takes a small step toward the door.

"Wait," Emaline says, rising from the stool.

"I'll go. I'm sorry," says Alex, but doesn't take that next step. She wishes she could still feel revulsion for this woman, the fear of that first day. But she is conscious only of gratitude, and gratitude is a sentiment that begs expression.

"We'll talk, tonight," says Emaline. "Mr. James is still here, just waiting for more stories to write. No need to act suspicious. And a whole pack of vigilantes just left, not an hour ago. Looking for Jed. It's a long story, but they didn't get him."

Emaline smiles and Alex remembers the gunshot echoing off the ravine and back through the thin walls of the outhouse.

"Talk to me. Tonight. Bring gold. The boys won't know the difference, will they? We'll figure something out. All right?"

Emaline's voice is pleading, surprising Alex. She'd expected . . . She doesn't know what she'd expected, but uncovered secrets have consequences. She doesn't want to leave, not without smelling fresh-cut lumber from the new sawmill, not without watching the town grow and the mine prosper, since the one was surely dependent on the other. She doesn't want to leave Limpy, or Micah, or David. She doesn't want to leave Emaline.

"Not safe out there for a woman alone, or a boy. It's not! You were lucky, and now you gotta be smart." Emaline's hands rest on her hips, the position of authority with which Alex is comfortable. Emaline wants her to stay, at least for the night, and Emaline is in control.

"Okay, then," says Emaline, nodding. She strides for the door and closes it behind her, ending the conversation. Alex eases her pack to the foot of the bed.

"Thank you," she whispers, and slumps to the floor, closes her eyes and leans her head back against the mattress.

David walks toward the Victoria wanting only to sink into the comfort of frivolous conversations and a game of low-stakes five-card stud. The day has made him weary of controversy. He wants to forget about men with guns and Chinese chicken thieves, to forget about everything but work and rum; although lately even work holds little comfort for him. A wasted day, he thinks and stares out into the dark void of an overcast night. He can see the faint outlines of bats diving for insects, their beating wings like whispered sentences. Crickets warm their bowstrings, but their song is muffled in the muggy night and David too feels muffled.

The returns have been low the past few weeks, as if all the gold in the mine had been floating in the topsoil. The hard rock has yielded little but granite, hardly worth the work, and he's beginning to think the vein they're looking for, the vein that produced Alex's nugget, is lost further up the mountain among the brambles and the poison oak, and this too makes him weary. Weary of hope and weary of doubt, and as he climbs the steps of the Victoria and edges his way to the bar, the bodies around him remind him of mounds of discarded slag cast away to the river's edge, to the edge of the world, to California.

Jed slides him a whiskey and leans his elbows on the countertop. Wine-colored veins course the whites of Jed's eyes and his teeth grind beneath his lips. David can think of nothing reassuring to say, and so says nothing. He decides against cards, leaves Harry and Fred to their arguments and Limpy to his liquor, and does his best to ignore Alex at the other end of the bar. He turns to watch men's lips move, but only snippets of the conversation from the table in front of him gain purchase.

"You need . . . The only thing we need . . . Union's no good to anybody cut in half. North and South, we need each other. It's like King Solomon and the baby . . . Listen to you quoting the Bible . . . Gentlemen, please . . ."

In the corner, Klein mans his accordion; Mexican Jack and his guitar give the tune rhythm. Music and voices throb through layers of tobacco smoke, and David's attention wanders back to Alex. The boy has locked his feet around the legs of the stool as if holding himself in place. His eyes flit about the room and meet David's. David looks away. Boy Bandit! Absurd. But hadn't he seen the boy skirt the edge of the inn when the posse showed up? Only guilt could explain his absence when Emaline needed him. A man protects those he loves. David will tell the boy. A man defends what he cares for, defends his home, he'll say, even as the word conjures the smell of his mother's pasties, the sound of the sea. He'll take the boy aside, confront him with this Boy Bandit nonsense. He peeks back to find Alex adjusting himself, and David shifts uncomfortably on his stool. Not now. Talk to him later. After a few more drinks.

"Jed." He holds up his cup, swivels back to the bar. But Jed is swiping the counter like he means to shine the wood stain away. He gestures silently to the knot of men at the King Solomon table.

". . . sooner pray to the Pope," slurs one of the men, and David listens closer.

"All that commotion today? For nothing, you ask me. I know Hudson. A jackass, but an honest one, and not the type to be turned away, not when there's reward money involved. He'll be back, by God. More power to him."

"I'd like to know how that Negro's master up and died so suddenly. Haversmith, was it? Knew a Haversmit 'cross the county in Louisiana. Didn't have a brother, though."

"A good hanging would solve the problem real fast."

They speak as though Jed weren't right there, only a table-length away and hearing every word. Jed is one of the few people in Motherlode in whose presence David feels completely comfortable. Friendly is the word, and as the conversation penetrates his brain, his hackles rise. He stands to say something and Jed's hand catches him softly on the shoulder. "Don't," says Jed. "Won't help."

"Now hold on!" one of the men insists. "Can't just go killing Negroes like you're killing cattle."

"He's right. No, you're right. Can't eat Negroes."

"That is the t-tru—" The whole room hushes silent.

Jed's hand falls from David's shoulder. David turns to follow his gaze.

Emaline stands atop the staircase. She's wearing a dress he's never seen with a soft lavender hue that tinges her skin golden-tan. Beneath the fabric, her body speaks in tongues, her stomach folding upon itself, meeting her ample hips in a whisper of skin against skin, and every man in the room knows that there is no corset accentuating those breasts. Her hair curls in ringlets, framing her face, enlarging her eyes, enhancing the glow of her cheeks. The lamplight envelops her, painting a penumbra on the wall which moves above her, around her, with her, down the steps and into the saloon. A whiskey glass drops. David releases a breath in time to three men to his right. The accordion suffocates with a wail, and every hand of cards is revealed faceup, should anyone care to look.

It's Limpy who breaks the spell.

"I must say, Miss Emaline," he says, "I cannot recall you ever looking lovelier." Cards are pulled back, protected from eyes that have yet to wander from Emaline, and the accordion breathes new life. "I got me a bag of gold dust that's just begging to see what improvements you've made in that room of yours."

"Now, Limpy!" says Micah, joining the duo on the other side. "Tuesday is my night, and I'm still richer'n you, for all your digging."

David follows the direction of Emaline's stare to Alex and can barely endure sitting. He stands, adjusts himself under the counter and downs his drink.

"Richer, hell! We just getting to the gold, ain't we, Dave!" Limpy yells. But David is busy saying the Lord's Prayer beneath his breath. He unclasps the top two buttons of his flannel. Shameful visions move dreamlike before his eyes. Memories of Alex's weight in his arms; of Emaline, revealed in the shadows of her upstairs room; Alex grasping, pressing himself against David's chest; Emaline smiling, naked; Alex enfolded in David's quilt, his small face gleaming, pale, his lips parted for breath.

"Besides," continues Limpy, twining his elbow with Emaline's, "two eyes're better than one in beholding beauty."

"Oh now, let's not start with –"

"Boys," says Emaline. She raises both hands in the air and sheds both men with the gesture. "I am promised to another."

She moves slowly through the crowd, splitting conversations, halting card games. She looks men in the eye as though considering possibilities, then moves on. She runs a finger down Mr. James's cheek, and his mouth falls open.

She nears David. He trembles. He watches the careful

224

placement of her feet – around table legs, over whiskey glasses – afraid to make eye contact. On this night he will go with her up those stairs. Tonight, he will not resist. He presses himself into the counter. Her hand brushes against the grain of his stubble and shivers squiggle to his toes. He leans close. Her breath teases his neck; her lips smack his and then – are gone?

His eyes blink open. She is moving away from him, continuing down the bar. She is stopping a foot from Alex and offering her hand. And Alex, Alex is laughing, with her or at her, with joy or stress, David can't tell. Alex takes her hand. The little runt takes her hand and allows her to lead him up the stairs.

New images: Emaline and Alex. Oh Lord. The Lord is my shepherd, I shall not want . . . Alex risking his soul? Damn Emaline for tempting him. For tempting them all. Only he, only David has been strong enough to resist. He downs another drink.

"Well, I'll be goddamned!" yells Limpy. "Attaboy, son! Be a man by morning! Round on me!" He changes his mind. "Round on Alex."

All serious talk is banished in favor of speculation. Memories circle the room, catching men like a sneeze or a yawn.

"I remember the time . . ."

"What you bet he cain't . . ."

"Care to put money on that?"

"She weren't pretty, I won't lie to you, but this girl, oh lordy, *this girl* . . ."

Sweat drips from David's forehead into his whiskey. His breath comes fast and his erection remains resilient. A heavy hand slams his shoulder. Limpy's foul breath descends.

"Got money on the boy. You in?"

David wrenches himself away and limps out into the humid night.

\* \* \*

225

"Good Lord!" says Emaline, and closes the bedroom door with her rump. "Didn't think I was going to make it up them stairs. 'Bout peed my pants! You see David's face? You the envy of every man in that saloon believe you me. Better give 'em a good story tomorrow – or no! Don't tell them a damn thing. Just smile real big and embarrassed like, just like that. Let 'em use their imaginations. A man's imagination is a woman's strongest ally, if you know how to use it. Hell, sit down, sit down. Don't looks so damn nervous. Didn't ask you up here to bite yah."

Alex sits. For all the renovations that have been done to the rest of the Victoria, Emaline's room has remained virtually untouched. The walls are bare. A modest mirror, rimmed with tarnished silver, reflects a porcelain washbasin sitting atop a narrow dressing table. She has allowed herself the luxury of a pulled-yarn throw rug of subdued autumn golds and browns like her curtains. They suit her coloring, but it's a contrast to the vivid reds decorating the rest of the inn. Emaline crosses the room. She unbuttons the lavender dress, pulls it up over her head, and wears nothing but her chemise. Alex turns away. Emaline smiles.

"What's this?" she asks. "Got the same parts. Am I right?"

Alex looks from her own chest to Emaline's, comparing the shape of their bodies, but finds as few similarities as a pumpkin and a pine pole. Emaline is right, of course. They do have the same parts, as she put it. No amount of clothing could change that. But the sight of skin seems to demand an open honesty Alex isn't sure she's ready for. She still doesn't know if the story she is about to tell will be the truth, or another fabrication, a new disguise that she will embrace as her own true identity. She sits on her hands, ignores the ache in her stomach, and anticipates Emaline's questions.

"I was thirty years old when I left Missouri," Emaline says, pulling on her nightdress and taking a seat on the chair by the dressing table. "Two weeks married, happy as a cow to pasture. It was foolish, leaving so late in the spring like we did, but Harold was itching to get to San Francisco, and he was older and I trusted him. So I packed up everything I thought I couldn't do without, left my mamma, and Missouri, and set off for California."

As she talks, Emaline releases her hair from its bonds and long amber strands fall, one after another, around her shoulders, framing her head in the lamplight. She pauses a moment, looking at herself in the mirror as though a stranger stares back, then continues, her voice lower now, shifting from an even conversational rhythm to the deep throaty flush of nostalgia.

"From the first there was trouble," she says, nodding in agreement with her image. "Two oxen pulled up lame in that first week. One had to be put down right then. And the wagon train we were traveling with was already conflicted when a Mormon man offered to wed his wife's sister after her husband took ill and died with the cholera. I got myself all agitated over that, swearing crimes against God, but when I think back, I reckon he done it as much out of kindness as anything. Ended up splitting into two parties, one traveling directly behind in plain sight of the other, coming together during Indian scares. Silly."

Emaline stretches her feet in front of her. Years peel from her face, and weight melts from her arms until she sits before Alex a younger, trimmer, naïve stranger.

"Then Harold got sick, coughing with such a rattle in the lungs, worst I'd ever heard. Insisted that we keep going, and there really wasn't much else to do. By this time we'd already passed Pikes Peak, and home was as far away as California. Truth be told, I didn't want to go back. Never worked so hard in my life from sunset to sundown, but the country was so big and beautiful. Words never do them natural beauties justice, leastways not my words, or Harold's, bless him. Bet

227

them English poets couldn't even say it right. Not tame enough for words. Not small enough. Level prairie as far as you could see in any direction for weeks, and the Rockies rising like Adam's curse, jagged and white capped. Like climbing to meet the clouds.

"It was in the Rockies that Harold died. The high plateau took his breath right away and he never got it back. Buried him next to the bodies of the four remaining oxen, just short of the Continental Divide. Grass was all eaten up by other wagons traveling early in the year like the guides tell you. Barely enough even then to feed the horses, and all them things I couldn't do without ended up stacked around Harold's grave like he was setting up home. A maple table that was my nana's. My mamma's porcelain dishes. I only kept the clothes on my back, and the little bit of money we had left. I cried then."

But her voice inflects only residual emotion, as though she is telling of someone else's loss. It's Alex's eyes that sting. A lump of indigestible emotion forms in her throat. She tries to focus on Emaline's story, but words are growing in her stomach, boiling up from the ache in her abdomen, from the tension just behind her temple. She feels Emaline's eyes settle upon her, so she looks at the floor. Emaline continues, growing into herself with every word. Her face filling out, her arms and hands gaining weight and muscle.

"Was afraid for myself – a woman alone, you know. 'Course you know. So I went on with that Mormon man and his wives. Isaiah was his name. Never agreed to the marriage part of it, mind you. Might have, if he'd convinced me to stay in Utah with him. But freedom had a hold on me, so I traveled on, doing the cooking and washing for a couple of cousins. North Carolina boys, one dark headed and coarse as Cane, and the other as blond and delicate as Abel. Was with them I discovered my talent for pleasing men.

"Now, I know what you think," Emaline says, her tone

sharp. Her eyebrows make a straight line across her brow, but she's too consumed with her own story to notice the heaviness of Alex's breath, or the muddy line of sweat Alex swipes away with the back of her hand.

"But it wasn't about lust or greed – both deadly sins, I understand. I gave 'em comfort, made 'em feel big again on a trail that made everyone feel so small. I made 'em feel important in a place where man was just another trifle on God's plate. And by the time I got to San Francisco, I was quite capable of taking care of myself. Offered a service much needed in a place starved for women.

"A service," Emaline says again, and opens the bottom drawer of her dresser. She pulls out two glasses and a bottle of New England rum. She offers some to Alex, who drinks it down in one gulp, holds out her glass for more and swallows that. The liquor burns a track through Alex's sinuses, coming to rest at a point just at the base of her neck. Emaline crosses her arms in front of her as if waiting for a response. Alex sets her glass on the floor by her feet. Her heartbeat thumps in her temple.

"Jed didn't kill nobody. No, dysentery got Haversmith, Haversmit, whatever his name was, in San Francisco, where I met Jed. Jed come into the Imperial with ol' Haversmith and after Haversmith passed out, Jed and I . . . well, we got acquainted."

Alex's insides begin to swell, cresting and breaking. Her throat is dry, her eyes damp as the liquor, loosens unspoken memories.

"Jed came with me to Sacramento, and that's where they came looking for him. Claimed he was a fugitive under the Fugitive Slave Act. Claimed he was property of some long-lost Haversmith brother gonna take him back to Alabama. Woulda never found him if Jackson Hudson hadn't gotten it into his head to marry me. That's when Jed and me came to Motherlode, though it weren't nothing but a valley with a

229

creek running through. Came to live in peace and a town sprung up around us.

"I love him," she says, looking just past Alex now. "I ain't never told nobody. Never told my mamma when she was still alive in Missouri, or my Aunt Flo. Thinks I'm running a goddamned orphanage out here," she chortles, then becomes serious. "I never told him. But I love him."

Emaline downs her rum, pulls a strand of hair from her mouth. But Alex is elsewhere, a room in her head kept dark these many weeks, a room where dead things locked away release waves of sickness. Her backbone bends upon itself and her legs lock together beneath the chair, anchoring her to something solid, as the floor rolls in waves around her.

"Terrible things . . ." she says, bringing her knees up to her chin now, closing up.

"Now, it weren't all that bad –" Emaline starts. "What things? Alex?" She places her hand on Alex's shoulder and Alex, feeling the touch through every organ, springs away, tipping the chair with a crash.

"I have to leave," Alex says and her mind flashes moving pictures: the white of an eye, a purple mound of bloody flesh, the glint of a knife, and closing her eyes does not bring darkness. She backs away toward the door. "I have to go."

"What things?" Emaline repeats. Alex grips the door handle. "Alex!"

She sees Emaline through distorting tears that refuse to fall. Emaline's face fractured like a reflection in a broken mirror, the color of her nightdress blurred and indistinct. Alex is speaking to an aberration, a ghost or an angel, and the words come of their own accord, casting away the protective shell of silence that served her for so long.

"It hurt so much!" she says, hissing the words at first. "Like my insides were turning out, and Gran could barely look at me, wouldn't hold my hand, and Peter never came. After he said all those beautiful things, he never came, and

I was glad it was dead 'cause Peter wouldn't marry me, and Gran didn't want me, and I held it, bloody and blue against my chest. I held it, but I didn't want it. Gran didn't say the word, like *he* did later, but that's what she meant, what her eyes said, and her frown. *Whore.* 'For out the heart come evil thoughts, murders, adulteries, fornications.' Murders, out the heart, she said, and put her hand on my stomach, pressing so hard, squeezed till all my blood was gone. My cycles, gone. She said I was barren, said it was better that way. 'Out of the heart comes evil inclinations, natural and evil.' And I always thought natural was good, was God.

"When she died, I didn't cry. I wouldn't – and I was so proud of myself."

"Alex, sit down."

Alex remains standing, tipping and swaying with the room.

"I put chrysanthemums on her grave 'cause I hate the smell of them. Can you smell them?" Alex thrusts her nose into the scent of fermenting flowers. "I pulled them up, roots and all, from around the porch, and piled them high on the tomb-stone, and they let me because she was the only thing I had left in the world, they said. I heard them, I overheard, and I never felt so relieved. Like a brand-new person.

"She was still there," Alex whispers. "Still floating in the walls, in the linen, squeezing. So I left for a new place where Gran couldn't find me, couldn't stop my cycle. I told the temperance lady who came round that I was a maid and fit for a bride, and she set me on a coach, set me off for California. California – I just liked the sound of it. California."

The waves dip and crash, and Alex sits down hard on the chair, grips the legs with her ankles, holds on to the seat. Emaline hovers above her.

"She followed me. Her face in every frown I saw, in *his* frown. But I was going to be a bride: Mrs. Hanson Minford. The old name, Gran's name, Thompson, gone. White dress, flowers. California flowers. Bright orange poppies instead of

231

red. And violets. No chrysanthemums. But I still didn't bleed, so he called me a whore, said he'd make me bleed, and when he hit me with his fists I could hear Gran laughing in that silent breathy way. Her hand on my stomach, pressing, pressing . . . I think I wanted to die, but he only hit so hard, you know. I tried to run away, to escape, but he kept the key. I had no choice. I had to stop her laughing. Do you understand that I had no choice? And I never cut off his fingers or his, his . . ." Emaline nods. "And I left him there. Took his money and left him there, and I thought that would be it. They'd look for Alexandra, but they'd never find Alex, and Gran would be gone."

The room is rocking gently now, then calms altogether. "I could still hear her at first, at night. But not for a while now, a long time, months. Gran is silent and I'm bleeding again. Do you understand that I had to stop her? I should be happy. I *was* happy. Alex was happy, I think. Golden Boy, Alex. Now, I don't know. I don't know . . ."

Her voice fades. Her eyes droop. Never so tired. The weight of her shoulders pulls her down and there is nothing but the accordion playing a wordless jig downstairs, the scrape of crickets calling, the humid air peeling sweat from her temple, her heartbeat like retreating footsteps in her ears. She can tell nothing from Emaline's expression; the tip of her tongue between her teeth, her eyes cast on the floor. Alex has said too much, but she couldn't stop. The truth, framed by words, seemed so short, like a storybook tale with witches and evil husbands and young, foolish girls.

"Emaline?" says Alex.

Emaline's lips purse. Her eyes narrow. She puts her hands on her knees and stands, retrieves her dress from where she had laid it on the bed, leaving Alex open, bloody.

"Did you like my dress?" she asks. Alex balks. "Lavender suits me, I think. You'd need a brighter color for dark eyes."

Alex opens her mouth but no words come.

"I bleed. Every month I bleed," says Emaline. "Barren is such an ugly word, don't you think?" She nods her head in agreement with herself. "The thing about dresses is, dresses can be changed, torn up, used for rags. Just put a new one on. Put on trousers, if you like. But people, people don't change like clothing. Not that easy. Mostly, we just discover parts of us we never knew we had, maybe never knew we needed, maybe never wanted. People don't change at all. We just unfold parts of ourselves while we fold other parts away, hide 'em. I imagine you haven't quite figured out what needs folding and what needs airing out. Would you do it again?"

"Would I . . . ?"

"Would you kill him again?"

"I'm not sad he's dead. I didn't want to kill him . . ." But this is not the answer to the question asked. "Yes. I'd do it again."

Emaline nods her approval. Downstairs, a sudden silence erupts into laughter. Limpy's deep guttural chuckle carries up the stairs and down the hall.

"What you gonna do?" Emaline asks finally.

"Leave."

"Where to?"

"I don't know. North."

Emaline sits and rests her elbows on her knees. Her lips purse in thought.

"You gonna need a plan," she says. "You been lucky, like I said. Go rushing off, and you'll go rushing into trouble, more than you're in now. So far, no one knows nothing. But can't count on that lasting. Mr. James is convinced you're this Boy Bandit – but you leave Mr. James to me. No reason you shouldn't just stick, for a while, at least. Like you say, they ain't looking for Alex, and as far as everyone's concerned, that's just who you are, understand? Stick till you know what's what. Okay? And when you get your direction, what you're doing, how and when, tell no one. Now, I can keep secrets.

Got more of 'em than is healthy. But I don't want to know where you going or who you are when you get there. You gotta make those decisions yourself, and the only person you can trust is yourself. You need anything in the meantime, you let me know. Anything. But don't go rushing off without knowing where you rushing to. Chances are, this whole thing'll just die out like a tall tale; newspapermen taking liberties with the truth. The law ain't strong enough to have a long memory round here, but San Francisco – San Francisco will never forget. He wasn't rich, was he?"

Alex nods. "Owned a share in the Union Bank."

"Don't change nothing. Some men . . . some men just need killing. Now, best get off. No one stays the night. And when you get up tomorrow, you're still Alex. Just Alex. Okay?"

# 17

From the softness of her tick mattress, Alex stares at the ceiling and the woodgrain's whorled eyes stare back at her. Her arms and legs are languid, her stomach tumid, heavy, pulling her down from her center, warming her at her center. Outside wagons clatter by. Thin human voices compete with the throaty calls of crows and scrub jays and a dog barks in a long emotionless rhythm as though it has forgotten why it started barking in the first place. From the street sounds, she can see the whole town in her mind, beginning with the oak carved sign, the letters newly sanded, the wood newly stained, offering a one-word welcome. MOTHERLODE, it says. No "welcome to," no unnecessary pleasantries. Just like Emaline. She allows her eyes to close, her arms to stretch out and over her head, her toes to point and flex. From here, breathing her own stale breath, she feels at once part of the commotion outside and separate, protected, the insulating familiarity of the room surrounding her like a warm liquid. If she could stay here, if it were possible never to leave this room, she would become this liquid – shapeless, faceless, unbreakable. She sits upright. She does not want to be shapeless or faceless.

She swings her legs over the side of the bed, finds her boots still on her feet, her shirt tucked into her trousers. She follows the rectangle of light to the window, braces her elbows against the frame, and looks out.

With every blow Minford struck she simply grew away from herself, unsnapped the corners of her skin and crawled out, leaving only the body to beat. She was somewhere else, or else locked so tightly inside her own skin, inside her very marrow, that he could not reach her. He died trying.

The sun is stretching itself over the lip of the ravine. The cedars on the ridge are outlined as morning silhouettes. Had a morning ever presented such a welcome? She can see the tops of heads – bonnets, hats and bald spots – and jumbled conversations tickle her ears like the twirl of the vireos flitting this way and that, and the barn swallows swooping down from the trees to their mud nests plastered beneath the rim of every roof. The wagons kick dust into the air and it falls in layers, giving the sun palette enough to paint streaks of diagonal light. She can see Harry making his way toward the Victoria from his cabin.

"Hi, Harry, hi," she calls, but before he can look, she pulls away from the window, resting her back flat against the bedroom wall. You're still Alex, she thinks, staring across the room where the mirror rests upon the floor. Just Alex. Quiet Alex. Neither boy nor woman; nothing. A nothing with the curse, she thinks, becoming all too conscious of the rag between her thighs, soiled, sticky, thick with the smell of her. She retreats further back into the shadows of the room.

She'll have to get rid of the rag, bury it or burn it. But for now she wraps another rag around it, shoves it beneath her bed with the dust devils and the short wooden safe Micah sold her to store her gold, and secures another rag between her legs. She adjusts the nugget, shivers as her fingers brush bare skin. Her body is coming back to life from the inside now, reasserting itself. The blood was proof of this, and she's not yet sure it's a good thing. It may just be safer to remain dead inside, if only to preserve the life outside. She's just now becoming accustomed to the Golden Boy, if never entirely comfortable. Surely, she thinks, buttoning her trousers, comfort was never an option. Surely she has never felt at ease with herself, except perhaps as a child climbing trees or running her hands through the clear spring water as the polly-wogs squirted this way and that. As a child, she didn't know any better.

She reaches down, lifts the mirror from the floor, holds it at arm's length. She places it up upon the washstand, behind the basin. This urge to look surprises her. She has resisted the temptation to catch more than a glimpse of herself in shop windows, or in the rippled distortion of the creek. She sensed that it was dangerous to look too closely. She was afraid she would dislike what she saw. Or, worse, that she too would become infatuated with the Golden Boy until those pieces of herself buried with her hair and her dress by the banks of the Sacramento River would rot and die there in the dark.

Her eyes trace the rose pattern of the mirror's frame, the dips and swirled branches gilded in bright gold, and only then does she allow herself to center on the reflection. She sees, at first, the face of a stranger. But her hair, hanging to her jaw and sun bleached to a lighter brown, carries with it the memory of that long braid falling heavy to her hip, or wound round and round her head like the coiled serpents of Gran's sermonizing. Her skin is brown, flaking in places, her cheekbones high, more defined than she remembers, and her jaw is square, jutting out over the wiry muscle of her neck. Her nose points just to the left of center, and bears a rounded knob of bone on its bridge. But there remain the small dark eyes of her mother as they gazed at her from the daguerreo-type by her bed. There are the eyes of Alexandra. This is not what she expected, though she can't say exactly what she expected. Utter transformation, perhaps.

237

She looks again, coming close enough that her breath paints patches of moisture on the metal. There, in the shape of her mouth, the thin upper lip forming a wry line atop the lower, there in the set of her eyebrows, is another face. Gran is staring back. Alex does not draw away from this image, but stares at the old woman in the mirror, lets the old woman stare back, indifferent at first, as if failing to recognize the busted nose, the burned skin of her granddaughter. Then Gran draws a quick breath, pulls herself up to a height her arthritic back resents. She doesn't smile, or frown. Instead, Gran begins to hum that tuneless kitchen melody, softly at first, as if struggling to find her voice. Alex is an infant again, toddling down the road away from the cottage, and then gathered into Gran's corded arms, hearing the old woman's heart flutter, her breath rasp. She feels the weight of that desiccated hand easing a fever with a touch, remembers how Gran smelled after chewing peppermint and strawberries from the garden, and Alex begins to hum, bumping along with Gran's tuneless melody by some trick of harmony. She stops herself. She turns her back on the mirror. She can look no longer.

"Morning to you, Alex. Sleep well?" Micah says, as Alex clumps down the stairs into the saloon. "Sleep at all?"

"Wondering if you were ever gonna get yourself up," says Harry, stirring his coffee. He brings it to his lips, decides against drinking, and starts stirring again.

"Alex had pressing business last night, isn't that right, Alex?" says Limpy, making room beside him at the table. David is not in the room but she decides not to ask where he is. Emaline, wiping cups behind the bar, flashes Alex the tiniest wink, then goes about her business with a sideways grin on her face that falls only when Jed walks through the door. Jed's hands are thrust in his pockets. Tired black bags hang beneath his eyes.

Alex doesn't remember much after leaving Emaline's room

238

last night. She stumbled down the hall, bracing herself against the wall so her legs wouldn't collapse beneath her, and passed a dark figure whose voice reminded her of a bullfrog, whose words made about as much sense. When her senses finally made contact with her brain, she realized it was Jed in the hall, and that she had nodded her head in affirmation to a question she hadn't really heard. His whole body frowned at her response. His shoulders slumped. His hands hugged his shoulders as he gazed down the hall toward Emaline's door and Alex wanted to say, "She loves you." Wanted to say these words so much that her chest ached. She hopes he knows. She hopes this kind of knowledge is possible without words.

"Expected you to be singing bass this morning," says Limpy, and Jed pushes through the kitchen door, fails to look back when Emaline calls his name. Emaline follows after him, and only after the door closes behind her does Limpy lean in, beckoning the men around him closer.

"She take matters into her own hands, or . . . ?" he asks, nodding his head as though "or" was all he needed to get a story from her. "Come on, spill it, boy. Details."

She smiles, in spite of herself, and wonders what to tell them. She remembers Emaline's advice to tell them nothing, but doesn't think they'll settle for this, and she isn't sure she'd be able to "use" a man's imagination even if she could somehow capture it. "It was . . . It's . . . It's just . . . private," she says finally, enduring the expelled breath of all four men.

"The hell it is!" says Limpy, turning Alex by the shoulders to face him. "Listen to me now, son, listen. You go upstairs with a woman that's looking like that, it ain't private!"

"She called me Golden Boy," Alex offers, and Limpy's eyes become marble round. Preacher, sitting silent in the corner, groans.

"She – by God, boys! We got ourselves a natural! By God,

a natural. What else? Don't blush, son. A man's duty to educate his peers. Duty, I say –"

"Did she bite yah?" says Micah. Only Emaline's return saves Alex from more explanation.

"I don't care what you do with your own time," Emaline says, "but if you're just sitting and not eating or drinking, you're wasting mine."

Emaline reaches the front porch in time to see six men riding out of town, pistols in the air. "Nigger whore!" yells a small man in a voice she recognizes and when his piebald excuse for a horse bucks, leaving him stunned on the ground, she makes no attempt to choke down her laughter. She hoots out loud with more vigor than she feels as he hobbles away, and while this is a paltry revenge, it's something. It takes several moments, and a bouquet of curious stares before she realizes she is standing in a mixture of blood and soft down feathers, and another moment to comprehend that the noxious soup was slopped on the entire porch. When the boys come rushing up from the creek, their faces more festive than concerned, her feet have already begun to stick. Limpy is smiling, goddamn him. He opens his mouth to speak, but Emaline cuts him off.

"Not a word, Limpy. What are we going to do about this?"

That sparks a whole mess of hogwash and fancy talk. They make threats to footprints, brag about what they'd do if they caught *them*, string *them* up, curse *them* with Chinese hocus-pocus, but no one offers to saddle up and give chase. No one mentions the law. Probably are the law. Hudson with a badge to go with his bravado. Whipping and lynching; tarring and feathering – there isn't much difference. Emaline raises her hand for silence, feeling like a schoolmarm in a class of over-grown teenagers.

"They say anything?" asks Jed.

"Nothing," Emaline replies, biting her lip. Jed eyes her

suspiciously. Concern dragging his whole face downward and Emaline grows aware of her unconscious gesture.

Too many secrets. She collects them like buttons: big ones with shiny surfaces that look good enough to eat, miniature ones too tiny for use which she preserves for novelty alone. She knows that Limpy keeps a picture of his mamma in his trouser pocket, that he never knew his daddy, that he mysteriously blames his propensity for chatter on this fact. She knows that Klein is a Lutheran pastor's son who fled Germany in order to marry a peasant girl with the misfortune of being Catholic. The girl died a hundred miles from the California Coast on a steamship, prompting him to forsake his name, Gunter Kranz, for Klein, a name whose meaning Emaline assumes carries some significance. She even knows secrets no one has told her; about Harry and Fred, for instance, that the reason they never come upstairs to see her bears no relation to David's claims of piety. She suspects that eventually they'll tell her outright, confirming her suspicion, or Fred will. Harry takes too much pleasure in the social game, playing with the town's unwillingness to acknowledge the relationship. It's the same with her and Jed. Ignorance, even self-perpetuated ignorance, is easier than outrage, if less intriguing. The town is not yet established enough for such scandal, although Mrs. Dourity, Erkstine and Waller and her sister Rose are changing that. Outrage comes from stable places like Grass Valley. And David? She's seen the way he looks at Alex. Should put the poor sap out of his moral misery, but what fun to watch him squirm, flailing himself with guilt. Besides, she would never tell Alex's secret. Of all her secrets, she knows that this one will lie with her in the grave.

She squints down from the porch at the small form she knows to be Alex. Her head barely reaches the level of Limpy's armpit. All other details are a blur, moving into and out of focus. She feels a headache coming.

Vultures congregate to the smell of blood, chasing each other in circles, taking pieces from the sun like the blades of a giant windmill. If Victor Lane weren't populated by a crowd of people trying to appear casually disinterested as they stroll past for a second and a third time, the big ugly birds might land, displaying for Emaline their featherless heads, red and wrinkled like the rotting flesh they eat. No one place or person deserves so much attention two days in a row, she thinks. Mrs. Dourity and Mrs. Erkstine, standing a safe distance across the street, probably believe Emaline planned these spectacles; a variety show that Lola Montez, the infamous spider dancer herself, would envy. Orphanage? Hell. Emaline considers herself a patient woman, but there are limits to the virtue. She sucks in her breath and her belly, letting both out at once in a rush of air and flesh as Limpy leads a silent retreat back to the mine. Emaline doesn't try to stop them. They'd just track blood across her floor. Be more of a mess than a help. Only Alex and Jed remain.

"Go on, Alex," she says. "You paid me plenty last night. Go on now."

Alex hesitates, showing a genuine concern that Emaline appreciates but doesn't need right now. She winks, gives Alex a smile, and watches her trudge back down Victor Lane, passing Rose and a well-dressed man with a striking resemblance to Preacher John. The Preacher tips his hat, receives a poke in the ribs for his civility, and continues down toward Sander's dry goods.

"Well," says Jed, pulling her eyes to him. She hardly expects him to stay. All day, he had been so distant, hostile even. This baffled her. Last night she'd been too tired to give him what he wanted. And when he'd asked her what was wrong, all she could say was, "Alex." His anger was unexpected. She was afraid at first that he would force her, shove her back against the wall as they had done more than once in passionate play, asserting a physical dominance he had never before taken advantage of.

Instead, he left her, closed the door behind him, so quietly, with such painful restraint, when all she wanted was to hold him all night until no explanations were necessary.

"You don't have to stay," Emaline tells him, hoping he'll stay, not so much for his help as his closeness. But she knows very well his aversion to anything resembling witchcraft. Emaline supposes this qualified. At the very least, it is a warning. "I know," he says. "I want to stay."

"Gonna need water. Lots of it," says Emaline though this is not what she wants to say. He turns to fetch the buckets. "Jed . . ." but the words catch in her throat.

"There's no one like you," she says finally.

He only nods and disappears around the corner of the inn.

By the time Emaline and Jed have cleaned the mess from the front porch of the Victoria, the day has faded to evening. She sits alone on a bench, picking feathers from her hair. Blood crusts on her dress in variegated patterns. Blood under her fingernails. Blood streaked across her face like war paint. She hasn't thought about dinner, and the evening's bread has burned to coal in the oven, and if she ever catches the sons-a-bitches who did this, she's gonna rip them limb from limb, starting with their smallest and fondest. Cowards, the lot of them, riding through town like a bunch of savages, masks hiding their faces, as if it wasn't obvious who they were.

She rises to the sound of her knees popping and heads inside. The saloon is empty of all but her regulars. Chicken blood and feathers have a way of putting customers off, but tonight she doesn't mind. The last two days have been more exciting than is healthy. A glass of whiskey, a wash, and bed. She will deny her worries for a few hours of sleep and maybe by morning the smell of blood and the pink residue left on the wall outside will have vanished.

She makes her way to the bar and glances at Alex, who lounges, legs apart, on the settee. Quite unladylike, she thinks. No doubt quite comfortable, too. She has no reason to doubt Alex or her confession. Emotion rarely lies. Emaline is almost envious – not of Alex's past, but her present. Just one of the boys, her boys. How many times has she wished she could just sit and play poker, eat someone else's cooking, make messes for someone else to clean, bask in the smelly camaraderie of men. Their acceptance and respect wouldn't be rooted in need. She could be sexless, thoughtless.

A glass shatters on the floor behind her. Harry's voice rises above the level of her thoughts and Limpy replies in protest. Even Alex leans forward into the argument.

"You lying sack of shit!" says Harry.

"Now listen!" says Limpy, raising his big hands to no avail. "I ain't made anything for sure yet. We just talking."

"*We* nothing. You and Mr. James were the only ones talking," says Harry, and Micah speaks up.

"Well now, let's not get carried away. There's nothing in writing, remember that."

"You knew about this?" David asks, standing up, and Micah eases back in his chair, putting his feet up as if to counteract the aggression in David's voice.

"I told you: hydraulicking," says Fred, looking to Alex for confirmation. "That was my idea."

"Well, not exactly hydraulicking," says Limpy, talking so fast now that his hands can't keep up. "We don't mine the gold, see. Leave that to some other poor bastards. And what does every poor bastard with a pick need to get at his gold, whether he's got the richest vein in California or the ore tailings of another man's claim? Water, of course. Water. And what we've got here is a year-round supply and a whole slew of folks dependent on it for their washing. No, hold on, let me finish, Harry. Mr. James explained it all to me. See, what we do is, we start our own water business: dam up part of the creek, sell water by the miner's inch to all them claims below this valley. We –"

"You can't sell water," says Harry.

"You can, though," says Fred, standing up next to Limpy.

Emaline rests her elbows upon the bar, stares off into the quiver of the lamplight, barely listening. If it is an argument worth her attention, one night won't see the end of it.

"We –" says Limpy again, motioning with his hands to everyone leaning into the circle – "we take a percentage of the profit of every claim using our water. It's a 'vestment, is what Mr. James called it. If we don't do this, someone else going to. And with the way the mine is playing out . . . No offense, Alex, but that nugget might just be the richest thing in the mountain. Now, water, water is gold and –"

"What have you done?" says David, and the circle goes quiet.

"Done? I ain't done nothing. What we doing? We talking."

"You're talking," says Harry. "I'm finished talking about this."

"Mr. James was here about water?" Alex asks.

"How much?" says David. "How much money *are* we talking?"

"My idea. Hydraulicking," says Fred, and Harry jolts from the table, knocking his chair over and spilling his whiskey.

"We are not talking hydraulicking, Fred!"

It's comic really, the two men's poorly matched bodies squaring off, but Emaline is not in the mood. She stands up straight, places her hands on her lower back and leans into the stretch. She steps up on a stool, then up on the bar.

One quiet night. One night without drama. Emaline's head brushes the crossbeam. Her toe taps against a whiskey jug on the counter and Jed gapes up at her, holding his arms out as if he could catch her. Squinting, she can see the bald spot on Micah's lumpy head, the muscle near his temple moving in time with his mouth, and Harry's cowlick rising like an exclamation point as he brandishes one of her new upholstered chairs. Couldn't use one of the old stools. Wants to break something precious. Precious. Emaline taps the whiskey jug closer to the edge of the bar as Limpy backs out of Harry's reach. Jed tenses but makes no move to catch the jug as it falls, breaking into two unsatisfying pieces on the floor.

Stillness. Cricket song. Emaline is on stage.

"If there's any messes to be made tonight, I'm gonna be making 'em."

She reaches to the shelf behind her, grabs a bottle of rum by its gooseneck, takes a long drink, spilling none, then slams it to the floor in an explosion of glass. "I'm tired," she says and smashes another bottle and another. Five tumblers are sacrificed, two of which bounce, two break, one does both. Whiskey on the counter. Whiskey soaking her shoes. Rum diluting whiskey on the floor. Glass and ceramic bits surrounding her as she reaches out for Jed, who helps her to the ground. She can feel their eyes as she climbs the stairs. She falls into bed too worn to enjoy their shock, their blessed silence.

# 18

With a stool in each hand, Alex steps from the Victoria to find Emaline hurrying in the opposite direction.

"Thank you, m'dear," says Emaline. "By the fire pit. Follow your nose," and bustles off without even slowing down.

The anniversary celebration was Emaline's idea. "Just a change," she said, "to bring us together as one town." Alex wonders if this effort isn't futile in the face of the Ladies Temperance League, now five members strong with the inclusion of Gerald Sander's wife, fresh from Boston. Mrs. Dourity and Mrs. Waller linger in front of the cigar shop, brown packages under their arms. Alex crosses to the other side of the street.

The last three days have found Emaline in four places at once, baking pies, skinning the hog, cooking the usual breakfast and dinner, and serving drinks and men each night. Her smile is willful, and Alex wonders if she's the only one who sees the tension pulsing that vein on Emaline's temple. She had Jed whitewash the Victoria and it glares garish white even in the evening. She's aired mattresses, washed the linen, even shined the mirrors, disregarding Alex's observation that no one was likely to notice the Victoria when the pig roast was in the clearing across the creek. "I'll notice," she said.

Alex rests a stool on the ground to wipe sweat from her forehead. She readjusts her hat and continues past the general store and Sander's dry goods.

Two weeks have passed since Alex's cycle ended, and true to her word, Emaline hasn't once asked about her plans. Alex is content not to make any plans. She's still the Golden Boy. Just Alex. The perpetual youth. All she's sure of is this town. The slant of the steeple, the ornamental balcony and the raucous noise of the saloon. Everyone she cares for sits down to Emaline's dinner each night: Limpy, Jed, Micah, Harry, Fred.

And David.

She no longer tries to emulate the way he sits in a chair or holds his whiskey cup, just watches and feels him grow more remote. Even he's been asking questions about this water company Limpy has been endorsing every spare breath. At the mine, he no longer tastes the soil for richness and his eyes no longer scour the ravine face for gold lodes; instead they linger on the ridgeline where the cedars sway. The physical distance he has always maintained has extended into silence. She's tempted to walk right into his cabin, slam one of these stools on the ground before him and stay there until he has to tell her to move. The thought only adds to the stagnant funk of this air sitting like a cap on the valley.

She reaches the creek, steps over the buckboard bridge into the clearing. A large circle of grass has been scythed and trampled flat. She sets the stools next to the plank tables, breathes in the scent of roasting pork. The sound of digging is so familiar she has to listen for it. She sits, watches smoke from the fire coil up in dizzying spirals. Across the valley and gliding closer are two cumbersome foreigners.

Yesterday she'd watched the gulls wobble over the lip of the ravine and into the valley on wings ill suited for the breathless air. Limpy bet Micah three ounces of gold they wouldn't be able to fly out again, and so far every attempt has failed. The air's too heavy and too still. They jaunt into the clearing, with that petulant head-first strut, then pause to shift foot to foot. The sight takes her back to the deck of the *Sea Sage*, almost a year ago. Boston Harbor had become wood splinters in the horizon. Gulls swarmed, their warm droppings christening the scrubbed deck, baptizing the shoulders and bonnet of a dreamy young woman. And then San Francisco Bay, so crowded with ships that passengers had to be rowed to shore. She can visualize both scenes, a leaving and an arrival. She's touched two different faces of the same continent. There should be some sense of accomplishment, but what she feels is lucky – lucky to be alive; lucky to be alive in Motherlode – and she has no desire to go anywhere else. Like those gulls, she has no lift, no reason. Motherlode just might be as good a place as any; a better place, she thinks.

"Hi, Alex. What are you thinking about?"

Lou Anne, fast approaching, stops just feet away. Her hair is curled and tied, no longer dangling free in the manner of young girls. Only a corset could hold her back so straight. Alex wonders if Lou Anne is capable of understanding the direction of the Golden Boy's thoughts.

On the girl's face is a naïve playfulness that Alex can't help but resent. She resents the way Lou Anne can sashay up to anyone, charming with her very boldness, while Alex must remain ever hidden and silent. It makes her angry. She wants to slap the girl, to break that perfect straight nose. Instead, she points to the gulls.

"Daddy says they're good luck," blurts Lou Anne, "that they protect sailors at sea. But Mamma says –"

"We're not at sea."

"That's what Mamma says." Lou Anne's face brightens.

Alex turns and walks away.

Gunshots ricochet off the ravine walls and Emaline's ivory-handled shotgun blows smoke with the rest. The sun has set behind the ravine, but she's no longer cold and she wishes Jed hadn't left to fetch her shawl. She bounces through the crowd, grabbing, dancing with, then discarding man after man, breathing in their pork-and-whiskey breath, embarrassing Mr. Waller by kissing him on the lips with a bit of French flavor. Idiot damn near bit her tongue off, but whiskey cures all, and she wheels around the dance floor to the rhythm of the fiddler's foot. The guitar and accordion have long since given up on harmony, and it's just as well, for half the boys are singing "Old Dan Tucker" to the tune of "Buffalo Gals." Voices compete as everyone seems determined to be heard above the rest. Emaline makes her choice and belts:

> Tucker he had cash a-plenty
> Dressed to death – his old trunk empty.

She grabs Harry by the collar with her free hand. If he steps on her toe again, she'll shoot his foot clean off. She tells him as much as they twirl around the dance floor, past David, enjoying himself in spite of himself, past Limpy and Mrs. Waller, her bun relinquishing strand after strand of slicked-back hair until a brown tiara surrounds her face. The woman bites back a smile as though it's a sin to show teeth. Emaline kicks up her skirt, exposing her flushed white flank. The cool air rushes in under the folds of fabric, sending a chill from the tips of her ears to the tips of her toes. Forgive that, she thinks.

"Dada, dada, dada, dada," Harry sings, forsaking lyrics altogether, but clinging to the eight count. His arms are damp with sweat and his smile turns the corners of his eyes downward.

"Toes," warns Emaline for the fifth time, and bangs him on the thigh with the muzzle of the shotgun. She discards him for a drink and a breath.

God above never threw such a party, she thinks, catching her breath before knocking back a drink. Terrible stuff, whiskey. She watches Limpy lumber about the dance floor, dragging Mrs. Erkstine with him. Mrs. Dourity is standing by the whiskey barrel, a big horsey grin on her face. No, God never threw such a party – and where the hell is Jed? Think I'd sent him to Grass Valley.

She leans against the plank table, squints out into the twirling mass of bodies. David, the fool, is making a great show of bowing low and kissing the hand of that Lou Anne gal, whose corset is just a-pressing her small breasts toward her ears. In a town like this, twenty men to every woman, that gal might never discover just how plain she is. Spitting image of her mamma, minus the ramrod up the ass, but give it time.

"Shave his belly with a rusty razor!" shouts Preacher, who stumbles through the crowd with a tumbler in hand while Rose frowns from a bench. She holds her hand up like a shield whenever a man asks her to dance. The music veers off to "The Drunken Sailor."

> *Shave his belly with a rusty razor,*
> *Earlye in the morning!*
> *Hooray, up she rises,*
> *Hooray, up she rises,*
> *Hooray, up she rises,*
> *Earlye in the morning!*

The words rise up to bounce back and forth across the ravine until hundreds of voices fill the valley.

Emaline gulps her whiskey, pushes herself to her feet with her shotgun, leads Micah through a romping two-step and trades him for a dewy-faced young man – she grabs his crotch – yes, a young man. Then she bounds over to David, flings him around the cut-grass dance floor, ignoring the sweet-and-sour smell of herself as her armpits drip. Her mouth aches from smiling and she lets her head fall back, trusting David to

251

support her. The stars are overpowered by the bonfire, which throws sparks to the sky, and the tangy mix of singed grass, charred meat, liquor and cedar pine thickens her tongue. She kisses David on the mouth and then discards him for Alex.

Emaline in the lead. They whirl around, spinning, dipping and twirling as lantern light follows behind in blurred streaks of color. Small teeth, she thinks, squinting down at Alex, but a pretty smile. Dimples.

"You're still here," she yells, and reaches for Alex's crotch. Alex grimaces. Just checking. Just making sure. Brave young woman with trousers and a pretty smile. Ones to watch out for: brave ones with pretty smiles, she thinks, and the double warmth of pride and whiskey spreads through her, making her heart feel big enough to split.

"Still here," Emaline says again and stops dancing. Where is Jed? Her arms fall to her sides. She passes Alex off to another and waves Klein away. For a moment she stands, panting and swaying like a wind-blown cedar, then stumbles back over the bridge to town.

Alex leans back. Hot breath on her shoulder. She turns to face David, his arms at his side as though weighted; his eyes cold, resistant.

"Dance?" she asks, surprised at the pleading sound of her voice. David takes a step back as though to turn away. His hands form fists and, for a moment, Alex fights the urge to step away, afraid he will hit her. She should leave him alone, but she doesn't. There is no reason he should act this way to her. She is "just Alex" to him, and what had stupid, helpless "just Alex" ever done to David? The boy doesn't deserve to be treated like some kind of criminal when all the boy wants is to be held, to feel David's arms around her. She means *him*. The boy. She's not making sense to herself, and it's his fault. She belches and tastes liquor and half-digested pork. She spits, aiming for his boots, but misses wide left.

He's jealous. Like John Thomas. Jealous that he didn't find the gold.

Alex holds her arms out in a dancing position. "Dance," she says. A command this time.

She knows he can – watched him bow to Lou Anne, kissing her hand like some kind of Cornish knight, if there were such things. Lou Anne's petticoats swished across his legs as she batted her eyes at him and laughed too loud at nothing. What Alex wouldn't give, right now, for a dress, for long hair in braids. No corset. What Alex wouldn't give to be strong and loud and respected and beautiful, and she wouldn't care if anyone approved of her, so long as they loved her and did what she said and never left her lonely.

Couples swirl around them. Limpy with Micah, Klein with Mrs. Erkstine, Fred with Lou Anne, and Harry with Mason Dourity. Countless other bearded partners dance: Frenchmen with Germans, Englishmen with Irishmen, Northern boys with Southern. Even some of the uninvited Chinese are present, their queues swinging behind them with lives of their own. David's eyes jump from couple to couple, as though dreaming wide awake, and Alex lifts her boot and slams it hard against his shin. No yelp of pain. No reaction. Nothing. She kicks him again, harder, and his hands fly to her shoulders.

"Stop!" His face inches from hers.

They begin to move together, swaying back and forth in one place until their mechanical movement becomes fluid. David's grip on Alex's shoulder relaxes and she can feel the blood rush back to the indentions left by his fingers. Bodies migrate around them in a random, self-absorbed disarray. David and Alex are alone, treading countercurrent in a human stew. He smells so familiar. Earth, tobacco, whiskey and sweat. Her head rests upon his shoulder; his hand warms the small of her back.

The song ends and David pulls away. His breath comes heavy again and his eyes avoid hers. Words weigh on Alex's tongue. If she told him, David would never tell, would he? Just David. No one else.

Limpy clears his throat and stands astride the pig carcass with his hand in the air for attention. A giddy silence fills the valley and Alex snaps her mouth shut.

"Now, it's been a 'ventful couple months, boy, I tell you!" Limpy says. "And what I hear is most of you didn't come to town for the gold, after all. Y'all heard about the pig roast – and let me tell you, there'd be a whole hell of a lot more pork to go around without you!"

Laughter rumbles up in chorus. A high-pitched giggle squeals from the back and Mrs. Erkstine clamps her hand over her mouth, embarrassed.

"I'm not complaining, mind. Hell, no! Good to have yah. Two pigs next year and three after that, all goes well. Now, there's just a couple of people we might oughta be thanking, and while I no doubt deserve a large chunk of any credit in this town –"

"Dear Loward!" bellows Preacher from the middle of the crowd. His hands rise to heaven. His face is bright red, his nose would be at home in a cherry tree. Rose tugs on his sleeve a few times but soon gives up to shrink back into the crowd. Alex grins. New clothes hadn't changed Preacher so much.

"Father God! Heavenly, Heavenly Father, we thank you for it all!"

"Aaaaymen!" someone yells from the back.

"For the gold, Lord, that brought us here . . ." His eyes are closed, but his eyeballs move beneath his lids, searching for words. His voice begins to crack and pinch. "And for this here pig that gave its life to feed us in your name, Lord God. Dear God . . ." A pause. Silence. Alex waits for him to speak again. Waits. And waits. Preacher's face turns skyward. His mouth opens and his eyes close as though sleeping in place.

"SIT DOWN!" comes a voice from Alex's immediate left.

254

"Sit down you son-of-a –" replies another on the right, and a bubble of drunk anger percolates through the crowd.

"Women present, y'all! Women present," Limpy interjects, reclaiming his audience. He winks at Mrs. Erkstine, his most frequent dance partner. Her hand still covers her mouth as though afraid of the intemperate sounds that might escape. Alex wishes that she would yell or scream or belch, if only to release her from the obvious pain of holding back.

"I think Alex needs a round of applause for his damned dumb luck," Limpy continues. "Come on up here, Alex . . . No?"

She's shaking her head no, but the attention warms her and she searches through the faces for Emaline. Hands and elbows give good-natured jabs as she passes through them.

"And where would we be," says Limpy, "without my darlin' Emaline? Where –"

Her town. Buildings on either side stand as sentries in the darkness, welcoming her. The road's flat expanse is her marble courtyard. Silence in front of her. A constant fluctuation of white noise behind. Her eyes blur, dilate and open like a mouth too small for the bite.

She feels the kiss of a breeze in the heavy air. Drought or no drought, this will be a good year. Drought or no drought, Bobcat Creek will flow and she'll plaster the kitchen walls. The creek will flow and she'll install shutters, and cover even the stairwell in worsted damask, and hire one or two girls, add a few more rooms. She jumps at the movement up the road.

Jed with his shiny half-grin, his arms crossed before him, one hand to his chin as if trying to hide that grin. This is what she sees in the darkness. Coarse hair beneath her fingers, the calm, steady sound of his heart next to hers. This is what she feels as she stumbles forward, giggling like that silly Lou Anne. Jed in braces, tailored gray trousers, a top hat to make him tall. So hard to see the future . . . just versions of the present or the past dressed up in other clothes. She'd rather not think beyond the man beneath the tattered trousers, his soft voice as rich as strong coffee. She squints ahead in the darkness, ahead to the shape. Shapes.

Too many moving shapes, too solid for imagination.

"Jed?" she whispers, covers her mouth, and finds the forgotten weight of her shotgun in her hand. A horse whinnies and a man's voice follows, inaudible except for its tone: deep, sober, almost soothing. The warm buzz at the back of Emaline's neck quiets and cools. Her ears pick new sounds from the air, distinguishing them from accordions, fiddles and drunken laughter.


Alex pushes through the crowd and over the bridge to town. Behind her, Limpy's voice rises and falls; laughter breaks and sputters over the sound of the creek. Before her, the silence is thick with movement. Emaline is a dark smudge plodding toward the Victoria. Alex follows.

Sweat dries in cold streaks across her forehead. She's forgotten her hat at the bonfire. She feels naked without it, wonders if she should just leave Emaline be, when a man's voice, then another, freezes her in place.

She picks out the clink of bridles, the groan of leather on leather. An orange-red flash lingers as sight. A mass of horses with human voices. Someone falls squirming on the ground at the base of the inn.

"Jed?" Emaline screaming, and Alex's body stumbles on without her brain. Her heart pounds out her presence and, as the shapes become larger, her breath comes shorter. Men without faces, riding horses. Horses shaking bridles, dancing, nervous, foot to foot. Emaline rushing forward, stopping yards from the figure on the ground. Gunshots from the pig roast echo sharp staccato in the clearing, but when Emaline fires, Alex hears nothing and sees only the flash of light bursting from the mouth of her gun.

A faceless man falls.

White-hot gold explodes from the mass of men on horse-back. Alex hears herself scream. Emaline's shoulders give as if shoved. She stumbles back a step, then forward. A torch is lit and held aloft by a young man with wide frightened eyes.

"A fucking goddamn," says the man in front: Jackson Hudson. His gun shakes in his hands, the barrel breathes. "For a nigger? Emaline?"

Alex bursts into the circle of torchlight. Pistols hold her in place. Jackson Hudson looks from Alex to Emaline to Alex. He points with the gun.

"You see this?" he says. Emaline slumps down next to Jed's prostrate form. Crimson circles bloom on her dress. Alex doesn't know if Emaline has seen her, doesn't know if Emaline is seeing anything but Jed as she hauls his limp weight toward her so that his head rests in the softness of her belly. Blood pumps from the holes in her chest, into his hair.

"See what she's done?" says Hudson. "Boy, look at me."

But Alex hears only her own breath coming fast and weak. Sees only the squint of Emaline's eyes and the barrel of Emaline's shotgun pointing like a finger. The barrel belches powder, kicks back. Jackson Hudson falls head over heels from his saddle to the ground. A cackle of pistol fire from the men on horses. Hudson pulls himself to his knees. Emaline lies still.

Falling forward, past smoking guns and the gaping mouths of vigilantes, to the open arms of the porch steps, Alex sinks down beside the torn bodies. Her fingers close around the barrel of Emaline's shotgun, slick with blood and bits of hair. Hudson staggers to his feet. Alex pulls the trigger, pulls the trigger, pulls the trigger. Hudson sways, unaware he's just died three times. He stands above her. He clutches his bleeding shoulder with his good hand, a pistol with the other. His eyebrows furrow.

"Give me the gun," says Hudson.

She shakes her head, no.

"Don't make me shoot you, too," he says, and cocks the pistol.

She shakes her head again, closes her eyes when his finger tightens on the trigger, ready for the flash. She's not ready for his boot in her gut. He yanks the shotgun away, dismisses her with a backward glance. "Gave her the goddamned thing in the first place." He motions to the wide-eyed young man with the torch.

"Burn it," he says. "Burn it all."

# 19

She tucks her mind in her pocket and lets muscle memory transform her movements into a thoughtless routine. She's just digging a coyote hole, six feet long, three feet wide. Just looking for gold. On her lips must be the salt of sweat. No one cries when looking for gold.

"That's enough." Limpy's hand on her shoulder. "Alex, that's deep enough."

Alex rubs red earth between her fingers and touches it to her tongue, wishing she could taste the hope David always seems to find there. She dusts her hands on her trousers, leaving fingerprints on her thighs, and leans on her shovel. Limpy's hand dangles before her. She grabs it and lets him haul her to the surface.

Behind her, the citizens of Motherlode, California, tiptoe around hot embers. The fire burned all night, sucking up the pine sap of the new wooden walls, and filling the air with a disgustingly pleasant cedar scent. Only by will and luck was the blaze stopped just short of Heinrich's shoe store on the south side of the road. The livery, David's flimsy cabin and the cigar shop stand apologetically untouched, while the Victoria Inn and the entire north quarter of town, including the chapel, have been reduced to smoldering ruins.

The flames dazzled her at first. The sight was the opposite of sobering, and, even when others arrived to help put out the flames and drag the bodies away from the Victoria's crumbling balcony, her throat was thick with a nauseous intoxication. She stood in a line of people as buckets of water passed hand to hand with ant-like sedulity. Wet blankets flapped up and down like one-winged birds. Had thought been possible, had her eyes seen anything but the flames, had she the perspective of the owl overhead, she might have recognized the surreal beauty of the night. A hundred forms, black against the red-yellow flames, gyrating in some elemental dance.

But now the sun has risen, the flames have been quelled, and three dead bodies lie blistering by the creek. Alex takes off her hat, places it over Emaline's face, and shoos the flies away. She stands to the side when Harry and Micah lift Emaline's body onto a clean white sheet that they wrap around her like a cocoon. They manage ten yards before stopping to rest her girth against their knees. David and Limpy arrive to help.

"What we do with Jed?" asks Harry. But for Alex there is no question. They all know what Emaline would want and, as improper as it seems, they lift Jed and carry him down Victor Lane, turning left at what was once the chapel, and lay him next to her. The other body remains creekside with a blue bandana covering the face and a bloody red hole through the heart. Of course Alex recognizes him. Few grown men have hair that fair or a frame that small and stocky. They will bury him later, behind the chicken coop, near the outhouse, but only because they feel they have to. A human being, after all, if a rotten one. David picks up his shovel and begins to dig another grave. Alex sits by Emaline's stiffening body. She is waiting for Emaline's mouth to open and orders to come out. Waits and waits as her eyes travel up and down with David's shovel.

By the time David is done, the whole town has gathered in a disorganized group, waiting for someone to take charge. Limpy's jaw juts outward and quivers with force enough to shake his whole body. Micah looks at his boots and chews a hole through his bottom lip. Harry's head tips skyward. His eyes are shallow flooded lakes, and Fred stands close to him, breathing through clenched teeth. Lou Anne grips her mother's skirts and cries. Above them, a single vulture is circling lower and lower, and in the chicken coop, behind the smoking remains of the Victoria Inn, the Rhode Island Red lays an egg.

Preacher John steps forward, parting the throng with touches on shoulders. He reaches down, brings Alex to her feet, helps David out of the second grave, and turns to face his congregation. He swipes his hat from his head. He digs in his pocket, finds his Bible, flips through. He purses his lips as though ready to speak, then shakes his head and mumbles something to himself. He closes the Bible, gazes out over the crowd.

"Well," he says, "my mamma, she wouldn't have liked Miss Emaline none. Would have called her an unholy woman, the kind to stay away from, the kind that opens wide the gates of hell."

He colors as if sensing he's gone too far. "But then, Mamma didn't want me coming here, neither. Said California would ruin me, as I was never inclined to virtue in the first place. Said I'd find gold at the price of my soul, and she was right, at first, I guess. I was heading to no good and know'd it, and, long story short, I decided 'bout time for a change, but didn't know quite how to go about it."

He wrings his hat like a wet rag, his voice taking an upturn. "Emaline, she saw things different from most. Saw me different, better than I was, am. Saw the man I was trying to be. Think that's how she was with everyone."

A murmur rumbles through the crowd and Alex takes a

step to the side and presses back against the turned-soil smell of David. She imagines Emaline in the kitchen, the sound of her humming, the heady grace of her efficiency, each movement deliberate, controlled as she kneaded the bread, or peeled potatoes, or sewed a seam, never feeling the need to make a task harder than it was, never feeling the need to make an art out of a chore. As Alex swept, pushing the dirt around to settle in much the same place, she'd felt the vital energy of the woman surrounding her like a hug. She wishes now that it had been a hug, wishes she had felt those arms around her, holding her close until the systematic execution of small tasks surmounted all fear of larger troubles. But Emaline was not one to give away a hug, not even that night in her room with her hair undone around her shoulders. Her face had been passive, not bent on understanding, just accepting. In her nightshift, with her hair down, the full flush of her radiance had bubbled from within her, coating Alex in its afterglow. And if she wasn't before, she is now and forever in Alex's memory, a beautiful woman, a queen with a thick middle and bad eyesight. Emaline is gone, and Alex is again alone with her secrets. Her sinuses pulse with the pressure of tears, but she cannot cry. The urge to leave Motherlode comes sudden and violent.

"She just gave us time and didn't take no shit, no excuses, and never blamed you for failing – again and again, in some cases, in my case," Preacher says. "Long as you tried like she tried, worked like she worked. A first-class inn she was building. The envy of the National Hotel, with the name of a queen, Victoria. You heard her talking. Gonna welcome everyone from President Pierce hisself to Jaquin Murietta, play no favorites. Everyone was her boys. And all she did every day was cook, clean, and take care of us piss-poor sons-a-bitches when all we had was mud in our pockets. Never made excuses. Knew what she was doing, and expected everyone, God included, to understand. And I think he did . . . does. I think he does."

Preacher pauses and a memory presents itself as a smile on his lips. "Was her who taught me to read. Back in Sacramento. Paid my fifty dollars for her . . . well, her services, and mentioned that I was seeking a change in myself – into what, I didn't know – and after we was done, she give me this Bible."

He holds up the tattered gray book. "Says she's only giving it me 'cause her eyes were going and she about had the damn thing memorized anyway. Then looks at me real stern, like she does, did, shit."

He looks around as if in apology, but no one can meet his eye. It's not so important what he says, just as long as he says something.

Alex closes her eyes to the pressure building there. No tears, no release. David's breath warms her neck. She feels his hand on her shoulder and her body tenses, then relaxes into the contact. The ground, which had been bucking and rolling, stills. Preacher continues:

"She tells me how dangerous it is to read before thinking, before feeling, asks me if I done either or both lately. Tells me she was giving me the Bible only for learning, and when I was done learning, I should close it, and only open it when I come up empty of the right words. I come up empty a lot." He looks down at the Bible, lets it fall open where it wants. He smiles.

"'In my father's house are many dwelling places, I go to prepare a place for you.' I go and prepare a place for you," he repeats. His voice rises clear and confident. The phrase echoes off the ravine. "She always had the right words, didn't she? Was her that named this town Motherlode, saying anything worth finding is worth digging for. Ain't that the truth?

"Now, I can't be sure she found all she was digging for. Can't say if it was worth what she lost. But I tell you what she told me – that this land don't settle for nobody who ain't

263

both a dreamer and a worker. And she may not have got what she was looking for, but she died trying, and, hell, that's all anyone can ask. Let us . . . let us pray."

One by one the citizens of Motherlode drift away to sift through their gutted businesses, leaving the Victoria Inn regulars to see Jed into the ground. Nothing is said, beyond a short prayer, and soon only Alex and David remain. The air around them is warm and still lacking in body and lift. Breathing takes effort. The cedars on the ridge stand like sentinels, overlooking the dusty ashes of a town they were helpless to protect. The sun has yet to reach nine o'clock.

The rest of the day Alex and David wander. They trudge through hot embers, salvaging what they can from where they can, but spend most of their time near the smoldering foundations of the Victoria. Here Emaline's presence is almost tangible. Her scent lingers, if only in Alex's imagination. Dust, baking bread, whiskey. The balcony has crumbled to the ground. Two stories have become one. Porcelain washbasins from the upstairs rooms lie in pieces; though one, with a painted vine of green ivy reaching out and over the rim, remains intact. Shards of reflective silver are all that remain of the mirrors. Scraps of clothing litter the ground. Alex recognizes a sleeve from one of her own flannels. A strip of Emaline's lavender dress has draped itself across what used to be the bar. Ceramic jugs and glass bottles, whose contents exploded in the heat, lie in a clumsy mosaic on the floor. Bits of tapestry float as red ash with every step.

The cast-iron stove is too heavy for David and Alex to lift. It stands on its four solid legs in defiance of flames, in scorn of wood's fragility. Its vents are two round staring eyes. The open oven door is a laughing mouth that Alex kicks closed. The clang bounces off the far valley wall, echoing back a softer version of itself. Down the road, vultures gather around John Thomas's body, picking at his eyes, nibbling his fingers, hopping into the air and resettling like sediment in a gold pan. The Rhode Island Red tiptoes around the grave mounds, flaps its wings, lets out a disgruntled series of clucks, each one louder, more frantic than the last.

Small piles of salvaged goods are forming all along the side of Victor Lane. Buckets and pots, pick and shovel heads missing their wooden handles. By Micah's shop sits a small iron safe and several barrels of whiskey. Limpy ambles past, taking a thirsty look at the barrels.

"I tell you," he says, wiping his mouth with the back of his hand, "I sure could use a drink."

David hands him a ladleful of water from a bucket. Limpy smirks, takes a sip, swirls it around his mouth, spits. "It's wet, all right."

That night the regulars gather in the road near the remains of the Victoria Inn. David sets a lantern on the ground and they sit upon three-legged stools dipping tin cups into an open barrel of whiskey. The lantern light mushrooms up and outward, spreading a dim orange glow on black-streaked faces.

Micah says, slouching on his stool, "Sent an order today for wood, nails and such. I might rebuild in brick."

No one speaks. It seems too soon to start rebuilding, David thinks, disrespectful. Off in the distance a coyote howls and David raises his hands to the moon and yawns. A glass of whiskey lays untouched near his boot. Alex sits within breathing distance to his right. The boy has been close all day and David hasn't discouraged him, doesn't feel guilty about it.

"Don't know," says Harry. A dribble of whiskey dampens his beard. "Been hearing good things about Colorado." He glances over at Fred, who studies the ground. "Don't know," Harry says again.

"Well, y'all wanna know what I think?" slurs Limpy, already long past drunk. He lets out a giant puff of gas but is the only one who thinks this is funny. His hee-haws turn to hee-hees, then quiet all together.

Ash and grit scratch David's eyes. He doesn't know either. A stubborn core of him wants to stay, to dig and blast until his arms fall off from the effort. Maybe rebuild with a solid roof, something permanent. But another, larger part of him is hungry for more; more gold, yes, he thinks, but also to explore another part of the country, and perhaps gain something he's never had: land. He's sure there's still gold in these hills, sure that someone is going to get rich. Maybe Mr. James and those hydraulicking folks Fred is always talking about. David's father would think it ridiculous, washing whole mountainsides away. Half the pay dirt would be swept right down the creek. But that is the way things are going here in California. No one cares how much is wasted, so long as someone gets rich in the process. Could learn a lesson from those Chinamen who hunker down washing every last ounce of gold from the dirt before moving on.

A glow from the Chinese huts across the creek is just visible. Without those Chinamen, he knows the rest of the town would have been lost last night. They hauled buckets and blankets and fought the flames, even though their homes were well out of the fire's reach, then disappeared by morning. Probably afraid of being blamed for it. Probably smart to be afraid. Rumor around town held that those chickens weren't attacked by any raving Chinamen, though that was the convenient answer. David thinks there might be a greater significance to this observation, but is too tired to speculate what it might be. His mind leaps sideways to the coast of Cornwall. The year-long green of the cliffs competes in brightness with the blue of the sky, and a circle of standing stones vibrate and straighten to a regimental line.

"We need gravestones," he says. "For both of them. Jed was a good ol' guy."

Silent nods all round. He was a good ol' guy. The fact that

he was black hadn't made much of a difference until today, until they dug his grave and, in broad daylight, laid him next to the white woman with whom he spent most of his nights.

Limpy giggles again and David rises. Best get him home. He'll never get him to bed if he passes out here. As if on cue, the others stand and the circle disperses. David helps Limpy zigzag toward the cabin and Alex hustles ahead to open the door, then follows them in uninvited.

"Close the door," says David, letting Limpy fall unconscious into bed. His convictions, his fears and reservations, slip like raw ore through hopper holes. He's tired of fighting himself. Alex closes the door and stands in the darkness, breathing as one asleep.

"Go on," David tells Alex, motioning to his own bed. "I'm not tired." He takes a seat on the stool in the corner, crosses his arms at his chest and falls asleep.

Alex's mother died when memory was only strong enough to grasp and hold misted images. A face so close as to consist only of a nose, a limitless warmth of skin on skin, a heartbeat slower and counter to her own, a dangled brightness, swinging back and forth like a pendulum in a golden blur, and a flaking, powdered-skin smell, corrupted by tobacco and peppermint. Alex coveted these memories, called them Mother, and kept them separate from all others until they assumed their own context, their own identity. And later they became her definition for something equally abstruse, became her definition for love.

Now, lying in the warmth of David's bed, with his quilt wrapped around her, she again hears a heartbeat, and a doubt enters her cache of coveted memories. The smell of skin, a sun-splotched hand with large knobbly knuckles like a living skeleton, a pipe smoked only in private, the tobacco tamped, lit and relit until the odor escaped underneath the bedroom door to the kitchen where Alexandra dressed her doll. Lips, cracked and abrasive as wool, kiss her forehead as she pretends to sleep, and suddenly the intangible blur of her wordless definition of love breaks apart into visions of a tired old woman with arthritic hands. And though she didn't at Gran's funeral, though she couldn't at Emaline's, Alex begins to cry. Tears ooze from the corners of her eyes like water from cracks in granite, building in intensity until her shoulders shake. The blanket only buffers the sound.

Then her grandmother's arms, like corrugated wires, wind around her, holding her, rocking her, squeezing her unexpected guilt into a manageable shape, a cylinder to tuck away in a closet corner. The old woman's hissing breath softens, her voice deepens. "Shhh. It's all right. Shhh."

Fingers augment to match gout-swollen joints. Palms grow leather-tough calluses. Legs elongate. Shoulders and chest widen, becoming dense and heavy. Lips make warm indents on Alex's temple, on her cheek, her neck, her lips. Hands roam, cupping her buttocks, sliding up to her neck and down to her breasts, then pull away, leaving behind a heat signature and a chill.

Alex shivers and opens her eyes to David staring at his hands. He's barely breathing. Moonlight penetrates the canvas roof. Alex can see the whites of his eyes as his mind works through exhausted confusion. Too much thinking. She lunges for his legs, wraps her arms around him and holds on until his knees bend and hairy knuckles skim the back of her neck.

"Please," she says.

She healed, and then she bled, and she could not change this. But the blood was still someone else's blood, the return of someone else's cycle. The curse of Alexandra of Pennsylvania. Alex is finished with curses, she's finished with lies. She was ready to bury herself with Emaline, to jump into the grave and close her eyes, letting roots and worms take what was left. But she knew then, and she knows now, that this is not what Emaline would want. It's not what Alex wants, though at this moment her desire stretches no further than David.

Ash thickens the stale air. Across the room, Limpy snores. Alex pulls off her flannel. David opens his mouth to speak. No words come. Alex rises to her knees, kisses his open mouth, runs her hands behind his head where hair gives way to the nape of his neck. Her fingers tingle. The sensation spreads, giving weight to empty muscles, and density to hollow bones. Her tongue dampens his chapped lips. She guides his hand to her chest and her hands roam, discovering in the length of his back, the arch of her own. Discovering in the hollow of his neck, the voice of her own. She moans, lets her head fall back, lets his tongue redefine her collarbone and color in her ears. His tongue meets hers. The quilt is cast to the floor. They lie back. The bed frame groans. His hands make circles around small breasts and edge downward, finding the nugget in its pouch. He follows the leather cord, easing his hands behind her to the knot. The pouch falls with a thump to the floor. She scrapes her cheek against the stubble of his chin, arches when he twists black hairs between his fingers. She tastes the salt of his navel, runs her tongue to the top of his trousers. He shivers. "Alex," he says.

# 20

She stands above him. His chest is bare and the thin fuzz of blond hair curls this way and that. His right arm is slung to the side where the imprint of her body remains.

There is, Alex thinks, only conditional love. Or if unconditional love were possible it could only arise if one could manage unconditional faith. Alex never has. So many things larger than she, stronger than she, have shaken her faith like sand from a pair of boots, and yet she marvels as she stands there, watching David's breath tease the hairs of his arm, something like faith always seems to reappear at the least predictable of moments. She wishes he would wake, and hopes that he will not. She wants to bend, to trace her hands along the contours of his chest, to hide there in the warmth of him, to hear only the beat of his heart. Instead, she reaches down for the leather pouch, frees the nugget into the palm of her hand, marvels at the density. In her other hand, a green stone from the scales above the stove, the polished skin so smooth.

Across the room, Limpy's snoring changes cadence from the even rumble of deep sleep to short choppy snorts. Alex tucks the green stone into her pouch and lets the nugget fall into the open mouth of David's boot, sitting as if placed by his bed for that purpose. The gold is not a gift. An invitation to forget her, or to remember her only as the Golden Boy? To follow her? She doesn't know and she wishes she didn't care. David gave Alex her body back, and she won't ask any more of him. Already, the lonely road is weight enough on her shoulders. Already she can feel the heat of blisters, her tongue parched with thirst. She can't remain in this town that knows her only as the Golden Boy, cannot watch as Emaline slips away beneath the walls of new buildings, or rots with the remains of the Victoria. There is no Motherlode without Emaline. There is no Golden Boy without Motherlode.

Outside, the ash has settled, and a thin layer of dew masks the smell of the embers. Smoldering serpents of smoke hiss softly, and it feels as if she's looking through a movable fog, a haze on the inside instead of out. She blows cabin air from her chest and rubs the crust of tears and sleep from her eyes. She scuffs her feet through the damp ash, unearthing the dry underlayer, making a cloud about her. The birds are just now waking. The morning light loosens the darkness to shadows, and on the lip of the ravine cedars sway against a breeze. Two seagulls rise on an air current and disappear to the west.

She picks up her feet now, a tentative optimism filling her, and tiptoes past a makeshift tent filled with sleeping men, past the debris of Micah's store and Sander's dry goods, past the charred chapel ruins to stand in the spot where the Victoria should be. The Rhode Island Red rouses itself from the singed blanket where it slept the night, looks sideways at Alex before scampering off. The hen's feet make three-pronged tracks as it goes. Alex looks back, following her own tracks through the soot to the cabin where David sleeps. No one stirs. Limpy's snoring is barely audible next to the murmur of the creek and, as she turns back, her feet brush something hard. The broken fragment of a frame.

From a mirror, she thinks at first, but looks closer to find a corner of parchment sticking out under the ash. She shakes the parchment free of char and coal, finds Queen Victoria's gray-blue eyes squinting off into the distance. Apart from one scorched corner, the painting is undamaged. The queen's full cheeks droop into a double chin, and her ears are heavy with jewels. When Alex squints she can almost see the shadow of a mustache darkening her upper lip. On her head is a veiled crown, but neither this, nor the jeweled pendant around her neck, nor the baby blue sash draped across her frock, can match the regal image of Emaline descending the stairs in that lavender dress nearly three weeks ago. She sees the set of Emaline's broad shoulders; her breasts, a burden all on their own; her hair, a cascading crown around her head. Alex holds the portrait before her, wishing there was a body to fill the space between the parchment and the ground.

Beyond the chapel where the twin mounds point north up Victor Lane, Alex kneels, smoothes the earth and lays the portrait of the queen like a mantle over the grave.

"Emaline," she says and places her hand flat on her stomach. She looks about for the presence she feels but sees no one and nothing but the hesitant movements of the chicken picking its way back through the ashes of the Victoria across the street.

She wishes it were Jackson Hudson lying there instead of Emaline. Some men, Emaline said, some men just need killing; she can see his face, the wide set of his eyes, his beard trimmed and clipped to a square on his pointed chin, the set of his shoulders. She can see him as clearly as the portrait, and if they meet again . . . If they meet again, there will be bullets in her gun.

She leans down, touches her lips to the cheek of the paper face, whispers "thank you" into the paper ear.

The town is stirring now. Loud pneumatic coughing makes her anxious. If she sees the sun come up over the lip of the ravine, she might just stay. She stands, dusts off her knees, and turns to find David standing in her path. He says nothing, but offers the lump of gold in the palm of his outstretched hand. She shakes her head and reaches into her pocket for the green stone she took in exchange.

"Serpentine," he says. His eyes bore into her, searching for the woman, searching for the boy, or a combination of the two; she doesn't know. His hair is disheveled, his feet bare and covered in a film of dust and ash.

"Emaline," is all she can say, and even this word catches thick in her throat. They stand close, without touching.

"You're leaving?" he says.

"Yes."

A few resilient miners are making their way to their claims, as if by digging they can tunnel away from the charred remains of town. Alex yearns for a pick, a shovel, for the repetitive, mindless exertion of the mine.

"If they dam the creek, for the water," says David, shifting his weight, "they'll flood this valley."

Alex doesn't answer, but she can see the water rising, drowning the summer grass, lapping at the foundations of deserted buildings, reflecting in flashes of white when the sun rises above the ravine wall. It feels like another death, a death she's glad she won't be here to see. She looks back at David, but he is elsewhere, perhaps envisioning a similar landscape.

She can feel his breath brush the top of her head as she moves past him. She closes her eyes against the impulse to stop, to stand there before him for a few moments more, warding off the loneliness already clutching at her pant legs. She can feel him watching as she walks up the road. No pack, no pan. Only the clothes on her back, and a pouch of gold dust. She's leaving with less than when she arrived.

She walks past the high grasses, tall enough now to brush the lowest branches of the scrub oaks skirting the ravine. She keeps to the hard-packed earth between the wagon ruts until the road becomes steep and the sounds of the creek are hushed. She slows her pace, not waiting, she tells herself, afraid even to hope, just easing into the journey, one foot in front of the other. When she hears footsteps behind her, she doesn't stop to wait, but keeps the same steady rhythm, swinging her arms, careful to avoid tripping in the ruts and holes, until their elbows brush and his heavy breath is the only thing she hears.

He carries a large canvas pack, a bedroll strapped to one side, an iron pot on the other. A pick and a shovel extend over one shoulder like tree branches, and he lugs the big rifle from the wall of his cabin in his free hand. She takes the rifle, balances the muzzle like a yoke across her shoulders, and continues on, weaving back and forth along the switch-backs of the road until the wind brushes cold on her face.

"I couldn't stay," she says. He doesn't ask why.

"Where are we going?"

She stares off into the valley. The wind weaves between the cedars on the opposite ridge, and the smoke curls of a camp-fire rise from the valley floor. She leans in closer to David. His arm finds its way round her shoulders and she feels his body relax and his breath ease, as if this simple embrace had confirmed something his mind could not. She shades her eyes from the sun, and points to the parallel path cutting its way eastward into the Sierra Nevadas, to what, to where, she doesn't know.

Reading Group Guide
# *Crown of Dust*

1.  Although Alex is the most notable example, most of the characters in *Crown of Dust* are haunted by and running from their pasts. Do any of these characters succeed in escaping their pasts?

2.  "Some men," says Emaline, "some men just need killing." Do you believe that Alex's first crime is justified? If she ever meets Jackson Hudson again, would she be justified in killing him? Do you think she would kill him?

3.  Discuss the unique social order in Motherlode when Alex arrives. Who governs the place? How are disputes settled? How are nineteenth century notions of religion, spirituality and morality revised to fit the needs of this community?

4.  What freedoms does Alex enjoy by living as a man that Emaline and Lou Ann do not enjoy as women? What must Alex sacrifice to live as a man? Upon leaving Motherlode, do you think Alex will choose to live as a man, as a woman, or both?

5.  In what way is Emaline's authority, and the town itself, threatened by the discovery of gold and by the quick arrival of "polite" society? Is this threat adequately illustrated by the conflict between Emaline and Mrs. Dourity? Are women like Mrs. Dourity to blame for perpetuating rigid gender roles in society? What attitudes and fears motivate Emaline and Mrs. Dourity?

6. "She no longer minds the fatigue, the rough calluses forming on her hands, the solid indentions developing where she never dreamt muscles lurked. With each new ache, she discovers a new, living part of herself. Filling out, the men call it, but to Alex it feels more like filling in…"

   While Alex cannot physically become a boy, hard physical labor in the mine does transform her body and her mind. Describe how this transformation changes her perspective of her own worth and of her place in the town. How does this transformation change the way others view her?

7. If David had not discovered that Alex is a woman, do you think he would still have allowed himself to love her?

8. In spite of her love for Jed, Emaline's treatment of the Chinese miners reveals she is not free of racial prejudice. Do her actions disappoint you? Why does she feel justified in mistreating the Chinese men? What does her behavior reveal about the complicated nature of racial prejudice?

9. What profession can you imagine Limpy assuming in the twenty-first century?

10. Before reading *Crown of Dust*, what did you know about the California gold rush? How did this novel shape your understanding of the daily life, the prevalent biases, prejudices and hardships prospectors endured during the gold rush? Were you aware of the role women played in shaping new gold rush communities?